For my Mother and Father

THE
KING'S BISHOP

THE OWEN ARCHER SERIES
BOOK FOUR

CANDACE
ROBB

DIVERSIONBOOKS

The Owen Archer Series
The Apothecary Rose
The Lady Chapel
The Nun's Tale
The Riddle of St. Leonard's
A Gift of Sanctuary
A Spy for the Redeemer
The Guilt of Innocents
A Vigil of Spies

The Margaret Kerr Series
A Trust Betrayed
The Fire in the Flint
A Cruel Courtship

Diversion Books
A Division of Diversion Publishing Corp.
443 Park Avenue South, Suite 1008
New York, New York 10016
www.DiversionBooks.com

For more information, email info@diversionbooks.com

First Diversion Books edition July 2015.
Print ISBN:978-1-68230-104-3
eBook ISBN: 978-1-62681-978-8

ACKNOWLEDGEMENTS

I thank my editors Lynne Drew and Hope Dellon for insightful critiques and Victoria Hipps for a sharp eye for detail; for advice and information about the period I thank Jeremy Goldberg, Pat Cullum, Betty Garbutt, and the medievalists on the Mediev-L, Medsci, and Chaucer discussion lists. Thanks to Karen Wuthrich for asking just the right questions, and Charlie Robb for being a terrific sys-op and mapmaker.

Research for this book was conducted on location in Windsor and Yorkshire and at the University of York's Morrell Library, the British Library, the University of Washington libraries and the Seattle Public Library, with additional critical materials from the York Archaeological Trust, English Heritage, and the National Trust.

GLOSSARY

bailey: castle wall enclosing the outer court, also the court itself

compline: the last of the seven canonical hours, after sunset

grange: an outlying farm-house with barns and other outbuildings belonging to an abbey, originally staffed by lay brothers

hospitaller: in a religious house, the person whose office it is to receive pilgrims or visitors

houppelande: men's attire; a flowing gown, often floor-length and slit up to thigh level to ease walking, but sometimes knee-length; sleeves large and open

jongleur: a minstrel who sang, juggled, tumbled

the King's road: highways under the King's protection

leman: mistress

liberty: an area of the city not subject to royal administration; for example, the Liberty of St Peter is the area surrounding York Minster which comes under the Archbishop's jurisdiction

the Marches/Marcher Lords: the borders of the kingdom and the lords to whom the King granted jurisdiction over them

mazer: a large wooden cup

minster: a large church or cathedral; the cathedral of St Peter is referred to as York Minster

motte: the mound on which sits Windsor's Round Tower

nones: the fifth of the seven canonical hours, or the ninth hour after sunrise

pandemain: the finest quality white bread, made from flour sifted two or three times

prime: the first of the seven canonical hours, or sunrise

solar: private room on upper level of house

the wards: at Windsor, the lower ward is the court west of the Round Tower, the middle ward is the area enclosing the Round Tower, and the upper ward is the court east of the tower, enclosing King Edward III's new royal apartments

vespers: the sixth of the canonical hours, towards sunset

white monks: Cistercians, an offshoot of the Benedictine order; their aim was to more strictly observe the rule of St. Benedict

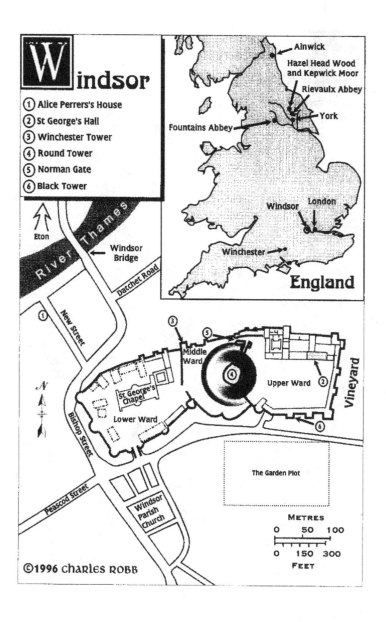

Windsor

1. Alice Perrers's House
2. St George's Hall
3. Winchester Tower
4. Round Tower
5. Norman Gate
6. Black Tower

Eton

River Thames

Windsor Bridge

Datchet Road

New Street

Bishop Street

Peascod Street

St George's Chapel

Lower Ward

Middle Ward

Upper Ward

Vineyard

Windsor Parish Church

The Garden Plot

METRES
0   50   100

0   150   300
FEET

©1996 CHARLES ROBB

Alnwick

Hazel Head Wood and Kepwick Moor

Rievaulx Abbey

Fountains Abbey

York

Windsor   London

Winchester

England

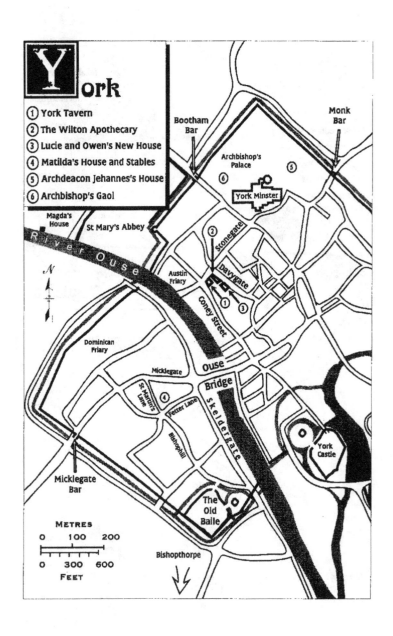

York

1. York Tavern
2. The Wilton Apothecary
3. Lucie and Owen's New House
4. Matilda's House and Stables
5. Archdeacon Jehannes's House
6. Archbishop's Gaol

Bootham Bar

Monk Bar

Archbishop's Palace

York Minster

Magda's House

St Mary's Abbey

River Ouse

N

Stonegate

Davygate

Austin Friary

Coney Street

Dominican Priory

Micklegate

Ouse

St Martin's Lane

Fetter Lane

Bridge

Skeldergate

Bishophill

York Castle

Micklegate Bar

The Old Baile

METRES

0   100   200

0   300   600

FEET

Bishopthorpe

1

A BODY IN THE MOAT

WINDSOR CASTLE, MARCH 1367

St George's Hall was aglow with torches and lamps, creating a firmament of stars in the glazed windows lining the far wall. The voices of the King's courtiers rang in counterpoint to the music, their silks rustled as their feet caught the rhythm. There was an exuberance of aromas—roasted boar, exotic spices, delicately scented hair and clothing, melting beeswax, smoke, sweat, and now and then icy air as revellers slipped out to relieve their wine-bloated bladders in the privies.

A latecomer impatiently pushed aside a stumbling lord, then paused as his senses, having adjusted to the dark silence of the snowfall outside in the upper ward, were now ambushed by the noise, the heat, and the smoky glare of the torches that made him cough and blink. As he shook the snow from his brown hair, Ned Townley searched the faces at the long tables near the door, where the pages and lesser officials huddled over their food. He was looking for a young face that had become all too familiar of late. A face seen too often bent towards Mary, Ned's betrothed.

He should not have left it so long. But the signs of Mary's turmoil had been subtle. Frowns shrugged off as nothing, a distracted air, unexplained tears. By the time Ned had suspected and had begun spying on Mary she had reached a level of comfortable intimacy with Daniel, a page in Sir William of Wyndesore's household, that Ned had taken months to achieve. Not that he had caught them embracing; Mary was too loyal to let it come to that without confessing all to Ned. He could see that Mary was aware of her shifting loyalties and tormented by guilt.

But he had no intention of losing Mary. His rival was a mere page, recently come to court from Dublin. What could the pup know of love? Ned had sampled women's charms in many lands and knew that Mary was the one God meant for him. How serious could the lad's affections be? Ned judged it would take little to frighten him off. Some sharp words, veiled threats, no more than that.

As he caught sight of Daniel, Ned felt a twinge of doubt about his suspicions. In contrast to the retainers surrounding him, the page looked a pale, delicate creature. What woman would lose her heart to such a lad? Was it possible Ned exaggerated the lad's threat to his happiness? But it was no time to weaken. Ned must do what he could to ensure his happy future with Mary.

He squared his shoulders, put on a threatening visage. Had his old comrades in arms been beside him tonight they would have laughed and slapped him on the back, calling him a fool for love. But behind the teasing façades, Owen and Lief would have understood; they were equally besotted with the women they had coaxed to the church door.

Ned had not reckoned with the solidarity of Wyndesore's men.

Daniel stared at his feet, his head and shoulders weighted down by remorse. He wished he were anywhere but here.

The page's grief centred on the tall, handsome man who had faced Sir William's retainers with disdain. "I am not such a fool as to attack a man in full view of his fellows! And a lad at that." But the retainers had been ordered to protect their lord's page and they meant to do so.

Glancing up, Daniel saw that the comely face of his accuser was red with indignation, his elegant clothes dishevelled by the men's rough handling. Daniel wished it were he being escorted from the hall, not Ned Townley. Daniel admired Townley. He was all the page might wish to be. He was a spy for the King's powerful third son, John of Gaunt, Duke of Lancaster. He was a proven warrior, renowned for his skill with daggers. Yet he was no oafish brute—not like Sir William's retainers; Townley was a courtier in dress, manner, speech. And with his gentle brown eyes and perfectly proportioned face and form, Daniel thought him the most handsome man he had ever seen. He would never have knowingly angered the man.

But moments ago Townley had informed Daniel of his inadvertent transgression. The warning had been delivered with an energy that had startled Daniel. Townley had grabbed him by the neck of his tunic, lifting him off his feet. "I will pin you to the tapestries if you persist in your attentions to my betrothed."

"Your betrothed?" Daniel had squeaked.

"Mary. Mistress Perrers's maid."

"No! I pray you!" Daniel had cried, hoping to be lowered to the floor so he might explain that his feelings for Mary were fraternal, nothing more. But his exclamation had drawn the attention of Sir William's bullies, who now led Townley from the hall.

"He'll bother you no more, Daniel. Rest easy," Scoggins said, filling the lad's tankard with ale.

Daniel lifted his tankard towards Scoggins and nodded, then both drank. It was the gesture Scoggins wanted, and so Daniel made it. But he was hardly grateful. If Scoggins had minded his own business, Townley would have pounded the table a few times while he threatened to tack Daniel to the rafters with his daggers, then he would have stomped off into the night, satisfied that he'd put the fear of the Lord in Daniel. And come morning, it would have been plain to Townley that Daniel had understood and meant to stay away from Mary, and all would have been forgiven and forgotten. But Scoggins obviously felt honour-bound to protect his lord's page.

In faith, Ned Townley had every right to be angry. Daniel had been foolish; he could see how his attentions to Mary had been misinterpreted. He had not known that Townley was the Ned Mary spoke of incessantly. Not once had she mentioned that her love was Lancaster's spy. Not once had she spoken of his remarkable skill with daggers. He had just been Ned, "beautiful Ned", "gentle Ned", "tender Ned", "tall, strong, dashing

Ned". A mythical being. Not the Duke of Lancaster's spy.

Daniel drank down his ale, pushed his tankard aside, listened half-heartedly to the conversations round him, all about how his lord, Sir William of Wyndesore, had met with the King that day. It was said Sir William had boldly blamed the troubles in Ireland on the Duke of Clarence's poor judgement. Some said the King was angered; Sir William was to be banished to the Scottish border. Others said the King knew his son Lionel, Duke of Clarence could not be trusted; Sir William was to be promoted to a Marcher Lord and sent to protect the Scottish border.

Daniel pricked up his ears. Punishment or reward, what everyone agreed upon was the likelihood of marching north to the border country. His mood lifted. That meant they would soon be far away from Windsor Castle and his humiliation. He absentmindedly reached for his tankard, remembered he'd drained it, found it full again. Had he imagined he'd downed the contents? No matter, he took a long drink. His head was beginning to hurt, so he took another long drink. And another. Then someone filled it up, laughing at Daniel's slurred protests.

"Come on, lad, drink up. Scoggins saved your hide. Drink to him."

Daniel remembered the snow that had begun to fall before the evening meal. It was a long, treacherous walk from the hall to Sir William's quarters. Already he dreaded trying to stand. How would he navigate through the snow?

"Lift it, lad, drink it down!" A face floated in front of Daniel's eyes, but he was so far gone he could not tell who it was. He blinked to focus. How many times had they filled his cup? He shook his head to clear it, felt the bile rise in his stomach. Oh Lord, he was going to embarrass himself yet again this night. He was cursed, that was certain.

Though it was March, the harsh winter persisted. Brother Michaelo found last night's snowfall lovely to behold at this early hour, while the pristine white lay undisturbed on the mounds and ledges within the walls of Windsor Castle, but underfoot the snow made the rutted mud treacherous. He stepped cautiously, his entire body bent forward, focusing on his boots and the hem of his habit. He intended to reach Archbishop Thoresby's chambers dry and presentable.

Not that it mattered; Michaelo would not be mingling with courtiers today. He would be hunched over a writing desk preparing letters from the Archbishop to the abbots of Fountains and Rievaulx, letters recommending William of Wykeham to the see of Winchester. A depressing task, for if the King succeeded in having the appointment confirmed, Wykeham would be poised to replace Archbishop Thoresby as Lord Chancellor. A dreary thought. Not that it was not an honour to be secretary to the Archbishop of York; but an archbishop was not so London-bound as the chancellor. Michaelo sighed at the prospect of more time in York. He preferred Thoresby in his dual role. If winter seemed endless here, it was far worse up north. His only hope of salvation from such a bleak future was that despite letters enthusiastically recommending Wykeham for the bishopric the Pope would stand firm in his determination to make Wykeham the first casualty in his war against pluralism. Pope Urban believed that the practice of conferring on clergy multiple benefices resulted in neglected parishes and pampered clergy who paid more heed to their debts to their benefactors than to their responsibilities to their flocks. His Holiness referred to William of Wykeham as the richest pluralist in England. Which was apparently quite true.

A shout from below the Round Tower startled Michaelo from his thoughts; he straightened suddenly, tottered, regained his balance. Three men at arms ran towards the commotion. The man who had called the alarm stood over the ditch that bordered the motte on which the tower squatted. The snow that blanketed the steep slope was scarred as if something had slid from the top. Curiosity propelled Michaelo closer.

When he was but ten feet from what was now a small crowd, Michaelo saw three men lifting a body from the ditch. The lifeless form dripped ice, water and filth. The heavy rains had filled the ditch, making it a shallow moat, and the freeze had crusted it with ice. Poor soul must have slid into the freezing water and drowned in a cold stupor before he got his wits about him to crawl out. But how had he come to be on the slope?

One of the men lifted what looked like a cloak from the mud, sniffed it, handed it to his companion. "Smell this, would you."

His companion sniffed, recoiled. "Phew! Better in the tankard than soaked into the wool. What did the lad do, dive into the barrel?"

"Drank a bellyful and thought he'd try sledding, I'd wager."

Ah. Now Michaelo understood the scar in the snow. Sledding down the motte, unable to stop—a scenario many a mother had rehearsed with her wayward children in the past months, warning them of the danger. "Who is he?" Michaelo called out.

"Daniel. The page of Sir William of Wyndesore."

"Are you certain?" Michaelo knew Daniel. A sweet-faced, gentle lad.

"Looks like Daniel to me," the man said.

Michaelo pressed closer still, cutting across the mud without a thought now for his boots. The lad lay on the ground, eyes opened wide, his hair caked with mud, his arms outspread. As Michaelo squatted beside the body to lift the stiff hair from the face, he noticed something that did not belong on a drowned man: red welts on the wrists, just visible beneath the sleeves of the lad's tunic. Michaelo wanted to push up a sleeve for a better look, but he resisted. He brushed back the hair, gently closed the lad's eyelids.

"So? Is it Daniel?" The man held the cloak at arm's length.

Michaelo straightened up, made the sign of the cross over the body. "Yes. Yes, poor lad." He hurried away without a word about Daniel's wrists. Better mentioned to someone he could trust.

Sir William of Wyndesore instructed his servants to leave the lad's body covered and to keep away the curious. Then he went out to speak with his men. He cursed under his breath as pale winter sunlight burned his eyes and a chill wind wrapped icy fingers round his bones. Wyndesore was a tough, seasoned campaigner, powerfully built; but he was no longer young, he had awakened with a head that felt several times its normal size thanks to some fine brandywine last night, and that awakening had been sudden and unpleasant, his servants distraught at the news of Daniel's drowning. His men were assembled in the outer ward, some hopping from foot to foot trying to get warm, some dabbing their eyes, but many frowning fiercely and demanding Ned Townley.

"Who?" Wyndesore asked his squire.

Alan leaned close. "Ned Townley. He is Lancaster's spy, left here to be the Duke's ears while he's fighting in Castile, so they say."

"Do they now? So what's his sin, besides being Lancaster's spy?"

"I know not. But I saw Scoggins with him last night."

Wyndesore straightened up, squinted out at his men, picked out Scoggins scowling with the best of them. "Well, Scoggins, what has this Townley done?"

"He's murdered Daniel, that's what he's done, my lord." The men muttered their approval of Scoggins's explanation, their combined voices echoing against the stone walls surrounding them.

"You witnessed him doing this, did you?"

Scoggins spat in the mud, shook his head. "Nay, my lord. But I saw the two of 'em last night arguing over one of Mistress Perrers's maids, that little Mary. And Townley told Daniel he'd pin him to the wall with his daggers if he found him round Mary again. That's what he said, and that I can swear to, my lord. I called some men to escort him from the hall. He must've come back, waited for the lad without."

Wyndesore closed his eyes. "And was Daniel stabbed?" Scoggins was a gossip and troublemaker, but a good fighter, and loyal. Fiercely loyal. "Eh, Scoggins?"

The man shrugged. "I did not see the body, my lord."

Wyndesore looked round. "Who did? Who found him?"

"One of the King's guards," Alan whispered. "But Bardolph and Crofter helped drag him from the ditch."

"Crofter!"

A fair, square-jawed man stepped forward. "I saw no stab

wounds, my lord. The lad drowned, no doubt of that."

Wyndesore nodded. "Then enough of this nonsense about Townley."

Crofter shook his head. "Who's to say Townley didn't change his mind and make it look like an accident, my lord? Who's to say?" His tone was matter-of-fact, not argumentative.

Wyndesore scowled. "Stick to the facts, Crofter."

Crofter bobbed his head in good-humoured deference. "He drowned, my lord."

"Thank you."

But Crofter was not finished. "If it please you, my lord. His cloak reeked of ale. He must have spilled it all over himself. I suppose he might have been too drunk to judge what he was doing, my lord."

Wyndesore turned to Scoggins. "Was Daniel drunk when he left the hall?"

Scoggins shrugged, looked down at his boots. "A bit, my lord."

"He was not accustomed to much drink, Scoggins. Did you encourage this?"

Scoggins faced his lord. "I did, my lord, and for that I shall do much penance."

"So you were drinking, too?"

"Aye, my lord."

"Did someone offer to help young Daniel back to his bed?"

"I did not see him leave, my lord."

"Too drunk by then?"

"Aye, my lord."

Wyndesore shielded his eyes against the sunlight as he looked back out at his men. "Go about your morning duties. You will have a chance to pray for Daniel at mass tomorrow morning." He turned on his heels and marched back inside, shouting for Alan to go wake Mistress Alice Perrers.

"And Ned Townley, my lord?"

"First Mistress Alice, damn you!"

Alan hurried away.

• • •

John Thoresby paced in his chamber waiting for his secretary. Michaelo's tardiness was particularly irritating this morning. Thoresby had decided how to reconcile the King's request with his own interests and he wished to complete the task. Where was his secretary? Admiring himself in his mirror?

When at last Michaelo arrived he was breathless, his face was flushed, and much to Thoresby's surprise the hem of his habit was soggy.

"Where have you been?"

"Your Grace, there has been a terrible—" Michaelo shook his head, sat down at the writing desk, and dabbed his face with a cloth, closed his eyes, took a deep breath.

"A terrible what, Michaelo? You are all atremble."

His secretary nodded, blotted his upper lip.

"Michaelo!"

"Forgive me, Your Grace. I wished to catch my breath." Michaelo shook his head. "It is the marks, Your Grace. And his cloak. He was floating in the moat, not an ale-cask. How does one spill so much ale as to *soak* an entire cloak? Even stranger, why wear a cloak while drinking?" Michaelo bowed his head, pressed the cloth to one temple, then the other.

The Archbishop studied his uncharacteristically dishevelled, babbling secretary. "Have you overindulged this morning? One of your headaches?"

Michaelo raised his head slowly, frowned up at Thoresby as if puzzled. "No, Your Grace. I was making my way here when they discovered him and pulled him from the ditch."

"*Who* was pulled from *what* ditch?"

"Did I not say? I pray you forgive me, Your Grace. It was Daniel. Sir William of Wyndesore's page. Down below the Round Tower. Drowned, Your Grace. Or worse."

Worse? "Drowning is rather final, I should think. What could be worse?"

Michaelo's brows pulled together. "I said nothing to the men who found him. I do not wish to make something of nothing. But there were marks on his wrists. As if his hands had been bound, Your Grace."

That could be troublesome. But it was the victim's identity that set off alarms in Thoresby's head. His secretary had a weakness for handsome youths. "Daniel. A rather pretty young man, as I recall. You have not been breaking your vows again, have you, Michaelo?"

The question seemed to clear Michaelo's head. He sat up, suddenly alert. "Your Grace! I was merely walking past."

"I do not doubt that, Michaelo, but your agitation bespeaks an attachment."

Michaelo's nostrils flared. "I kept my distance as always, Your Grace."

Deo gratias. Thoresby hid a smile as Michaelo lifted his chin, his back stiff with indignation, raised his quill pen and sat with it poised above the parchment.

"Shall we begin, Your Grace?"

His secretary's injured feelings reassured Thoresby. "Indeed. I have resolved my approach to the letters our King has requested."

It was a matter of emphasis, Thoresby had decided. Praise those aspects of Wykeham's service of which the Cistercian abbots least approved—how in his past post of Clerk of Works and presently as Keeper of the Privy Seal the King found him indispensable, which, of course, emphasised Wykeham's worldly loyalties. The King could not deny it, nor could he deny that Thoresby couched his words as praise. Thoresby smiled to himself as he began to dictate to Michaelo.

Rather elegantly gowned for an early morning walk, her brown hair carefully coiffed beneath a gossamer veil, Alice Perrers swept through the Norman Gate from the upper ward clutching a fur-lined cloak round her shivering body. It was too early to be abroad; the blood was not yet warmed in her extremities. The guard bowed to her. Her page hurried after her carrying a goblet and a flagon of watered and delicately spiced wine. Alice intended to wake properly with her usual morning refreshment no matter who had been found floating in the moat. After attending Sir William she must return to the apartments of the ailing Queen and attend her. There would be no time to see to Alice's own needs. Not that she resented her duty to Queen Phillippa. Alice owed her position to the aged Queen's affection. But she must also take care of herself—no one else would. She was nineteen years old and would soon lose the bloom of youth that so enchanted the King if she did not have a care for her health. She did not delude herself; she was no beauty. Her power was in her youthful, well-formed body, her understanding of men's desires, and her cunning ambition.

At the door to Sir William of Wyndesore's chambers Alice turned, eyebrows raised. "Gilbert?"

Her servant rushed forward, shifting the goblet to the hand with the flagon, and rapped sharply. He had learned that to spare his knuckles threw his lady into a temper.

As the door opened, Alice swept past Gilbert into a comfortable yet austere parlour, obviously furnished by a military man: two high-backed chairs, two companion tables, and a chest for storage. The chairs were arranged in front of a large brazier that radiated a pleasant heat from its dark corner. Sir William occupied one of the chairs, his feet stretched out towards the fire. He looked up lazily and nodded. He was a handsome man, over twenty years Alice's senior but still a physically powerful man with rich dark hair—succumbing to silver streaks, but still abundant. How like him not to rise, Alice thought. When he served under the Duke of Clarence in Ireland had he behaved with such insolence? An intriguing question. She must pursue it. "Sir William."

Wyndesore waved Alice over to the other chair. She sat down with a regal sweep of her skirts. A servant rushed over to place a small table by her. Gilbert came forward, poured the wine.

"You carry your refreshment with you? As a precaution?" Wyndesore grinned.

"I have a particular thirst in the early morning, and, as we decided last night—" she glanced up with a coy smile "—my cellar is excellent." Alice lifted her goblet as if toasting him, then drank.

Wyndesore watched her with amusement. "The King's pampered pet."

Alice bristled. "Not a pet."

Wyndesore touched his heart and bowed his head. "Forgive me, Mistress Alice. I have the clumsy manners of a soldier."

Alice paid no heed to his false apology.

Wyndesore looked bored with the game. "So. Ned Townley. He fancies your maid Mary?"

Alice ran her finger idly round the rim of her goblet. "Why do you ask?"

"You have heard about my page?"

Alice made a sad face. "Poor Daniel. Sledding. Everyone has been expecting such an accident, but involving a child, not a young man." She lifted her eyes slowly. "Why do you mention Ned?"

"Perhaps it was not an accident. Ned Townley threatened Daniel last night—about being with Mary. Was Daniel dallying with your maid?"

"Sir William! Have you been consulting common gossips?"

Wyndesore leaned forward, impatient with Alice's teasing. "Was he?"

Alice pouted and folded her hands like an obedient child. "Daniel had made a pest of himself of late, that I can say, though I dislike speaking ill of the dead. But he was not wooing Mary. That was clearly not his intention."

Wyndesore sniffed. "Why else does a man spend time round a pretty woman?"

Alice feigned surprise at his comment. "She cannot be a friend if she is pretty?" She tilted her head and tsked at Wyndesore.

He laughed.

Alice sipped her wine, serious again. "What are you thinking?"

Wyndesore drew his feet back, snapped his fingers for a cup of ale. "What I'm thinking does not matter. It's my men. They think Townley killed Daniel." He took a long drink, watching Alice over the rim of his mazer.

Alice shook her head. "Ned did no such thing. I can vouch for him, and so can Mary. He was with her last night when I went up to bed—you will recall that was rather late." Alice sighed. Mary was a pretty child; Alice had plans for her—and they did not include a nobody like Ned Townley. "I have little hope for the preservation of Mary's maidenhead."

Wyndesore grinned. "There was never any hope for it, Mistress Alice. A pretty girl at court? Come now." Wyndesore drank down his ale, took a cloth from his sleeve and wiped his mouth like a gentleman. Manners of a soldier indeed. "Well, your word is enough for me, but my men will not agree. They were fond of the lad—he was their pet, I suppose. They're angry he's dead, they want blood, and Townley's a man they delight in hating, with his courtly clothes and his swagger with his fancy daggers." Wyndesore laughed at his witticism.

Alice smiled politely; Wyndesore was handsome and powerful, but he was no wit. "Ned is also resented because he is Lancaster's spy. The common folk have no love for the Duke." Gilbert refreshed Alice's goblet. She used the interruption to consider the situation. "I wonder whether Ned knows he's in danger?"

"You may be sure he does. I'll warn my men that any harm comes to Townley, they'll pay. But he'd be best away from here."

"That was not the Duke's plan for him," Alice said. The Duke of Lancaster had left Ned at court, while he fought in Spain, to polish his manners and his skill at letter-writing, informing the Duke of the news of court.

"Devil take the Duke!" Wyndesore growled.

Alice winced. Wyndesore should have a care. In Ireland, he had been second in command, too important to offend. But here at the King's court he was insignificant. And many felt he had betrayed his lord to the King. Men neither respected nor trusted such an opportunist. Wyndesore should tread softly.

"How goes the King?" Wyndesore asked, changing the subject.

Alice frowned, glanced towards Wyndesore's servants. Hers was also a precarious perch at court. As the King's mistress she was showered with gifts from him and wielded some power. But should he tire of her—or more likely, considering his age, should he die...Alice took great care to be discreet. She trusted her own servant, but what did she know of Wyndesore's men? How carefully did he choose those who surrounded him? They certainly had no cause to be loyal to her.

Wyndesore snapped his fingers, dispersing the servants. "So?"

Alice shrugged. "He spits venom at Pope Urban at the moment."

"Wykeham is not yet a bishop, I know."

"Thomas Cobham has returned from Avignon with the news that His Holiness is pleased to allow Wykeham to handle the temporalities of the seat of Winchester *until the successor is named.* You can imagine Cobham's red ears. The poor man was visibly trembling when he entered the King's presence. And he was far worse before he backed away."

"Wykeham seems a suitable man. I do not understand the Pope's resistance."

"All this is just a convenient way for His Holiness to show his power over the King. Two old men hitting each other with sticks."

They shared a smile.

Smarting from the hostile glances all about him, Ned went in search of Mary's sympathetic ear. She knew where he'd been last night; she of all people would bristle with righteous indignation on his behalf. He found her sitting by a tall window in Mistress Alice's parlour, transferring pearls from one of her mistress's fine dresses to another. Mary was a lovely young woman with a cloud of softly curling, raven-black hair, a face of such sweet innocence Ned had been amazed by the passion with which she'd responded to his kisses from the first, and the tiniest waist he had ever had the pleasure to wrap his arms round. Mary possessed his heart completely. Never again would he tease his friend Owen Archer about his devotion to his wife. Ned understood now.

Mary glanced up at Ned, revealing eyes red from weeping. She sniffed. Her heavenly hazel eyes filled with tears.

Ned dropped down to his knees before her, dismayed. "Oh, my sweet Mary, do not weep for me. Their unjust accusations are naught to me."

Mary put aside her sewing to blow her nose.

"Let me fetch you some wine," Ned offered.

Mary shook her head. "No. I must finish my work. Wine will lead to pricks that stain the dresses. You would not suggest it had you ever had the chore of removing bloodstains from fine cloth."

Always practical, his Mary. Sweet Heaven, how he loved her. Ned took her hands.

Mary snatched them away.

"What's this?" Ned sat back on his heels, confused. "You reject my comfort?"

"Oh, Ned. 'Tis your stubborn jealousy caused it, you know it is true. Daniel would never have drunk so much if you had not threatened him. Why did you do it? There was no need. No need. I'd told you, I'd sworn you had nothing to be jealous of. Daniel was kind to me, was all. He was my friend." Mary sniffed, hiccuped.

His fault? "Kind to you, was all, was it? Why? Why was Sir William of Wyndesore's page so kind to the maid of Mistress Alice Perrers?"

Mary flushed. Her eyes flashed with anger. "Oh indeed. The lowly maid of Mistress Alice could not possibly be considered a friend by the handsome young page of Sir William of Wyndesore."

"How did he befriend you, Mary? I cannot think of a reason why Sir William's page and Mistress Alice's maid would even meet."

Mary gasped. "Even in death you distrust him! Oh shame, Ned. Shame on you!" She rose and hurried towards the inner door.

Ned groaned, hurried after her, caught her elbow. "For pity's sake, Mary, we are to be wed. You should be comforting me as the victim of unfounded gossip, not accusing me of something you know full well I did not do."

Mary stood stubbornly with her back to him, looking down at the floor. Ned heard her catch her breath and knew the tears flowed once more. For a friend? He'd be a fool to believe that! He let go of her arm. "Forgive me, Mistress Mary. I have misunderstood. I thought you loved me, but I see my error." He strode from the room to the sound of Mary's sobs. Devil take her, she could be so stubborn. It was Mistress Perrers's doing, he'd wager. She did not like him—had other plans for Mary, no doubt. He must find a way to free Mary from the whore's service. He wished Owen Archer were not so far north in York. Ned could use his advice in this.

2

MATTERS OF CONSCIENCE

YORK, MARCH 1367

Owen Archer laughed as his daughter pulled at his eye patch, then his beard, her efforts accompanied by a low, throaty laugh. "You've a grip to make an archer proud," Owen said.

His wife's head was bowed over the rows of seeds. "I'd thought Gwenllian might learn my profession," Lucie said. She had been named Master Apothecary after the death of her first husband, Nicholas Wilton. "But Gwenllian is to be an archer, not just carry your name?" Lucie retained her first husband's surname to acknowledge that she held her position as Nicholas's widow, not Owen's wife. "It is settled at five months?"

Owen walked over to Lucie, peered over her shoulder. "She shall learn the art of the longbow if she wishes. If everyone in this household becomes your apprentice, you will have little to do and will lose your skill. Some of those seeds look as if water got to them."

Lucie shrugged. "The river damp is ever a problem. So Gwenllian is to serve under you as one of the Archbishop's retainers?"

"Never that," Owen snapped.

Lucie glanced up, hearing the change in her husband's voice, and caught the telltale twitch in his left cheek. "You are angry, I know, though I do not understand it. Surely you knew you would owe His Grace service?" At Christmas, Archbishop Thoresby had named Owen captain of his retainers and Steward of Bishopthorpe, his palace south of the city. "Why did you accept the posts if you meant to go into a rage whenever he called upon you?"

Owen met Lucie's eye and said simply, "It seemed an honour at the time."

"And so it was. And is." Lucie did not look away.

But Owen's eye slid from Lucie to his daughter. He lifted Gwenllian into the air and murmured, "What makes you prouder—Owen Archer, Spy, or Captain Archer, Steward of Bishopthorpe?"

Gwenllian gurgled as she tilted towards him, grabbing for his face.

Bess Merchet hummed a tune as she made her way back to the York Tavern from market. As she approached Wilton's apothecary she noted Owen Archer striding off in the direction of the minster. By the time he'd turned up Stonegate he had ignored the greetings of two neighbours, a singular lapse in courtesy for Owen. Bess read it as the aftermath of a heated argument in the household, certainly not a rarity, but odd at this early hour, when Tildy, Jasper, and Gwenllian would be witnesses. She hurried home to drop her purchases off with the cook, then slipped next door to see whether Lucie needed a friend's perspective.

Tildy greeted her at the kitchen door holding Gwenllian on her hip. "Oh bless you, Mistress Merchet, you are the answer to my prayers." She handed Bess the baby, who immediately grabbed one of the ribbons on Bess's cap. "Mistress Lucie has gone into the shop to give Jasper some instruction and the broth needs stirring." Jasper was Lucie's apprentice, an orphan who was considered part of the family.

Bess bounced and chucked her godchild and followed Tildy into the kitchen. "You are in need of an extra hand round here, I can see that, Tildy. Has your mistress done aught about hiring another girl?"

Tildy shook her head. "Most days I find a hand ready when I need it. And Gwenllian is often in the shop with Mistress Lucie and Jasper. But Jasper dropped something that must be swept up with care, so Gwenllian stayed with me."

Bess considered all the facts. "The Captain is off to the minster?"

Tildy nodded as she wiped her hands and took up a long wooden spoon to stir the bubbling broth.

Lucie came through the beaded curtain. Gwenllian immediately screwed up her face and began to bawl for her mother.

Bess handed the squirming, squealing baby into Lucie's outstretched arms. "She has you all dancing to her tune, Lucie. Have a care she does not become a burden."

"You mind the inn, Bess, I shall mind my daughter," Lucie said with a smile as she settled on a cushioned chair by the fire to nurse Gwenllian.

Bess sat down near Lucie and kept her peace until the child was ready to be winded. "Owen went off in quite a temper."

Lucie rubbed Gwenllian's back. "His Grace has a mission for him, something that will take him away. 'Tis nothing unusual, but you would think Archbishop Thoresby had ordered Owen to slay us all in our sleep. He is convinced that all the evil in the world will be unleashed on this house as soon as he steps away."

Bess sniffed and nodded vigorously. "I thought as much. Thoresby's retainers stopped at the inn last night. I guessed they had been here too." She closed her eyes, made more connections. "From London, eh? There are rumours John Thoresby will not be chancellor much longer."

Lucie nodded towards the shelves behind Bess. "Look at the silver cup he sent for his godchild."

Bess was not surprised by the change of subject. Lucie had been raised in a convent school and abhorred gossip, probably the only pupil who had taken the warnings against gossip to heart. Bess turned round to see the cup, rose with an exclamation. It was an extravagant gift for a child, obviously meant as a keepsake, not to use. "I am glad that Owen bit his tongue and agreed to the Archbishop's offer to stand as her godfather. Already Gwenllian has riches to carry her comfortably through life." The cup was exquisitely decorated with doves and flowers. Bess used her apron as a cloth to protect it from fingerprints as she turned it this way and that. "So. What does Owen fear will happen?"

"He says he cannot leave me with a babe in arms and an

apprentice who is but eleven years old. Who will protect us?" Lucie tucked the now sleeping baby into her cradle. "We have gone round and round about it. I cannot make him see reason. We live in a walled city surrounded by friends, under the protection of a powerful guild, and surely God will watch over Owen's family while he is serving the Archbishop." Lucie settled back in the chair, pressing her fingers to her temples. "He hovers over us, Bess. He will drive me mad."

Bess nodded. "I saw it coming while you still carried Gwenllian. Remember his silences, the frowns when he thought you did not see him? You thought he was sorry he was to be a father."

Lucie smiled, remembering. "How wrong I was." Owen had been worried that a child would be frightened by his scarred face and his patch. "And how wrong he was; Gwenllian adores him." Lucie sighed. "I had hoped that he might thus see the futility of worry."

Bess smiled at her friend. Levelheaded Lucie expected all mankind to think as she did. "A worrier is a worrier, Lucie. Wait for Owen to change and you *will* go mad. So what is this mission?"

"He is to escort Archdeacon Jehannes and a small company to Fountains Abbey. The King wishes to convince the Cistercian abbots to support Sir William of Wykeham as Bishop of Winchester. The Archdeacon will carry letters from the King, from Thoresby as chancellor, and from Wykeham himself, I trust."

Bess sat forward. "Thoresby is doing this for Wykeham, the man poised to take his place as chancellor? I thought John Thoresby loved his power."

Lucie reached down, smoothed her daughter's unruly hair, dark and soft as down. "It is strange. But with the King so keen on Wykeham's promotion, Thoresby has little choice but to support the effort."

"So Owen is off to make plans with Jehannes?"

"More likely to complain. I pray God Jehannes has his usual calming effect on my husband."

"It is passing strange Owen complains so about his work for the Archbishop, yet grows bored when he is too long at home."

Lucie smiled, though her blue eyes were melancholy. "Owen is a riddle, Bess, one that I doubt I shall ever solve. To him, Captain of Archers was a noble profession. Spying for the old Duke of Lancaster was the least he could do for his lord's loyalty in keeping him in his service after he lost the sight in his left eye. But his work for the Archbishop of York"—she shook her head—"he thinks a man of God has no business retaining spies. In Owen's opinion Thoresby is too much the Lord Chancellor and not enough the man of God."

Bess leaned over and patted Lucie's arm. "Then if the rumours that Wykeham is to become chancellor prove true, Owen might be a happier man."

Lucie chuckled. "Trust you to find the bright side of gossip, Bess. But the Archbishop of York is still a powerful political force. Owen will still be called away. And worry all the while."

"You know, Lucie, if an obsession to protect his family is the only thing you find to fault in your husband, you are a lucky woman."

"You will not find me denying that."

Jehannes paced his parlour, hands clasped behind his back. When Owen was shown in, the Archdeacon spun round, hurried forward, arms outstretched, his youthful face brightening. "Bless you for coming so quickly, my friend," Jehannes said breathlessly, putting an arm round Owen's shoulders. "Please, sit with me by the fire." Though outside the day was warm, the stone house had not yet caught the heat, being in a dark street.

Owen settled into the chair, stretched out his long legs, steepled his hands before him. "I am curious about what is not explained in the letter."

Jehannes sat down stiffly, perched at the edge of his seat. He nodded towards a flagon of wine and two goblets. "Take some refreshment while we talk. We shall eat afterwards."

Owen leaned over to pour. "And you?"

Jehannes frowned, shook his head. "Not yet." He looked agitated. Owen had rarely seen him like this. "As I presume His Grace informed you, we are to carry letters to the abbots of Fountains and Rievaulx." Jehannes tapped the arms of the chair as he spoke.

Owen leaned back with his wine. "That is the mission. But what is behind it?"

Jehannes cleared his throat. "You have heard that the King has named Wykeham to the see of Winchester?"

Owen nodded. "And Pope Urban has refused to approve it. That should please the Archbishop."

Jehannes flashed a tight smile.

"What is your role in this?"

Jehannes raised his eyes to the ceiling. "I am to add my voice to the arguments in favour of Sir William of Wykeham."

Considering the Archdeacon's agitation, Owen doubted it was that simple. He would return to that. Of Wykeham he knew only that the King's partiality to the man was owing to his architectural talent. Many at court claimed he was a commoner who had finagled his way into the King's confidence, but Owen imagined they were simply jealous. "I agree with His Holiness that a bishop should be a devout man of God."

"That is precisely the irony of the situation," Jehannes said. "Wykeham may be a devoted churchman. But His Holiness sees only the number and value of the benefices Wykeham holds, all gifts from the King, particularly his position as Keeper of the Privy Seal. And, of course, everyone knows that the appointment is the first step towards his promotion to Lord Chancellor."

"At which time he would no doubt be the King's man."

Jehannes nodded. "The King's bishop. Precisely."

"I do not believe Archbishop Thoresby sincere in his support of Wykeham."

Jehannes closed his eyes, pressed his fingers against his lids. "You know His Grace too well. In public he proclaims his support; in private he plots with Lancaster to overturn Wykeham. Echoing the Archbishop's strategy, I am to find subtle ways to remind the abbots why Wykeham is unsuitable." He dropped his hands, gave Owen a weary look. "I am not a dissembler, my friend. I shall disappoint His Grace."

Owen was outraged. "You are put in an impossible position!"

Jehannes rose to pace again. "Impossible indeed."

"His Grace is the dissembler. Why can he not do this?"

"He is Lord Chancellor and Archbishop of York. He cannot be pulled away from London and court at a time like this."

Owen watched his friend pace back and forth several times while he absorbed the information. "So what is my part in this?" he asked at last.

Jehannes paused, gave Owen a puzzled look. "Undoubtedly, His Grace recommended you."

"That I can see. But why? Why the captain of his retainers leading the escort? He expects trouble?"

Jehannes nodded as he grasped Owen's point. "Oh, yes. Trouble. Yes, I daresay. You must understand that this issue has inspired more than rivalry. It has brought to a head feelings that have divided the Church in this kingdom, one side believing that the Pope has sovereignty over the Church in England, the other that King Edward has sovereignty over all in his kingdom, be they soldiers, farmers, or clergy. A friar has even circulated a paper—anonymously, of course, the coward—declaring that the King has forfeited his right to govern by refusing to pay tribute to the Pope. The King fears that with tempers flaring there might be danger."

"And His Grace generously suggested me for the job."

"His words were that he trusted you implicitly."

Owen grinned. "His Grace has a honeyed tongue when it is to his purpose. What do you mean to say to the abbots?"

Jehannes shook his head, a desperate look in his eyes. "I have no idea. Somehow I must undermine the man while appearing to praise him. I am not in the habit of saying one thing, meaning another. My face and voice will give me away."

"It sickens me to hear you berate yourself for being an honest man. For pity's sake, Jehannes, you are a man of God. You *must* be honest!"

Jehannes smiled at his friend's indignation. "You note His Grace has not asked *you* to dissemble."

"He would not dare!"

They shared a laugh over that.

Then Owen grew serious again. "Do you ever regret serving under Archbishop Thoresby?"

Jehannes looked surprised. "Never. He is a good man." When Owen's eyebrow rose, the Archdeacon shrugged. "As good as the circumstances allow him to be."

"That smacks of cynicism."

"It is not meant that way, truly. You are a fortunate man to serve His Grace."

Owen could see that his friend was in earnest. Having nothing polite to reply to that, he chose to move on to practical plans. "When will the letters arrive?"

"I should think fairly soon."

3

A HUSHED ARGUMENT

Delayed by a bilious stomach, John Thoresby now hurried to a meeting with the King, his robes sailing round him, his eyes squinting to see ten steps ahead. He cursed the indignities of age that made him so much more conscious of his mortal shell than ever before—stomach, eyes, joints. The disintegration of his body seemed to be accelerating of late. So why was he plotting Wykeham's disappointment? Would it not be a relief were Wykeham to take the chancellor's chain from round his neck and lighten his load? In comparison, his duties as Archbishop of York were nothing.

Round the corner he hastened, down shallow stone steps, pushed open the heavy door, gasped as the cold, damp air hit him. It was not so much colder without than within, but it was damper, with a brisk wind that rushed the chill to the bone. Down through the winter garden the chancellor walked, a bit slower now, the air sharp in his lungs.

Thoresby slowed as he noticed a couple standing in the shadow of the doorway just ahead, hissing at one another in loud whispers. He was disappointed that he could not make out their words, for the woman was Alice Perrers. Even with his failing eyesight, Thoresby found her hated form unmistakable. But he could not make out the man's features. He stepped closer.

Alas, the two caught the movement and quickly separated, rushing in different directions. Disappointed, Thoresby continued through the doorway, consoling himself with the thought that the court might yet be rid of that strident-voiced, meddling commoner, Alice Perrers.

In fact, it spurred him on to his meeting and his resolve to deliver to the King his carefully worded letters, calculated to make the abbots uneasy. The ploy was underhand and deceitful, but Thoresby felt the end was to the country's benefit. He plotted against Wykeham not so much to keep the office of chancellor, but to win Lancaster's support in his efforts to separate the King from his despised mistress.

Thoresby told himself that he was defending the Queen's honour, but it was Phillippa herself who had first shown Perrers preference. Had Alice not been the Queen's favourite, she might never have been placed in such constant contact with the King. The Queen feigned ignorance of the affair by never mentioning it. But everyone at court knew that Perrers's little bastard was the King's. It sickened Thoresby to think of the hurt that the kindly Queen hid so well.

The unpleasant truth was that the Queen's honour accounted for only part of Thoresby's animosity towards Alice Perrers. The other reason was shameful. He lusted for her. No matter the prayer, the penance, the staunch resolve, when he looked on her his blood ran hot. Which made him hate her all the more. Her presence at court was a constant torment. And thus he was resolved to rid the court of her. Or to leave himself.

At the door to the King's chambers Thoresby paused, checking his clothes, dabbing the sweat from his upper lip and temples, straightening his chain of office, clearing his throat. He then nodded to the door warden to knock. A servant opened the door from within, announced Thoresby. Sweet Heaven, when had the King adopted such ceremony in his own apartments?

Thoresby was disappointed to see William of Wykeham, ascetic and sombre in his clerical robes, already seated near a window, his long, slender hands folded calmly in his lap, heavy-lidded eyes cast discreetly down. Thoresby had thought he was to see the King alone, a chat between old friends.

"Ah, there you are, John." Edward came forward, arms outstretched, stopping short of touching Thoresby. He made a sweeping motion towards the table at which Wykeham sat. "Come, sit with us. We have much to discuss."

A servant brought wine, which Thoresby accepted but let stand for now. Wine taken too soon after activity would bring on a cold sweat, and he must not appear nervous or even uncomfortable in front of Wykeham.

The King settled himself in a well-cushioned chair. As soon as he sat, out came the dagger with which he increasingly expressed himself in conversation, stabbing here, jabbing there. It was as if with the stooping of his once mighty shoulders and the clouding of his once piercing eyes Edward had chosen the dagger to instil fear in his people. "So. Well met, my counsellors. You have something for me, John?"

"I have indeed, Your Grace. Letters for the abbots of Fountains and Rievaulx." Thoresby pulled them from his purse, handed them to the King's servant, who waited beside the Archbishop's chair.

Edward squinted at the documents, then back to Thoresby with raised eyebrows. "Already sealed?"

On second thought, Thoresby had decided that the King would see through his crafty prose and had sealed the letters. The King might yet open them, but he might not. Thoresby creased his brow in an expression of concern. "You did not wish me to put the seals of chancellor and archbishop on them, Your Grace? Forgive me, I misunderstood. I thought you wished to impress on them the weight of my opinion."

The King said nothing, holding Thoresby's eyes with his old power. Thoresby regretted the ploy. Wykeham gave a nervous cough that echoed in the lengthening silence. The floorboards creaked as the servant shifted his weight. Thoresby's own heartbeat thundered in his ears. The King sat with his back to the window, so that the light caught the coarse white hairs on his ears, the seams in the royal neck.

Oh Edward, Edward, we grow so old. Please, my King, be wise in your last years. Put that she-devil from you and comfort sweet Phillippa, Thoresby prayed silently.

The King suddenly smiled. "Of course that was the point, John, and you did well to seal them. You are as competent as ever."

Now Thoresby yearned for the wine, but he must wait until his heartbeat slowed, else his hands would tremble and give him away.

Wykeham, however, was not so wise. He grabbed his goblet and took a good, long drink, returning it to the table with a nervous clatter.

The King grinned unpleasantly at his protégé. "What, William? Did my silence make you nervous?" He sat back, studied Wykeham, who dropped his eyes to the table directly in front of him. "Are you easily bullied, William? How then will you stand up to His Holiness?" Edward turned to Thoresby. "Am I making a mistake, John? Is William too gentle to be my bishop?" Thoresby thought Wykeham's rising colour could as easily be caused by anger as by fear. But Edward did not wait for a reply; he closed his eyes, shook his head. "God will guide me." He opened his eyes, leaned forward, pointed the dagger at Thoresby. "Captain Archer is standing ready?"

Thoresby hesitated only a second, accustomed to the shifts in the King's moods. "By now he has received his orders, Your Grace."

"And the Archdeacon of York?"

Thoresby bowed towards Edward. "And the Archdeacon, Your Grace." Calm now, he lifted his cup to his lips, drank deeply.

"So," the King continued, "we have the letters, the York contingent, all that is still to do is send the letters north, eh?" He nodded to himself. "Townley, Gaunt's spy, is to lead the party north."

Thoresby choked on a second sip of wine, managed to mask it as a cough. John of Gaunt's spy? Was this Lancaster's move to foil Wykeham?

Before Thoresby could think of a comment, Wykeham jumped in with a protest. "But, Your Grace!"

Edward turned slowly towards Wykeham. "You disapprove?" The ice in his voice was unmistakable.

Wykeham's already heightened colour deepened. "Forgive me, Your Grace, but Ned Townley...Perhaps you have not heard the rumours, but surely you have heard of the drowning of Sir William of Wyndesore's page?"

"Ah." The King rolled his eyes. "*That* nonsense. Mistress Alice assured me that Townley could not be guilty, he lay with her maid that night."

Thoresby closed his eyes. Mistress Alice. What was she up to?

"Still, Your Grace, there are those who yet whisper..." Wykeham began.

"Indeed. That is just the point, William. He is condemned when he is innocent. Townley is best out of the way until Wyndesore convinces his men of their mistake, or at least until tempers cool. We would not want my son's spy attacked, would we?" Edward pointed his dagger at Thoresby again. "And his man Archer was Townley's captain, did you know that, William? Archer was Henry of Grosmont's captain of archers. Who better to take charge of Townley for now?"

Wykeham's tall frame trembled. With rage, Thoresby was certain. The privy councillor's usually expressionless face registered indignant disbelief. "Your Grace, I beg you. I must protest for yet another reason."

King Edward sighed, leaned back in his chair, studied his nails, cleaned one with the tip of his dagger. "You grow tedious, William."

Thoresby drank his wine and thanked his good fortune. The King might rethink his preference for Wykeham if the man proved intractable.

Wykeham licked his lips. "Your Grace, I am quite sure that the Duke of Lancaster opposes my promotion. And as Ned Townley is his man, I am frankly uneasy."

"So I can see." The King glanced at Thoresby. "This Townley. Was he not the one who found that rogue Sebastian for me?"

"With Captain Archer's aid, yes, Your Grace."

Edward grinned, turned back to Wykeham. "He has been trained to obey orders. He is my son's man. He will obey me, William."

Wykeham nodded, lifted his cup to his lips with surprisingly steady hands, and sipped carefully. "Who travels north with Ned Townley, Your Grace?"

"It will be the same as with the other groups I have dispatched. Soldiers, a priest or a friar—several in some cases." Edward suddenly pounded the table. "I know what will let you rest easy. Don Ambrose will accompany Townley. He is loyal to you, and an Austin friar— though they like to preach against pluralists, here is one devoted to you. That should impress the saintly Cistercians. What do you say, William?"

Thoresby was puzzled. An Austin friar on such a mission?

Wykeham's long face wore a pained expression. "Your Grace, I had thought to take Ambrose into my household."

"All the better. Knowing he is to reside in your household on his return, the man will be doubly dutiful."

Wykeham glanced over at Thoresby, who closed his eyes slowly, opened them, gave one almost invisible nod. *Accept the King's plan. There is nothing you can do.*

Wykeham understood. He gave the King a little bow. "Forgive me for questioning the plan, Your Grace. I can see now that all will be well."

Well, he was a fool if he meant that, Thoresby thought. Something odd was behind this plan. He could not help suspecting his old enemy, Alice Perrers.

4

THE KING'S BISHOP?

Early the following day Thoresby received an invitation to dine with Wykeham. He had expected the invitation; it had been obvious that the King's choice of escorts for the journey to Fountains had disturbed the privy councillor. Thoresby accepted the invitation with a mixture of curiosity and caution.

He made his way to Wykeham's quarters in the early afternoon, amused by their location in the same tower in which Wykeham had resided as Clerk of Works, supervising the renovation and expansion of the King's castles. Wykeham lived among the guards, lesser clerics, and servants. As Keeper of the Privy Seal, it was an inappropriate residence. Thoresby assumed it artful humility.

The building was at least of sturdy stone, and the windows were glazed. It was not one of the typical lower ward wattle and daub structures that periodically burned. A clerk led Thoresby up to the main chamber. The Archbishop bowed his head and stepped through the doorway; within, he brought his head up to gaze round in surprise. It was a far more comfortable room than he had expected, of generous size, with a curtained bed in the corner to the left of the doorway, a brazier and a table with chairs nearby, a writing desk beneath a south-facing window.

"The councillor is up in his workroom," the clerk said, leading Thoresby up yet another flight. Thoresby entered the room and paused, amazed. On makeshift counters along the wall and tables in the middle of the room stood models—towers, turrets, stairways, porches, window tracery, archways, gates, a small house, a mill—

some tall, some quite small, some visible only by peering behind or over one of the others. Thoresby slowly wandered through the maze, marvelling at the care that had been taken with even the simplest model. He touched nothing for fear he might do damage. Few of the models seemed intended for display—most were unpainted, made from salvaged wood, stones, obviously whatever came to hand—but all had been assembled with careful measurement.

Was this Wykeham's purpose in inviting him here, to his rooms: to give Thoresby a glimpse of his heart? For surely this was evidence of the overriding passion of Wykeham's life. But why would Wykeham care to impart this to him?

Thoresby found his host at the far end, kneeling in front of a clever model of the Round Tower. The tower stood on a mound fashioned from layers of mud and pebbles. "Welcome to my workroom," Wykeham said as he noticed Thoresby standing behind him.

"This is a remarkable collection."

Wykeham nodded. "Years of my life." As he rose, unfolding his tall, angular body, his knees made popping sounds. "I knelt too long. This tower is always cold and damp. I should pull up a stool, but that requires planning, and I never know what will catch my attention."

Thoresby could understand. His eyes were drawn here and there, making new discoveries. "You are considering repairs to the tower?"

Wykeham glanced back at the model he'd been studying and shook his head. "No. I was thinking of Daniel's accident." He crouched down again, picked up a wooden peg approximating the page, Daniel, and placed it at the top of the mound. The moment he took his hand away, the peg tumbled down the slope. "You see, that is the problem. One does not easily stand there, certainly not in the snow. Not to mention the fact that if he had climbed the mound he would have left footprints, yet there were none that I could see, only the scar of his fall."

Thoresby considered that. "Daniel fell from somewhere on the tower itself?"

Wykeham rubbed his chin. "Perhaps." He placed the figure atop the tower, let it tumble from above. It hit the slope halfway down and followed an erratic course.

"You believe Ned Townley is guilty?"

Still crouched before the model studying it, Wykeham shook his head. "No. It is not that." He pointed to the top of the mound, where the tower rested. "The snow melts up there during the day, freezes once more come nightfall. By the time I asked to examine it, I could no longer distinguish the scar or any footprints."

Thoresby found Wykeham's curiosity surprising. "You climbed round the tower looking for footprints?"

Wykeham straightened up again. "I do not seek to point a finger at Ned Townley. What I do not like, cannot account for, is the lack of interest in finding the cause of the lad's death."

"You do not believe it was an accident?"

Wykeham shrugged. "I cannot discount an accident. But what I do not believe is that the page got drunk, walked out into the night and was inspired by the snow to try sliding down the mound. If he'd been drunk, he would have given up any attempt to climb the mound with the first slip; drunks have no patience."

"So he climbed the steps."

Wykeham shook his head. "Had he climbed the steps up to the tower and walked round, he would have slipped closer to the steps." Wykeham leaned over, pointed to the location of the scar in the snow. "His fall occurred out of sight of any of the guards. Did you note that?"

Thoresby was surprised by Wykeham. He seemed a different person from the man who had made the King so impatient. More confident. "You have considered this with care."

Wykeham shrugged. "God forgive me, but it is the tiny details that fascinate me. In incidents as well as buildings."

Thoresby crouched down, studied the mound, the tower. It was true, the guards were stationed out of sight of that very spot. He rose. "So tell me this. If the lad did not climb the mound, and he did not gain access to the tower, and he did not try skirting it, what happened?"

Wykeham threw up his hands. "I do not know."

"If it was murder, how was it carried out?"

Wykeham shook his head. "I do not know."

Thoresby stared down at the model, feeling a bit of a fool for thinking of none of this himself.

"I built this model when the King spoke of heightening the tower, but now I doubt that will happen in his lifetime." Wykeham's voice was sad.

Thoresby turned back to his host. "The funds have been expended for the war in France?"

Wykeham's expression matched his voice. "The war has emptied the coffers. Whatever we finally win from France, it will have cost too dearly."

"In lives as well as building projects."

Wykeham turned a startled eye on the Archbishop. "You cannot think I am unaware of that."

Thoresby held up his hands, palms out, shook his head. "Forgive me. I intended no insult. We may be tearing at the same bone, but I do not think you a heartless man."

Wykeham bowed slightly, then motioned towards the steps. "Shall we descend and sit comfortably? Peter has wine waiting for us, and in a little while he will amaze us with a pie he has coaxed out of the guards' cook."

Thoresby followed his host down the narrow stairs. As he took a seat by the fire, he reached out towards the heat, rubbing his hands together. He had grown quite cold up in the workroom. "I was not aware that the post of Clerk of Works went to men educated in architecture, appropriate though that may be. I thought it usually a political appointment."

Wykeham smiled as he settled into the chair nearest the brazier and turned it at an angle to the table, facing the fire. "My knees," he explained. Peter stepped forward to pour the wine. "Not all Clerks of Works have shared my interest in architecture. But when I was appointed, the King had plans for much building." The sadness had crept back into Wykeham's voice.

"You miss the work?"

Wykeham settled back in his chair. "We accomplished a great deal. Improvements to Eltham and Sheen, much of this castle..." he shrugged. "I am content."

Thoresby glanced over at the bed. "You work on the models when you are wakeful?"

Wykeham smiled. "When prayer fails to calm me to sleep, yes, I rise, light the lamp, find a problem I have not resolved."

"And you eventually grow drowsy?"

Wykeham laughed. "A wiser man would choose what made him drowsy, but I am usually still staring at the problem when Peter comes to wake me for mass."

Thoresby was intrigued. "What keeps you awake at night?"

Wykeham leaned forward. "We come to the point so quickly. Good. We are both busy men." He motioned to Peter for more wine. When it was poured, Wykeham sat bent slightly over his cup for a moment, his long, thin fingers wrapped round it.

Thoresby wondered whether Wykeham was back at the Round Tower, puzzling over Daniel's death. "It is about our interview with the King?"

Wykeham looked up, his eyes no longer sad, but wary. He sat back, tasted his wine, set the cup carefully on the table, as if it were very important to arrange it in a specific position. Only then did he reply. "I want to know how you have arranged for the King to send your spy, Captain Archer, and his friend, Ned Townley, on this mission. And why." He held Thoresby's eyes with his.

But the show of strength meant nothing to Thoresby. The substance did. It suggested a surprising insecurity. "I was under the impression that our King had no secrets from you."

The pale face reddened slightly, but the eyes did not waver. "That is no answer."

Thoresby lifted his eyebrows. "That is because I have none for you."

Wykeham sat back with a disbelieving sniff.

Thoresby relented; after all, he had accepted Wykeham's invitation. "In faith, I can answer part of it. His Grace is sending so many small companies out on your behalf that he is running short of trustworthy retainers. I therefore offered the captain of my retainers for this particular mission. York is a natural rendezvous point before riding to Fountains Abbey." Thoresby lifted his hands, dropped them. "That is all."

Wykeham glanced aside, obviously annoyed and doubting Thoresby's words. But he did not challenge them. "And Ned Townley?"

"I had not heard of his involvement until the King announced it to us. For that you might ask Mistress Perrers. Surely she would tell you?"

Wykeham bent over his wine again, his eyes closed.

Thoresby waited.

Without looking up, Wykeham suddenly said, "Lancaster thinks I hold too much power already. He has arranged for Townley to make trouble on this mission—I am certain of it."

Thoresby had imagined the same when he had heard of Ned's involvement. But since then he had seen the flaw in that idea. "Were the mighty Lancaster plotting against you, he would devise a subtler scheme. No, I think you must look to Mistress Perrers for the architect of your uncertainty."

Now Wykeham looked up. "What would be her purpose?"

"Only God knows her heart, I think."

Wykeham studied Thoresby. "I have heard that there is something between you."

Thoresby did not wish to comment, but he must not appear to avoid the topic. "I make no secret of the fact that I believe her presence at court is an unforgivable insult to the Queen. I have angered the King with my opinions."

Wykeham swirled the wine in his cup, his lids low while he followed the motion. "I doubt you are alone in your feelings."

He despised her, too? "Merely more outspoken than most." Thoresby sat back in his chair. "What are your suspicions about Daniel's death?"

Wykeham directed Peter to bring on the food. "It is the lack of attention his death brought. A brief outburst against Ned Townley, then—forgive me for bringing her up again, but it is necessary in order to answer your question—Mistress Perrers steps forward and swears that he was with her maid, and then, as if Townley were the only possible culprit, everyone agrees to agree that it was an accident. That is what bothers me."

Thoresby studied the man. Should he mention Michaelo's

observation about the page's wrists? And the quantity of ale on the cloak? "Have you discussed this with anyone else?"

Wykeham nodded. "I brought it to Sir William of Wyndesore's attention."

"And?"

Wykeham's expression had soured. "An arrogant, ill-mannered man, Wyndesore."

Thoresby grinned. "You soon became fast friends?"

Wykeham started, then caught the grin and laughed. "Indeed." He was quiet while Peter served the food.

Thoresby tasted the pie. "The guards are fortunate in their cook."

Wykeham nodded towards Peter, who sat quietly on a bench against the wall. "He is so slender, you would never guess, but Peter lives for his food rather than by it. When he hears of a good cook, he befriends him. I fear he trades gossip from the high table for tasty titbits. But discreetly, choosing with care."

They ate in silence for a while. As Wykeham paused to refill his cup, Thoresby asked, "What did Wyndesore say?"

"Oh. Wyndesore." Wykeham nodded. "He could not be bothered with it. 'The lad's dead. Pity. I had trained him well. But he could not hold his drink.' That was it. Not a pause to consider. He had made up his mind and that was that. An appallingly ignorant man to hold such a high station."

Thoresby raised an eyebrow. Wykeham certainly had made up his mind about Sir William of Wyndesore. "No different from most military men." Still, he liked the sentiment. This meeting was changing Thoresby's opinion of his host. "Concerning Daniel, my secretary saw the lad's body as it was carried away."

Wykeham looked up from his food, leaned forward with interest. "Did he notice anything out of place?"

"Indeed he did. Daniel's wrists showed signs of having been bound. And his cloak had been soaked in ale. Difficult to imagine how that might happen."

Wykeham put down his knife, bowed his head, crossed himself. Thoresby did also. "I am afraid I paid it little heed. But your analysis has given me pause."

"Do not blame yourself. No one else made note of the wrists. No one else has questioned that it was an accident, except those who dislike Ned Townley and wish him to be guilty."

Thoresby walked back to his own quarters in a thoughtful mood. Who would have thought the ambitious William of Wykeham would be such a decent, conscientious man? Indeed, he seemed a man admirably suited to the position of bishop, someone with a heart, mind, and soul that worked in concert. He might even make a good chancellor; though Thoresby wondered what he knew of the law.

It was a pity, really, that Wykeham was the King's man. He would feel the conflicts as Thoresby did, the frustration when a compromise was necessary to please the King, a compromise in morals or justice.

Did Wykeham understand that? Did he see the price of becoming the King's bishop?

Thoresby paused at his door, shrugged. If he had not been the King's man, Wykeham would never have risen so high. He could be nothing but the King's bishop.

Pity. The man would undoubtedly someday regret it. But not now.

5

MISTRESS MARY

Ned spent the days before departure banished to his small room. *For your safety*, Wyndesore had explained. For his safety. Hah! Sir William meant to torture him. Ned had gone to Brother Michaelo in the hope that Chancellor Thoresby might intercede and recommend his freedom, but the secretary told him it was in his best interest to stay away from Wyndesore's angry men. In truth, Michaelo's behaviour towards him had been less than courteous. Everyone condemned Ned despite Mistress Perrers's testimony that he was with Mary the night of Daniel's death.

So Ned spent his days practising with his daggers, throwing them at a straw target until his wrists and eyes ached. Or staring out of his small, unglazed window at St George's Chapel and especially the yard before it, where men bustled about their tasks with the confidence that God was pleased with their industry. As Ned gazed out on the life in the lower ward he thought back over the past few weeks, examining his behaviour towards Mary and Daniel. Gradually he came to see that his misery was his own fault. It was true that time and again he had discovered Daniel sitting with Mary when he'd gone to call, but he had seen no embraces, no fond touching, no meaningful looks. It was not until after he had lost his temper several times that Mary and Daniel had seemed at all uncomfortable about his finding them together.

Ned had to see Mary before he left, to beg her forgiveness, to ask whether there was any hope for him. Twice he sneaked to her quarters, twice she refused to see him. How could she be so cruel?

Was not his beloved to stand beside him when all deserted him?

And then, miracle of miracles, Mary appeared at Ned's door the afternoon before he was to leave.

"Mary! Sweet Heaven, I am glad to see you." Ned dropped down to his knees, wrapped his arms round her legs before she had time to back away. "Mary, my love, forgive me for my foolish jealousy. It was only that I could not imagine a man looking on you and not wanting you as I do. I should have listened to you. I vow I shall be your obedient servant all the rest of my days."

Mary smoothed his hair. She had the gentlest touch. "Peace, my love. Peace," she whispered.

My love! Ned rose and, cupping her lovely face in his hands, looked deep into Mary's eyes. "You love me?"

"You know that I do."

"You turned me away, Mary. Twice! I could never turn you away."

Her sweet eyes swam with tears. "Oh, Ned, I have been so miserable!" She stood on tiptoe and kissed him.

Blessed Mary, Mother of God, thank you for hearing my prayers. Ned covered Mary's face with kisses. Then, holding her close to him, he edged slowly backwards, drawing her into his room.

Breathlessly, she whispered, "I must not stay long. Mistress Alice will miss me."

"Just a little while, my love," Ned begged as he closed the door with his foot. He let her go, brought the lamp closer to see her.

Mary pushed back the hood of her cloak, shook out her hair. The dark cloud fell softly round her face, tumbled about her white shoulders, which were partially bared by her low-cut gown—his favourite silk. It whispered at her slightest move and gave off her exquisite scent. "Say but that you shall remain at Windsor and all is forgiven," she whispered, moving towards him.

Bless her innocent heart that beat so softly under those white, white breasts. Ned had to clear his throat before he could speak. "Sweet Mary, would that I might say yes. Ask me anything else. But I cannot stay; I am ordered north on the King's business. I must go." He reached for her hands.

Mary hid them behind her back. Her face was flushed. "Is that truly the only reason you go?"

"What other reason could there be?" Ned could think of none.

"That you fear what Daniel's friends might do to you."

Ned's heart sank. Still she gnawed on that bone between them. "You know that is not so, Mary. I am no saint, but neither am I a coward. I do not run from my troubles. In better times you worried that I was incautious."

Mary bit her lip, which Ned read as a hopeful sign that she was listening. "I think the King is sending you away to protect you," she said, "because Mistress Alice told His Grace that you could not have followed Daniel from the hall that night."

"That may be His Grace's reason, but not mine."

"Then stay." Mary said it with a thrust of her chin, challenging him. "Do not let the King make you act the coward."

Would that Ned might accept the challenge. He gently pressed Mary's shoulders. "Please, Mary, let us not argue. I must obey the King; I am in his service."

Mary retreated from him. "You are in the service of the Duke of Lancaster."

Ned nodded. "And the Duke left me here at court to learn from and serve the King, his father. Now the King has need of me. The Duke would expect me to obey."

Mary turned away from Ned, stood with one hand to her chin.

"Mary?" Ned whispered.

She tossed her hair, took a deep breath, spun round prettily on her slipper, her silk rustling. "Perhaps I can change your orders."

Ned grinned. "You, Mary? And how would you do that?"

She stood quite straight, her hands clasped behind her. "Mistress Alice might intercede for us. I shall tell her I cannot bear to be separated from you."

In her innocence she was but a child. "You have forgotten what your mistress thinks of me. She would never succumb to such a plot. She does not support our union. In truth, it may be Mistress Alice who suggested me for this mission. And once I am away up north she will distract you with a more suitable man. A nice, elderly knight who can provide for you."

Tears swam in Mary's pretty eyes, her lower lip trembled. "I do not want an elderly knight. I would hate that."

"People would consider such a man more suitable for you, Mary. Far better than a young spy with neither land nor title."

Mary's tears flowed freely now. She wiped them away angrily. "You must not go, Ned!"

"I must, Mary. And it will not be the last time you must accept my absence. If we wed, you must reconcile yourself to a life of separations. As Lancaster's man I shall often be called away. It is the nature of my work."

Mary crossed her arms, stomped a pretty foot, hung her head.

Ned stood there stupidly, hands at his sides, wondering how to proceed. Suddenly, in the gathering quiet, he saw Mary shiver, heard a trembling intake of breath. In one stride he had her in his arms.

"Mary, my dearest love," he whispered, "I shall return. Never doubt it. With you waiting for me, I could not do otherwise. And when I return we shall be wed."

She looked up into his eyes. "But how long, Ned? How long must you be away?"

He squeezed her hard. "Oh, my sweetness, my love."

Mary clung to Ned. He picked her up and carried her to the bed, fumbled with the clasp of her cloak, drew it off her, tilted her head back. Her tears had stopped. Her mouth parted. He kissed her hungrily. Soon he held her soft, naked body in his arms.

"I am afraid," Mary whispered, pressing herself against him. "Oh, Ned, I am so afraid."

"You have nothing to fear, my love. I would never hurt you."

Ned woke to the sound of someone quietly weeping. Disoriented, he glanced round, discovered Mary lying beside him with her hands over her eyes. "Mary, my love. I am not yet gone. Do not weep while we are so happy." He gathered her into his arms. "Do you not know how much I love you? Do you doubt that I shall return to you?"

She kissed his chin. "I do not doubt you, Ned."

"Then what is it?"

She did not answer at once. "I shall be so alone without you."

"And I without you, my love. But soon we shall be together always."

"But while you are gone, Ned. What about while you are gone? Am I strong enough to stand up to Mistress Alice and her ambitions for me?"

"You have stood up to her so far, my love. I have not played your protector in this. She thinks it beneath her to speak to me."

Mary sat up with a sigh. "I weary of butting heads with Mistress Alice."

Ned pushed himself up on one elbow, touched a finger to Mary's cheek, catching a tear on the tip of his finger. "You are a strong woman, Mary."

She attempted a smile, with modest results. "Ned, my love. Are you certain that Daniel's death was truly an accident?"

Ned fell back on to the pillows with a groan. That again! "You *know* I did not do it!"

"No, no, please, Ned, what I mean is—well, do you believe it was an accident?" She leaned over him, her hair caressing him. Her eyes did not smile now, nor did they weep. She was quite serious.

Ned wearied of Daniel, even in death. He put a hand over his eyes. "*I* don't know, Mary. They said he drowned. They accused me of murder. That is all I know for certain."

Mary lay down facing him, propping her head up on one elbow. "Why would it have occurred to them to accuse you? Why did they not assume at once that it had been an accident? Folk drown all the time."

"It was because of our argument in the hall. I threatened him. Meaning naught by it, I swear. But I did threaten him—with the daggers."

"I have heard no talk of knife wounds," Mary said, "nor wounds of any sort." She grew quiet.

Ned stole a peek at Mary. She was biting her lip, deep in thought. "What is it?"

"He did drown, didn't he?"

"I did not see his body." Ned stroked her hair, kissed her forehead. "Why does it worry you so?"

"I—" Mary looked confused.

Immediately suspicious, Ned grabbed her shoulders. "What was between you?"

"Nothing! For the love of God, Ned, I am fearful because if he was murdered, whoever did it might be in the castle. And I am in the castle. And when you leave, I've no one to protect me. No one to run to if I'm frightened."

Ned pulled her to him, hugged her hard. "You have nothing to fear, Mary. You are in the King's court, under Mistress Alice's protection. You will be quite safe."

Alice Perrers returned from an exhausting morning with the ailing Queen to find her bed unmade, her chamber not yet aired.

The elegant Mistresses Cecily and Isabeau sat near the window using the daylight for their embroidery.

"Where is Mary?" Alice demanded of them.

Mistress Cecily rolled her eyes. "Whimpering on her bed…my lady." Cecily always paused on the last two words. It rankled her to serve Alice, who was of lesser birth than she. But as the King's mistress, mother of his bastard son, Alice must be treated with respect. It was the King himself who had insisted on Alice's serving women calling her "lady".

"On her bed? At midday?"

Cecily and Isabeau dropped their eyes to their embroidery, tittering at poor Mary's misfortune. Their needles did not move. Alice had no doubt they had sat there all the while in their elegant silk gowns and gossiped.

"Mary is worth ten of you, you lazy ornaments!" Alice hissed as she left the room. What had Queen Phillippa been thinking when she'd asked Alice to take them into her chambers?

Mary was different. She had been Alice's choice, an orphan like herself, only two years younger. Alice trusted Mary, understood her lot in life. Ned Townley had upset the balance. He had been warned to stay away, but the damnable man had kept returning, swearing his undying love, turning Mary's pretty head.

Well, if one considered a handsome man with pretty speech an ideal knight, Ned was that, and more. Lancaster would never have trained him as a spy if he were not brave and cunning. But he was a nobody. And would ever be a nobody. His sort never acquired property. Never advanced in rank beyond captain. Already it was plain that what little money Ned made he squandered on clothes. It was true he had an eye for colour and fabric, but clothes did not appreciate in value. Mary deserved better. Mary required better.

Alice found Mary sitting in a dark, airless room. She threw open the shutters. "For pity's sake, Mary, how can you breathe?"

Mary blinked, then held her hands before her eyes to shield them from the sudden light. "Forgive me, mistress."

Alice knelt down, lifted Mary's face towards the light, pushing her hair back from her face. "*Mon Dieu*, what a pitiful sight!" Mary's lovely face was swollen and red, her eyes bloodshot. "Enough of this, Mary! I will stand no more. You must put your knife-thrower out of your mind. I have plans for you."

Mary twisted out of Alice's grasp. "I shall wed no one but Ned."

Alice sat back on her heels. "You little fool. You do not understand your fortune. I know what it is to be an orphan. I know the uncertainty." Her parents had died of the plague the year Alice was born. Until her uncles had devised the plan to educate her and call in favours to establish her at court, she had been brought up by a merchant and his wife, whose own children oft reminded Alice of her temporary status in their home. Alice knew all about uncertainty. She took Mary's hands in hers. Cold hands. The child was not eating. "Trust me, Mary. I want what is best for you. And I can give it to you."

"Then help me be with Ned. He loves me and I love him, Mistress Alice. He will take care of me."

Alice dropped Mary's hands, rose. "For pity's sake *think*, Mary.

He has no money but that given him by Lancaster. No house, no land, no name."

Mary sat up straight, chin jutting forward. "Townley is a fine name."

Heavens but the child's heart was loyal. Most inconvenient. "You are not so simple as that, Mary. You know what I mean. The name brings nothing with it."

"I don't care."

"No, not now. And why should you? But you will care soon enough—when the babes come. They must be fed, clothed, kept warm and safe."

Mary folded her arms across her chest. "I shall marry no one but Ned."

Alice shook her head at the girl's stubbornness. "We shall see about that."

"You would treat me as your uncles treated you? You would make me a whore?"

Alice slapped Mary's face. "You do not win an argument with insults. Now get to your chores. I cannot abide slothfulness."

A whore. Did Mary hear nothing? Alice meant to find a good husband for Mary, not a royal lover.

It was early evening, a time Mary saved for chores that required either thought or space, as Cecily and Isabeau accompanied Mistress Alice to the great hall for supper. The silence of this time of day was a particular blessing. Cecily and Isabeau could not abide silence; they filled any room they inhabited with incessant chatter and the rustle of their lovely clothes as they paced, fidgeted, rearranged, fussed. Ned had often kept Mary company during these quiet hours while she completed her chores, entertaining her with tales of his life of action. Mary must not think of that now, for thoughts of Ned churned up the sea of emotion she was trying to ignore while she finished her work.

Tonight Mary was rearranging Mistress Alice's gowns and shifts in the wide, shallow chest that allowed the gowns to be laid flat.

The contents had shifted when the chest had been moved a few days before. Mary shook out the shifts and shawls, folded them with care and stacked them on a bench; then, one at a time, she lifted the gowns of softest wool, silk, and velvet out of the chest and arranged them on Mistress Alice's bed. Then one by one she returned the gowns to the chest, lovingly smoothing them with her hands. On top she placed the folded linens, shawls, and stockings.

All the while Mary had been thinking about her plan. Now she knelt down and prayed for courage. It was a brief prayer. She must not dally, else Mistress Alice might return before she was away.

Mary gathered some clothes and sundries and put them in a leather pack. She moved quickly, with an efficiency born of Mistress Alice's frequent impulsive decisions to leave court and move to her house in town. For protection, Mary took the knife Ned had given her, an elegant weapon with an ivory hilt that arched into the neck of a swan. She tucked the knife into her girdle; she wanted it quick to hand in case of trouble. Tonight she was travelling only the length of the King's castle, but it was dark, and Daniel's death was on her mind. Best to have a weapon handy.

Now she was ready. Donning her cloak, she bid a silent farewell to her comfortable life and slipped out into the dimly lit corridor.

As she left the protection of the building, Mary pulled up the hood of her cloak and hugged her pack to her for extra warmth. The knife pressed against her hip, giving her a sense of security. Her plan was to stay concealed in Ned's old room until dawn, then hide near the gate and wait for a party of servants or merchants to mask her departure through the castle gate. She had once thus escaped the castle to meet Ned down on the Thames; it should not be difficult. There was nothing about her appearance to call attention to herself. The journey beyond Windsor would be more difficult, but it was her only hope—to make her way to Lucie Wilton's apothecary in York, where she knew she would be safe until Ned returned.

Mary stood uncertainly in the dark courtyard of the upper ward, wondering how best to sneak down into the lower ward. To her right loomed the motte and bailey of the Round Tower and the gate through which she usually passed; the gatekeeper knew her and might question her carrying a pack at this time of the evening. She remembered that at the opposite side of the ward, farthest from the river, the builders had cleared a narrow path between the wall and the edge of the ditch, just wide enough for one person pushing a cart of bricks or timber. It was dark there, made darker still by the huge earthwork that blocked out any light from the inhabited parts of the castle wards. Mary shivered as she chose the dark path. It frightened her, but for her plan to succeed she must not be seen.

Early the following morning Sir William of Wyndesore made ready to depart for the Scottish border, where he was to assist in protecting the Marches. Alice did not know why Sir William must leave now, before Easter. She had looked forward to watching him joust. He was impressive in his fearlessness. She could imagine him on the battlefield. Tall, steely-eyed.

This morning his eyes were almost as bloodshot as Mary's had been yesterday. Impetuous Mary. Where could she have gone? Alice had sent Gilbert out at first light to search the castle precinct for her. So far he had found only Mary's dagger in the lower ward.

"You are gathering wool, Mistress Alice," Wyndesore said.

She shook herself. "I am indeed, Sir William. I am remembering a certain strong knight, the firelight reflected in his eyes." She handed him his stirrup cup with a smile. "Your eyes betray your late night. Perhaps it is best that you leave court. You will get some rest."

He grinned, took a long drink. "You are most generous, Mistress Alice."

Alice looked round, noticed that Wyndesore's squire was busy securing one of the pack horses. "Sir William, I must speak to you privately."

Wyndesore glanced round, nodded, drew her to the side of his horse away from the crowd, gave her waist a little squeeze. "Why did you not ask it last night?"

She put a hand on his shoulder, leaned close. "I did not wish to spoil the evening."

"Spoil the evening? What is amiss?"

"My maid, Mary—she disappeared last night."

Wyndesore looked unconcerned. "She is off keeping a vigil for her lover in some chapel."

"No, Sir William. She took clothing. I fear she has gone in pursuit of Ned Townley. His party is far from the castle by now I should think?"

Wyndesore drank down the wine, handed Alice the cup. "Too far for her to catch up, if that is what you ask." He gazed off in the distance for a moment, then nodded. "So you think she's gone after him? I suppose it is the sort of thing she might do." He shook his head. "Poor, foolish girl. If she does not find him, she will find trouble instead." He touched Alice's cheek. "I shall keep a watch out for her as we ride north."

Alice straightened the brooch on Wyndesore's cloak. "Nothing must happen to her, Sir William."

Wyndesore took Alice by the shoulders, looked her in the eye. "She has removed herself from your protection, Mistress Alice. By her own free will. You cannot be to blame if aught happens."

Alice shook her head. "By her own free will, perhaps. But she willed it because I told her that Ned was not good enough for her. I had ambitions for her."

"Then she is an ungrateful child. All the more reason why you cannot be to blame." Wyndesore touched the tip of Alice's nose. "Forget her, eh?" He suddenly frowned, cocked his head. "'Tis troubling, though, her running away. You said Mary was loyal to you."

Alice bristled. The touch on the nose was the gesture of a man to a child. "She *is* loyal to me."

"More so to Ned Townley."

Alice shrugged. "She is of the age when love for a man blinds a young woman to all else."

Wyndesore smiled. "I cannot imagine you blinded by love!"

"You are a charmer, Sir William."

"And you, Mistress Alice, are not as clever as you think. To run from you is an odd way to show loyalty." Wyndesore flicked a finger under Alice's chin, then moved away from her, prepared to mount.

"Take care, Sir William," Alice said softly. "It is a cold, lonely road you travel."

His glance told her he had heard. She smiled sweetly and waved.

Gilbert continued his search of the castle, asking for news of Mary. Alice waited on Queen Phillippa as usual, but her distracted manner concerned her mistress.

"What is it, child? What troubles you?" the Queen asked, leaning forward on her cane.

"Mary, my maid, disappeared last evening."

The Queen smiled indulgently. "Now, Alice, it is a grand castle and such a dreamer as Mary might lose her way."

"I thought of that. But Mary packed clothes, Your Grace. I fear she is running after her lover."

Now the Queen's kind face registered concern. "Young hearts can be too fond. Too fond. What has been done to find the girl?"

Alice told her of Gilbert's search and Sir William's promise to look out for her on the road north.

"Who is her lover? Where is he?"

"Ned Townley, one of the men headed north to York on the King's business."

The Queen shook her head, her eyes sad. "And the child could not stay put. What does she think, that she may travel with her love on the King's business? Foolish girl."

Alice dropped her head. "I am worried, Your Grace. They argued bitterly over the young man who drowned. What if her lover now rejects her?"

The Queen rested a swollen hand on Alice's head. "My poor child. We waste time. I shall order a full search of the castle and the town." The Queen chucked Alice under her chin, kissed her on the forehead. "You have a good heart, sweet Alice."

Oh no, not a good heart. That had been put to rest when Alice's uncles had taken her from her foster parents and announced that she was to be their key to riches. A good heart would not have come so far, would never have reached the Queen, would never have usurped her in the King's bed. But sweet Phillippa, born far above Alice's station, had no need to understand such things.

6

MATTERS OF THE HEART

Jasper burst through the shop door, his flaxen hair darkened with sweat and clinging to his flushed face. "Mistress Lucie! I've seen them! The King's company!"

Lucie caught him by the shoulders before he slid to a stop against the shop counter. She forced a smile as she smoothed back his damp hair, tweaked his nose. "The King's company is here? How do you know that, love? Your errand should not have taken you near Micklegate Bar." *Holy Mary, Mother of God, let him be mistaken.*

"Master Merchet called out to me as I passed the tavern," Jasper said, his eyes shining.

"Ah. Well. If Tom Merchet says it is so, it is indeed." Lucie tried to hide her disappointment. She understood Jasper's excitement. His friends had been much impressed when they'd learned that Owen was to lead a company of the King's men to Fountains Abbey. He had already asked and received permission to hand Owen his stirrup cup at departure, which would guarantee that he met the men when they were in full gear. The boys would later hang on Jasper's every word as he described the company's dress, their weapons, their speech, and Owen's part in the expedition.

Owen's part; that was what troubled Lucie. The company's arrival meant Owen's departure was imminent. And despite her confiding to Bess that Owen was driving her mad with his litany of worries, that she prayed for a respite, Lucie did not wish him to go. If this was the answer to her prayers, they had been misinterpreted. She had meant to pray that he would realise their little family was as safe as any family in York, not that he would leave the city.

Already she missed him, thinking of the cold bed, the nights when she needed his ear and must write instead, the countless possible dangers he might encounter that would haunt her throughout her days and nights while he was gone: Scotsmen on the road—they were not wont to observe the King's peace; packs of wolves—folk said they were hungry after the hard winter and moving in larger packs than usual; men jealous of Owen's favour with the powerful John Thoresby who might cause an "accident" in order to take his place; even such mundane matters as spoiled food, and no one with her skill with physics to care for him if he should fall ill. When Owen was at home Lucie did not fret over such things, but the moment he rode out of the city her imagination betrayed her. She had thought it would be easier to part with him in time, but instead it grew worse. He was more and more a part of her. And now there was Gwenllian. She was growing so quickly. He would miss so much while he was away.

"Will they come here directly?" Jasper wondered, climbing up on to a stool with Crowder in his arms. The ginger kitten swatted at a fly that buzzed past. Jasper lunged to catch the unbalanced kitten and they both crashed to the floor, the stool following with a clatter. The kitten squirmed out of Jasper's grasp and hissed at the stool. Jasper lay on his back and giggled.

Lucie stood there, hands on hips, knowing she should caution Jasper that Crowder was safer tumbling through the air than clutched tightly, but too thankful for the boy's laughter to bring herself to chide him. "I doubt they will come here directly. They have ridden a long way and will wish to rest."

Jasper sat up, brushed himself off. Bits of dust and herbs clung to his pale hair. "I should like to see them come across the bridge." Eyes wide, smile eager, he willed her with all his energy to consent.

"Why?" Lucie teased, picking the debris out of his hair. "You have seen King's men before."

Jasper's pale eyebrows came together; he stretched his hands towards her, palms up in supplication though she had not yet said no. "I want to see the men the Captain is going to lead."

Lucie made a great business of whisking the last bits of debris from Jasper's hair. "But surely you mean to be there to watch when they depart? You will see them then."

Jasper's shoulders slumped, his head drooped. "And I have work to do."

Lucie could tease him no further. "You may go as soon as you tell me how fares Mistress Thorpe." Jasper's errand had been to Gwenllian's first godmother, the wife of Lucie's guildmaster. Mistress Thorpe had taken a fall with a cauldron of hot washing water a few weeks past and had scalded her left foot. Jasper had delivered a second jar of salve for the terrible blistering.

"Mistress Thorpe says that she has not awakened with the pain in two nights, which is a blessing. And she was most grateful you had sent the salve. She blessed you for knowing she had used the last of it this morning. She has the children helping with the washing and cooking and did not know when she could spare one to come to the shop."

Lucie could tell nothing from that; Gwen Thorpe believed that to complain of pain was to criticise God's judgement. Even when she had almost died in childbirth last year she had suffered the pain with a white-lipped, white-knuckled silence that had so angered Magda Digby, the midwife had threatened to leave the birth chamber, for how was she to help if she did not know the condition of her patient. But Lucie knew Jasper was a keen observer. "Did you see her foot?"

Jasper shook his head. "She did not show me."

Still badly blistered then, else she would have shown him. It was time for Magda Digby to visit Gwen Thorpe. "All right. Off with you."

Lucie stepped back into the kitchen to check on Gwen's namesake and found Owen lounging on a bench, cup in hand. The cradle beside him was empty. "Where is Gwenllian?" The excited pitch of her own voice surprised Lucie.

Owen grinned. "And you call me a worrier. I am tempted to tell you a tale of Scotsmen crashing into the kitchen, but the truth is Tildy took Gwenllian out in the garden to watch the clouds. No harm will come to her."

Lucie trusted Tildy; it was coming upon Owen unaware and remembering the separation to come that had tightened her throat, but perhaps it was better to let Owen think she was just a fretting mother. "Is it warm enough for Gwenllian in the garden?"

Owen sat up, handed Lucie his cup to taste. "You must trust Tildy, my love. She is very good with our child. You cannot do everything in this house, though I'm damned if I know how to keep you from trying."

Lucie took a sip of the cool well water, handed Owen the cup. "It is Tildy who tries to do everything in the house. I worry that with cooking, cleaning, and tending Gwenllian she is overworked."

"Tildy will tell you when she has need of help, my love. When she fears that things are not as perfect as they might be." They both knew that Tildy would ask for assistance only if she felt the quality of her work was disappointing them.

Lucie studied her husband, so handsome, so much a part of her. He was sweaty and covered with a fine film of rich earth; he looked content. "The work is going well?"

"I have one more bed to prepare. God help me, the rocks I dug out last year are back, and with a year's extra growth." His damp linen shirt clung to his muscular chest and back as he flexed and stretched.

Lucie never tired of looking at him, such a fine man. Already she missed him so keenly that the quiet, companionable joy of the moment pained her. "Rocks growing indeed, Owen! I'll ask you to hold your tongue with nonsense such as that or Gwenllian and Jasper will grow up with unholy notions of God's creation." She could see at once that her effort to sound jolly had failed.

Owen's eye held hers. "What is wrong?"

Lucie allowed herself to go to him, stroke his wiry dark hair. "The King's company has entered the city. We've little time together before you leave."

Owen wiped his hands on a cloth, draped it over his lap, clean side up, and pulled Lucie down. "I won't pretend I'm sorry to hear you are already missing me. I've been thinking you wanted me out from underfoot."

Lucie took a cloth and gently wiped his face. "You drive me mad at times, 'tis true, my love. But I would have you no other way. And I would have you home and safe, not riding north in this uncertain season on the King's business."

Owen grabbed the hand that held the cloth, kissed Lucie's palm. "How do you know the company is here?"

"Tom Merchet told Jasper."

The bell on the shop door announced a customer. With a groan, Lucie began to rise. Owen held her down. "Let Jasper see to them."

"He has gone out to watch the company come across the bridge." Lucie stood, brushed her skirt, kissed Owen's forehead.

"Mistress Wilton? Captain Archer?" a young, reedy voice called from the front of the house.

They looked at each other. "Harold," they said together. Archdeacon Jehannes's clerk. Owen rose, hugged Lucie, went into the shop. Lucie followed with a heavy heart, knowing Harold would be summoning Owen to meet the company.

Harold bowed to them. "God go with you, Mistress Wilton, Captain Archer. I am sent to ask the Captain to come to my master's house after vespers. The King's men are to arrive shortly."

Vespers, Lucie thought. And then Owen's mind would be filled with the coming mission. His eyes would shine with the prospect. For though Lucie had no doubt that Owen loved his family, she knew he could not be happy long without a battle, or at least a good problem to solve, preferably outside York. She had warned him when he chose to stay in the city as her apprentice that he would tire of the life. And since Lucie had predicted it, Owen tried to hide his yearning for action from her—but she knew him far too well to miss the signs, the pacing, the stretching, the cutting of too much firewood.

Owen nodded to Harold. "Tell the Archdeacon I shall be there."

After Harold departed, Owen held his arms out to Lucie. Grateful that he understood her mood, she stepped into his embrace.

Their quiet moment did not last long. Soon Jasper came puffing in, obviously winded from a good run. "God go with you," he cried, then hesitated at the door.

Lucie could see that he was about to burst with news. She moved away from Owen, smoothed her apron and the kerchief holding up her hair. "What is it, Jasper?"

"It's Ned leading the company! Did you know? Was it to be a surprise?"

Owen frowned. "Ned Townley?" The boy nodded. "Are you sure?"

"I would not mistake him," Jasper said. The lad had been quite taken with Ned when he had met him the previous summer. "So you did not know. And I have been first to tell you." Jasper was pleased.

"Why would he be part of the company?" Lucie asked, suddenly adding another worry to her growing list. Was this a matter requiring more armed men? "You did not tell me that there would be need for two such fighters as you and Ned."

Owen squeezed Lucie's shoulder. "We do not know that is the case, though it is possible." He shrugged. "We shall know soon enough. It would be very like the Archbishop to lead me into trouble with nary a word of warning."

As Archdeacon of York, Jehannes had a substantial house near the minster. It was simply furnished, his spiritual life being that which drew his attention. Neither hangings nor painted plaster softened the walls, nor embroidered cushions the chairs. But the fire was welcoming and the food and wine were good.

However, this evening the room seemed more ascetically furnished than usual, with Ned Townley's elegance radiating from the corner, standing as a contrast against the dark walls. Even in his travelling gown and leggings, Ned looked too elegant for the room, the clasp on his travelling cloak a heavy circle of bronze, his leather belt intricately tooled and clasped with a silver buckle, the sheath of his dagger tipped in silver, his boots of fine make, his hair precisely cut to frame his handsome face.

Owen lounged in the doorway as he took in Ned's appearance. "So you've taken to baiting the thieves in the forests, flaunting

Lancaster's generosity to his spy?"

Ned had begun to cross over to greet his friend, but he hesitated at the comment, his smile frozen. "Baiting…?"

Owen nodded towards the ornate scabbard. "A bit of silver to lure them?"

Ned glanced down, then laughed and slapped Owen on the back. "I must keep the King's men in fighting form, my friend. How better than to invite attack?"

"You will not wear the silver on the road?" Jehannes asked with a worried frown.

Ned wiped the grin off his face when he saw the Archdeacon's concern. "Fear not. I am no fool."

Owen slapped his friend on the back, nodded to Jehannes. "He is a good man, I assure you." He turned his good eye on his friend. "I am glad to see you, Ned, never doubt it, and glad to have you riding with me. But knowing you as I do, I know there's a story to why you are part of this company. And the others who join our company in York will ask. It is common knowledge that Lancaster opposed Wykeham's advancement to the Privy Seal, believing he climbed too high. Bishop of Winchester, Lord Chancellor—the titles would make Wykeham even more powerful. As Lancaster's spy, it's passing strange you would come with us to speak for Wykeham in this matter—unless Lancaster has had a change of heart?"

Ned raised an eyebrow, burst into hearty laughter. "Nay. The enmity goes too deep for that."

"Then come, my friend. Sit down and tell us how it is you are here." Owen joined Jehannes near the fire, motioned to Ned.

Ned returned to his seat, settled back in his chair, nodded. "It was not my design to hide the sad circumstances that bring me here. I merely waited for the proper moment."

Jehannes asked Harold to pour wine. "You may speak in front of my clerk, Master Townley. Harold can be trusted."

"To be sure, it is nothing so horrible that I need worry about Harold," Ned said. "My fault is merely loving too well and acting a fool." As he sipped his wine he told them of his unfortunate argument with the page Daniel on the evening of the lad's death. "His protectors in Wyndesore's household did not believe my assurance that I could not have followed him from the hall and murdered him. It seemed wise to remove me from Windsor Castle while Daniel's death was fresh in people's minds."

"But you are most unjustly accused," Jehannes said with a look of dismay. "Had no one a thought to clearing your name?"

"Oh, aye, my lady's mistress, Alice Perrers, declared me innocent, and that was enough for the King. And more than that they could not easily do, eh? Even the King cannot return to that night and follow Daniel. Would that he could. I would be grateful for a means to prove to my Mary that I did not touch the lad."

"*Your* Mary?" Owen grinned. "You do sound as if you have lost your heart at last." And to someone in Mistress Perrers's household.

"Aye."

"You look a bit sad for such good fortune, Ned." Owen could always read Ned's eyes.

"'Tis a painful thing, love."

"But you said you were with her that night," Jehannes said. "Does she share the blame?"

"'Tis not that sort of blame. What she says is that he drank too much that evening because of our argument; and the drink killed him."

Owen thought that a bit of wrongheaded reasoning. "But surely you do not believe that? Are we to be blamed for another's mistaken impression of us?"

"Of course I do not agree with Mary. In faith, had I frightened Daniel, had he feared for his safety, he would have stayed sober. Else he was a fool. Either way, I cannot see how I am to blame."

Jehannes sat forward. "And all this has naught to do with the Duke of Lancaster? You have no secret instructions to subvert our mission?"

Ned glanced at Owen with raised eyebrows. "First Mary, now the good Archdeacon. I find myself a man much distrusted of a sudden."

"Forgive me," Jehannes said, "but I must know."

"He has understandable concerns," Owen agreed.

"Rest easy, sir. My lord knows naught of this mission, or shall hear of it too late to prevent it. I tell you it is my suspicion that Mistress Perrers put my name forth. She is eager to separate me from my love. When I am out of sight, she will try to shift Mary's affections to someone more suitable."

"The mighty Alice Perrers has ambitions for Mary?" A selfless affection? Owen found that interesting indeed.

Ned looked weary. "Mistress Perrers told Mary I shall lead her down a path of poverty and disappointment."

Owen was happy for his friend's new-found heart. He made a decision. "Then you must prove yourself worthy, Ned, that is all. Archdeacon Jehannes should ride directly to Fountains; I prefer not to risk his eminence and the important documents he carries. So I need a separate company to ride to Abbot Richard at Rievaulx and escort him west across the moors to Fountains for the meeting. I shall appoint you captain of Abbot Richard's escort."

Jehannes let slip a chirp of dismay. As heads turned towards him, he lifted his hands, palms up, his expression one of apology. "Forgive me, but am I not to be consulted? We had not discussed dividing the company."

"I assure you Ned is a good man," Owen said. "I can think of no one better able to deliver Abbot Richard safely."

Ned cleared his throat. "I am honoured by the sentiment, my friend. But I think it best the Archdeacon choose his man. Only Our Lord might guarantee a choice of men. And the Archdeacon is closer to Him than you or I."

Owen was pleased. It seemed love had steadied his headstrong friend. "You grow wise, Ned. I agree. It is best to let Jehannes decide."

Jehannes rose, clasped his hands behind his back, moved over to the fire, stared down into it. The room was quiet while he considered. After a long while, he returned to his seat, lifted his cup. "To Ned, second in command."

Owen grinned, raised his cup. "To Ned."

Ned beamed. "Then it is agreed."

• • •

Lucie did not share Owen's certainty. "Might there not be enmity hidden among the others that would flare up once they are up on the moors, far from witnesses?"

"They might as easily have struck on the road to York. Yet they did not."

"They were on the King's road to York and know full well the penalty for breaking his peace. But the road to Rievaulx Abbey is a different matter." Lucie spoke softly and in pleasant tones while she nursed Gwenllian. But the expression on her face said, "Beware."

Owen struggled to concentrate on tactics rather than the appealing scene before him, Lucie's hair tumbling down over her sleepy-eyed daughter, her finger held tightly in Gwenllian's dimpled hand. The room smelled milky, a calming scent from a time when fear is unknown in the presence of mother and father. "Let us not discuss it now, Lucie."

"Just think on this, Owen. If aught happens, Ned will be blamed. And if aught happens to him, with only his enemies about, we shall hear of it too late, and perhaps never know the truth."

Trust Lucie to have expanded Jehannes's argument. "What might happen for which Ned would be blamed?"

"I know not. I just warn you that any misadventure will be his to explain."

"I shall consider this."

Lucie sighed. "I speak thus, knowing full well my warning will go unheeded. You have decided. You will not turn back."

"No. I admit to having been caught up in the idea of Ned being changed by his love. But perhaps I read too much into it. He has ever been quick to anger, quick to speak his mind. Both faults that were at work in his latest trouble. With Easter upon us, he must wait at least four days to depart. I shall watch him and consider."

Lucie looked surprised. "I am glad to hear you retain an open mind, Owen. It is all I ask."

7

PREMONITIONS

The afternoon sun brightened the solar and Alice hummed as she dressed. She liked it best here, her small house by the Thames. Though it was close to the river and wattle and daub above the first storey, the house seemed warmer than her chambers in Windsor Castle. Perhaps it was the absence of watchful eyes and incessant whispers. Here she could quietly enjoy the fruits of her labours.

Though Alice hummed, she was not gay. She awaited the King, who was coming to see their son John and to discuss the boy's education. He had chosen a household for John in which the boy would be tutored and brought up as a gentleman. Alice did not like parting from her son—he was but two years old. But he was the King's son, bastard or no, and must be raised properly.

Lifting John from his play in the sunbeam, Alice cleaned his face and then carried him to the window. From her vantage point on the second storey she spied a cart clattering up the slope from the river, driven by a man in the livery of the castle guards. In the cart was a draped bundle the shape of a body. A fisherman followed, his head bowed, his gait melancholy. Beside him walked William of Wykeham. Alice crossed herself. A week past, Mary's pack had been found down by the river. Since then Alice had waited in dreadful certainty.

As Alice watched the curious procession, the King's party drew up beside them. Wykeham hurried to the King, who leaned from his saddle with a grave face. Handing John to his nurse, Alice hurried from her private chamber down the ladder to the parlour. "The King and his privy councillor are without, Gilbert," she called to her servant. "Invite them in."

Alice called to Katie to bring John. The child fussed as his nurse lifted him. He preferred to descend the ladder from the solar by himself. But it would not do to greet the King in ripped and soiled clothes. In the end, John discovered that Katie's arms were a perfect launch for leaping into the outthrust arms of King Edward as he entered with his company and William of Wykeham.

"Praise God, what a strapping fine lad!" the King roared, throwing back his head and laughing. John's chubby hands clasped the King's wool-clad shoulders.

Alice stood back, taking in the sight. Her son was as fair as his father had once been, pale blond hair, hazel eyes, a straight body, long in the limbs. You could see John was a Plantagenet. He had a promising future, for the King doted on him. And she would ensure that future while the affection lasted. For the King could be inconstant in his affections.

Edward spun round with John, who giggled and hung on to his father's beard.

Wykeham cleared his throat. "My lady…"

Alice gestured towards a cushioned window seat. "Come. Sit beside me and tell me of the curious group I saw without. Who is the fisherman? What is in the cart?" She fought to keep her tone light.

Wykeham glanced questioningly at the King.

Edward's face changed. He handed the confused child to Alice, who handed him to the nurse.

"Come back when I call for you, Katie," Alice said.

John chirped, reaching back towards the King as Katie carried him off.

But Edward had turned away, the boy already forgotten. John screwed up his face and let out a howl of disappointment. The nurse hurried up the ladder with him.

Gilbert had pulled up a high-backed armchair for the King, who settled down into it, comfortably at home. Alice returned to her seat on the bench beneath the window. Wykeham went to the door, called to someone, paused, returned with the fisherman, who bobbed nervously when he realised he was brought before the King.

Edward turned to Alice, levelled his faded blue eyes at her, leaned over and took her hand. "We have news of your maid, Mistress Alice." He turned to Wykeham. "William?"

Alice brought her free hand to her throat, glanced over at the King's councillor.

Wykeham's eyes flicked towards Alice, back to the fisherman. "This man found her, Your Grace."

The King nodded. "And you identified her?"

Wykeham closed his eyes and nodded. "I did, Your Grace."

"Sit down, William. It is civilised to sit at eye level with a person when you give them evil news."

Wykeham lowered his long body on to the bench beside Alice, who sat stiffly at the edge. "Mistress Alice…" He hesitated.

Alice pressed her hands together. "This fisherman has found Mary. Which means she was in the river. Drowned."

Wykeham nodded, his eyes discreetly on Alice's shoe.

Alice pressed cold fingers to hot eyelids. "How long?"

The councillor cleared his throat. "Perhaps ever since she went missing. She was caught in the weeds in an inlet. This good man found her early this morning."

Alice glanced up at the man who pressed one dirty foot down on the toe of the other as if so to force himself to remain in this uncomfortable place. His hair and clothes were grimy, but his face was clean, as were his hands. Alice rose and took his hand. "God bless you for ending my search, however horrible the outcome," she said. "Has she been much— Have the fish—" Sweet Heaven, why did she ask such a thing? She could see by the distress in the fisherman's eyes that Mary was not whole. Alice shook her head. "No. Do not tell me. God bless you."

"Give him a purse for his troubles," the King shouted to his servant by the door.

The fisherman grinned, showing healthy teeth but for a broken one on the top and a gap on the bottom. "Your Grace," he murmured. "My Lady. Father William."

"You may go now, Rafe," Wykeham said.

The man gladly hurried out, the servant following.

Alice turned to Wykeham. "Thank you for going down to the river, councillor. I would fain not see Mary so."

The eyes upturned to her were sympathetic. "I deemed it best you did not see her."

Alice shivered, aware of the river flowing just below the garden, its icy waters blackening as the sun set.

The King rose and put an arm round her. "Let us save John's future for another day. Are there any women from court might keep you company tonight in your grief?"

"No," Alice whispered. "I am best alone tonight."

Owen bought drinks for Ned and his company at the York Tavern to observe his friend with the men he'd travelled with from Windsor. Having been a captain of archers, Owen had developed a sixth sense for troublemakers. He took a dislike to two of them, large, coarse men who seemed to itch for a brawl. Bardolph and Crofter. He would warn Ned to watch them. Ned's second, Matthew, looked like a clumsy pup and acted much the same. Completely devoted to his master. The others were nondescript. All looked to be good fighters. One was lacking a thumb and two fingers on his right hand. "Dagger tricks?"

A puzzled look, then a blush. "Nay. Helping my father at the sawmill. And your eye? A lass poke it out for winking?"

Owen slapped him on the back. He liked a man who let you have it with wit, not muscle. "We're even now, Henry."

"In faith, Captain. Tell us the story."

Owen groaned.

Bess Merchet, never far away when her handsome neighbour graced her tavern, leaned over. "'Tis a good story. Give us a treat."

Ned lifted his cup to Owen and nodded.

So for the hundredth time Owen found himself telling the sad tale of betrayal that had led him here from his comfortable, honourable career as captain of archers in the service of the great Henry of Grosmont. He told them of the Breton jongleur whose life had been spared on Owen's orders; and how the following night Owen had found him in camp slitting the throats of the prize hostages. When Owen had attacked, the jongleur's leman had come from behind and in the struggle dealt the blow that blinded him.

"How did they die?" Crofter asked.

"Swiftly. By my hand," Owen said quietly. He did not like the gleam of approval in the fair man's eyes. "But enough about me. There are far more heroic tales to tell about Captain Townley." And so the evening went, fighting men showing off their battle scars. What else were such permanent reminders of death good for?

Gwenllian's cries broke Lucie free from her nightmare. She sat up, rubbed her eyes, wondered how long she had slept.

Owen turned on his side. "Bad dream?"

"Are you asking me? Or Gwenllian?"

"You. You were thrashing round. I almost woke you."

The bad dream had left her edgy. "Almost woke me? There's no almost about it. You've lain there and let Gwenllian cry so long she dragged me from my sleep. And listen to her. She is hoarse! Why did you not comfort her?" Lucie rocked the cradle with one hand. The movement was not enough to quiet Gwenllian.

"You're the one she wants," Owen said. "She's hungry."

Would that it were so simple. "How do you know? Oft-times when she's wakeful she refuses to nurse. She wants to be held and walked. You can do that."

"You sing to her, too."

"You are the one with the voice of an angel."

"But I don't know the songs you sing to her."

"She is not particular, Owen. It is our voices that comfort her, not the words. Now come round here. Pick her up."

"But you are up now."

"Owen…"

He rose with a sigh, shrugged into a linen chemise, picked up the squalling child. Gwenllian hiccuped, grabbed her father's finger, and quieted to a feeble whimper. Owen began to walk.

Lucie, more awake now, propped herself up and smiled at the incongruities in the scene, Owen's scarred face bent over the perfect face of his daughter, who looked no more than a doll pressed against his broad chest. "What keeps you awake?"

"I have decided I cannot withdraw the captaincy from Ned. I put myself in his place and I cannot insult him so. Perhaps I was too hasty in offering it to him, but now I have and he shall not suffer from my hasty tongue." When Lucie said nothing, Owen glanced over at her. "You disagree."

"Ned would accept whatever you decide without question, Owen. But I knew you were set in this. I do not know why you pretended otherwise."

"You are angry."

"No. In truth, I merely tire of the subject." Gwenllian had been up most of the previous night with a mysterious complaint, and Lucie with her. She knew that her mood was partly lack of sleep.

"I should not bother you with my problems."

"Of course you should. We are husband and wife. Your problems are my problems."

"You think he will come to harm. Or fail me."

Remembering her dream, Lucie shivered and hugged herself. "I pray my fears are unfounded. Ned is a good man. He is our friend. All I said was that he would accept your decision."

"I know that he would. But it would be there between us, Lucie. Offered, then withdrawn. He would feel the sting. I cannot do that to Ned."

"Then you should not. Have I argued?"

Gwenllian chose that moment to register her complaint that Owen had stopped his pacing. "Hush, Gwenllian, hush," he murmured, gently rocking her as he resumed his pacing.

Lucie slipped back down under the blankets and fell asleep.

• • •

Come morning, Lucie clearly recalled her nightmare and wondered whether to tell Owen. If it was merely the outgrowth of her fears she should not, because Owen trusted her dreams and she did not wish to influence him by turning her own reasoning—however sound—into portents. Lucie took care to tell him only those dreams she truly believed to be warnings, answers to her prayers for guidance.

In the dream, Lucie stood on a hill watching Owen descend towards a burning village, his longbow ready. Lucie could hear nothing, not the crackle of the fire down below nor the whisper of the breeze that blew smoke into her eyes. And then, all of a sudden, sound engulfed her. She stood in the midst of a crowd murmuring and gesturing angrily. They did not appear to see her. Their eyes were fixed on the village, and now Owen and Ned, their clothes smudged and bloody, their arrows spent, came out from the cloud of smoke that surrounded the village.

"'Tis them," a woman said. "They be the ones, Father. They be the murderers."

"No!" Lucie screamed. But the woman did not hear her. Lucie threw herself at the woman, crying, "It was not them. Owen went down to find Ned."

The woman stared ahead, her arm outstretched, her finger pointed towards Owen and Ned. Lucie pounded the woman's chest, tore at her hair. But the woman did not notice. How could Lucie touch the woman and yet the woman feel nothing? The woman pushed Lucie aside and began to move forward with the others. Lucie fell and was trampled by the surging crowd.

She crossed herself as she sat over her morning ale.

"What is it, Mistress Lucie?" Tildy asked. Owen was still abed, having slept only after Lucie had woken to give Gwenllian her early morning feed.

"Remembering a nightmare is all, Tildy. You should have seen Owen last night, walking Gwenllian, cooing at her." Lucie smiled at the memory.

"He's a good father is the Captain. He worries if Gwenllian as much as frowns. Talks to her whenever he's near her. Mine was nothing like. I think he looked at me for the first time when I was grown. Saw this mark I've had on my face since birth and said, 'What's this, girl? Did you fall?'" Tildy touched the red birthmark that spread across her left cheek. "But the Captain is different. He'll fret all the while he's gone that Gwenllian will forget him."

"Owen worries too much."

Tildy shrugged. "There's no changing a man's nature. The Captain is just a worrier. 'Tis naught to be done about it."

No changing a man's nature. Lucie wondered. Had Ned steadied, as Owen thought? "Some say a man is changed by love. You would disagree?"

Tildy rolled her eyes. "Women marry rogues believing that. I hope I'm never so daft."

When Ned's company had arrived in York, Don Ambrose had left them to stay with his fellow Austin Friars in their house on Lendal. He would join the company once more for the journey to Rievaulx. Or would he?

Don Ambrose read through the letter he had just received, dropped it, stared off across the cloister. Sweet Heaven, he had been right. He sat quite still, staring at nothing, considering what he must do.

For surely this letter was a sign that God had not forsaken Ambrose. Had it been delayed one day, it would not have reached him before he departed York. It must be a sign from God that he might still save himself.

No time to lose; he snatched up the letter. He must speak to Archdeacon Jehannes at once.

Owen leaned on the counter, watching Lucie attack a dried root with mortar and pestle. "Would you like help, or are you doing away with someone?"

She looked up, startled. "I did not hear you come down." Her hair was slipping from her kerchief. There was a dusting of powder on her nose where she must have rubbed it.

With a soft cloth Owen wiped her nose, kissed it. "Want some help?"

Lucie pushed the work towards him. "You are welcome to it."

He bent to it. "What was your dream last night?"

"Last night? Something about a fire. Can't remember."

Owen glanced up, caught Lucie biting her lower lip. "About Ned, was it?"

Lucie shrugged. "Thank you for last night. I needed sleep."

"I told you I should not leave."

"It cannot be helped, Owen, and there's an end to it."

Owen studied her with his good eye. She hugged herself and turned to study the wall of jars. "A nightmare, it was. Tell me about it."

Lucie shook her head. "I was just dreaming my worries, Owen. The dream meant nothing."

Jehannes looked up from his work with poorly hidden impatience as Harold stood aside for Don Ambrose. There was much to do before tomorrow's departure. Letters to write, last minute orders to give Harold. "*Benedicte*," Jehannes said.

"*Benedicte*," Ambrose replied.

Jehannes motioned the friar to be seated. "You are prepared for tomorrow's departure?"

Ambrose leaned forward, pressing the table with his fingertips. "It is of that I wish to speak, Father. I pray you relieve me of the mission. I would remain in York."

Holy Mary, Mother of God. "You would remain in York? Why is that?" Jehannes had not guessed that Ambrose was of a nervous humour. But there was no denying the beads of sweat standing out along the friar's receding hairline. And he did not face Jehannes directly, but up through his lashes.

"Forgive me, but I cannot say, Father. I assure you that I mean to harm no one in this."

Cannot say. That made the cause clear. "Your superiors object to your support of William of Wykeham, I presume. They took their time protesting."

Ambrose's eyes widened in surprise and dismay. "Oh no, no, they have nothing to do with my request." He dropped his gaze to the fingers that pressed down on the table. "It is a...personal matter, Father."

Jehannes sat back, steepled his hands. The man appeared to be lying. An Austin friar had no personal business. And the Austins hated rich pluralists like Wykeham. His sweat and his indirect look were not signs of nerves then, but deceit. Well, he would not have it. If Jehannes had to swallow his pride on the King's business, so did the friar before him, and all the friars in his house if that was the truth of it. "I am sorry, but I have my orders, as you do yours. The King chose you to accompany us. I have neither the time nor the inclination—you have given me no motivation, you must admit—to release you and find another. You ride to Rievaulx tomorrow. If you do not, you shall be guilty of a grievous sin."

Ambrose pressed his hands together. "Then please, Father Jehannes, allow me to accompany you to Fountains. Send someone else to Rievaulx."

Jehannes was a patient man, but today was not the day to try him. "You do not wish to cross the moors, is that it? Rievaulx has been situated in the moors since the conception of this mission. Why did you not protest before?"

The friar's hands kneaded each other. "It is not the moors. Truly." At least now he looked Jehannes in the eye. "I pray God you heed me. I must not travel with the company to Rievaulx."

"So it is the company to which you object. Any particular person? Or the lack thereof?"

Ambrose sat back, obviously seeing Jehannes was losing his patience and realising that he must answer the question with care.

"Well?"

Ambrose shook his head. "I cannot explain. If I am wrong I might slander an innocent soul."

A most revealing reply. Jehannes guessed that the friar objected to Ned Townley, having been poisoned against him in Windsor. "The men have been carefully chosen. I shall accept no objections. You are dismissed. God go with you, Don Ambrose. And if you do not ride with the party to Rievaulx on the morrow, you shall answer to the King."

The prior of the York Austins shook his head at Don Ambrose. "And no wonder the Archdeacon refused to grant your request. In the name of our prior provincial so shall I. A personal matter, indeed. The King chose you and you must obey. It will benefit our order to have a member in Wykeham's household, a man with the King's ear. I cannot in truth think of a reason you might give that would change my mind, save Divine intervention. And I am sure you would admit if you'd had a vision."

"I have had no vision."

"Then you must go, Ambrose. God grant you a speedy and safe return."

Ambrose bowed his head. Safe. He would make sure of that. It was up to him now.

8

PRIVATE DEVILS

Alice did not wish to dine in the great hall, but the King insisted. "Two days you have closed yourself in. Enough. The girl chose her fate. Your brooding changes nothing." Artfully applied paints and powders concealed her sleepless vigil, careful dressing gave her colour and shape, but only Alice herself could force her spirits. Her mourning need not be concealed; the Court expected it, encouraged it. But her anger must be laid aside with her private face. A difficult discipline.

Someone had placed Alice beside the privy councillor. A sly comment on their being the King's toadies? She did not smile at the thought. Wykeham smelled of incense and sawdust as usual; but he was making more of an effort with his attire of late. Tonight he had forsaken his clerical robes for a discreetly colourful houppelande. The King would make a courtier of him yet.

They spoke little during the meal, but as Alice rose to leave, Wykeham rose also. "May I escort you, my lady?"

How might she refuse politely? "You must not leave on my account, Sir William."

"I beg your patience. You afford me an excuse to leave early." The sensitive mouth turned up at the edges, in a smile not cheerful but meant to reassure.

Alice bowed slightly. "Then I would be honoured."

He said nothing until they were outside and Gilbert had gone on ahead of them to tell Alice's new maid her mistress was on her way. Then Wykeham turned to Alice. "Forgive me for broaching the subject when it is still painful, my lady, but I must know your thoughts on your maid's death."

Alice squared her jaw, forbidding tears, and took a deep breath. "You are right, it is a painful topic. I grieve for Mary as I would a sister. But that was not your question, was it?" The torches surrounding the courtyard created moving shadows. It was impossible to read Wykeham's face. "What are you asking me?"

Wykeham dropped his chin to his chest, pressed his long fingers to his forehead. "Do you believe that she fell into the river, my lady?"

She saw where this led, but wished to force Wykeham to state his suspicion clearly. "How else would she get into the Thames, Sir William?"

"Was she likely to despair of finding her lover and jump into the river?"

"No."

Wykeham raised his head, gave one nod. "I thought not."

"Therefore she stumbled."

"Is that what you think?"

"I am more curious to hear what you think."

"Daniel, Sir William of Wyndesore's page: do you believe his death was an accident?"

Alice's heartbeat quickened. "Their deaths are connected?"

"What if they were?"

"That would be a terrible thing, Sir William."

"I agree. I would ask you to share with me any thoughts you might have on this possible connection, Mistress Perrers."

"Why? What were Mary and Daniel to you?"

"God's children."

"As are we all, Sir William."

"Just so." He turned, offered her his arm. "Now I must deliver you to your servant else he shall tell His Grace I have chilled you with my chatter."

Chilled her he had, indeed. But to confide in him was out of the question.

• • •

Ned's company rode from York four days before Owen was to set forth. Archdeacon Jehannes had sketched out the route, but once they climbed up on to the moors the way was not so clear. According to Jehannes, Rievaulx lay in a deep vale surrounded by high moors; but Ned had not expected the track down to the abbey to look so like a ravine, and with no abbey in sight. Surely something of the reportedly magnificent church would be visible from here? In doubt, Ned consulted Don Ambrose, the one member of their party who had been here several times.

Don Ambrose nodded as he edged his steed away from Ned with a scowl. "'Tis the track to the abbey."

A friendlier response was not to be expected. The friar had circled Ned warily since York, as if he expected an attack. It had not been so on the first part of the journey, riding up from Windsor. Ned wondered what had happened in York to change the friar's behaviour towards him.

"And horses can descend without harm?"

Ambrose hunched his shoulders sullenly. "Aye."

"You are certain?"

"I am not in the habit of lying, Captain." He did not meet Ned's eyes.

Ned shrugged, ordered the men to dismount. "Safer to lead our horses down this slope," he said. He trusted the friar only so far.

The descent was sudden. Ned was uneasy. If attacked, the company would not move quickly, certainly not surefootedly. It was as if they were being swallowed up by the land. The only comfort was that an enemy would be likewise handicapped.

The vale soon coaxed him into noticing its beauty, thickly wooded and echoing with birdsong. But wild. Could there truly be a community as large as Rievaulx down below? Thinking to ask how far before they should see signs of the community, Ned glanced back at Don Ambrose, who sensed Ned's gaze and lifted his eyes to meet it. Ned slowed and edged over to the side of the track to let the others pass him. "This track is too narrow for carts, Don Ambrose. You stand by your assurance that this is the track to the abbey?"

The eyes were coldly challenging. "I do."

"But it is not the only way."

The eyes slipped sideways. "I never said it was."

Ned took a deep breath to calm himself. "Why have you led us down such a dangerous path?" He was glad to hear his voice so low, reasonable.

Ambrose looked him in the eye. "As God is my witness, I did not lead you, Captain. You paused at the top and asked whether this was the track to the abbey. It is one of them."

"You might have corrected me when I passed the safer way. You are meant to be our guide."

"The cart road is farther on." The ghost of a smile trembled at the corners of the friar's mouth.

Ned gripped the reins in his hand tightly. "Damn it, man, if you have some grudge against me take it out on me, not my men!"

Ambrose glanced down the track at the disappearing backs. "All are well so far."

"You arrogant b— When shall we glimpse something of the abbey?"

"Anon." Still the eyes challenged.

Ned had never met with such insolence. "What is it? Why do you hate me? What happened in York?"

"I see through your plan, Captain," Don Ambrose snarled. "You waited until the others were out of sight to ask." The pinched mouth spread into a cold grin. "You must think me a fool." The friar took a step forward.

Ned fought a desire to punch the smile off the friar's face. What was his sin? He had done nothing to the man. And that sly, knowing grin. Ned grabbed at a branch, snapped it off the tree, broke it in two across his knee.

The noise startled the friar. He lunged into the dried leaves and bracken, missing the track. Ned cried out to warn him, but Ambrose yanked at his horse's reins and continued. As Ned started down the track after him, the friar quickened his pace and stumbled. His horse stumbled. They both began to slide in the dense mat of old leaves, so thick and unstable on the steep slope that neither man nor beast could find a purchase.

Ned hurried along the path, shouting, "Let go the reins, you bloody fool! The horse will crush you!" He threw the reins of his own steed round a sapling and headed off into the bracken towards Ambrose. But it was no use with the horse between Ambrose and Ned, and both tumbling slowly, slowly through the leaves.

Two of the men who had gone on ahead came running back up the track, hesitated as they saw the avalanche upon them. "Let go of the reins, Don Ambrose!" one yelled.

Ambrose did so. The horse slid a bit farther, but with its head free it managed to twist itself round and dig in its hooves. With a snort, the horse rose and stood panting, its eyes wild. The men managed to grab Ambrose and pull him back on to the track.

Seeing the immediate danger past, Ned eased down the slope, calmed the friar's horse, led it back to the track, got his own, led them both down towards Ambrose and his rescuers, who were asking the friar whether he was injured. "As long as he can walk, let us continue," Ned said. "The infirmarian can see to him."

Ambrose looked up at Ned with an expression of fear and loathing. "You almost had me."

Ned shook his head. "You almost had yourself, you bloody fool. I tried to warn you."

"Warn me? Coming after me with a switch?"

It was no use. "Help him down," Ned ordered his men. He went on ahead. Damn the man. He now heard faint sounds of a community echoing from down below, the hammer of a smithy, the lowing of cattle. Praise be the Lord. He rode out from under the canopy of trees and came upon the rest of the company, sitting their steeds now as the incline lessened, gazing on a huge complex of honey coloured stone that rose out of the peaceful valley. They moved forward together, still descending, and suddenly, as they rounded a bend, the church towered to the left, tucked on a slight rise above the rest of the buildings, its roof soaring to compete with the bluff beside it. The afternoon sun shone on the lead roof, the tall, arched windows. Ned was almost glad he had come upon it this way, such a dramatic approach.

But his pleasure was checked by the fear and hatred in Don Ambrose's eyes. He must ask Abbot Richard to let the friar stay at the abbey. Someone else could escort the man back to York.

Owen held Gwenllian up, studying her dear face. She laughed and grabbed at his earring. "My angel." He kissed her, handed her to Lucie. "I would remember her just like that."

Lucie crossed herself. "For pity's sake, Owen, you speak as if you shall not see her again, yet you insist there is no danger on this mission. Have you lied to me?"

He cursed himself for voicing his thoughts. "I meant only that I wish to burn Gwenllian's face into my memory so that I might see her whenever I close my eyes."

"You must take care, Owen. We depend on your return." Lucie's clear blue eyes were levelled at his good one, watching for a flinch.

"I have every intention of returning, my love." He put his arms round her. She lifted her chin for a kiss. He sniffed her hair, kissed her forehead, her eyelids, her lips. She slid her fingers up through his hair while her body pressed against his. Sweet Heaven, why must he always be leaving her?

He was still thinking about that kiss as he joined Jehannes and the company he was to lead to Fountains Abbey.

"You look as if you come to meet your doom, my friend." Jehannes grinned, looked round him. "I see here no enemies. Do you?"

Owen looked the men over, nodded to Jehannes. "Clearly I am mistaken. No enemies here."

"It is difficult to leave your family, eh?"

Owen grinned. "Nay, foolish. I ask myself how it is I choose a life of constant farewell. Why can I not stay put?"

"Because you have a questing soul, Owen. And because Lucie loves you the way you are. You know, were she a man I believe she would be much like you."

Owen laughed. "So I fell in love with my own reflection?"

Jehannes grinned. "Now I have chased the shadows away. Shall we depart?"

They were well on the road when Jehannes mentioned Don Ambrose. "I pity Ned Townley, riding with the secretive friar."

"Secretive?"

"He came to me the day before he was to depart, begged to be relieved of the task."

"On what grounds?"

"He would not say. The King's orders and he would not say why he wished to remain in York." Jehannes shook his head.

Owen felt a prickling under his eyepatch. "He said nothing more?"

"Nothing."

"Austins have no love for worldly clerics. But why were they so slow to protest supporting Wykeham?"

"I thought perhaps to delay us," Jehannes said.

Owen turned his head to study Jehannes. "You do not believe that."

"Why did he wait so long to come to me? I had enough to do without bowing to his whim." Jehannes winced under the piercing gaze of his one-eyed friend. "In truth, I sensed a private devil somewhere within him. It made me uneasy. But with no explanation…" The Archdeacon's voice trailed off. "I was indulging in righteous indignation."

"You chose a poor time to indulge yourself. A man with a private devil, asking to be relieved of the mission—why in God's name did you not tell me of this before they rode out?"

Jehannes looked surprised. "You are angry?"

"Ned Townley has enough trouble without the friar's private devil. But Ned's as much to blame. He said nothing to me."

"I did not tell him."

Owen reined in his horse. "For the love of God, why not?" he shouted.

Jehannes glanced back, turned his horse round to face his angry captain. "King Edward wished the friar to be in the company. Why should I poison him to his captain?"

"You warn a captain of trouble in his ranks, Jehannes. You warn him!"

"He might have refused to ride with him. You soldiers have no patience with cowards."

Owen bit back a curse. "What does it matter to the King whether Ambrose accompanies us or not?"

"He had a reason for choosing him."

"And we had a damned good reason to leave him behind."

They rode on in an uncomfortable silence, Jehannes feeling unjustly criticised, Owen wondering what bedevilled the friar.

9

SIGNS OF TREACHERY

It was late afternoon when the breeze stiffened and a scent of salt air brought Abbot Richard's head up sharp. He turned to Ned, who rode beside him. "I feel a storm coming."

Ned had noticed the change, and from the look in the Abbot's eyes it must be a storm and not just rain approaching. "Will it overtake us before we reach tonight's resting place?" They were a day's ride from Fountains Abbey.

The abbot paused, studied the sky all round. "I fear it will, though our goal is a grange house belonging to Fountains, not Rievaulx, so I am not certain of the distance. I think it close enough to reach by sunset, but not before the storm. May God protect us."

"By sunset is good enough," Ned said. The company had departed Rievaulx Abbey the previous afternoon and had spent the past night in one of Rievaulx's grange houses along the way. The shepherds had been out with the lambing ewes, and were thus absent hosts. But they had left wood for a fire, fresh water, salted meats and hard bread. Ned had thought it quite comfortable. "If we get wet, a fire will soon dry our clothes."

Abbot Richard nodded. "There is no mistaking you for anything other than a soldier."

Ned was unsure whether that was praise or criticism, so he kept his peace. As the wind picked up and whipped his cloak round him, he rode through the company warning the men of the coming storm, softening it with the Abbot's reassurance that they would reach shelter before the light faded.

Don Ambrose received the news with a look and posture that blamed the bearer for any mishap. Ned wearied of the man. "I shall be glad to part company with you, to be sure," Ned muttered as he rode on, feeling the friar's hostile eyes upon him.

When Ned had asked Abbot Richard's permission to leave Don Ambrose at Rievaulx, to be sent back to York with the next messenger headed that way, the Abbot had replied with questions: "What happened as you rode into the vale, my son? What is the trouble between you?"

Ned had been taken aback; it was clear that the Abbot thought them both at fault. "In my mind, we have no quarrel," Ned had replied. "Ask my men. From Windsor to York, the friar was—in faith I would not call him friendly, but cordial. Since York he has acted as if I were an enemy. What befell him in York I know not."

The Abbot's expression had been enigmatic, though he kept his voice kindly enough. "Don Ambrose told me he asked the Archdeacon of York to relieve him from his duty to accompany you, but as he could not break an oath of silence to explain his request, it was not granted."

Ned stared at the Abbot, dumbfounded. Archdeacon Jehannes had not told him. Nor had Owen. "I did not know."

The Abbot smiled.

Ned saw the Abbot was amused by what he perceived to be a clumsy lie, as well it might seem. It was incomprehensible why the Archdeacon had withheld information critical to the peace of the company. "I swear I did not know!"

Still Abbot Richard smiled.

What curse had befallen Ned that he was so misunderstood? By his gift of pleasing speech Ned always drew people to him, like a flower draws bees, a candle moths. Many had so described his gift. Why was he suddenly unable to speak on his behalf and be believed? Abbot Richard seemed determined to mistrust him.

"Come now, Captain Townley. It would be foolhardy for the Archdeacon to keep such a request from the captain of the company."

"Indeed it was!"

The Abbot's smile grew tired. "You have made the friar swear silence and he fears you will accuse him of breaking that oath. It is quite obvious."

"But not true, my lord abbot. Not true." What could Ned say to convince the Abbot of his ignorance in the matter?

Abbot Richard pressed his hands together, shrugged. "You must search your conscience for the truth in this, my son. It is between you and God." He had risen from the table.

"It is between me and Don Ambrose," Ned said to the Abbot's retreating back.

They had not spoken of it again. But Ned felt not only the friar's eyes on him, but the Abbot's. Constantly. It was enough to make a man mad.

The trees bent in the wind, the brush flattened. The travellers pulled their hoods low over their faces and leaned close to their beasts for warmth. At last the rain came, cold, sharp, penetrating. Cloaks were soon sodden and slapped wetly against the flanks of the steeds. It was with a hoarse cheer that the forward rider announced the grange house and barn were in sight.

Mercifully, a fire had been left to smoulder under a layer of ashes. The men stirred it into flames and added dry wood. Ned looked round, counting the company. All there. He bowed his head and silently gave thanks. He did not need the Abbot to blame him for another mishap. Ropes were strung from the rafters and the wet clothes hung to dry overnight. It was a shivering, weary company that crowded round the fire to chew on bread and salted fish. The men spoke of other miserable journeys, as if to convince themselves that this, too, would pass. At last, bellies sufficiently filled, the company bedded down for the night. Ned offered the main room with the fire to the Abbot and his monks, but Richard chose the far room, explaining that white monks were not accustomed to sleeping in heated rooms.

Nor was Ned. He fell asleep with his nostrils full of the stench of damp wool and his own sweat. Still, it was a small price to pay for dry clothes in the morning.

Someone shook Ned, pulled him out of a dream of marching to battle in the hot sun. He jerked awake, shot up to attack, met a restraining hand.

"*Benedicte.*" Don Ambrose knelt over him, backlit by the fire.

"What the Hell...?" Ned reached for his daggers.

Ambrose put a hand over Ned's. "Peace, Captain Townley. I would speak with you alone. Please. Come out to the stables with me."

"Out to the stables?" Ned rubbed his eyes. The room was so curséd smoky and his lids so heavy with sleep he had trouble keeping them open. "We can talk here. I have no wish to go out in the rain."

The friar put a finger to his lips. "We cannot talk here, among our sleeping companions. I pray you come quickly. The way to the stable is roofed, you will stay dry. We must resolve the trouble between us."

Grumbling at the friar's choice of nights to interrupt his sleep, Ned was enticed by the prospect of peace. And by the covered arcade connecting the house with the stables—at least he would not be soaked again. "I will come." Ned wiped his sweaty chest with the blanket, pulled on his chemise and leggings.

Ned and Don Ambrose moved silently among the sleeping men. Outside, the rain fell steadily, but the wind had died down. "Clear tomorrow, I wager," Ned said, pausing to fill his lungs with fresh air. The moon cast little light through the clouds. The landscape revealed itself to Ned's ears rather than his eyes. Behind him, the stream they'd crossed on arrival boiled over rocks. Nearby, water gurgled in a gutter, pushing round some obstacle, and dripped from the eaves, hitting the rocky ground with wet plops. Ned heard the stable door open and shut and turned to follow, thought better of it. It was too dark to be walking round unfamiliar surroundings without a lantern; and he did not fancy sitting in the dark with a man who distrusted him. He returned to the grange house for a light.

Back at the stable, Ned opened the door cautiously, shifting the lantern in his hands to open the shutter. The horses whinnied softly as the light moved over them. Where was the friar? Ned set the lantern on a shelf just within and was closing the door when something grazed him on the back of the neck. He whirled round. Don Ambrose lunged forward. Ned threw his arm up to protect his face from the friar's dagger while reaching for his own with his other hand. His dagger was not there. Of course not. He had not expected an attack. The friar came at Ned again, this time shouting, "You'll not advance yourself with my blood!"

Ned kicked out. The friar stumbled, then righted himself enough to butt Ned in the groin with his head. As Ned fell back, the dagger grazed his leg. "Bloody idiot!" He lunged at Ambrose, gripped his right wrist and shook the dagger out of his hand. The friar twisted out of his grasp and rolled over the dagger. Ned stood, pulled the friar up by the back of his habit, grabbed for his right arm, thinking Ambrose had retrieved the dagger. But it was still on the floor. Ned stepped on it, Ambrose tried to kick his foot away. They toppled, Ned grabbed the knife, sliced across the palm of the hand that tried to steal it from him. "What is wrong with you?" Ned cried. "I'm here to protect you, you bloody bastard!"

"Protect me?" Don Ambrose spat at Ned. He held his bleeding hand away from his habit. "Poor Mary. She thought you loved her. Who did it, Townley? A friend left behind?"

Ned sat on the ground pressing the wound in his thigh. "What are you blathering on about? And why did you ask to stay in York? Why didn't you just disappear?" He started to rise. Ambrose kicked him in the face and went running out into the night. Ned rolled over, spitting blood. "Damned good fighter for a friar." On the ground near him was the pouch the friar kept close to him. Ned picked it up as he climbed to his feet, then staggered back to the house clutching the pouch against his bleeding thigh. He left the lantern behind.

Matthew, his second in command, woke as Ned stumbled towards him.

"Come, Matthew. I need you to tend a wound."

Their rustling woke the other men. Outraged to hear what had happened, two ran out into the night after Don Ambrose.

Ned cursed himself for the foolishness of going off with a man who so obviously despised him. What was it he'd cried? Something about advancing himself with the friar's blood? What did that mean? And what did Mary have to do with the friar? While Matthew cleaned and bound the wound, Ned fidgeted and fretted.

"Why not open the pouch, Captain? See what the friar guarded so well, then left behind," Matthew suggested.

Ned opened the courier pouch. A breviary; a few coins; a seal; wax; a letter, seal broken. He unfolded the paper, spread it out where the light might illuminate it, squinted over the words. Reading did not come easily to Ned, but fortunately the hand was clean. Or unfortunately…

Matthew glanced up as Ned moaned. "What is it, Captain? What's ado?"

"Mary. My Mary." Ned raised his eyes, stared at the terrible image the words had conjured.

"What of Mary?"

Ned moved his eyes to Matthew, tried to focus on him rather than his nightmare vision. "They have killed her," he whispered, for such a thing should not be spoken aloud.

Matthew crossed himself. "What are you saying?"

Poor Mary. She thought you loved her. Who did it…a friend left behind? "He thought *I* had her murdered," Ned whispered.

Matthew reached into his medicine pouch, drew out a bottle of brandywine, dropped it on Ned's lap. "Drink some of this, Captain. You are shivering."

Ned glanced down at the bottle, but did not touch it. "Mary is drowned."

"Someone wrote this to Don Ambrose?"

Ned nodded slowly. "Another friar. Paulus. He says he saw her. Told no one. 'God will lead them to her, not I.'"

"This friar wrote to Don Ambrose and told him he had let your Mary drown?"

A movement in the next room brought Ned back to the present. He stuffed the letter in his waistband and picked up the bottle. He took a drink, coughed.

"Why did he carry such a letter? Why would someone write to him about Mary?" Matthew asked.

"The bastard carried this letter from York and never a word to me."

Abbot Richard approached, his right hand outstretched, his eyes fixed on Ned. "Give me the letter you hid in your belt, Captain Townley."

Ned stared up at him. What did these churchmen care about Mary? How was her death any of their business? How would Abbot Richard misinterpret this? It was clear that Ned had been wronged, but the Abbot would find a way to blame him. Already his voice, eyes and that outstretched hand accused.

Ned took another drink. "What letter?"

The Abbot looked right at the spot where it pressed into Ned's side. "That one."

Ned touched it, shrugged. "It has naught to do with our mission."

"You can read?"

Ned bristled. "I can indeed."

"Most admirable."

"Most necessary in my work for the Duke."

"What have you stolen from Don Ambrose?"

"Stolen? Don Ambrose attacked the Captain," Matthew protested.

The Abbot looked not at Matthew. "You conceal the letter at the risk of your immortal soul, Captain Townley."

"At the...You do not understand, my lord abbot. I have done nothing but read a letter that should have been shared with me. The friar—"

The Abbot turned to Matthew. "You say Ambrose attacked the Captain?"

"Aye, my lord. I have cleaned a deep wound in the Captain's leg."

"Where is Don Ambrose now?" the Abbot demanded.

"Crofter and Bardolph are searching for him," Matthew said.

Abbot Richard turned back to Ned. "What did you do with him?"

Despair pressed down on Ned's head and shoulders, twisted his gut, pulled him away from this pointless interrogation. He took another drink, stared into the fire.

The Abbot laid a hand on Ned's shoulder, shook him. "What did you do with Don Ambrose?"

Ned shrugged out of the Abbot's grasp. "For pity's sake, he woke me. Asked me to come to the stables, he would make peace. So I followed."

"And attacked him? What is in the letter? Why did you take it from him?"

"He attacked me. Hid while I went for a lantern, hit me from behind."

"A friar bested a seasoned soldier?" The Abbot closed his eyes, shook his head. "It would go better for you if you spoke the truth, Captain Townley."

"I am telling the truth," Ned said. "But you are not listening. You chatter and jape at me like a bird does a cat for merely being in the garden."

"Indeed. Like the cat, it is your nature to attack. It is unlikely the birds would attack the cat. Give me the letter."

Ned saw no gain in refusing any longer. He pulled the letter out, handed it to Abbot Richard. "If you were not already set against me you would find it odd that such a letter would be exchanged between two friars."

The Abbot's servant shone a lantern on the letter. Quickly the Abbot read, his disapproving lips moving slightly, then pursing as the eyes lifted to meet Ned's. "We must search for Don Ambrose."

"Two men are already out looking," Matthew said.

"If they return empty-handed, four will stay behind to search, the rest will continue with me—and Captain Townley, who will be kept under guard at all times."

It was Matthew who protested. Ned knew better.

The Abbot looked amused. "You are loyal to your Captain, but you shall soon see your error. It is plain that Don Ambrose told the Captain of Mary's death, then ran from Captain Townley's rage. Or perhaps the Captain attacked Ambrose. God shall reveal all in good time."

"He knew nothing of Mary's death until he read the letter."

"And how did he get Don Ambrose's pouch? The pouch he guarded so jealously?" the Abbot demanded of Matthew.

"Don Ambrose dropped it, my lord abbot."

Abbot Richard tilted his head. "Come now, my son. After guarding it so carefully, he dropped it and ran?" He shook his head.

Ned silently emptied the skin, trying to obliterate the image of Mary floating in the Thames. But there was not enough drink in the world to do so.

10

BLIND RAGE

A cock crowed, waking Matthew. He lay there for a time, listening to the wind, listening for rain battering against the grange house. Had the rain stopped? His eyes and mouth were dry from the smoky room. His hair damp from night sweats. Man was not meant to sleep in such a warm room. He rolled over to find his boots, noticed the other men beginning to roll about and stretch. All the others but the one who should lie beside him.

Matthew sat up, rubbed his eyes. He had not been mistaken: Captain Townley was not where he should be. Nor were his cloak, boots or daggers. *Think. Think. When did I last see him? What was he about? Where was he?* Matthew closed his eyes, moved back to the past night. Abbot Richard had retired, charging Matthew to watch the captain. What had there been to watch? The captain had sat there hugging the brandywine, already bleary-eyed. *They murdered my Mary.* Over and over again. Matthew had coaxed him into lying down. *You have lost much blood, Captain. When bled, one is always told to lie down and let the humours calm. You must lie down.* Captain Townley had lain down. He had seemed to sleep. Reassured, Matthew had gone to sleep beside him.

But the captain was not lying beside Matthew this morning. And his belongings were gone. What would Abbot Richard say? *Blessed Mary, Mother of God, let it not be what I fear.* Perhaps the captain was getting his horse ready for the day's ride.

Matthew needed a plan. While he relieved himself he would look about, see whether Captain Townley was just up betimes,

getting some air, readying his mount. After much drink, cool air—
wet or no—would feel good. *Let him be outside, merely clearing his head.*

Matthew picked up his cloak and slipped out of the door. The
air was chilly and damp, just right after the stuffy house. But his
damp hair soon had Matthew shivering. He shook out his cloak and
draped it about him as he hurried down into the bushes by the beck.
His urine steamed in the cold air. It was too cold to stand out here—
so the captain would have hurried to the barn as soon as the chill
had penetrated his clothing. Matthew turned to climb the slope back
to the barn, stopped with a gasp of dismay.

Abbot Richard stood above, his servant and Brother Augustine
behind him. The Abbot's eyes were fierce, even with his face shadowed
by the white cowl. He looked like Death come to collect Matthew.

"*Benedicte*, Matthew. Where is your captain?" The Abbot's voice
was quietly threatening. Matthew's father had spoken just so before
he whipped him.

Death. His father's whip. This was no time for fear. Matthew
must think how he might protect his captain. But if the captain
were gone, there was no protecting himself from the Abbot's wrath.
What might Matthew say? "The Captain must have slipped out to
the barn while I slept, my lord abbot. He always readies himself so
he may help the others." Which was true.

The Abbot signalled his companions to check the barn. Then
he fixed his dark, unfriendly eyes on Matthew.

Sweat ran down Matthew's neck, down his back. It tickled. He
wanted to squirm or reach back to scratch. *Sweet Jesu, already I do
penance for my lie.* But was it a lie? Was the barn not where he had
imagined the captain? Was he not always ready before the others?

Brother Augustine hurried from the barn, shaking his head.
"Pray God protect our poor brother, Don Ambrose. Captain
Townley's mount is gone."

Abbot Richard seemed to grow another foot beyond his already
considerable height. "Take Matthew inside and guard him, Brother
Augustine."

Matthew's legs wanted to collapse under him, not carry him up to where the Abbot stood, but he willed them to carry him to the top. He would not let the Abbot see his fear.

Ned's lungs burned, but he urged his steed on, faster, faster. His leg throbbed; he felt a wetness spreading from the wound. It had opened when he had fallen in the dark, leading his horse up the rocks, away from the grange house. Foolish to have fled in the dark, but best that he had gone quickly, best to ride through his fury, though it meant he rode his horse and himself to exhaustion. Riding to where? Ah, that was obvious. To nowhere. To forgetfulness, he hoped. To death, more likely. Mary was dead; why should he live?

Abbot Richard paced the main room while the men quietly gathered their clothes and prepared to depart.

"I want four to stay and search for the friar and the Captain," the Abbot said.

"May I?" Matthew asked.

"No." Without a pause, without considering, so easy to deny him, like swatting a fly. Matthew hated him.

Bardolph stepped forward. "Crofter and I were sent along on this mission to watch Captain Townley, my lord abbot. We shall search."

The Abbot's eyes narrowed. "Sent along to watch him? By whom?"

Bardolph glanced back at Crofter as if seeking permission to answer. The man blinked once, slowly. Matthew saw the exchange. He doubted the Abbot could see it. Bardolph turned back to the Abbot. "Sir William of Wyndesore, my lord abbot. Some say the Captain murdered Sir William's page." He shrugged.

Abbot Richard bristled. "Then was it not irresponsible to send him on such a mission?"

From the darkness, Crofter said, "Mistress Alice Perrers cleared him of the charges, my lord abbot."

"Mistress Perrers!" the Abbot murmured with a disapproving sneer. "Come forward. I should see you when you speak."

Crofter stepped forward. "After Mistress Perrers spoke up for Townley, His Grace the King wished him sent away from court until those of our fellows who still believed him guilty had time to calm down."

"Do you believe him guilty?" Abbot Richard asked.

"No, my lord abbot, I do not."

The Abbot paced away from Crofter, returned to him. "Why were you to watch him?"

Crofter tilted his head and averted his eyes for a moment, as if considering how to reply. "In case Mistress Perrers—" An exasperated sigh as he faced the Abbot once more. "In truth, there are those who do not trust her."

Abbot Richard gave a satisfied grunt. "Including your lord?"

"I took the orders to mean that, aye."

Matthew closed his eyes and cursed Crofter. He had made a point of connecting Captain Townley with a woman the Abbot was sure to despise. Cunning bastard. The Captain had warned him to beware Crofter. *That fair face is a mask, Matthew. His eyes are mirrors, not windows. Watch how Bardolph jumps to do his bidding.* What was Crofter's game?

Abbot Richard saw nothing amiss. "You two shall indeed stay behind to search for the Captain. Gervase and Henry shall stay with you."

"There is no need for you to sacrifice your escort to the search, my lord abbot," Crofter said. "Bardolph and I gladly take it upon ourselves."

Abbot Richard indulged in a fleeting smile. "You searched once and failed to recover Don Ambrose."

Bardolph took a step forward. "But it was—"

Crofter silenced him with a hand on his arm. "We are grateful for the chance to participate in the search, my lord abbot. I did not mean to question your decision."

"Good. May God guide the four of you."

Matthew watched as Bardolph and Crofter backed into the shadows. He was very worried for his captain.

. . .

When his horse stumbled at a ford, Ned realised his folly. He had ridden for miles. It was already midday. He gave himself and his deserving mount a rest. Drank deeply, cooled his head. Sobered.

Mary was dead. Her murderers must be found and punished. Fleeing across the moors would not accomplish that. And Ned's death would leave the matter as it was. He owed it to Mary to stay alive until she was avenged.

Why had Don Ambrose hidden the letter from him? Why had he attacked? What did he know?

After a brief nap, with a few hours of daylight left, Ned turned his horse round. Flight was not the answer.

11

TWO MEN TOO FEW

Owen leaned against the bridge and gazed down into the foaming water of the River Skell where it rushed forth from the abbey mill and caught the sun before disappearing beneath the dormitories and the infirmary. It was his second day at Fountains Abbey, but his first opportunity for a solitary walk. Yesterday he had settled the men, dined with Abbot Robert Monkton and Jehannes, attended services in the abbey church. By the time he'd had the leisure to slip outside, Owen found the sky louring with storm clouds and a cold, damp wind whipping down through the bowl of Skelldale. The valley had seemed too vulnerable for habitation.

Jehannes said the Cistercians had purposefully built in isolated countryside, the more desolate the better, to test themselves in their resolve to serve God with a simple life. With a storm coming, Skelldale had indeed seemed a place of trial.

But this morning the valley was utterly different, the sun lighting the trees atop the bluff and in the valley, sparkling on the rushing river, glinting off the lead roofs and warming the damp stone walls of the maze of buildings. The stone bridge on which Owen stood gave him a broad view of the abbey complex. He moved his good eye left along the expanse of the two storey lay brothers dormitory and beyond to the great west door of the church with its Galilee porch, then up, up to the steep lead roof of the long church nave. To his right were two guest houses and the lay brothers infirmary. Behind him was the mill, a wool house, a malt house and more—far more outbuildings than at St Mary's in York.

It was members of the Benedictine Abbey of St Mary's, protesting against the pampered life within its walls, who had fought for and won permission to come to the valley of the Skell and live simply, closer to God. The small company of monks had spent the first winter shivering in the caves tucked into the bluff above the church. From where Owen stood he could not see across the valley to those caves; the maze of buildings, particularly the church, blocked the view. Was this what they had intended? To fill the valley with their material presence? Yet despite the bustle of the large community, Owen sensed a joyous peace here.

Owen was not a stranger to abbeys. He had once spent a fortnight in St Mary's, York, seeking—but not finding—just such a peace as he felt in Skelldale. Here, away from the stench and noise of the city, where work, song, bells, prayer and devotional readings were the only noises of men competing with wind, birdsong, and the rushing river, Owen felt that peace. Was it the descent into the valley and the wild countryside all round, the sense of leaving the world behind? Was it the symmetries of the grand yet simple, unadorned stone buildings, the way the soaring arches echoed one's footsteps? Or had the white monks tapped into a celestial paradise in this valley?

"God smiles on the valley this morning," Jehannes said as he approached on Owen's blind side.

Owen turned so that he might take in the Archdeacon with his right eye. "It looks to me as if God smiles on this valley more often than not. It takes prosperity to build such a complex."

"The white monks have almost been destroyed by their unplanned prosperity," Jehannes said. "Even these worthy brothers have succumbed to the lure of riches."

"Tell me nothing of their failings," Owen said. "Come round where I can see you and still look out on the church." He disliked having anyone on his blind side.

Jehannes moved round to Owen's right. "I came out here not to disturb your peace but to tell you the party from Rievaulx has been spotted by a shepherd. They should arrive by midday."

Owen smiled. "Good. Our business can be concluded quickly."

Fountains might be a paradise, but York sheltered all those Owen held dear. He was anxious to return to his family. "Pray God the friar caused no trouble."

Jehannes rested his forearms on the bridge with a sad sigh. "I, too, am eager to know the outcome. And yet I confess it seems a pity they arrive so soon. I should like more time here."

"Stay too long and you will be tempted to leave the world entirely," Owen warned.

Jehannes glanced round, surprised. "You feel the power of this place."

Owen nodded.

"Yet you wish to leave quickly."

"Aye. My family pulls me ever back to York. But I do sense a peace here. I feel I should whisper and step softly. God is near."

The Archdeacon's expression was wistful. "It is bewitching."

Owen laughed. "I should have thought it more a blessing than a bewitching."

"I have no gift for eloquent speech."

"You were eloquent enough on Wykeham's behalf. Abbot Monkton listened to your arguments most keenly. In truth I fear you were too eloquent. 'Sober habits, tireless industry...'" Owen shook his head. "His Grace the Archbishop would be disappointed. You make Wykeham sound the ideal bishop."

Jehannes winced. "I told you I was no dissembler."

Owen leaned his left elbow on the bridge and studied Jehannes's profile. "The underlying problem is your heart, not your tongue, eh? You believe Wykeham well suited to be Bishop of Winchester."

Jehannes did not reply at once, and when he did it was in a whisper almost lost in the sound of the rushing river. "I fear that I do. A better dissembler might argue less effectively, but I am bound to disappoint Archbishop Thoresby."

"Take heart, my friend. If you fail John Thoresby in this mission, you shall make a friend of the King."

Jehannes shook his head. "John Thoresby shall make a friend of the King. My role in this will be overlooked."

"Do you ever wish you had chosen a cloistered life?"

Jehannes shrugged. "When I am in such a place as this, yes. But I quickly forget when I am back out in the world."

The world. As if an abbey were not in the world. Clerics had odd notions. "What would it take for you to give up the world?"

"A loss of self."

Owen frowned. "Should you not have lost that to your calling?"

"I am an archdeacon, Owen. An administrator, a financier, a politician as well as a clergyman. Selfless men of God make good saints, not archdeacons."

It reminded Owen of Thoresby's defence of the former Archdeacon of York, Anselm. In Owen's mind Anselm had been a disgrace to his position, but Thoresby had called him a fine archdeacon, responsible for collecting the bulk of the donations for stained glass in the minster.

Owen turned towards the sound of someone approaching at a run. It was a lay brother, who reached them gasping for breath. "I am to tell you that the party from Rievaulx are come. There has been trouble. My lord abbot asks you to come quickly."

A white-robed cluster took up the centre of the abbot's parlour, pristine robes encircling travel-stained ones. From their midst, a cool voice could be heard saying, "As I had predicted…"

The voice hushed and the monks parted as Owen and Jehannes joined them, revealing in their midst a tall monk with deep-set eyes who carried himself with a haughty authority. Owen guessed this to be the speaker.

Abbot Robert Monkton stepped forward. "Captain Archer, Archdeacon Jehannes, this is Abbot Richard of Rievaulx."

Jehannes bowed and spoke most courteously. Owen bobbed his head and asked after the escort.

"They shall be lodged in the guest house with you," Abbot Monkton said. His eyes did not stay on Owen's face.

Owen looked round at the waiting faces, noting all eyes focused on him. Uneasy eyes. It took no wit to sense trouble. "What has happened here?"

With a bow to his fellow abbot, Monkton said, "Abbot Richard had just begun to explain. It seems that Don Ambrose disappeared, and Captain Townley after him. Four men were left behind to search for them."

"Sweet Heaven!" Jehannes murmured.

Well he might. Why hadn't the bloody fool warned Ned about the friar's request to quit the company? Owen closed his eye, clenched his hands. *First hear all, then blame.* "If you would be so kind as to tell me what happened. All of it."

The Abbot of Rievaulx bowed to Owen with a chilly smile. "I shall begin again." He started with the incident on the bluff above Rievaulx. "Each had a different story, and I deemed both stories plausible, so I resolved to watch both men on the journey. Don Ambrose invariably exhibited a fearful wariness when the captain was near. Such strong emotion is difficult to mask. And, of course, Captain Townley revealed his guilt when he fled."

"Forgive me, my lord abbot, but you jump ahead," Owen said, winning a sniff from Abbot Richard. "Did you ever witness Captain Townley doing aught to warrant the friar's behaviour?"

Abbot Richard sighed, lifted one shoulder slightly as if to dismiss the issue.

"I thought not," Owen said. "Then whatever the problem, it began with the friar."

Abbot Richard drew a piece of paper from his sleeve. "This letter reveals the connection between the two men."

Abbot Monkton took the letter, read. His carefully neutral expression changed and by the time his eyes had moved from the letter he was quite agitated. "I would speak privately with the Captain, the Archdeacon, and my fellow Abbot."

Once the others had shuffled out, Monkton quickly read through the document again. "It is a letter from Don Paulus, a fellow Austin friar, to Don Ambrose concerning the drowning of a young woman at Windsor—Mary, maid to Mistress Alice Perrers, a member of the Queen's household. Paulus writes that he observed the body in the river but did not report it. He knows that Ambrose will understand his reluctance." The Abbots' eyes met. "What I read here condemns Don Paulus and implicates Don Ambrose. What has this to do with Captain Townley?"

The drowning of Ned's beloved. Owen crossed himself, turned to Abbot Monkton. "The young woman was Captain Townley's betrothed, my lord abbot."

Monkton's eyebrows registered interest. But still he looked at his fellow abbot. "What was the friars' interest in the young woman?"

"I do not know," Richard said.

"This letter was in Captain Townley's possession?" Owen asked.

Richard inclined his head. "I took it from him, yes. He claimed that the friar had attacked him during the night, then dropped the letter as he fled." Another eloquent sigh. "A friar attacking a soldier." He shook his head as if pitying Ned. "You see why I believe otherwise."

"You suspect Captain Townley of wrongdoing," Owen said. "What is it you think he did?"

"I believe he discovered the letter in York and accused Don Ambrose of being a party to the girl's accident. Threatened him."

"Do you have proof of this?" Abbot Monkton asked.

Abbot Richard reared up. "The friar's behaviour."

Monkton shook his head at Owen's scowl, turned back to Richard. "That is all?"

"How might it be explained otherwise?"

Monkton turned to Owen. "It is said that you and the Captain are friends. You were together in York. Is it true? Did he see the letter, or hear of it, in York? Did he know of his lady's death?"

"I am certain he did not, my lord abbot."

"He would have told you?"

"He would. Instead he spoke of Mary as his future wife."

"It is true," Jehannes said. "He spoke about the living, not the dead." He pointed to the letter. "That was written by an Austin friar?"

Abbot Monkton checked the letter. "Yes. The Austins are no

friends of Wykeham. Might Don Ambrose have hoped to distract us from our purpose?"

"No," Abbot Richard said in an impatient tone. "Don Ambrose told me he was to join the privy councillor's household on his return."

Monkton studied his fellow abbot with a sad expression. "You are convinced of the friar's honesty and the Captain's deceit." He shook his head. When Richard opened his mouth, Monkton held up a hand. "Peace. We must consider this after prayer and meditation. You must all rest from your journey. We shall meet again tomorrow morning."

Owen and Jehannes walked back towards the guest house in silence according to the custom of this place, but as they approached the Galilee porch at the west entrance to the church, Jehannes paused. "I would pray," he said.

Owen followed him in, though he itched to find Matthew and the men and to hear their accounts of Ned's disappearance. Jehannes knelt before a statue of the Blessed Virgin placed high on one of the nave piers.

Back in the shadows, Owen knelt and said a prayer for his friend, then one for himself, though he ought rather to have cursed himself for ignoring Lucie's warnings. She had predicted the situation precisely—anything that went wrong would be blamed on Ned, an easy scapegoat because the seeds of suspicion had been sown at Windsor, and once sown would require little sustenance to take root. Owen should have kept Ned by his side so he might be witness to anything that happened. How had Lucie seen it and he had not? What did he lack? He prayed for whatever it was. It was not necessary to know its name. God knew his failings well enough.

When Owen's knees numbed with the cold, he rose and began to pace slowly round the nave. Stone screens extended from the first to the sixth piers on each side, backing the lay brothers' choir stalls. Owen sat for a while in one of the stalls, his eye raised to the high roof, following with his ear the plight of a trapped bird. He assumed it was a bird—it was far too dark to see so high. The frantic wingbeat sounded otherworldly. How easy to believe an angel hovered above, listening to his prayers. But the truth of the trapped and frightened bird broke his peaceful meditations.

He rose and lifted a torch from the first pier, walked slowly down the outer aisle, studying the walls, and the scalloped and waterleafed capitals of the piers and corbels, the perfect stonework of the arches. Even the wall painting drew one into quiet contemplation, repeated lines mimicking masonry, nothing more.

Jehannes joined him. "I hear a bird above."

Owen returned the torch to its sconce. "Come. Let us leave the door ajar and hope the bird sees its freedom."

In the guest house, Jehannes sank down on a chair, refused wine. "I should have warned both you and Ned about Don Ambrose the moment he came to see me."

"Aye, that you should have." Owen sat down beside Jehannes, his anger forestalled by his friend's admission. "But I, too, am at fault. Lucie warned me. She said Ned would be blamed for aught that went wrong on the journey." He accepted the wine the servant offered, asked him, "The men who escorted the party from Rievaulx, where are they?"

"The four soldiers are up in the chamber next to yours, Captain. Matthew is in there." The servant indicated a door at the far end of the parlour.

Owen eased himself up, started for the door.

"It is locked," the servant said in a timid voice.

"Locked? Why?"

"Abbot Richard said he must be confined."

"Unlock it for him," Jehannes said.

The servant looked uncertain. "You will keep him inside, Captain?"

Owen nodded. The door was duly opened. Taking up an oil lamp, Owen stepped into a small, dark, airless room. Matthew, lying on a cot, threw up a hand to shield his eyes from the sudden light.

"You need a good meal, eh?" Owen settled at the foot of the cot.

Matthew lifted himself up on one elbow, rubbed his eyes. "I have little appetite at the moment, Captain Archer."

That was plain, and understandable, but Owen could not allow Matthew the peace to lick his wounds. "You must eat. I have questions to ask you. And we've more travel before we're through."

"Abbot Richard hates Captain Townley."

Owen shook his head to silence Matthew while the servant brought in bread, cheese, and ale. When the servant was gone, Owen swung his long legs off the cot, reached for the pitcher, filled a cup, handed it to Matthew, who drank thirstily.

Owen filled a cup for himself. "Now, tell me in your own words what happened with Captain Townley."

Matthew proved to be a careful recorder, noting conversations with Ned, his observations of Don Ambrose. He recounted what he remembered of Ned's encounters with the friar. "By the time we left Rievaulx, Captain Townley was uneasy. Watchful. *Something* made the friar fearful, and it had something to do with the Captain, you see. That much seemed plain."

Owen was quiet a while, thinking. But unless Matthew left out some critical detail, there seemed nothing to note except a nervous friar who—what? Was worried Ned might find the letter? And do what? Was Abbot Richard correct? Was the friar worried that Ned would blame him? Imagine he was implicated in the drowning? Ned's temper was quick to ignite and burned hot. "Don Ambrose kept the letter in his pouch, you say?"

Matthew nodded.

"He kept it close at all times?"

"Yes. I think that is why Abbot Richard did not believe he dropped it in the barn."

Owen, too, found that passing strange. "The friar received the letter in York and his odd behaviour began then." Owen sighed. "I must agree with Abbot Richard, much as I dislike agreeing with the man. You saw no evidence of the friar's unease before?"

"He was nervous from the start, but not of anyone in particular. Or perhaps of Wyndesore's men, Bardolph and Crofter."

Owen remembered Crofter's cold eyes. But would the friar have understood the danger in such a man? "Why them?"

Matthew shrugged. "I think it was their speech. They have been on campaign of late, with Sir William and the Duke of Clarence. Rough, rude, bawdy speech and songs."

"They gave him trouble?"

"Not that I saw. They're up to something, though." He told Owen of Crofter's effort to associate Ned with Alice Perrers in Abbot Richard's mind, and their claim that Wyndesore had set them to watch Ned.

"What madness was this?" Owen growled. "I've never encountered such a pack of scheming fools." He was frustrated. All the threads seem to head nowhere or into a knot. But seeing Matthew's alarmed look, he put his anger aside. "Once Don Ambrose had the letter it was Captain Townley he watched?"

"We saw him little in York. But once we had headed out towards Rievaulx, yes, he was fearful of the Captain; watched him all the time." Matthew rubbed his eyes, rumpled his hair. The ale was warming him up. "Why would friars exchange such a letter? About a young woman?"

Why indeed?

"I'm damned if I know. Would they have known Mary was to wed Captain Townley?"

"Most like. After the death of Daniel—Sir William of Wyndesore's page—everyone at the castle must have known. Courtiers love their gossip, and their confessors hear it all, I imagine."

Owen disliked how he agreed with the Abbot more and more. He leaned over, refilled Matthew's cup. "What was Captain Townley like when you last saw him?"

"Drunk as a lord, sir," Matthew said. "I did not like to think of him riding through the moors in such a state."

"Nor I." The account left Owen with much to ponder. "Eat something, Matthew. I will be taking you with me when we escort Abbot Richard to Rievaulx."

"Escort him back?"

"My man Alfred will escort Archdeacon Jehannes back to York. I wish to see where Captain Townley and Don Ambrose disappeared. So I shall lead Abbot Richard's escort back to Rievaulx when the meeting is over."

"I do not know what else I might have done." Matthew's huge eyes implored. He looked like an awkward puppy.

"I see nothing to blame in your conduct, Matthew."

A sigh. "Abbot Richard hates the Captain."

"Aye. You have said that twice now. I doubt he hates him. I doubt he has made much note of him at all. My guess is the trouble between the Captain and the friar came as an opportunity to question the integrity of our mission."

"But how can it?"

"It does not need to make sense to work in his favour, Matthew." That Owen had learned from his work for the Archbishop.

Another storm had moved in overnight. Archdeacon Jehannes was chilled when he joined the two abbots in Monkton's parlour, and the smug expression on Abbot Richard's face did nothing to warm him.

Owen had agreed that the Abbot of Rievaulx might be friendlier to Jehannes if he attended alone, but it appeared they had been wrong. Jehannes fortified himself with spiced wine and settled in for an unpleasant round of argument. "I am sure the issue needs no further explanation," he began.

"No," Abbot Monkton said with a smile meant to soften what was to come. "In fact, it requires no further discussion."

Abbot Richard made no effort to mask a smug grin, and Jehannes knew what was coming.

Abbot Monkton winced, as if experiencing, too, the pain he imagined Jehannes must feel. "Abbot Richard and I do not agree about Captain Townley and Don Ambrose..."

"They have nothing to do with my purpose for being here," Jehannes said, interrupting. It was either this mild aggression or throw wine in Abbot Richard's smug face, which would distress Abbot Monkton.

"The Captain and friar *are* to your purpose," Abbot Monkton said, holding up his hands for silence when Jehannes began to protest. "I have prayed over this, my son, and I am quite confident in my assessment. This unfortunate circumstance is a sign given us by God that we are right to stand firm against pluralism." He paused as Jehannes shook his head. "You cannot see it?"

How could he? There was naught to see. "I cannot."

"Were Wykeham a simple parish priest, conscientious in ministering to the souls in his care, His Holiness would have readily agreed to his appointment, Wykeham would have been consecrated, and all would have progressed quietly, efficiently. Instead, the King pushes his favourite at His Holiness, a favourite on whom the King has already lavished an array of benefices that bring him indecent wealth, a favourite who has attracted enemies. Naturally His Holiness sees this as a dangerous situation; such a prominent, wealthy, political man, a man so important to the King, will not suddenly change his allegiance and withdraw his attention from the court to focus on the see of Winchester. His diocese will become a pawn in the King's hands."

"I understand His Holiness's objections," Jehannes snapped. The Abbot tried his patience. Together they had been through all this already. "But your point? The connection between this and Don Ambrose's attack upon Captain Townley?" Obviously Archbishop Thoresby was going to get his wish and be assisted in his work against Wykeham by these two men, and Jehannes knew he should not protest too strongly. But the argument must make sense. "I do not yet see how to explain this connection to the King."

Abbot Monkton sighed. "Patience, my son, patience. Simply put, had the King's candidate been a simple man of God, these companies of men would not be riding through the kingdom collecting support for him. Because the King's candidate is already a man of great wealth and power, and none of that his by birth or simple hard work, he is a man with many enemies. The entire situation begs the kind of discord and danger we now see."

"Which is precisely our point," Abbot Richard added in a falsely sweet tone.

Jehannes did not allow himself to glance at Abbot Richard;

it was not his purpose to make an enemy of these men. "My lord abbot," he said to Monkton, "surely you do not think the young lady's death had anything to do with Wykeham's advancement?"

"Not her death, though even that might have been avoided had Captain Townley remained at Windsor, but the letter from Don Paulus to Don Ambrose which so incensed the Captain…"

Jehannes took a deep breath and managed to stay calm and polite throughout the rest of the meeting, which continued far too long. Two questions kept rising to the surface of his mind: *What had the maid to do with Wykeham's advancement? What was Abbot Richard's purpose in seizing that connection?* In the end, Jehannes merely smiled and nodded and took his leave with admirable calm and courtesy.

"Abbot Richard never meant to support Wykeham," Owen said. "I see no riddle in that. But I too find it puzzling that Mary's drowning should concern the friars—on that we agree."

Jehannes paced the guest house parlour, hands behind his back, head bowed forward, brow furrowed. "I think we owe it to Captain Townley to find out more about the friars' interest in his lady's death," he said at last, pausing before Owen.

Owen nodded. "I agree. I had begun a letter to the Archbishop for Ned, to learn as much detail of the incident as possible. I shall put the friars' involvement to him as well."

Jehannes's brow suddenly smoothed, his mouth widened into a smile. "Owen Archer, you sly one. You do unto him as he would do unto you."

Owen slapped his thighs, rose with a grin. "Aye, Jehannes. His Grace shall be my spy for a change."

12

A GRAVE MATTER

Owen had imagined the grange house in a meadow, with gently rolling hills about it. But in reality it sat in a rock-strewn valley whose steeply sloping sides were choked with thorn trees. "Not a place through which I would have chosen to run on a stormy night," he said. "And Captain Townley was drunk, you say?"

Matthew stood beside him, his face screwed up, remembering. "Drunk. Oh, that he was." Matthew truly looked a puppy, with his wide, flat nose, receding chin, and huge ears. And when he concentrated he was uglier yet. "We came on this place in the storm. In the dark. We none of us knew what to expect. But the friar is mad, Captain Archer, so it did not surprise me, his running off in the storm. I told you how he almost brought his horse down on him when we rode into the vale of Rievaulx. And it was he who led us down the steepest way."

"But running off into unknown dangers in a storm is not what you would have expected from Captain Townley?"

Matthew shook his head, almost more of a shiver than a negation. "He would have scolded me for even thinking about it."

That was the problem. As Owen saw it, Ned had not been thinking. Not clearly. The pain of losing Mary would have dulled his mind.

They stood in the covered walkway between the house and the stable, looking down at the rushing stream.

"Perhaps Don Ambrose was waiting to tell Ned about Mary. Wanted to spare him the sad news for a while…" Owen suggested.

Matthew turned, looked Owen in the eye. "Do you think that? Truly?"

Owen would have liked to think that. He would have liked to think all the missing men awaited them at Rievaulx. But he did not for a moment expect that. "No, Matthew, I do not think he meant to spare Ned."

Owen took off to explore the valley; soon Matthew was puffing up behind him.

"If you would not mind, Captain, I should like to come."

Owen shrugged.

"What are we looking for?"

"What does Abbot Richard have men searching for in the barn? I cannot say, nor can he. Captain Townley and Don Ambrose? The four men searching for them? A sign of what happened that night? Blood? Ned told you he had wounded the friar in the hand. A good bleeder, the hand. You know, I thank you for joining me. With one eye it's difficult enough for me to stay upright along the stream and out of the thorns on the slope."

"Does it bother you, then, having just the one eye?"

"Every moment of every day, Matthew. Now come. Talk distracts us from our search."

Atop one of the ridges, Matthew found a cap. He ran to catch up with Owen, who had wandered on. It was a felt cap with the King's arms. "Several of the men wore these, Captain," Matthew said breathlessly. "Proud of wearing the King's livery, they were."

"Which men?"

"Ah. Which ones." Matthew screwed up his eyes and clutched the cap to him as if it might prompt his memory. Which it must have done. "Gervase, Henry, and Bardolph," he suddenly barked with a pleased expression.

Owen took the cap, examined it. No blood, though it was damp from the rains so any blood might have washed out. "Show me where you found it."

Matthew led him back up the slope to a small clearing with a thin layer of brush, so thin that the rock beneath poked through in many places. "It was caught in that bush." He pointed to the far end of the clearing.

"Footing would be slippery up here in the rain," Owen said. He walked slowly round, poking at the brush, examining the trees. Several small thorns had been trampled, trunks showed signs of reins having been tied to them, including the one beside the bush that had caught the cap. The cap was significant, but what did it tell them? That one man lost a hat and did not think it important to return for it? That he was in a hurry? Involved in a struggle?

"This sort of clue is almost worse than none at all, eh Matthew?"

The young man looked disappointed. "I thought it promising."

"How so? It merely tells us they climbed up here, which they should have done. No surprise in that. They were left behind to search for Don Ambrose and Captain Townley, they *should* have covered this entire valley." Owen shook his head. "Let us walk over the ridge a bit, see what else we see."

But it had been days since the incident, days of rain and wind. There might be clues aplenty up there, trampled in the mud, blown beyond their sight, hiding from the men who needed them.

As they scrambled back down the slope towards the ford of the stream, Owen noted a scar in the earth. A mud slide? He paused, looked more closely. The debris below the scar—rocks, uprooted bracken and heather—were appropriate, and Owen almost continued. But there was something else, something towards the bottom of the debris. He crouched down. A muddy piece of cloth. He gave it a tug, which loosened some more dirt and uncovered more cloth, but did not budge it. As if it was attached to something much larger.

Owen looked up at the scar. If he were going to hide a body, not a bad idea. Easy to dig near the stream, easy to mask it as a mud slide. But someone had not counted on the heavy rains since.

He stood up. Matthew was already over the ford, waiting on the other side. "Fetch Abbot Richard and the rest," Owen shouted. "Tell them we must do some digging. Bring shovels or something like."

Matthew hesitated, looking doubtful.

"I believe a body lies under this mud slide, Matthew."

That spurred Matthew up to the house.

Owen spent the wait clearing the debris, but he did not dig. He would first ask Abbot Richard's permission.

The Abbot arrived before the others, managing to ford the stream without wetting the hem of his habit or letting any mud mar its whiteness. Owen was keenly aware of his own sweat- and mud-stained garments, his dirt-encrusted hands.

"What is it?" the Abbot asked, nodding towards the exposed scar. "A grave?"

"That is what I'm thinking, my lord abbot. And I ask your permission to dig it up."

The cold eyes took in the pile of debris by Owen's feet. "You cleared that from it?"

"I did."

"Then someone meant to hide this."

"I'll not contradict you there."

The Abbot closed his eyes, bowed his head, pressed his hands together.

Owen crouched down and splashed his face with cool water from the stream, washed off his hands. He took care as he rose not to splash the Abbot.

The Abbot opened his eyes as the rest of the men came across the ford, two with shovels, one with a rake, one a large spoon. "We must know who it is, Captain Archer," the Abbot said. "We must learn whatever the body may tell us. And then bury it once more, in a Christian way." He turned to the men. "Dig where the Captain orders you." Then he stepped back across the ford to wait and pray.

The mud was quickly scraped away, revealing a body, as expected. Ralph dropped his shovel and crossed himself. Matthew stood with his shovel in mid-air and gulped for air, his face ashen. "What a stench!" Curan cried, backing away with his sleeve to his nose, the rake dragging from the other hand. Brother Augustine stepped forward and made the sign of the cross over the body.

Abbot Richard quietly joined Owen. "It is just as I feared. And I doubt any prayers were said over him. He was pushed in, covered up."

It was true. No shroud covered Don Ambrose. No coins covered his eyes. His hands and feet were bound, his mouth open, as if crying out.

Owen nodded. "The mud makes it difficult to guess the cause of death. May I cut the habit?"

The Abbot closed his eyes. "Do what is necessary."

Owen knelt, slipped his dagger under the neckline and slit down. He did not need to go far. He could feel the fabric clinging to the body hair. Dried blood did that. He knew that all too well. He ripped the cloth free. Three wounds on the chest. He lifted the hem, examined the friar's legs and the bottom of his torso. No more wounds. He stood up. "He was stabbed three times in the chest."

The Abbot crossed himself. "Captain Townley is known for his skill with a dagger."

"Throwing daggers, not stabbing with them. And Captain Townley would not bind the man. He would insist on a fair fight."

The Abbot sighed. "We shall talk later. Let us see to Don Ambrose first." He turned to Brother Augustine. "Find something to use as a shroud and move him to the barn. We shall set a watch over him until we leave the wretched place."

"You will bury him at Rievaulx?" Owen asked.

"He was a consecrated priest. He deserves burial in consecrated ground."

Owen nodded. "I had not thought, but it is fitting."

The afternoon's grim work had brought a gloom on the company. Owen and his men sat silently round the fire while the monks said their evening office in the next room.

"Abbot Richard has tried and condemned Captain Townley," Matthew said, more to his cup of ale than to the others.

"I can't say I blame him," Curan said. "Quick temper, has Captain Townley."

Matthew's shaggy head shot up. "So do you, you—"

"Men!" Owen shouted, rising.

"There are other men missing as well," Ralph said. "I don't know as I believe one man overcame him, bound him, stabbed him, and then brought the slope down atop him."

With that grim recitation of the events, the men grew silent once more.

Later, Abbot Richard sent Brother Augustine and his servant to join the men at the fire and invited Owen into the more private room. Several oil lamps sat on the floor near two benches. A small bottle and two cups sat beside the lamps.

"Would you take some brandywine?" Abbot Richard asked.

"After this day's business, I should dearly love some," Owen said.

The Abbot bent down, filled the cups, handed one to Owen. "My compliments on your discovery today, Captain. I doubt I would have noticed that it was no natural slide."

The comment relaxed Owen. They had progressed beyond their pointless sparring. "One-eyed and all, I have trained myself over the past years to make note of things, my lord abbot."

"Ah. Your work for Archbishop Thoresby."

Owen nodded. "I propose to escort you back to Rievaulx before we continue our search."

While the Abbot sipped his brandywine, he fixed his deep-set eyes on Owen. "Why is that?"

"You might be in danger."

The ghost of a smile. "I might indeed. But so might you."

What was he after? "It is my duty to protect you. And you are shifting a body someone wished to hide."

"From whom do you think you protect me, Captain Archer?"

Ah. There it was. "Perhaps Captain Townley. Perhaps the other men. Perhaps someone we have not yet encountered."

"So you accept that your friend might be involved?"

"As you said this afternoon, he is known for his skill with daggers." The Abbot made a move to protest. Owen shook his head. "No need to withdraw the comment. It was made and it should be considered. My wife would tell me I am too fond of Ned Townley to trust my judgement."

The Abbot inclined his head. "A wise woman. How are the men?"

"Truth?"

"Of course."

"Matthew believes you have tried and condemned Captain Townley. Curan is eager to blame the Captain and head back to Windsor. Ralph does not think Don Ambrose's murder and burial were the work of one man."

"What do you think?"

"I think we do not know what happened. I must talk to my captain, hear his story. For all we know—God grant that it is not so"—Owen crossed himself—"my captain, too, lies in this valley."

"I misjudged you, Captain Archer."

"Indeed you did, my lord abbot."

"I gladly accept your escort to Rievaulx."

They journeyed to Rievaulx without incident. The hospitaller crossed himself at their tidings, shook his head at their unhappy burden. "May Our Lord God welcome Don Ambrose into the Heavenly City."

"You have seen none of the other men? The search party?"

The hospitaller slowly moved his head from side to side. "But there is a shepherd to see you, Captain. He waits in the parlour."

"A shepherd? What does he want?"

"He said his business was with you. I did not press him further. It is not our way."

Owen stepped into the parlour, nodded to the man in russet tunic and leggings. His hair was grizzled, shaggy as the sheep he tended, and so redolent of them they must often have mistaken him for one of their own.

The man grasped his crook and supported himself as he rose. "Captain Archer?" His voice was gruff with age.

"And you are?"

"Nym, sir."

It seemed wrong for the elderly man to call him "sir". "Would you take some refreshment?"

"I never say no to a drop of ale."

Owen went to a cupboard and returned with a pitcher and two drinking bowls, poured for both of them, handed a bowl to his guest, who had resumed his seat.

Nym drained the bowl, leaned forward to set it down. The movement was awkward, and Owen noticed the shepherd had a malformed foot. He rose and took the bowl from the shepherd, who nodded in thanks, settling back on the chair.

Owen drank some ale. "Brother Hospitaller said you had business with me?"

A subtle nod. "It is said you seek six men travelling on the moors."

"Five."

The bushy eyebrows drifted up, a broad shoulder shrugged. "You have found one of them?"

Nym obviously knew something. "Where did you hear about us?"

"I was sent to lead you to one who might help."

"Where? Who?"

"Hazel Heath Wood. Widow Digby."

Owen blinked. "Magda Digby?"

"Widow Digby. Aye. Comes up here collecting roots and herbs, seeing to old friends. You know her as midwife in York."

Owen could not believe his fortune. "And she knows something of these men?"

"Aye, she said so. Sent me to bring you to her."

"When do we leave?"

"Tomorrow would be pleasing to me."

"Tomorrow it is."

13

MAGDA'S SECRET

Mist hung low in the Vale of Rievaulx. The abbey seemed to float on clouds. But for the company standing beside their mounts awaiting the Abbot's blessing, the damp ground was all too substantial. Moisture found the seams and tears in their boots and chilled their feet. Only Nym seemed comfortable, leaning quietly on his crook. Ralph stamped his feet and flapped his arms and muttered curses under his breath. Geoff repeatedly blew on his hands. Matthew's nose dripped; he stood with his hands up his sleeves and occasionally pressed his arms up to blot his nose. Curan shifted from one foot to the other in a steady rhythm. Edgar held his cloak tight about him with gloved hands and stood as close to his horse's warmth as the beast would allow.

Owen paced and swung his arms. His left shoulder ached in the damp, an old wound. It was far too early to be standing about. Yet as his eye travelled up the bank, he saw that the mist thinned, revealing the trees that clung to the steep sides. And high above, the sky was blue, as it should be in early May, the sun touching the lead roof of the church and setting it aglow.

The horses snorted and stamped, their breath blending into the mist.

A door opened nearby, heard but not seen.

"His royal highness at last," muttered Matthew.

A procession of white-robed novices appeared out of the mist, followed by Abbot Richard in his mass robes. The night before, he had questioned Owen's judgement in riding up on to the moors to consult a midwife.

"What can a midwife do for you, Captain Archer? Cast a spell? Weave a charm for your friend?"

"I seek facts, my lord abbot. Magda Digby will know whether there is news of my men."

"So she is more than a midwife."

"As are we all more besides our callings."

"I intend to notify King Edward of the circumstances."

"I never doubted you would. And I shall send a complete account to Archbishop Thoresby and to you when I return to York."

The Abbot had been satisfied with Owen's reply; his presence here this morning was testament to that.

"*Benedicte*, Captain Archer; Nym; Matthew; Ralph; Curan; Edgar; Geoff." Abbot Richard made the sign of the cross over each man as he spoke his name. "Our Lord God shines His light upon this company. Let us pray it is a sign of a safe and productive journey."

The men had grown still with the blessing, now they bowed their heads, pressed their hands together. Abbot Richard did not prolong the prayers overmuch, but neither did he skimp. When he was finished, the men crossed themselves and moved towards their mounts.

Abbot Richard took Owen aside. "You have the trust of powerful men, Captain Archer. Do not ruin your future by misguided loyalty."

"Do not be so confident you are right to condemn Captain Townley, my lord abbot. I would delight in proving you wrong."

An eyebrow raised, a smile flickered and died. The deep-set eyes looked sad. "God go with you, Captain."

Owen found the Abbot's blessing disquieting. He was silent as he joined his men. The company mounted, made secure the reins connecting them to the packhorses carrying food, gifts from the infirmarian for Nym's family and a bottle of brandywine for Magda Digby, and rode off towards the north.

Nym led the company up along the Rye River valley. The ground was sodden and muddy from recent floods. The shepherd assured them his ears were trained to hear the warning sound of a flash flood, which could come at any time now that the snow cover on the high moors was melting. They rode prepared for a sudden gallop up on to the high ground.

Owen rode at the rear, Matthew beside him. The puppy-faced man kept glancing up and about at the rolling moorland.

"Nym has not lived to two score and ten by acting the fool, Matthew," Owen said. "Have faith that he does not mean to be washed away."

"'Tis not just that, Captain. Along the Thames, where I was born, a man may look out over many miles and see whence he came and where he is headed. But this…" Matthew made a sweeping gesture over the surrounding heights. "Hills. Mist. Abbeys hiding in valleys where the traveller comes upon them like giants lurking. 'Tis a queer, dangerous country. There are too many hills from which the enemy might watch, valleys where they might hide." He screwed up his puppy face. "How might a man live here without forever glancing about, ready for mischief?"

Ah. Owen remembered such fears among his archers in Normandy. Unfamiliar terrain held unpredictable dangers. Some men eased into the new, learned it. Some resisted it, always feared it. "Knowing that men are missing, that someone murdered Don Ambrose, makes it all the keener, that feeling."

Matthew ducked his head, embarrassed. "It does that, Captain."

"We are fortunate to have a guide who knows the land. I have faith he will get us there safely." Owen glanced over at Matthew, saw less fear in his eyes. Owen would not mention what bothered him, the uncertainty of what they sought.

Matthew glanced at Owen. "This Riverwoman. What is she?"

The man was a bundle of worries, to be sure. "A midwife," Owen said. "She brought my wife into the world. And my daughter."

A puzzled frown. "What need have we of a midwife?"

Owen laughed. "Abbot Richard asked the same question. Her skill as a midwife is what most folk seek her for. But I think her the finest spy in the land. Folk hear of something out of joint, they tell Magda. Magda seeks knowledge of something, she spreads the word. If anyone has seen aught of Captain Townley or the other men up on the moors, Magda will know. Or will find out."

"Let us pray she knows something that will help Captain Townley."

"Magda would not send Nym for us if she had naught to offer."

They reached the hamlet at the edge of Hazel Head Wood as twilight faded into night. A fire burned in front of one of the houses, its brightness making the darkness in which the company rode seem blacker still.

Matthew stared straight ahead. As the sun had set he had told Owen that the moorland hills on either side seemed like dark, crouching beasts, and the sky was too broad.

Owen had glanced up to the twilight sky, stars beginning to twinkle palely. "The Thames shares the same sky."

Matthew had shaken his head. "Not the same. Not at all."

Owen, however, felt at home riding into the hamlet. The smoky fire with its welcoming crackle, the soft bleating of the sheep, the wind sighing down from the moors and whispering in the trees, voices murmuring. It felt like the village of his boyhood. Nym dismounted and nodded for Owen and the others to wait. He ducked into the low doorway of the house directly ahead and quickly returned to beckon the men to dismount. He walked over to Owen.

"Widow Digby welcomes you and says you and your men may settle yourselves in the far house. There is fire and water for your needs. She will come and talk to you there."

Owen looked down the houses to the far one. "That is Magda's house?"

Nym shook his head. "'Tis empty for now, is all. Asa is away."

The men led the horses to the stable end of the house. It was a long building with a third of it separated from the living space by a wood partition. Straw was spread over the floor and the place had the strong scent of animals. The rest of the house held a fire pit under the hole in the sod roof, a much mended table, a chair, a bench that might seat three grown men, a milking stool.

A flimsy wooden partition created a private sleeping chamber. A simple shepherd's house, perhaps larger than the average. But what caught Owen's eye were the wall decorations, images of the moorland life: not the simple flowers and borders in repetitive patterns that most commonly decorated walls, but sketches of animals, trees, rocks.

Nym entered, dragging two benches, one of which needed to be pressed down on to the packed earth floor to be steadied. Owen asked him about the painting.

Nym glanced at the walls, shrugged. "Asa's work." He stooped in the doorway. "There is wood by the fire. You are welcome to what you need."

Owen glanced at Ralph, who motioned for the men to follow Nym out to fetch wood and a burning ember for the fire.

They were settling in, their rations spread out, eating and drinking and letting the quiet of the moors descend upon them, when Matthew, glancing over at the doorway, called out, "Who goes there?"

Owen turned, then rose. A short figure swathed in a plain wool cloak stood there, head covered with a linen coif. The clothing was unlike Magda's usual attire, but no one else had such eyes. Certainly no one so old. "Bless you, Magda. The house is comfortable after our long ride."

"Thou hast need of Magda." She stepped into the room, nodded towards the other men, who had all risen. No one confronted by Magda doubted her powerful presence. She inspired respect without asking for it. "Sit thee down, sit thee down. Magda despairs of her shrinking frame enough. Thou needst not tower over her." Her eyes laughed.

Owen handed her the bottle of brandywine. "From the cellars of Rievaulx."

Magda opened it, sniffed, nodded. "The white monks fled luxury, they say." She threw back her head and barked with laughter.

The men all grinned and relaxed, sinking back down on to their seats.

Magda perched on the milking stool, loosened the cloak from round her wrinkled neck, then tilted her head back and savoured a mouthful of brandywine. Only then did she speak. "How goest thy daughter, Bird-eye?"

Owen was impatient to hear why she had sent for him, but he would not rush her. It never paid to rush Magda. "God has granted us a healthy child. Already Gwenllian has a strong grasp and a straight back."

Magda bobbed her head from side to side in a merry gesture. "Like thy apothecary wife, eh?" She took another sip. "And Jasper? He pleases Lucie?"

Would they make their way through all in the household? "Jasper learns and remembers. He is quick to obey, cheerful. Lucie could ask for no better."

"Good." Magda sighed, stoppered the bottle and tucked it into a pouch at her waist, stretched her arms wide, extended her feet towards the fire. "Good and warm. So. Magda and thee shall ride up on to Kepwick Moor tomorrow."

"Why?"

"To visit a shepherd."

"Someone with news of Ned or the others?"

Magda shrugged.

"Kepwick Moor. Surely my men did not travel so far."

With a piece of kindling Magda poked the fire. "Thou sayest not so far." She turned to look at him with her shrewd eyes. "And if they were lost? Or in flight? On horseback?"

The men were quiet now, straining to hear.

"What do you know, Magda?" Owen asked.

"Magda can take thee at dawn. But just thee and Magda. No others."

"Why not my men?"

"Thou seekst answers from a shepherd? They are not fond of strangers. Nym is different, so Magda might send him to the abbey. But this one would not speak to a company of men. To just one…" She shrugged. "Mayhap." She rose, fastened her cloak. "Magda shall ride like a lordling tomorrow. Have two mounts ready at dawn." As she walked towards the door she paused in front of one of the decorations, a hawk, wings spread wide, head down, eyeing its prey. Magda sniffed, shrugged, departed.

• • •

After a day of riding across the high moor, just as the light faded, Magda said, "Canst thou see it?"

Owen squinted, saw nothing but heath that slowly lost detail in the dying light. "I hear a dog barking."

Magda nodded, pointed.

"Ah." He saw the buildings: two sod huts, not far from them.

By the time they reached the larger hut, a large-boned woman with flinty eyes stood in the doorway, arms folded before her. The strands of hair that escaped her linen cap were dark with light streaks, grey, Owen guessed, though he could not see colour in the twilight. The barking dog must be in the smaller hut, behind this one. Owen wondered how the woman could stand so calmly and ignore the sound.

"What is thy business with us, Widow Digby?" The eyes moved to Owen, back to Magda. "Is this the one-eyed spy who works for thy Archbishop?" The voice was low, unfriendly.

Magda walked up to the woman, stood quite close to her, hands on hips. "Captain Archer comes to speak with the shepherd, Asa." Magda's voice was as unfriendly as Asa's.

Owen recognised the name—this woman was the artist. She was not what he had expected.

The flinty eyes rested on Owen. Asa shook her head, stretched out her hands, clutching either side of the doorway to bar the way. "He has naught to say to thee, Captain."

"Let him decide whether he will speak to the Captain," Magda said firmly.

Someone grabbed Asa's shoulder from behind. "What is it?" A head peered over the woman's shoulder. "Widow Digby. Asa, step aside."

Asa turned and whispered something. The man pushed her aside, stepped forward.

"Ned!" Owen reached out for his friend, ignoring Ned's strangeness in his great relief to find his friend alive. For he was strange, the usually fastidious man unshaven, uncombed, gaunt, dressed in tattered, shapeless tunic and leggings, his fingernails torn and filthy.

Ned's eyebrows met in a frown. Even his large brown eyes were wrong, vague. "Owen? How did you find me?"

Praise God he recognised him. "Magda sent for me."

Ned lifted his head, peered out beyond Owen. "And the others?"

"They know nothing. They did not accompany us."

Ned took a deep breath, nodded, took one step back towards Asa. His movements were like his eyes, dulled, slow. A contrast to Asa's flinty stare.

"It grows dark and chilly," Magda said. "Wouldst thou invite Magda and the Captain inside?"

"Why should he?" Asa demanded.

Ned glanced back. "These are my friends, Asa." At last a spark of life. He stepped aside and invited them in.

Dark, smoky, tiny, but with a fire and a pot of something with a spicy scent cooking over it. Ned indicated a bench against the wall. "Pull it up, rest yourselves."

Owen held out a wineskin. "Will you drink with us? Something to warm you?"

Ned reached for the skin, Asa stayed his hand. Ned withdrew his hand.

"Why do you refuse wine?" Owen asked. He had never known Ned to pass up a drink.

Magda sniffed. "Because Asa, who calls herself a healer, has been filling thy friend's belly with remedies that dull his mind. Wine might rob his wits entirely."

"Be quiet, old woman. They calm him; they do not dull his mind," Asa said.

Magda rolled her eyes and sniffed again.

Asa knelt down by the pot and stirred.

Owen looked from one to the other, wondering what was between them. He had never seen Magda treated with such disrespect. And she gave it so little heed. "Why do you need calming, Ned?" Owen asked.

Ned looked down at his hands. "You know about Mary?"

"I do. I am sorrier than I can say." Owen nodded towards Asa. "Is that what you are helping him forget?"

Asa met Owen's eye. "Thou wouldst have thy friend suffer?"

"She has dulled my wish to die. There is no forgetting." Ned rose. "Come. I have something to show you."

"Not now." Asa stepped in front of Ned, hands out, barring his way.

He gave her a weak push. "Out of my way."

She did not move.

"In the morning, Dagger-thrower," Magda said. "In daylight." She touched Owen's arm. "Magda knows of a place for us to spend the night, not far."

"There is no need," Asa said with an impatient sigh. "There is room for thee here. But let Ned be for tonight. Ask no questions."

"If thou shalt promise to cease dosing him," Magda said.

Owen felt a tug of wills as the women faced each other with steely eyes.

It was Asa who looked away first. "I shall give him naught tonight."

"Then thou art kind to offer Magda and Bird-eye a bed for the night." Magda's voice held a smile.

Owen felt he had walked into a room in the middle of an interesting tale.

The dog's incessant barking accompanied the meal. At last Owen could bear it no longer. "What is wrong with the dog?"

Ned and Asa exchanged glances.

"Sheep dogs are trained to attack wolves," Asa said. "But some become confused and forget it is only wolves they are to attack. That one must be tied up when not working. He does not like it."

"Why tie him out of sight of his master?" Magda asked. "'Tis punishment to lock him away alone."

"What dost thou know of dogs?" Asa demanded.

"More than thee," Magda said, bending back to her food.

Ned put down his spoon with a clatter, picked up a lantern and headed for the door, motioning for Owen to follow. "Come along.

I will show you."

They headed for the smaller hut. As they stepped inside, the barking switched to a whimper. Ned shined the lantern on a stall. A dark dog, muzzle grey with age, was chained to a post. "Nym loaned me his old dog to help with the lambing," Ned said. "He is as vicious as he should be, but I did not tie him up for fear he would attack. He's a good dog. Trouble is he keeps running to the beck, and I cannot let him go down there." Ned's voice was stronger. It seemed the food had lessened the effect of whatever Asa had given him.

"Why keep him from the beck?" Owen asked.

Ned looked Owen in the eye. "There are bodies down there. He found them. He's much too curious about them."

Sweet Heaven. "That is what we are to see in the morning?"

Ned turned away, opened the stall, knelt down beside the dog, who fell on his new master, panting with joy. "Gervase and Henry in the beck. Aye." His voice was choked. He hugged the dog, as if for comfort.

"Gervase and Henry," Owen repeated. It grew worse and worse. "Were they caught in a flood?"

"Nay. They are bound hand and foot."

An unpleasant pattern was developing. "Had they come up here with you?"

"No. I came here alone."

"So what were Gervase and Henry doing here?"

"I do not know."

"Ned."

Ned turned to Owen. "I do not know, Owen. The dog found the bodies. It was the first I knew of their presence."

Owen found such a coincidence unlikely. "What happened that night, Ned? Did you find Don Ambrose?"

Ned rubbed his eyes, gave his head a little shake. "I rode off. Drunk. Almost killed myself. But I had to get away from Abbot Richard, fussing about everything but what was important. When I sobered, I turned back. To find the friar. Find out what more he knew about Mary. But I lost my way."

Owen had never known Ned to lose his way. He was accustomed

to life on the road. Anyone might have guided him to Rievaulx or Fountains. "Did anyone come after you?"

Ned still crouched by the dog, scratching him. "Must have, with two bodies in the beck so close by, eh?"

There seemed nothing wrong with Ned's mind now. He was managing to side-step the unpleasant parts of Owen's questions. Nothing at all wrong with his mind. "When did you find the bodies?"

"A few days ago."

"And you sent for Asa?"

"Nay. She came to check on me."

"And she told Magda?"

"She stayed. Asa has not been back to the village. She would not have told Magda anyway. She has no affection for your Riverwoman."

"The feeling appears to be mutual. So you just rode off that night and found Nym's village?"

"Eventually found it."

"And you just decided to stay here?"

Ned shrugged. "That woman. Asa. She said she could help me forget."

"Is that what you want to do? Forget what happened to Mary? Forget you loved her? Forget your duties to Lancaster?"

"Lancaster." Ned scratched the dog. "I've thought little of the Duke. But I do not mean to forget Mary." His voice broke; he buried his head in the dog's fur and wept.

Owen sat down in the damp hay, closed his eye. He would smell of tar and damp sod, and his behind would ache tomorrow from the damp, but he meant to stay here quietly and think until Ned was ready to go. He had to sort out his questions. What he believed and what did not ring true. But one thing was certain. Ned was leaving a great deal out of his story.

14

BODIES IN A BECK

The sod house drew in the damp. Owen woke with an aching shoulder and a taste of wet earth in his mouth. There was little light. He sat up and waited until his eye had adjusted to the darkness before moving about. When he could make out forms, he realised Ned was gone. He must have made a noise at this discovery, because Asa raised her head.

"He is out with the sheep," she whispered, "and letting the dog have a run. He has not slipped away from thee."

"I would walk out to him. How do I find him?"

"Walkst thou up into the sun. The ground here is too damp for sheep."

Owen heard the dog barking as he climbed out of a morning mist into the sun. Up yet another rocky outcrop and at last he came upon Ned, busy removing the woven mats that enfolded the flock during the night. The bleating sheep were moving about as if blind, bumping into each other and Ned. He patted them affectionately on their shaggy, long-tailed rumps and went on with his work, far more patient than Owen would have guessed. The dog was out beyond the slowly dispersing sheep, barking at something Owen could not see.

"What's the dog after?" he asked.

Ned looked round, seeming unsurprised by Owen's presence, and shrugged. "Perhaps he's gone silly with age. Or it could be Malcolm on his way. He should have been down here by now, and the dog knows it."

"Can I help?"

"What do you know of sheep?"

"What did you know till recently?"

"I watched sheep one summer when I was sent to help my cousin."

"My family had goats."

"Easier to manage than sheep. Smarter."

Owen looked at the shaggy, seemingly confused creatures. "Well, no danger of their outsmarting me."

The dog's barking changed. A man approached, hands up in the air, palms out.

"Malcolm," Ned said. "He can take over now."

Ned was silent as they walked back to the house.

The sun was still low in the sky when the four reached the valley. A stand of birch glowed whitely in the misty dawn. It was a sheltered valley through which the beck rushed, swollen from the spring thaw and the recent storms. As if on command the four paused, no one eager to continue. It was Ned who pushed on.

His friend's silence worried Owen. Ned had said he'd meant to find Don Ambrose and learn what the man knew about Mary's death, but he had not asked Owen whether the man had been found. Did Ned already know Don Ambrose was dead? How? And Gervase and Henry: Ned had not questioned why they might be up on the moors. Or why Owen was here. Was Asa's remedy still at work? Or was Ned avoiding talk that would reveal too much?

Lucie, Lucie, I have been such a fool. What had begun as a mundane journey to confer with the Cistercian abbots and report back to the King had become a nightmare. One that might destroy a friend.

Owen's fault? How might he have planned for the unexpected? How might he have guessed at Don Ambrose's strange humour in the brief glimpse he'd had of the man? Owen thought back. He had met the friar only as Ned's company had gathered to depart York. What had he noted about him? Slender. A long nose. Hunched shoulders which Owen had thought appropriate for a bookish cleric. He'd had the squinting eyes of one who spent his days with manuscripts, not men; and he had kept his gaze humbly averted. Had it not been humility? Had any of this predicted aught? Might a more cautious captain have read danger in the friar's demeanour?

The self-examination knotted Owen's stomach. He shifted his gaze from the familiar back of his friend, focused on the ground, the bracken, and heather. Right now he must steel himself for unpleasantness of a different sort. He noted a stone cross on the far side of the beck. "Does that mark a road?"

"Aye," Asa said. "The monks use it. They thrive all round us— Rievaulx, Rosedale—thou canst not fault their industry."

When they reached the beck, Ned pointed towards an uprooted tree caught upstream, where the course slowed and curved round a rock. "Up there."

From where he stood, Owen would have guessed the water was merely reflecting the brightening sky. But as he drew nearer he saw the bodies. Two, one slightly further downstream than the other, just beneath the water's surface, the other partly exposed. They must have lain there when the uprooted tree floated down upon them. The current was slowly dragging it across the bodies, the branches pitting and gouging the flesh, tearing away the clothing. What had Ned been thinking to leave them there?

"Could the bodies be seen from the track?" Owen asked.

Asa shook her head. "But a thirsty traveller might happen upon them."

"So whoever left them here meant them to be discovered."

"Aye. Were fools else."

The wind whistled past Owen's ears, an eerie dirge. "Ned. Come help me lift the tree from them." He handed his cloak to Magda, crouched down on the bank.

Ned joined Owen. Together they grabbed the tree, yanked, but branches were caught in hair and fabric. Owen sat back, shook his head. "We must wade in."

They pulled off their boots, then their leggings.

As Asa stooped to collect their clothing, she said, "Thou'lt freeze,

Ned. 'Tis melt water." Owen heard tender concern in her voice.

"How else are we to carry them out?" Ned asked sharply. Apparently Asa's affection was lost on him. He stepped into the water.

"See thou dost not stay in over long, Captain Archer," Asa said.

"Never fear. I do not mean to lose my toes."

Asa seemed satisfied, backed away with the clothing.

Owen waded in. Asa's warning had been unnecessary. He would not loiter in this icy stream. The current was brisk, too, so there was no warming of the water round them. A mixed blessing, for the stench of the bodies now teased his stomach. It might have been far worse in warmer water.

The two men worked silently, moving round the bodies, loosening the branches. At last, they nodded to one another, heaved, and tossed the tree far from the rock. Then they bent to the bodies. Carried them from the stream one at a time, stumbling on their numb feet.

When he was back on land, dried off, clothed, Owen knelt beside the bodies. Gervase had lost an eye, but otherwise his face was intact. The other face was so badly torn Owen could not make out the features. "How did you identify Henry?"

Ned, still fussing with his boots, glanced towards the body, shrugged. "He was not so when I first saw him. His face was as clean as Gervase's."

What havoc had been wreaked since! "Why did you leave them in the stream?"

"Who was to help me?" Ned rose, joined Owen, but did not meet his friend's eye.

Owen felt a stranger stood beside him. The Ned he had fought beside would have removed the bodies himself, taking what time he needed. As Owen would have done. "How could you just leave them out there? They might have been carried farther downstream."

Ned shrugged. Said nothing.

Magda crouched down beside Owen, carefully drew the tattered fabric away from the torso of the one Ned had identified as Henry, sat back on her heels. "Dost thou see?"

Owen nodded. "Knife wounds." Coupled with the bound

hands and feet, the mark of the same murderer or murderers as Don Ambrose's. Owen turned the body over. The back was too torn to discover anything more.

Ned rose and walked away. Asa followed him.

Owen looked after them, his anger barely contained.

Magda moved on to Gervase, proceeded carefully to peel the cloth from the torso.

Owen eased Henry's torn body over once more. Dead or no, torn face or no, he could not leave the body lying face down. And then he noticed what he should have see right away: the mutilated right hand, a thumb and two fingers, lost long ago, the skin smooth over the scars. This was indeed Henry. Owen glanced up at Magda, who watched him with a sad expression. "Henry need not have been so disfigured. Why did Ned leave them here?"

Magda shook her head. "Dagger-thrower is not himself. It does not take a Magda to see that." She inclined her head towards the other body. "Stabbed in the chest. But lookst thou."

Owen left Henry, knelt down beside Gervase.

Magda pointed to a wound on the right forearm.

Owen turned the body. Stabbed twice in the back, too. "He fought the attack."

Magda sighed, rose and kneaded her lower back with her fists. "Magda ages faster with each winter." She stomped her feet and rubbed her hands together, then drew the bottle of brandywine from the purse at her waist and drank. "So. Where shall the lads lie? Dost thou intend to carry them back to their mates or bury them here?" She handed Owen the bottle.

"We shall bury them here, then I must escort Ned back to the company and head to York." Owen took a mouthful of brandywine, swallowed slowly, letting the heat spiral downwards.

Magda grinned. "Thou art chilled, too, eh?"

Owen laughed as he handed her the bottle. "Of course I'm cold. I was in the beck."

"Thou wilt go back at once?"

"Aye. Where is Ned's horse?"

"In the village."

"And his clothes?"

Magda nodded, her keen eyes watching his reaction.

Why? What did it mean? "Asa meant to hide him up here?"

Magda shrugged.

That must be it. "Thus her anger. She meant for us to find his horse and clothes, but no Ned. Would she have shown us a grave, Magda? Told us a tale of death so that we might search no farther for Ned?"

Magda turned in the direction Asa and Ned had taken, shaded her eyes. "Asa's heart is unknown to Magda."

"You discovered Ned when you arrived and sent for us. That is the enmity between you and Asa."

Still poised as if searching the horizon, Magda said, "Find Ned. Bury these men before Nym's old dog goes mad and chews through his rope."

"Why does Asa treat you as she does?"

"Why art thou concerned with Magda and Asa?"

"Asa has influenced Ned. If I understood her, I might better understand what has happened to him."

"Asa has done naught to concern thee. She meant to calm thy friend. It is her way of healing. Magda does not call it such, but that matters not to thee. Thy friend has chosen his own way. He is thy concern."

Owen was not surprised that Magda turned the question back on him. But his curiosity was aroused. "What are you doing up here on the moors, Magda? You must have travelled up here when it yet snowed."

Magda gave him an enigmatic, sideways glance. "Thou hast enough to trouble thee without Magda's comings and goings, Bird-eye."

"That is all the answer you will give me?"

"Thou hast bodies to bury."

Owen grumbled, but went in search of Ned. He would try again anon.

• • •

The late afternoon sun coaxed Lucie from the shop and out into the herb garden. The fresh air felt soothing on her face. She stood on the path and surveyed her domain. The lavender and other woody plants needed trimming before the spring growth began. She smiled to herself. Jasper would call for her when a customer came, and Tildy kept Gwenllian's cradle close at hand as she worked, so why should Lucie not stay out here a while, trimming the lavender and perhaps the santolina, too, while she formulated her plans for Owen's and Jasper's spring chores?

Owen. Would he be here for the spring chores? He might have been out here today, planting the hardy seedlings that had been started in the garden shed in late winter. He would have been here had he not put Ned into the path of trouble. Perverse man. Why had he not listened to her? Lucie was not pleased to be proved right in this. She was troubled. More than that. Frightened for Ned.

Owen had sent a letter with Jehannes, delivered two days ago. Lucie knew of Mary's drowning, Don Ambrose's apparent fear of Ned, the disappearance of both Ned and the friar, and Abbot Richard's accusations. She prayed Owen would find Ned before he was found by someone less sympathetic.

She glanced up at noises coming from the house next door. John Corbett's house, now hers. The Corbett children had at last come to clear out John's possessions, much to Lucie's relief. She was not yet comfortable about her father's generous gift—Sir Robert had purchased the house for her growing family. But it was in deed her property and now she might find a way to make it her own. She looked up at the first storey of the house, creamy timber and plaster that overhung the street and almost touched her garden wall. A glazed window faced the garden. That would be their bedchamber, Owen and Lucie's.

"Mistress Lucie," Jasper called, standing in the kitchen doorway, "Master Fortescue is here for his eye drops. Shall I pour them?"

Lucie straightened, shaded her eyes. The clerk of the Mercers' Guild was a regular customer, the formula for his drops unchanging. Jasper had prepared it twice under her watchful eye. "I think you are ready, do you?" Jasper stretched tall with pride and nodded. "Good." When he was out of sight, Lucie crossed herself and said a little prayer. She suffered the anxiety of a chick's first flight, not distrust in Jasper's abilities.

Owen said little to Ned until they were back at the sod hut, warmed with food and ale. Then he suggested they might let the dog run a while. Ned followed Owen towards the other building.

As soon as they were out of sight of the house, Owen turned and punched Ned in the jaw, sending him sprawling. "What game are you playing, you addle-pate?"

Ned rubbed his jaw, checked his teeth, picked himself up, brushed himself off, resumed walking towards the barking dog.

Owen went after him, grabbed him by the elbow. Ned tried to shake him loose, but Owen held on.

Ned turned, shoulders slumped. "What now?"

"How long did you think to leave them in the beck—until there was naught to bury?"

Ned rubbed his forehead with the heel of his left hand. "I am confused."

"You're a poor actor, you are. What are you hiding from, Ned?"

"I need to be alone. Mourn Mary."

"The dead would not interfere with your mourning."

Ned shrugged.

Owen pushed Ned's shoulder. Ned clenched his fists. "Leave me!"

"I am your friend. Or I was. And your captain. But you act like a stranger. What has Asa done to you?"

"She is not to blame. She has been kind to me."

"No doubt, loving you as she does."

At last, a flicker of uncertainty in Ned's eyes. "You know nothing of Asa." The voice, too, was less assured.

"Lancaster must be a fool to use you as a spy. You walk about with your eyes closed. The woman is holding out her heart to you.

Have you tripped over it?"

"She helped me. I had to hide."

At last a crumb of truth. "You said you lost your way. You did not expect me to believe that, did you? You killed Don Ambrose and ran, didn't you?"

Ned's eyes blazed. "You know I would not commit such a cowardly act!"

Trapped. "You already know he's dead."

"I—"

Owen grabbed Ned's shoulder. "You have played the fool with me long enough, Ned. Now I want the truth..."

"You will not believe me."

"How can I know until you tell me what happened? Start telling the truth or I'll beat you till my knuckles are a bloody pulp."

Ned closed his eyes and clenched his fists. Sweat glistened on his upper lip. "I returned to the grange house the night after I'd fled. Found him shoved under some brush. Tied hand and foot. His chest was wet with blood."

"Don Ambrose?"

"Aye."

"It was yet dark?"

"Aye."

"Yet you knew it was he?"

Ned glared up at Owen. "For pity's sake. Put your doubt to work on something of use. You've ridden at night. You know how the eye adjusts. And I'd just fought with the man. I knew his form. His scent."

"And you were certain he was dead?"

"I felt no heartbeat."

"So you examined him."

"Aye. Got his blood on me doing it. And then I thought what a fool I'd been. Abbot Richard would accuse me as soon as he saw the blood. So I hid him."

"You hid him?"

"I thought his attackers would return to do likewise. I would tell the Abbot to put a secret watch on the place. Just Brother Augustine or his servant."

"You suspected someone in your own company?"

"It was the place to start, eh? But I found the grange house and the barn empty. I'd missed the company. So at dawn I buried him."

"You buried Don Ambrose? Yet you did not bury Henry and Gervase?"

"I did not bury the friar out of a sense of Christian duty. I thought to leave him as his comrade had left Mary…floating…" A pause, a deep breath. "But I reckoned the Abbot would leave a search party behind. If they did not know of Ambrose's death, they would be searching for two people. They would not put all their effort into pursuing me. And if they *did* know of his death…" he grunted.

"You would worry them."

A thin smile. Suddenly Ned grabbed Owen's sleeve, his eyes pleaded. "I must find her murderers before the trail is gone."

"What are you talking about?"

"I must return to Windsor."

"And so you shall."

Ned shook his head. "Without the company. No one must expect me. I mean to find Don Paulus. Find out who killed Mary."

"You bloody fool! Aren't you in trouble enough?"

"Trouble?" Ned made a wry face. "More than trouble. I am a dead man, Owen. No matter what I do. At least let me avenge her."

Owen shook his head. "No."

"If it were Lucie, you would feel the same."

Owen could not deny that, but he hoped his tactics would be better than Ned's, more likely to succeed. "Why are you so certain Mary's death was no accident?"

"She was frightened. At Windsor. She wanted me to stay. Who would protect her, she asked. I thought she was safe. Maid to Alice Perrers—who could be safer?"

"Who would have cause to harm Mary?"

"I don't know. She was so good, so kind. She could have no enemies." Ned covered his eyes with his hand, turned away from Owen. "Perhaps they meant to attack me through her. Perhaps she was their pawn."

"Whose pawn, Ned? Who are your enemies?"

"I know not," Ned whispered. "Lancaster has many enemies."

"What do you mean to do?"

Ned turned. Tears shone in his eyes, but his expression was excited. Hopeful. "I must find out from whom Bardolph and Crofter take their orders. They have done everything so that the blame fell on me."

"You think they murdered Henry and Gervase?"

"And Don Ambrose."

"Why?"

Ned shrugged. "I am Lancaster's man. That is enough."

"It is nothing, Ned." But his suspicion about Bardolph and Crofter was not so easy to dismiss. Owen had guessed them to be trouble the night he drank with the company in the York Tavern. Crofter had admired Owen for killing the jongleur and his leman. And Matthew had said that Don Ambrose had at first seemed to fear them, not Ned. "Bardolph and Crofter fought under Wyndesore."

Ned nodded. "And he under the Duke of Clarence, Lancaster's brother. Wyndesore has defamed Clarence to the King."

Owen shook his head. "I do not see the connection."

Ned shrugged.

"And you've no proof of any sort so far."

"I knew you would try to stop me. And now you know who I'm after."

"Why didn't you bury Henry and Gervase?"

"Asa and Malcolm have been watching them. To see whether Bardolph and Crofter return for the bodies."

"Not for you?"

Ned shook his head. "I don't think they knew how close I was. That stream, near that track on which folk travel between the moorland abbeys—word would have reached Abbot Richard soon enough. And who would he blame?"

"They did not see you up here?"

A filthy hand tugged at the knotted locks. "Would you recognise me had you known me only a short time?"

Owen looked his friend up and down. "Nay. And not from a distance even now, knowing you as I do."

"Now that you know, you must help me bring them to justice. Find proof of their infamy."

Owen shook his head. "Things have gone too far. I must take you back to York under guard is what I must do."

Ned looked disgusted. "I'll run."

"You did not run last night."

"In truth, I am relieved to be forced to action."

"You will not run. You are not yet so mad as to betray me."

"Friendship can be a heavy burden."

"I am the one has more cause to complain. But I swear, Ned, I shall find out all I can about Mary."

Ned grimaced. "I may yet change your mind."

Owen doubted it. If Ned were more himself, perhaps. But the lies and silences...

Word of their approach had arrived at the hamlet before Owen and company. The men heard that Owen shared his horse with the Widow Digby, another man rode beside him, a dog following. Who had joined the company? The men waited outside Asa's house, eager to see.

Matthew recognised him first. "Captain Townley!"

Ralph and Geoff moved forward to take the reins. "God be with you, Captain Townley," Ralph said.

Ned nodded to him, but said nothing.

"Any sign of the others, Captain?" Geoff asked.

"Two we buried, two we have not seen," Owen said.

A murmur passed among the men.

"Whom did you bury, sir?" Geoff asked.

"Henry and Gervase."

The men dropped their heads and crossed themselves.

It was Ralph who asked, "How did they die?"

"Murdered," Owen said.

Ralph turned to Ned. "Did you see who did it?"

"I did not see it happen."

Ralph studied Ned's face for a moment. "Ah," he said at last, nodded and walked away.

Watching Ralph, Owen expected trouble, but he and Geoff went off about their business. Still uneasy, Owen showed Ned into Asa's house. Matthew, Curan and Edgar followed them.

"So what's to be done now, Captain Archer?" Matthew asked.

"We shall escort Captain Townley back to York, where he will await the King's pleasure."

Curan strode up to Ned. "You snivelling coward. You killed them, and the friar, didn't you? What did they know about you, eh?"

Ned's fist connected with Curan's jaw before Owen could get between them. But Ned did not leave it at that. He threw himself on Curan, knocked him to the ground, and managed to bloody his nose before Owen grabbed Ned and sent him sprawling.

"Get Curan to Magda," Owen commanded Edgar and Matthew.

Ned slowly rose. Owen punched him back down. "I am losing my patience with you. Any more foolish behaviour and you ride to York bound hand and foot."

"Bardolph and Crofter have done a good job. Everyone believes I'm guilty."

Owen shook his head. "If you're right about them, your behaviour suits their purpose, you fool." He went out to see how Curan fared. It would be a long ride back to York.

15

HAUNTING FACES

Owen, Ned and Matthew spent the night in Magda's cottage; both Ned and Matthew were nursing sore noses and split lips from encounters with the other men that had failed to restore Ned's good name. Magda had ordered the separation so that she might have peace.

It was a crowded cottage. Magda shared it with a young woman, Tola, who was great with child. It was her imminent lying in that prevented Magda from returning to York in Owen's company.

Owen had seen little of the young woman until this evening. He talked to her while she prepared a meal for the five of them. Her husband was busy with the lambing and glad that Magda had come to assist Tola in the birth of their first child.

"Why did you send all the way to York for a midwife?" Owen asked. "Have you none up here?"

Tola, her back to Owen as she sprinkled dried herbs into the broth, said simply, "We thought it best." Thus had she answered all Owen's attempts to converse with her. A woman of few words. One might suspect her of being simple but for the eyes. The few times Owen had found her watching him it was because he had felt her gaze. As intense as Magda's.

As Owen lay in the dark much later, he noted something else: many of Tola's features were very much like Asa's. Asa and Magda. Of course. Lucie would have seen it sooner, recognised the relationship, no doubt.

He rose. Magda had gone out when everyone else had settled for the night. Owen found her at the edge of the clearing, sitting on a stone, her head thrown back to study the night sky.

"Thou shalt be back among thy family soon, Bird-eye. Art thou glad?"

"You know that I am."

"What keeps thee wakeful? Dagger-thrower's ill fortune?"

"Magda, is Ned telling me the truth about how he came to be here?"

Magda said nothing. Owen glanced over at her. She had resumed her star-gazing.

"You have nothing to say?"

"Nay. 'Tis not for Magda to tell thee whether or no thy friend can be trusted. Thou canst judge for thyself."

Owen raised his eye to the stars. "Matthew believes that the sky over the River Thames is different from this sky."

"The pup fears the moors, aye." Magda patted Owen's knee. "Many do."

"Why is your daughter living up on the moors? And why do they call you 'Widow Digby' up here?"

"Magda's daughter, eh? And who might she be?"

"Asa."

A wheezing laugh warmed the darkness. "Thou hast a habit of spying now, eh? So how didst thou guess?"

"I see both of you in Tola."

"Tola looks more like Digby than Magda."

"Potter? Not at all."

"Nay, Bird-eye, Potter's father."

"He was a shepherd?"

"Aye."

"But folk say you have always lived on the Ouse."

"Aye."

"You did not live with your husband? And yet you took his name."

The wheezing laughter was his only answer.

"Tell me about him."

"What wouldst thou hear? Magda was needed in York, Digby had his sheep."

"Asa lived with her father, Potter with you?"

"Aye. They chose. Asa was ever her father's child, at peace alone, up on the moors. Potter liked the river."

"But Asa, too, is a healer."

Magda snorted. "Healer? Asa plays with the dark arts as if they cannot hurt her. Spells. Potions. Foolish Asa. Magda warned her, but she hears nothing Magda says." The old woman rose, brushed off her clothes. "To bed. Thou shouldst sleep, Bird-eye. A long ride lies before thee, with angry men."

Owen rose. "When I asked Tola why she sent all the way to York for a midwife, she said they 'thought it best'. Why did she not tell me you were her mother's mother?"

Magda stood before Owen, hands on hips, shaking her head slowly from side to side. "Thou knowest nothing of the moorland folk. Why spew out thy heart to a stranger?"

"Moorland folk, or the Digby clan?"

Magda shook her head again, motioned for him to come along.

Owen followed, knowing full well he had learned all he would about the Riverwoman for now. It was enough to ponder as he fell asleep.

Archdeacon Jehannes had returned to York anxiously guarded by Owen's man Alfred and the rest of the men who had not accompanied Owen and Abbot Richard. After sending a messenger to Archbishop Thoresby with the sad tale of his journey, Jehannes settled into his customary routine. Several days after his return he spent a long morning with the master mason discussing the slow progress on the minster's Lady Chapel. Archbishop Thoresby would be disappointed, but the problem was with the quarry, not with the masons. Soon, very soon, they must find another source, particularly for the larger stones. There was no other as near, which meant higher costs for transportation. And funds were dwindling; Jehannes was embarrassed to admit that Archdeacon Anselm had been more successful in filling the minster coffers.

Frustrated, wanting to delay writing yet another unpleasant

letter to the Archbishop, Jehannes decided to spend the afternoon in the city doing errands. Perhaps he would add a visit to Lucie Wilton. He had not spoken with her since she'd received Owen's letter. She might have some insight into what had happened.

The day was overcast but with an invigorating breeze. Jehannes set off with his clerk Harold. It was Thursday market day, and though they were well away from the market square they found the streets crowded. As they left the minster gate and entered Stonegate, a man approached, hood up, head down, hands behind his back. Jehannes noticed him because he walked as if lost in thought, a quiet island in the midst of the bustling market day crowd. Possibly sensing eyes upon him, the man lifted his. When he met Jehannes's gaze, the man gave a little cry and turned to run away. Jehannes chided himself for intruding on the man's reveries.

But then, just as suddenly, the man spun back, dropped to his knees before Jehannes, bowed and raised his folded hands over his head. "I beg you, Father, give me your blessing," he said.

Jehannes did not find it an unusual request. What puzzled him was the cry and the momentary turning away. Nevertheless, he laid his hands on the man's head and gave his blessing.

"May God forgive me my sins," the man said, crossing himself. He rose and kissed Jehannes's hand. "Bless you, Father."

"Do you wish to come to me at the minster and make confession?"

The man shook his head. His hood slipped back.

There was a familiarity about the eyes, the voice. Might that explain the odd behaviour? A disconcerting thought, that he might have hesitated to approach Jehannes in particular. "Do I know you?" Jehannes asked.

The man shook his head, pulled up his hood, and slipped back into the crowd.

"Harold, who was that?"

"I did not recognise him."

The crowd had begun to jostle them. It was unwise—and difficult—to stand still in the street on market day. "Come, Harold, let us make our visit to Mistress Wilton before we go to market."

Jehannes hoped that by talking to Lucie Wilton and thereby putting the incident out of his mind, he might trick himself into remembering where he had seen the man before.

Seated at a table by the garden window, supporting a sleeping Gwenllian on her lap with her left arm, Lucie was making notes in the shop ledger when Archdeacon Jehannes appeared in the kitchen doorway. Lucie had left the door ajar to catch the fresh air.

"How lovely! Forgive me for not rising to greet you, Father, but as you see I cannot."

"Forgive me for interrupting your work, Mistress Wilton." Jehannes stepped back as if to leave.

"Oh, please do not desert me so soon. Tildy is at market, Jasper is minding the shop, and I need cheering. Come, sit and tell me how Owen looked when you left him. It is three weeks and more since he headed north with you and I am eager for news of him."

"You had the letter?" Jehannes asked, stepping inside. Harold followed him.

"Yes, but he hardly told me how he looked, and he told me very little about how he felt." Jehannes looked decidedly uncomfortable about that. "How he felt about Ned Townley."

"Oh. The poor man."

Lucie nodded towards Harold. "How is the earache?"

The young clerk put a hand to his right ear and nodded. "Much better, Mistress Wilton. I have slept these past nights without pain."

"I hope you cover your head with your cowl whenever you go out in this wind. It is important to protect your ears."

"I do, Mistress Wilton."

Jehannes sat down opposite Lucie. "Tell me why you need cheering."

Lucie wished she had not said that. She felt rather foolish telling the Archdeacon of York she missed her husband. She watched silently as he reached over and gently touched Gwenllian's hand. When the baby curled her chubby fingers round Jehannes's forefinger and pressed it to her face, his face glowed with joy. Lucie relaxed. Here was a man who understood matters of the heart.

"'Tis a bittersweet sadness. I am missing my husband."

Jehannes's smile was kind. "Did he tell you in his letter about the bird trapped in the nave at Fountains?"

"No."

Jehannes told the story, his finger all the while clasped firmly in Gwenllian's hand.

"Did the bird escape?"

"When I returned later that day, I heard nothing. And the door was still ajar."

Lucie smiled. The simple story had cheered her. "Would you like to hold Gwenllian?"

The Archdeacon looked surprised. "I shall not frighten her?"

"We can but try." Lucie rose, put the baby in his arms.

Gwenllian opened her eyes, screwed up her face to cry. Jehannes folded his hands round her and began to rock, all as if he had done it many times before. Gwenllian relaxed, blinked a few times, then closed her eyes and slept once more.

"You are good with children."

"I am fond of them."

"You were a good friend to Jasper when he was in need."

"He is a bright lad. You were good to take him in."

Always the compliment must be returned. Lucie closed up the ledger, offered Jehannes and Harold some ale. They were quiet while she poured. "It is a sad business about Ned," Lucie said, sitting down once more.

Jehannes's eyes darkened. He lowered the cup he had raised to his lips to drink. "I blame myself. I should have gone to Owen and Ned when Don Ambrose came to me. God grant that no evil comes of my mistake."

Lucie regretted broaching the subject. She had forgotten the Archdeacon's part in it. But now that she had erred…"You blessed Ned's company the day he rode from York, did you not?" she asked.

"Yes." Jehannes gazed down into his untasted ale.

"Did Don Ambrose behave oddly then?"

The smooth brow crinkled in thought. "A little. I see it now that I look for it. But at the time I thought him uncomfortable with the soldiers. They can be..." he shrugged.

Lucie laughed. "Owen asked me recently if he was so rude in manner and speech when we first met. Did Don Ambrose seem uneasy with all the men?"

Jehannes shrugged. "Not that day, but earlier I had noted he kept his distance from Bardolph and—" Jehannes's head snapped up, his eyes wide. "That was him. Today."

"Who?"

"Bardolph." Jehannes told her of the encounter in Stonegate. "I could not place him, but there was something familiar. And now it is so plain. Without a doubt." He took a drink.

"Just Bardolph? None of the others?"

"Just him. What was he doing here in York? Alone? Out of livery?"

"You must find out."

Jehannes nodded.

Lucie reclaimed Gwenllian, who immediately began to scream. Above the din, Lucie said, "You must send someone to search for Bardolph before he has time to leave the city."

Jehannes rose to go. "I am such a fool."

Lucie shook her head. "You are no fool, Father. God bless you for coming. Please come back and tell me what happens." As she watched the two hurry from the yard she shook her head at her improved spirits. But at last they might learn something.

John Thoresby did not like the rumour. It was said that Wykeham and the King had met with the Duke of Burgundy, a valuable prisoner of war who was held in comfortable quarters in London. According to the rumours, the King had offered Burgundy his freedom in exchange for using his influence on Pope Urban in the matter of the seat of Winchester. Thoresby did not find it surprising; the King had a penchant for creative finance. What irked Thoresby was that if the rumours were true, all the trouble at Fountains Abbey had been for naught. That made his blood boil.

And what a mess the meeting with the abbots at Fountains had been. Jehannes had written a full account. Though the outcome, the abbots' refusals to support Wykeham, was just what he had wished, Thoresby did not like the complications with Ned Townley and the Austin friar. They would be found, no doubt, but the situation required Archer to remain up north, and Thoresby had hoped to lure him down to court. Something was wrong, something that had begun with the death of Wyndesore's page, and Thoresby wanted to get to the bottom of it.

Archer's letter had been of more interest than Jehannes's. Archer had asked for details about the death of Alice Perrers's maid and copied the contents of Don Paulus's letter to the missing Don Ambrose. Thoresby must find an opportunity to speak to Mistress Perrers. It was said that she mourned her maid; her maid's death would be a delicate subject to broach, but he suspected Mistress Perrers's curiosity would outweigh her distress. If indeed her sorrow was sincere.

First things first. Thoresby needed to learn more about the friars. There could be no doubt the two were concealing something. Wykeham—he might prove knowledgeable; he had intended Don Ambrose for his household.

Thoresby waited until the King left the high table that evening, for the momentary commotion as the first wave of courtiers departed—hurrying towards rest or more private play—and those left behind reshuffled into more intimate parties. During the bustle, Michaelo was dispatched to invite Wykeham, seated at an adjoining table, to join Thoresby. While he waited, Thoresby entertained himself watching Alice Perrers dodge fawning courtiers seeking favours. Her back straight as a pike, head held high, precious stones in her gold circlet and sewn into her amber silk gown and veil glittering in the torchlight, those cat eyes sly and knowing. Notoriety made some slouch and slink, but not Alice Perrers. As her servant held open the tapestries at the end of the hall, Perrers turned; the cat eyes moved right to Thoresby. She smiled, inclined her head slightly, and slipped through the opening, the same through which Edward had disappeared. How had she felt his eyes upon her when so many others shared his curiosity? Thoresby crossed himself.

Wykeham approached with a nervous gait, his face flushed with colour.

Thoresby straightened, put Perrers out of his mind. "You are kind to join me."

Wykeham nodded. "You are kind to invite me." The privy councillor folded his tall, angular body into the seat beside Thoresby, adjusted his flowing sleeves. The colours might be dark and dignified, but the cut was courtly.

"Is it true about Burgundy?" Thoresby asked. Wykeham's surprise made the Archbishop smile. "I see that no one was to hear."

"I thought your spy was up on the moors."

"A wise chancellor has ears wherever they are needed. But if you prefer not to speak of it, never mind. It is about another matter I wished to talk."

"How did you hear?"

Thoresby motioned to Michaelo to bring them wine. "It is difficult to avoid the gossip, try as I will."

Wykeham took out an embroidered cloth and dabbed his upper lip. The gesture was graceful, so mannered as to hide its purpose. But Thoresby could see the sweat on the councillor's face. Wykeham's manners grew more courtly with each day, but so did the tension that accompanied his position. Was it worth it, Thoresby wondered? Michaelo set a cup of wine before Wykeham, another in front of Thoresby.

"I understand the mission to Fountains was fraught with misfortune," Wykeham said, sliding the cloth back up his sleeve.

"Misfortune?" Thoresby sipped his wine. "Far less innocent than misfortune, I think."

The privy councillor ignored his cup, leaned towards Thoresby with interest. "Less innocent?" He glanced round as if worried that someone might overhear.

"We are quite alone at this end of the high table, I assure you."

Wykeham's smile was refreshingly sheepish. "Forgive me. But, as you just pointed out to me, rumours spread with such speed at court."

Thoresby laughed. "You are right. Let us have done with the posturing. Abbot Monkton has written to His Grace the King and you have read his account. Being a thorough man, the Abbot will have included a copy of the letter Don Paulus sent your friend, Don Ambrose. It is of that that I wish to speak with you."

"My friend Don Ambrose?" Wykeham shook his head. "I thought to take him into my household but—" He waved the matter aside. "No matter. The letter, yes." Now he picked up the cup of wine and took a drink. "I found it puzzling, Don Paulus's behaviour reprehensible. But you obviously see something more—malevolent?"

Malevolent. A fitting word. "Do you not find it strange that the friars should take such an interest in the death of Ned Townley's betrothed?"

"Betrothed?" Wykeham sat back, still holding his cup of wine. "I am sure I heard of no such vows."

Thoresby grew impatient. Did Wykeham mean to question every word in their conversation? "Perhaps not betrothed, perhaps the vows were more private than that. But that is not my point." The privy councillor had the grace to look uncomfortable. "The point is that from the time Don Ambrose received the letter in York he behaved as if he expected trouble from Townley. Now why was that, do you suppose?"

"In faith, I do not understand Don Ambrose's behaviour. I am anxious to talk to him. He has much to explain before he joins my household."

"Was he, perhaps, ill at ease in supporting you against his fellow Austins? Might he have met with disapproval in York?"

Wykeham seemed suddenly distracted, fussing with one of his flowing sleeves, adjusting it so that it lay smoothly along the arm of the chair. Thoresby did not recall the privy councillor paying such attention to his clothes in the past. At last, apparently satisfied with his adjustments, Wykeham met Thoresby's eyes. "I take full blame for all the trouble regarding my favour with the King."

Jesu, give me patience. Thoresby pressed the bridge of his nose with both forefingers. "Quite noble, but beside the point. I am looking for facts, not apologies, Councillor."

Wykeham made a wry face. "I never know with you, Chancellor."

Thoresby laughed. Wykeham joined him. They lifted their cups and drank.

"So." Wykeham drew out the embroidered cloth, dabbed his lips. "Facts. Don Paulus has disappeared. Did you know?"

"I had heard. Vanishing is becoming quite the fashion at court."

"This Paulus has a habit of disappearing, it seems. A herbalist who does not practise discretion."

A herbalist. Thoresby tucked that away. "Do you know when he departed Windsor?"

Wykeham shook his head. "Alas, no. By the time I knew to look for him, he was gone. But how long before…" he shrugged.

Truth? Thoresby thought so. "Pity."

"I have asked the King for some men to help me search for him. His Grace has agreed."

"The King is generous. Why are you so interested? Because you feel responsible?"

"And to know my enemies, if that proves to be the case."

"You learn quickly."

Wykeham sipped his wine. "I understand that Townley accused Don Ambrose of attacking him."

"He did." What was he getting at? And when had the councillor taken control of this quizzing?

Wykeham flicked at an invisible speck on his sleeve. "To be honest, that is so unlikely that it makes me doubt the rest."

The averted eyes said otherwise. "Come now. Even Abbot Richard of Rievaulx attests to Don Ambrose's strange behaviour. What is there to doubt?"

"That Townley had not seen the letter until that night, or heard about the drowning and Paulus's failure to act, until after Ambrose's supposed attack."

"Do you have evidence to support these suppositions?"

"No."

Thoresby was disturbed by his own sense of relief. He was worried that Wykeham knew more than he. What in Heaven's name was wrong with him? "In any case, what difference would it make if Townley had known of his lady's drowning before that night?"

"Townley has a quick temper, they say. A violent temper."

"One might say that of any soldier."

"But not of Austins, I should think."

"No. They slink away."

Wykeham sniffed.

Thoresby had expected a chuckle. So be it; the man was bent on a point. "What are you suggesting, Councillor?"

"It is far more likely that Townley attacked the friar, perhaps merely because he wore the robes of the man who had seen his lady floating in the Thames and had left her there as food for the fish." Wykeham winced at the indelicacy of his own words. "Forgive me."

Fascinating to witness the metamorphosis of a decent man into a hardened courtier. "So you are inclined to believe Ned Townley attacked Don Ambrose. So?"

Wykeham sighed. "So I have won an argument. An empty victory." Pressing his fingers to his temples, Wykeham rose. There were dark hollows beneath his eyes that had not been there before. "I shall share with you what I learn about Don Paulus, Chancellor. And now I must say good-night."

Long after Wykeham departed, Thoresby sat in his chair, sipping his wine and examining his feelings. He had watched such a play of emotions wash over the councillor's face—pride, fear, ambition, uncertainty, regret. One might almost pity him. But how hypocritical, when Thoresby's own insecurity had made him play a silly game with the man. When had Thoresby himself become such a courtier?

16

AN INVITATION TO DINE

Thoresby's chambers at Windsor were in the new wing near the royal apartments, large and comfortable, with a hearth that served both the parlour and bedchamber. Queen Phillippa had seen to his placement here, one of her many acts of generosity towards him. Alice Perrers occupied the mirror apartment at the other end of the long hallway, also the Queen's choice. Did Phillippa ever regret inviting Alice into her household?

Tonight Thoresby and Alice would dine in the Archbishop's parlour. Quite civilised, enemies dining on food from the royal kitchen, fine wine from Thoresby's cellar, warmed by a fire burning in the hearth, the torches along the wall lighting the elegant tapestries depicting such courtly activities as tournaments and dancing in the great hall. Would Alice notice the tapestries? He remembered Archer's first visit to his London chambers, the hawk eye studying the hunt tapestries that had been designed for the parlour. Thoresby did not recall Alice studying these when she had visited him in his old quarters in the lower ward. He certainly could not remember noting the decoration in Alice's parlour when he had returned her visit; but she had been distraction enough.

She would not distract him tonight. Thoresby meant to impress Alice with his courtly manners, allow her every opportunity to display her infamous wit. He meant to sit back and watch, and listen, and make her so comfortable she would speak to him of Mary's death.

Thoresby's page, Adam, staggered into the room with a basket loaded with the first items for the supper. Michaelo followed him in.

Already the table was covered with a linen cloth, Thoresby's finest Italian goblets, silver platters, spoons, even a bowl of dried, fragrant herbs from Lucie Wilton's garden to scent the room. Adam now drew several bottles from the basket, a ripe cheese, a loaf of pandemain.

Thoresby was well pleased.

Michaelo proffered a tall, narrow bottle.

"Your family's liqueur?" Thoresby asked.

"I thought the occasion might warrant it." Michaelo lifted an inquiring eyebrow. His family was known for this exquisite concoction, but the last time Thoresby had heard of it was when someone had used the intense flavour to mask an unsavoury, dangerous additive.

Though it was true that Thoresby would have liked to see the last of Alice Perrers, a man in his position had to take subtler action. "It is quite safe?"

Michaelo smirked. "I assure you it is. A heady mixture of herbs and honey, nothing more. However, should you require…"

"I do not."

Michaelo erased the smile.

Thoresby glanced at the other items. "You have outdone yourselves, both of you."

Still nonplussed by the rebuff of his attempt to amuse, Michaelo bowed stiffly. "These are merely the accessories, Your Grace. Adam will fetch the kitchen servants to deliver the hot dishes after Mistress Perrers arrives."

"Let us hope she warms to the hospitality."

"If all is well, I shall leave the remaining preparations to Adam," Michaelo said, pausing by the door until Thoresby waved him away.

Adam opened the door with a flourish, bowing low to Gilbert and his lady. The young servant stepped back to allow Mistress Perrers a sweeping entrance. Resplendent in crimson velvet and silk, pearls sprinkled on the costly gown, in her hair, and on her transparent veil, Alice Perrers made the most of her arrival. The colour, Thoresby knew, had been chosen to be provocative. Which it was, it was.

"You do me honour, Mistress Perrers," Thoresby said.

"My Lord Chancellor, it is I who am honoured." Her voice matched her gown, all silk and velvet. "But will you not call me 'Alice'? You did so when I entertained you in my chambers." Her smile was playful.

Thoresby had not invited Alice Perrers for a evening of cat and mouse. He wondered whether honesty might halt the game. "I was drunk and discourteous at that meeting," he said. "I did not invite you to dine with me in order to repeat my shameful behaviour, but rather to begin again." The last part was not entirely honest, but it was plausible, and it suited his purpose.

The cat eyes twinkled with amusement. "You are a man of many surprises."

"Might we try to begin again?"

"Certainly, Your Grace." She made the formal address sound intimate.

While they dined, Thoresby kept to pleasantries about court, details about the wine, amusing stories of York. Alice, for her part, also kept to light topics, though she seemed unable to resist flirting with her eyes and gestures. It was not until the fish and venison had been removed that Thoresby turned to the real discussion.

"I have not had the opportunity to extend my condolences at the loss of your maid, Mary." At once the cat eyes lost their sparkle. "I understand she was more ward than servant."

Alice dropped her head, took a moment to reply. "I was fond of Mary."

"She was attending you at your house in town when it happened?"

Without looking up, Alice shook her head. "No." Now she raised her head. The cat eyes glistened, but with tears, not amusement. Thoresby could not remember having seen her thus before. "The silly girl had fallen in love with Ned Townley, as I am sure you know," Alice said, her voice strained. "I opposed the match. I pushed her too far. She ran away." She dropped her eyes.

"You blame yourself?" An unexpected twist.

Alice gestured towards Adam. "If your servant were to run from you, would you not feel responsible?"

"Forgive me for mentioning it." His apology was surprisingly sincere.

Alice lifted her cup, sipped the liqueur. "Why *are* we speaking of Mary's death?"

Never so deeply in mourning that she let down her guard. "I wondered whether you had heard of Ned Townley's disappearance after reading a puzzling letter about Mary's drowning?"

A flush of discomfort. "I have heard rumours. Have you read the letter?"

So she had not. Interesting. "I have. In fact, one of my men copied the contents. Would you like me to read it?"

A moment's hesitation. "Please do."

Thoresby found the pause, the tight voice, most intriguing. Apprehensive? Was the King withholding this information from his mistress? Or was this a sign of a more serious rift? Thoresby nodded to Adam, who disappeared into the next room for the letter. He had staged it thus so neither Alice nor her servant might see in which trunk Thoresby kept his papers. Perhaps an unnecessary precaution. Nevertheless...

While awaiting the letter, Thoresby told Alice of Don Ambrose's behaviour on the journey to Rievaulx.

"Don Ambrose?" Alice's hand moved up to her throat, her eyes mirrored the surprise in her voice.

He had indeed cracked Alice's seemingly impregnable shell. "You had not heard of Don Ambrose's part in this?"

Alice shook her head. "An Austin friar. That is all I heard."

Adam returned with Owen's letter. Thoresby read his transcription of Don Paulus's letter. As he finished, he glanced up, saw an Alice drained of colour. "You are shocked."

"How could he be so cruel as to leave her there?" Her voice was a whisper, her cat eyes were wide, battling tears.

Thoresby resisted a desire to console her. "Precisely why I wished you to hear it, Mistress Perrers. I thought you might be able to tell me why Don Paulus would write such a letter. Two things puzzle me— the assumption that Don Ambrose will understand why he neither pulled Mary from the river nor told anyone what he had seen, and why Ambrose and Paulus concerned themselves with Mary at all."

"Where is Paulus?" Alice asked.

"He has disappeared."

"And Ambrose, too?"

Thoresby nodded. "Were either of the friars kin to Mary?"

"Kin?" Alice whispered, shook her head. "I think I should have known. We *did* talk. I trust she would have said something."

"Can you explain any of this?"

Alice gripped the edge of the table with her hands. The gesture seemed to strengthen her. Her face took on some colour. "These friars must be found." Her voice was clear now, angry.

"The privy councillor has organised a search for Paulus, I believe. I have men searching for Ambrose."

"The privy councillor? What is Wykeham's interest in this?"

"Don Ambrose and Ned Townley were on a mission on his behalf when they disappeared."

Alice nodded. "I had forgotten." She took the last sip of her liqueur. "I would be grateful for any news."

Thoresby nodded. "I did have a thought. I wondered whether I might ask your opinion?"

"Of course."

"Is it possible that Mary's death is related to the death of Sir William of Wyndesore's page, Daniel?"

A flush. The amber eyes flamed. "Neither Mary nor Ned had anything to do with Daniel's accident."

"You are convinced it was an accident?"

Alice rose. "In truth, I have given it little thought. Daniel was not my concern."

Not true. She was trembling with emotion. But what emotion? "You vouched for Ned Townley."

"I stepped forward as someone who knew the truth. Ned had been with Mary that night."

"Do you know Sir William of Wyndesore very well?"

Alice's blush competed with her crimson clothing. So. Lovers, were they? He felt a disturbing stab of envy. "I know him," Alice said. Her chin up, she motioned for Gilbert to prepare to depart. "I went to him when his men accused Ned Townley of frightening Daniel into drinking too much."

"Is that what they accused him of?"

The cat eyes were wary. "What did you think?"

Thoresby shrugged. "A push from the tower?"

Alice closed her eyes, shook her head. "There was never any question of that." She stood tensed, as if awaiting the next uncomfortable question.

Was it possible only Michaelo had noted the marks on the lad's wrists? "Sir William never doubted it was an accident?"

Alice opened her eyes slowly. "I would not know, Your Grace." This time the last two words were icily formal.

Stalemate. Thoresby bowed. "Forgive me for ending the evening with an unpleasant topic."

"I thank you for reading the letter, Your Grace. I regret that I have been of no help to you. The excellent food, wine and company more than compensate for a little unpleasantness." Her smile was polite, but it could not hide the strain in the eyes, the voice.

Michaelo stood up as the door to Thoresby's chambers opened. He smiled in the darkness as he heard Thoresby's farewell, saw Alice Perrers's profile against the lighted doorway.

He watched Alice and Gilbert move down the torchlit hallway. As soon as they turned into the crossing corridor, he stole after them. He was disappointed to see Gilbert open the door to Alice's chambers. But perhaps she required a cloak. Michaelo ducked into an alcove, waited. At last the door opened, but it was only Gilbert, off to his bed in the servant's hall below. Michaelo followed him just to make sure. Indeed, Gilbert entered the room and did not leave.

Thoresby sat slumped in his chair by the fire, his stomach beginning to register a complaint at the rich food followed by a tense conversation. And his latest battle to resist Alice Perrers's attraction. Michaelo's disappointing report was shrugged off. It would have been convenient to identify another with an interest in this matter, but no matter. It was enough to see Alice Perrers's unease.

Adam coughed politely beside him. Thoresby glanced up. The lad held a drinking bowl nestled in a cloth. Something hot.

"What is it?"

"Mistress Wilton's tisane for the stomach, Your Grace. I thought perhaps with the rich food...?"

Thoresby made the effort to smile as he accepted the warm bowl. "You must be weary, lad. To bed with you. The rest can be removed in the morning."

"You are ready to retire, Your Grace?"

"Not quite yet. Prepare my bed, then go to yours. I shall drink this, think a while. I can undress myself, Adam. It is more important that you are awake to dress me in the morning, eh?"

Adam nodded, went about snuffing candles, then disappeared into the bedchamber.

Thoresby sipped the minty tisane and tried to slip into pleasant thoughts, tried to conjure up his goddaughter's face, her throaty laugh. But it was no use. The unhappy faces of William of Wykeham and Alice Perrers were burned into the insides of his eyelids. Two intelligent people made miserable by their ambition. It was no surprise that Alice Perrers was uneasy at court; the position of a royal mistress was only as stable as the King, and Edward was an old man with flagging powers. But Thoresby had not expected Wykeham to lose his peace of mind so soon.

Of late, it seemed the worst fate of a courtier was to win the confidence of the King. Yet who would utter such treasonous advice?

17

WHOM TO TRUST?

May warmed as the company rode south. By the time the towers of York Minster were in sight, Owen's back itched and he considered removing his cloak, but he resisted. He wanted no distractions. If Ned meant to escape, this was his last chance, and Owen could see the men were waiting for it, hoping for it. It was plain they believed Ned had betrayed their comrades and they ached for vengeance. Owen and Matthew rode flanking Ned.

But Ned made no move to escape. He stared straight ahead, watching the approaching city without expression, without comment.

"We will enter by Bootham Bar," Owen said, "right beside the minster liberty. The men would not turn on you there."

Ned glanced at Owen with sunken, uneasy eyes. "You mean to do this? Hand me over to the Archdeacon?" He flicked his hair from his face in a nervous manner.

"Jehannes is a fair man, Ned."

"It is not the Archdeacon of York who will decide my fate."

Owen, unable to deny that, said nothing, stared at Bootham Bar, the well built barbican. It reminded him of the Archbishop's gaol. Would Jehannes lock Ned in there?

Ned leaned towards Owen. "You are resolved in this?"

"What choice do I have?"

"Take me to Archbishop Thoresby."

Owen glanced at his friend, saw despair in the luminous eyes. "It is the King's business, Ned."

"And Thoresby is chancellor."

"So he is. But I swore that if I found you I would deliver you at once to the Archdeacon of York."

"Much has happened since you swore it."

"Nothing to make me break my oath."

A brief silence. "You have not decided whether you believe me."

Damn Ned for making Owen admit it. "No. I have not."

"The King's men will come for me."

"Yes. They will." And it looked bad for Ned.

Jehannes asked Harold to escort Ralph, Curan, Geoff and Edgar to the barracks by the Archbishop's gaol.

"First we should take Townley to the gaol," Ralph said.

Jehannes stood at the head of the table round which they had gathered. He tucked his hands in his sleeves. "No. Captain Townley will stay here."

Ralph shook his head. "He should be under guard. You do not know what he has done."

"Neither do you," Owen said. "You suspect, but you have no proof."

"There is more to tell, Captain?" Jehannes asked.

"Yes. But in private." Though one-eyed, Owen caught Ralph's sneer, glared at him until he dropped his gaze.

Jehannes nodded at the men. "Matthew will guard Captain Townley."

Owen had his doubts about Matthew's ability to guard his master and intended to offer some of his own men, the Archbishop's retainers; but he kept his counsel for the moment.

Ralph was not so diplomatic. "You will leave Matthew to guard Townley? His sworn man?" He fairly flung himself across the table towards the Archdeacon, his ruddy face dark with anger. "Why waste time? Why not escort him out of the city and set him free right now?"

"You will obey orders, Ralph. Quietly," Owen warned.

Ralph growled and would not meet Owen's eye, but he did

settle back on the bench.

"I have no intention of setting him free," Jehannes said. He sounded calm, certain of his judgement. "Neither do I intend to let you take the law into your hands. I understand your anger. Captain Townley ran from his duty. You men did not. But that in itself does not make him a dangerous man."

"They should have tried him in Windsor. Caught him with only the blood of Daniel on his hands," Curan muttered.

Ned, who sat between Owen and Jehannes, clenched his hands and began to rise.

Owen held him back. "Follow Harold, men," he said. "I shall come to you in the morning."

"It is not right," Edgar protested.

"I do not recall asking your opinion, any of you," Owen said with a look that silenced the men.

They shuffled out of the Archdeacon's house with grim faces. When they were gone, Jehannes dabbed his face.

Owen admired the show Jehannes had put on. There had been no outward sign that Jehannes was so nervous about the meeting until now. "You handled that well."

Jehannes dabbed again. "I do not enjoy such encounters. I could see by all your faces that there is much to tell me. A roomful of soldiers thirsty for blood…" He shook his head.

Ned threw his cap on the table. "Swine." He slumped into a chair, folded his arms, glowered at Owen and Jehannes. He wore his livery and had let Asa trim his hair before they set off, so he looked more like himself. Except for the eyes, which had taken on a wildness that Owen had never seen in them before.

"Are you referring to us as swine?" Owen asked, taking care to sound amused. He did not wish to give Jehannes any more frights.

"Don't play the fool with me, Owen. You know full well I mean Ralph and his curs."

"They are good men," Owen said, taking a seat opposite Ned.

Ned gave a nasty laugh. "And how do you see that, my friend?"

"They might have overwhelmed me at any time on the road. And they did not, Ned. They are mouthing empty threats. It makes them feel better. But they have not indulged in the bloodletting they thirst for."

Jehannes lifted the cap Ned had thrown on to the table, thoughtfully traced the badge with a fingertip. "I saw Bardolph in the city yesterday," he said into the sullen silence.

"Bardolph!" Ned straightened, leaned forward. "Where is the murdering bastard?"

Jehannes dropped the cap, looked taken aback. "He is a murderer?"

"Ned has a suspicion, nothing more," Owen said. "Where did you see him? Was Crofter with him?"

Jehannes told them of the encounter.

"You see?" Ned said. "He was asking absolution for his sins."

Jehannes got a faraway look in his eyes and nodded slowly. "He seemed frightened. Such a sin on one's soul would be something to fear. But as I say, I told him I could not absolve him there in the street, that he must come to me for confession."

Owen rose. "My men failed to find him?"

Jehannes nodded. "I sent for His Grace's guards as soon as Mistress Wilton suggested it."

With an impatient kick to the chair he'd just vacated, Owen left the table, moved towards the door, changed his mind, returned. "You went right to my house. How long were you there?"

Jehannes shrugged. "Long enough to have a small cup of ale. Not long."

"Then he knew he had made a mistake coming to you. Yet he was driven to ask forgiveness."

"You see?" Ned said. "A guilty conscience."

"Are we simpletons, Ned? Can there be only one cause of guilt?"

"I wish to God I had been quick enough to catch him," Jehannes said.

Owen shook his head. "I doubt you would have fared better unless you had had the men right there to take him. Do not blame yourself, Jehannes. At least we know Bardolph is alive, and bothered by something." He picked up his pack. "I shall send some men to help Matthew guard."

"So I *am* a prisoner," Ned said.

"No need, Owen," Jehannes said. "Matthew will guard his captain well."

"See that you do, Matthew," Owen warned.

"I will, Captain Archer. You can trust me."

Jasper stood on a stool, stirring a small bowl of wine while Lucie dripped juice of wild nept into it. "Why are you mixing it with the wine?" the boy asked.

"Caught by my apprentice!" Lucie said with a look of horror. Confused, Jasper stopped stirring. Lucie laughed as she stoppered the bottle. "I shall explain as soon as we are finished." She picked up a funnel and handed Jasper a bottle. "Hold this beneath the funnel while I pour." He assisted in silence. That finished, Lucie said, "When you take the bowl to Tildy for washing, tell her what we mixed in it. Wild nept juice is a strong purgative. Not something we want accidentally to consume at supper."

Jasper made a face. "Now will you tell me about the wine?"

Lucie sat down on the stool Jasper had vacated, glanced at the door to check there were no customers to overhear, then leaned close. "This is for Master Maldon. What have I told you about him?"

Jasper dropped his chin to his chest, chewed his lower lip as he thought. After a few minutes, he shrugged with defeat.

"He has a taste for remedies. He thinks if a little is good, a lot is much better. And no matter how I caution him, he will take more than he should." Lucie shrugged. "So I compensate for him."

"That's cheating!"

Lucie smiled. "Do you think so? The wine I use is almost as dear as the juice. But I charge him less than I do others for the same physick."

"The ways of a Master Apothecary are mysterious, eh, Jasper?"

Lucie's head shot up. "Owen!"

He stood in the doorway, pack in hand. Lucie jumped up, hurried round the counter. Owen dropped his pack and met her in the middle of the room, lifted her in his arms. She buried her face in his dusty hair. There was no scent she loved so well as Owen's, nothing that felt so right as being in his arms.

"I missed you, my love," she whispered to him.

He squeezed her hard, let her down on her feet, put his hands on her shoulders. "You received my letter from Rievaulx?"

"No. Only the one from Fountains."

"A pox on them. I've ridden up on to the moors and back down and they could not get a letter to you in all that time?" Owen's face was drawn, lines ran from his nose to the corners of his mouth.

Lucie traced the lines with a finger. "What is it? Did you find Ned?"

"I did indeed." Owen shrugged wearily. "There is much to tell."

And none of it good, Lucie guessed. "First you must refresh yourself. Come."

Jasper stood behind the counter, still encumbered by the bowl. "Welcome home, Captain."

Owen ruffled his hair, chucked him under the chin. "One day I shall return and think you a stranger, you are growing so quickly. Come into the kitchen and I shall show you what I brought you."

After Jasper and Tildy had gone to bed, Lucie and Owen went up to their bedchamber. Lucie sat by the window nursing Gwenllian. Owen stretched out on the bed, lying on his side, arm supporting his head.

"You are beautiful, you two," Owen said softly.

"You've not yet held your daughter."

Owen sighed, flopped onto his back, arms outstretched. "Think back to your last long ride. I was on horseback from dawn until you saw me, but for a pause at Jehannes's house. And two days before that. Every muscle in my back is twitching or aching. To sit still and hold Gwenllian..." he moaned. "But if you knead my back tonight with one of your soothing ointments I shall be able to hold my daughter in the morning, I am sure." He grinned.

Lucie laughed. "You might have just asked."

"I am steeling myself for our customary argument. I cannot yet divine whence it shall come, but to ask a favour might be just the thing to irk you."

"Do you dare accuse me of starting arguments?"

"Well…"

Lucie held Gwenllian up to her shoulder to wind her. "Tell me about Ned."

Gwenllian interrupted with a hearty belch.

Owen laughed. "She is not shy."

"Your daughter? Of course not." Lucie lay Gwenllian in her basket beside the bed. Already the long eyelashes rested on the chubby cheeks. "I must go down to the shop for the ointment."

"Never mind. Tomorrow morning is soon enough."

Lucie hesitated, tempted to slide into bed. But her professional self would not allow it. "Your back will be stiff when you wake. Best do it now. I have some ointment mixed. I shall be back before you've missed me."

When Lucie returned, Owen lay on her side of the bed, dangling his arm in Gwenllian's basket, one finger firmly grasped in his daughter's right hand. Lucie smiled, gave thanks. She had feared Owen had developed a new worry, something that would prevent his touching his daughter. "She looks so much like you when she sleeps," she said.

"Nay, like you."

Lucie pulled her shift over her head.

"What is this? You could not find the ointment?"

"I have it." Lucie nodded at the jar on the small table beside the bed. "I would rather not soil my shift with the oil."

"What a practical wife you are."

Lucie slid under the covers and ran her hand down Owen's side and up over his chest.

He rolled over on top of her, bit her shoulder.

"I thought your back needed a rub."

"First things first."

• • •

Gwenllian woke them with a hungry cry. Lucie wrapped a shawl round her shoulders and lifted Gwenllian into bed to nurse her.

Owen sat up, touched his daughter's damp curls. "She sleeps hot."

"Like her father."

"Will she soon sleep through the night?"

Owen disliked being awakened; a noise in the night could cause a day of complaints. Lucie did not sympathise. "I pray that she will soon sleep the night through, but it is impossible to predict a child's appetite." Quickly, to avoid more comments, Lucie asked, "Did Jehannes tell you he saw Bardolph?"

"Aye. He did." Lucie heard Owen's frustration in his voice.

"I had hoped that might be good news. Of some help. But it is one more problem?"

"Ned would say no. He believes—" Owen shook his head. "We shall not speak of such things while Gwenllian is suckling."

Men had the oddest sense of order, Lucie thought. "How did you find Ned?"

Owen sat up a little. She had chosen a good topic. "You will be amazed who found him for me." Already his voice had brightened.

Lucie could not imagine. She chose the first name that came to mind. "Don Ambrose?"

Owen did not answer at once.

"Well? Am I right or wrong?" His continued silence alerted her. "What is it, husband?"

"Nothing." He forced a bright voice. "Guess again."

Lucie groaned. "I dislike this game. Tell me."

Owen tickled her neck. "You don't care to guess?"

"Mmmm…" she smiled. "I shall only guess wrong. I cannot imagine who found Ned."

"You are certain?"

"Owen…"

"Are we about to have our argument?"

"Not if you tell me right away. You want to tell me. You will in the end. Why torture me when I am innocent?"

"You become choleric with too much work."

Lucie laughed. "Tell me or I shall tell Gwenllian you enjoy her crying in the middle of the night."

"Sweet Heaven but you are a cruel woman!"

"Well?"

"Magda Digby found Ned for me."

"Truly!" Lucie would not have guessed that. "How is that possible?"

Owen told her how Nym had come for them at Rievaulx.

"Though I am not surprised that Magda travels up on to the moors, I am puzzled by her being there now, in such an uncertain season," Lucie said.

"She went to be midwife to her granddaughter, something that occurs at its own time." A smug smile.

"Granddaughter! Owen, you monstrous man, to have such a story and keep it secret."

Owen laughed, told Lucie of Magda's family.

Lucie was delighted. She and Bess often wondered about Magda's past, who Potter's father might have been. "You discovered this for yourself?"

"None of the women spoke of it."

"I wonder why?"

"There is some rift between Magda and her daughter."

Lucie lowered the sleeping Gwenllian back into her basket. She prayed that no such rifts happened with her children.

"She falls asleep faster now," Owen noted.

"Tonight, yes. Tomorrow night might be another matter." Lucie snuggled up next to him. "You are eager to be done with the difficult part of siring children."

"Rub my back now?"

Lucie had forgotten. She blinked back sleep, forced herself upright. "While I work on your back, tell me about Ned."

"You thirst for bad news?"

"I want to know what troubles my husband."

"It is difficult to know what to say. I am so uncertain what to think."

"Then tell me all."

And Owen did. As Lucie kneaded his back, smoothing out the tight muscles, he told her of Ned's confusion when Owen had first seen him in the shepherd's hut, his half-truths about how he had come to be there, the fact that he had known of Ambrose's death.

"And you cannot judge whether he is lying or confused?"

"No. I think some of both, but I do not know." Owen squirmed under her searching fingers. "Don Ambrose's death is the worst that might have happened for Ned. Unless..."

Lucie had not realised the extent of his suspicions. "You don't think Ned killed him?"

A long silence. "It is possible. But it is so difficult to believe that of him. It would have been the act of a coward. Ned is not that. Or he was not before."

Lucie was shocked Owen would even consider the possibility. "His running away has made you doubt him."

"Aye. Another thing I would have said he would never do."

When such doubts began, where indeed did they end? "You blame yourself for giving Ned command of the men."

"I do. And Jehannes for saying nothing of the friar's request."

His left shoulder felt knotted, slightly swollen. Owen winced when Lucie kneaded it. "Chilly and damp up on the moors?"

"Aye."

She would talk to Brother Wulfstan, the infirmarian at St Mary's, and Magda; perhaps one of them knew of a salve that would bring more warmth to the shoulder at such times. For now, she tried a gentler touch, which seemed to help him. "Why did Jehannes say nothing?"

"To be plain, inexperience. And a stubborn streak he chose a wretched time to indulge."

"You do not think Jehannes is hiding something?"

"No. It would be against his nature."

"Has Ned lied to you before?"

Owen paused. "How can I know for certain? But I think not. He is a braggart, not a liar. I should have listened to you. You warned me."

That dream. What had it meant? It had seemed merely fear

before. But now? "For once I should have been happy to be wrong."
Lucie sank back on her heels.

Owen turned over on to his back. "Already I feel better." He
held out his arms to her, she sank down onto him, kissed him, then
rolled to the side, yawning and stretching. "I am keeping you awake,"
Owen said, letting her hear his disappointment.

"I have had many wakeful nights with Gwenllian. I cannot
remember when I felt truly rested."

"I should have waited till morning for you to tend my aches."

"No, silly man. I prefer to have you rise in the morning without
pain."

Owen kissed Lucie's forehead, then grew quiet for a while. Lucie
was drifting off when he said, "Gervase and Henry are dead, too."

"What?" Lucie opened her eyes. "Where?"

"Ned found them lying in the beck near where he stayed while
tending the flock."

Lucie sat up. "Do you think Ned…" She shook her head. She
could not say it. But why would someone go to such lengths to make
Ned look guilty?

"I think it highly unlikely one man could have overcome
both men."

"But, Owen. Ned was so far from Rievaulx or Fountains. How
did Gervase and Henry also stray there?" That it was not the work
of one man did not eliminate Ned. It merely required an accomplice.

"Ned believes their bodies were left there, near a road between
abbeys, so that word would reach Abbot Richard, and the details would
point to the same man the Abbot believes murdered Don Ambrose."

"Who would go to such lengths?"

"According to Ned, Bardolph and Crofter."

"Bardolph! So that is why Ned was glad of the Archdeacon's
encounter."

Owen said nothing.

"But Gervase and Henry were their comrades."

"On this journey only."

"Why would they do this to Ned?"

Owen sighed. "He cannot say."

"Will not?"

"I think cannot."

"Such an elaborate theory."

"I fear Mary's death has robbed Ned of his wits."

"I should like to talk to him."

"I should like you to."

18

NED TAKES ACTION

Rain tapped on the casement window above Thoresby's writing desk. For once he was glad not to be at his leaking palace at Bishopthorpe; last summer's heavy rains and this winter's snows had found all the weak spots in the roof and worried at them. Pray God the roof was fixed when he returned. With Archer busy chasing corpses and runaway captains he had little time for his duties as steward. Before Archer had left for Fountains he had given orders for workmen to fix the roof, but who was ensuring that the orders were carried out? Thoresby thought it wise to include a reminder in his letter to Owen.

He frowned over the papers spread out before him—letters he had dictated to Michaelo: one to Archdeacon Jehannes and one to Captain Archer, in Michaelo's beautiful, steady hand. The quality of Michaelo's work reflected well on Thoresby, in looks if not in content; he was not so pleased by the content, which was his fault, not Michaelo's. These letters would be carried by a messenger accompanying the King's retainers who would ride north today. To York. To arrest Ned Townley for the murder of Don Ambrose.

Thoresby found the arrest absurd. It was plain that there was no proof of Townley's guilt; however, though Jehannes had expressed his uncertainty to the King, Abbot Richard of Rievaulx had argued persuasively for the man's arrest. And the King, preferring an arrest over uncertainty, had been pleased. Townley was expendable; the morale of the King's retainers was more important. Thoresby's letters explained this to Jehannes and Archer, urged them not to despair, but to continue questioning the judgement; he promised them he would delay a decision about Townley's fate as long as possible. Admittedly, he had little hope of saving Townley, but nothing was impossible. Thoresby sighed, pressed the ridge of his nose, considered how to phrase his addition to Archer's letter so that he would not appear to be more concerned by the state of the roof at Bishopthorpe than by Ned Townley's arrest.

But perhaps Archer would welcome the opportunity to think of something other than Townley. In writing to Thoresby, Archer had told of finding Ned Townley up on the moors, as well as the corpses of two of the men left behind to search for Townley and Don Ambrose. To Thoresby it looked worse and worse for Archer's friend.

Except when one examined the supposed motive. Blaming Don Ambrose for keeping the news of Mary's death from him, killing Henry and Gervase to silence them. Only a very frightened man would be so foolish as to murder someone who had been known to fear him. And who could believe that Townley had been so addle-brained by the time Archer had arrived that he had willingly led him to the bodies he had disposed of so poorly? And what of the other men in the search party? Where had they been when Townley was murdering their comrades? Thoresby did not believe Ned was guilty. But he agreed with Archer—it was difficult to explain Townley's behaviour.

What of the other two left behind to search? Bardolph falling to his knees before Jehannes—what was that about? And where was Crofter?

Archer had sent a trustworthy messenger, Walter of Coventry, in haste to Windsor with instructions to learn what he might of Sir William of Wyndesore and the Duke of Clarence, under whom the two men still unaccounted for had served in Ireland. Thoresby had admitted to Archer in the letter that he knew little of Wyndesore, but intended to learn more. As for the Duke of Clarence, he was unlikely to have anything to do with such a subtle business.

Sunlight reflected off the letters beneath his hands. Thoresby had wasted so much time debating whether to add a note to Archer's letter about the repairs at Bishopthorpe that the rain had stopped. This was nonsense. Why not simply tell Walter to remind Archer of the work? It would give Thoresby an opportunity to speak with

Walter, find out whether he had heard anything of Bardolph in York, or knew either of the Austin friars. As a messenger, Walter would hear more than most people.

Thoresby chuckled as he gathered the letters. He began to enjoy this sleuthing; perhaps he ought to assist Archer more often. That would put another thorn in Archer's already heavy crown.

The rain had turned the lower ward of the castle into a sea of mud. Thoresby had not foreseen that. He regretted his excursion, particularly after leaving Walter's quarters none the wiser. But he was rewarded in other coin. As he hurried north-east across the yard from the guards' lodgings, his boots sucking disgustingly, he heard someone clumsily hurrying after him. He turned. It was Gilbert, Mistress Perrers's servant.

"Your Grace." The young man was panting, his face a glistening red.

"*Benedicte*, Gilbert. Surely you were not running to catch me? I do not walk so fast as that. Especially in such mud."

Gilbert wiped his sweaty forehead with his right sleeve while nodding. "Master Walter said I had just missed you."

"Walter? Indeed, I was just there."

Blinking to rid his eyes of sweat, Gilbert gave a little bow. "Aye, Your Grace. He said that I might catch you."

"You had business with Walter?"

Gilbert drew a sealed note from his purse, handed it to the Archbishop. "I was delivering a letter. As I am to you, if it please Your Grace."

Thoresby glanced at the note. "Your mistress has been busy." He smiled at Gilbert, who was still red in the face, his hair damp along his temples. "Did you run from Walter's lodging?"

"Aye, Your Grace."

"Had your mistress ordered you to make haste?"

Head dropped, eyes looked aside. "No, Your Grace. I thought to save time."

Thoresby would not ask for what. It was not Gilbert who interested him. "She is a good mistress?" He tucked the note in his sleeve.

Gilbert watched the note disappear with a troubled expression. "If it please Your Grace, I am to await your reply."

"Ah." Thoresby withdrew the note and broke the seal. An invitation to meet at his convenience. In private. At Mistress Perrers's house in the town. Intriguing. But no need to seem eager. "I might come just after vespers tomorrow evening. Would that suit your mistress, Gilbert?"

The young man had regained his composure and looked pleased with Thoresby's reply. "I am certain that it would, Your Grace." He bowed, hurried away.

Thoresby watched Gilbert disappear in the direction of the town gate. So Alice wished to discuss something away from the prying eyes and ears of the court. That both cheered and chilled him.

Sunshine and a fresh breeze had lured Owen to the writing table beneath the bedchamber window. He leaned against the table, at just the right height to catch the breeze on the back of his neck; Lucie kept the shutters closed during the night for fear of a draft on Gwenllian, and the air in the bedchamber never seemed fresh enough. Arms crossed, Owen waited for Lucie to finish fussing with the gown she had chosen to wear to the Archdeacon's house. Now she spun round, waiting for an opinion.

Sweet Heaven, did she know how she looked? Owen stared at the white rounds of her swollen breasts that pushed up from the low, tight bodice.

Lucie tilted her head to one side. "Why such a frown?"

"Do you mean to seduce Ned or talk to him?"

She glanced down the front of her dress and blushed. "I had wondered about it. The nursing has changed my figure. I mean to find cloth for an insert, but I have no time to do it this morning."

Owen was uncertain what to say. As Lucie's husband he would have preferred her either to delay the visit or to wear an old gown.

As captain of the Archbishop's retainers he could see it as a clever ploy: send a desirable woman to a rogue who has just lost his lady, have her coax the truth from him.

"My alternatives are the gowns I wear in the garden and the shop," Lucie said. "Do you think one of them more suitable?"

That depended on whether he was acting as husband or captain. What was needed was a hint of her mood. "Your beauty might inspire Ned to tell the truth..."

Lucie's chin came up, her blue eyes chilled. "You would use me so, husband?"

Ah. Now he knew the lie of the land. "I?" He grinned, shook his head. "How little you know me to ask that question. Your husband would ask you to wear one of your old gowns, or delay."

When Owen watched Lucie hurrying down Stonegate in her old gown, a pale shawl thrown over her shoulders, he knew himself for a fool. The gown was very like the one she had worn when he first saw her, and her hair was pulled up in a white kerchief as it had been that day, showing her long, delicate neck. He had won no victory. And the thought that Ned might reveal his heart to her was cold comfort.

When Matthew opened the Archdeacon's door, Lucie was glad of her choice of gown. He was tongue-tied and blushing. How much worse would he have been had she worn the other dress? Matthew hurried off to fetch Ned. Ann, the Archdeacon's serving girl, peeked in to ask whether Lucie wished for some refreshment. Lucie asked for water. She paced the parlour as she waited for Ned, listening for footsteps descending. When she heard them, she hurried to the foot of the stairs.

But only Matthew appeared, looking frightened.

"Will Ned not see me?" Lucie asked.

"Mistress Wilton, I—" Matthew swallowed, glanced back up the stairs. "The Captain's gone, mistress." He began to back up the stairs, his eyes wide, unblinking. "The window. He must have—Oh, Mistress Wilton, what have I done?"

Lucie closed her eyes for a moment, ordering herself to question the puppyish man gently, else he might bolt out the same window from which she guessed Ned had escaped. But it was hard. So hard. Because with Ned gone…Damn him. How could he do this? How could he so betray the trust Jehannes had shown? And Owen. Sweet Mary in Heaven. Damn. Now Owen, home just a day, would go riding off after Ned and she would be alone again. Was she never to have her husband to herself?

Her stillness must have worried Matthew, for he hurried back down the stairs. "Mistress Wilton? Are you faint?"

Holy Mary, Mother of God, give me the patience to get through this day. Lucie opened her eyes. "No, Matthew, I am fine. Take me to the Captain's chamber. Show me what you found."

There was little to see. Jehannes had trusted Ned even so far as to give him a room with a window that faced away from the street, so he might drop out of it with little chance of being seen. Just beyond the overhanging second storey grew a sturdy fruit tree. At St Clement's Nunnery Lucie had become adept at using trees to escape. Even now she quickly concluded that if one climbed out and stood on the window sill, clutching the edge of the roof above, then—with a prayer and a promise never to do it again—pushed off and reached out for the branch just below, one might use the tree for a reasonably quiet escape. Had Archdeacon Jehannes truly thought Ned would resist the temptation and stay put to be taken back to Windsor shackled?

"He had no guard?" Lucie asked Matthew.

He blushed, dropped his head. "I was to guard him."

"Then it happened when you came to answer the door? Hurry. We might—"

Matthew was shaking his head. "Most like it happened as soon as I left him, which was hours ago. He told me he had not slept during the night but felt at last he might. He must have the window shuttered. But I needed light; I was oiling my boots. He asked me was it likely he would go anywhere in his sleep. So why didn't I take the boots and go elsewhere, he would sleep until midday." Matthew's eyes were sad, not angry. "He was cruel to use me so."

"Perhaps a little. But you were foolish as well, Matthew. Did you believe he would do nothing to save himself from the humiliation of being taken a prisoner to Windsor?"

"Mistress Wilton?" Ann was in the doorway, holding a cup of water.

Lucie had forgotten Ann. Now she glanced out the window, back to the serving girl. Even had Ned managed a smooth leap to the branch, someone down in the kitchen might well have heard him, and would surely have seen him once he reached the ground. "How long ago did the Captain escape, Ann?"

The young woman quickly dropped her head, peered up through her lashes. "Mistress?"

"With what did Captain Townley buy your silence?"

The bit of cheek and neck visible to Lucie reddened. Ann was a tall, gangly young woman, awkward in this meek role. "What do you mean, mistress?"

Lucie walked over to Ann, took the cup of water out of her hands, lifted the sturdy chin until the nervous eyes met hers for an instance before flicking away. "Captain Townley has climbed down out of his window and disappeared, Ann. I doubt you have the kitchen door closed today. You must have seen him."

"I was busy, mistress. Getting your water."

Ann was not a practised liar. She'd forgotten to feign surprise about the escape. "Do you think me such a fool as to believe you would be so busy pouring water you would not notice a handsome soldier dropping down out of a tree into your kitchen garden?"

Ann snorted in the effort to stifle a laugh. She shook her head. "No, mistress." She eyed Matthew, dropped her head.

A kiss, Lucie guessed. She saw no need to embarrass the young woman. "Never mind, Ann. Just tell me how long ago, and what you noted him wearing, carrying, anything."

"By the minster clock, an hour past, Mistress Wilton." Ann screwed up her face. "I shall lose my job."

Lucie sighed impatiently. She had no time to comfort the silly woman. "If I tell him you have been helpful I doubt the Archdeacon will throw you out for one mistake. But you must help me."

"He wore the King's colours. Took his pack. Oh, he was bleeding badly, mistress. He should have come to you."

"Bleeding badly?"

Ann nodded. "A branch caught his leg, opened it up on the inside. He jumped anyway, went running, did not stop to see how bad he was. He's very strong, Captain Townley is."

Perhaps not strong enough to ride. Or run quickly. Lucie ordered Matthew to run to the Archbishop's retainers to tell them to alert the bailiffs and the gatekeepers to hold Ned if he tried to come through and to look out for an injured man.

She did not stay to witness Jehannes's reception of the news.

Bess Merchet, her starched cap and pressed ribbons riding high as she swept a new chambermaid down the hall to a lesson in dish washing, stopped in the kitchen doorway at the sight of her pretty neighbour hurrying past the gate looking grief-stricken. Bess rushed out, arms outspread, and gathered a startled Lucie to her. "My dear, what is it? Not my godchild, I pray?"

Lucie tried to shake her head, but she was held too snugly against Bess's fleshy shoulder. "Gwenllian is well. It's Ned. He has run away from the Archdeacon."

Bess tsked. "Well a day, 'tis not such a bad thing then. Owen will ride forth and find him, quick as can be. You know your man."

Lucie did indeed. "That is the trouble. Owen will be off again today, searching for Ned."

With a quizzical sound Bess held Lucie away from her until she could see her face, then shook her head. "And that's as must be, Lucie Wilton. How could you think else? How could you go on loving that rogue if he deserted his friend?" Gripping Lucie's arm, Bess led her to the tavern kitchen.

Lucie sank down on a bench inside the doorway. "Ned has no honour."

Bess shrugged, pointed the maid towards the tub of soaking dishes on a shelf just outside the door. "Show me what you can do with that," she said, waited until the young woman pushed up her sleeves and set to it, then returned to Lucie. "Honour is oft a deadly virtue; sense is what keeps a man alive. Ned has the sense to know he's a pawn and unimportant to the likes of the Archbishop and the King. They are anxious for someone to punish. It matters naught to them whether they accuse the right man."

"Ned knows Owen will come after him."

"Mayhap 'tis what he hopes. He and Owen might make short work of finding the true culprits." Bess crossed her arms and frowned at Lucie's silence. "Am I right, Lucie Wilton?"

Lucie raised her eyes to Bess's, shrugged. "Of course you are right, Bess, but I'm no happier for it."

Bess sat down next to Lucie. "You told me you'd come to accept Owen's work for the Archbishop. So why this pouting?"

Why indeed? Why this hot pain in the pit of her stomach? Was it still the dream of the burning village? "Before Owen left for the abbeys, I had a nightmare." She told Bess of the dream, the angry people shouting for Owen's and Ned's blood.

Bess crossed herself. "Such a dream is more curse than blessing."

Lucie nodded. "Only afterwards will I know how the dream was to be interpreted. But it is there in the back of my mind. I cannot forget it."

"I understand. And yet Owen must go after Ned. You know that."

Lucie sighed. "I know. But first Owen must find him. Ned's injured, Bess. He may be hiding in the city, unable to move too far. Who might hide him here?"

Bess frowned. "Where to begin? He broke several hearts when he was here last. But the one he returned to when he arrived here last month was Matilda. Her father runs the stables near Micklegate."

A nurse and then a horse. Perfect. "Can you send your groom for her?"

Bess nodded sharply. "By the time you've delivered the bad news to Owen, Simon will have her in your kitchen."

With a grateful hug, Lucie hurried home.

• • •

Owen pounded the shop counter with his fist. His face was tight with anger, the scar on his left cheek standing out lividly. "And if you had not injured yourself, you would be out of the city by now, eh?"

Ned looked taken aback. "I would not! I told you! I have a plan. A way to lure the bastards out of hiding. I need your help."

"So you jump out of the Archdeacon's window? Would it not have been easier on your leg to ask to speak to me? For God's sake, Ned, Lucie went to talk to you this morning. She would have listened."

"The Archdeacon is a coward. He would not allow me the freedom I need."

"Ah. We're to set you free to lure Bardolph and Crofter, is that it?"

"Yes." Ned winced at Owen's glare. "That's an unforgiving eye you have there, my friend."

"Are we still friends?" Owen asked quietly.

"God help me. When you take that tone..." Ned and Owen both looked up as Lucie entered the shop.

"Sweet Jesu!" she hurried over to Ned. "I am so relieved. I thought"—she glanced at Owen, saw his expression—"Ah, so did you. Well, no matter." She turned back to Ned. "The serving girl told me you were injured. Let me see." Lucie took a small knife from the counter, knelt down, slit open the blood-soaked legging. "Holy Mary, Mother of God..."

"He does not deserve your ministrations, Lucie," Owen said. "He means to convince us to set him free."

Lucie glanced up at Ned. "You will go nowhere with this leg."

"Not soon, I know. I've been a fool. But I have a plan to catch the bas—the men who mean to see me hanged. The men who murdered my Mary."

Owen groaned. "You'll not win me over by tugging at my wife's heart."

Lucie closed her eyes, shouted, "Peace! We shall talk about it after we have seen to this wound. These wounds. You've opened an old one, too."

"Aye."

"A knife wound?"

"Don Ambrose. We fought the night he disappeared."

Lucie rose. "I must fetch some warm water and a cloth to clean the wounds." She began to step aside to avoid Owen in his pacing trajectory, but he grabbed her shoulder. "Husband…"

"While you two politely discuss wounds, the Archdeacon's household must be in turmoil. Eh, wife? Or did you say naught when you found his room empty?"

"Oh dear." The blue eyes widened as they met Owen's eye. "Oh sweet heaven, a turmoil indeed. I sent Matthew to alert your men. They will have the gatekeepers and bailiffs watching for Ned by now."

Owen let her go and kicked a stool, sending it clattering against the counter. "You sent that mewling Matthew to give orders to my men? He'll tell Ralph and his men. When they find Ned here they'll hang him."

"For pity's sake, Owen. Do you always abuse the messenger? It was not I who let Ned slip out the window. It was not I who agreed to have Matthew guard him! And I did just what you would do, did I not? Alerted the city and gatekeepers?"

"I pray you," Ned cried, struggling to stand, "I will not be the cause of discord between you. I'll leave."

As quickly as Owen's anger had flared up, it died. "Sit down, Ned." Ned sat. Owen righted the stool by the counter and sank down on it, elbows on knees, forehead in hands. "I have a mind to wash my hands of this matter, Lucie. Jehannes has made a mess of it, first sending Ned out without warning of Don Ambrose's request, then trusting him to stay put in his house with only Matthew to guard him. 'Tis Jehannes's affair now. Let him answer to the Archbishop and the King."

Lucie frowned, shook her head slightly, brought a finger to her lips, then smiled at a customer coming through the doorway. "Have a care," she whispered, "Mistress Tarrington would love to spread word of our arguing in the shop. And of Ned's presence. I shall take him into the kitchen before she has a good look." Lucie nodded to the woman and helped Ned hobble out. "See to her."

Owen rose and beamed at the gossip. "How is Will's leg today, Mistress Tarrington?"

"Middling. Can you give him naught stronger for the pain?" The man had been savaged by a wild boar. Master Saurian had recommended amputation at the knee, but Will Tarrington wanted first to try prayer and time. "'Tis the thrashing about that's stopping his healing," his wife said. "If you gave him something stronger, he might rest and recover." She was a tiny woman with a rasping voice and the beady eyes of a ferret.

Lucie had already given poor Will a salve that often was used to numb a patient before surgery. Owen could do no better for him without endangering his life. "My wife has given him her strongest physick for pain, Mistress Tarrington."

"I wish to God Master Wilton were alive, he would have helped my Will."

Owen bit his tongue and waited for Mistress Tarrington to continue.

But the woman surprised him. Tears welled in her beady eyes, her pointy nose reddened. "He'll lose the leg, won't he?"

Owen wished Lucie were here. He was not good at handling such things. "I pray that he does not."

"What shall we do without him working at St Clement's mill?"

"There's many a man lost a leg in battle and found ways to move about. And what about yourself? Do you have something to calm you and help you sleep?"

The woman shook her head. "Not I, Captain Archer. I must be alert to his cries, mustn't I?"

"But a soothing tisane might help calm you and allow you to rest when he's asleep." Owen turned, lifted a jar from the shelf behind him. "Balm, mint, and just a touch of valerian root. A pinch heated in a cup of water, strained, and sipped slowly. It will not induce a deep sleep, just soothe you. You must get some rest else you won't be strong enough to help your husband."

Mistress Tarrington dropped her head, patted her nose and eyes with her sleeve. "God bless you," she whispered.

When she had gone, Owen stood a moment, thinking about the

frightened woman. Had he snapped at her, he would not have heard what she feared. He slipped back to the kitchen. Lucie looked up from Ned's leg with anxious eyes. "Mistress Tarrington went away content," Owen said. He nodded towards Ned. "Has he described his intent?"

"A little. You must listen to him, Owen."

"What do you take me for? Of course I shall listen."

The kitchen door flew open. Ned began to duck, then recognised Bess Merchet.

"The hussy claims she's not seen—" Bess stopped as she recognised Ned. "So you've set us a merry chase for naught?"

Owen and Ned exchanged puzzled looks.

"I asked Bess who might help Ned escape," Lucie said. "She sent Simon to the stables near Micklegate."

"Ah." Ned nodded. "Matilda. I hope you did not mention me in her father's hearing?"

"I am sure I do not know." Bess stood, arms akimbo, watching Ned with the stern expression she used on her serving girls.

"Poor Matilda. She'll not thank me."

Bess shook her head. "Such girls. I've had my fill of woolly-brained girls."

"Your new kitchen maid displeases?" Lucie asked.

Bess snorted. "Displeases? A dog has more sense." She nodded towards Ned, her caps ribbons trembling. "And you've no sense, neither. What is Captain Archer to say to the Archdeacon?"

What indeed? "Some of Tom's ale might help us sit down and civilly discuss this, Bess," Owen suggested. It promised to be a long afternoon.

19

DON PAULUS DISSEMBLES

Thoresby's new apartments at Windsor were in the north-east corner of the upper bailey, at the edge of the continuing construction of apartments for members of the court that would stretch along the east and south walls to the Black Tower. From his chamber window Thoresby could spy a small corner of sun-drenched vineyard through a section of the east wall that was under repair. After almost a week of scudding clouds and frequent showers, today had dawned with little fog, and by mid-morning the air was warm and sweet. Though the recently pruned vines bore insubstantial leaves as yet, the earth would be warm from the sun. Thoresby could almost smell the rich, pungent aroma. "I shall be walking in the vineyard," he informed Michaelo.

Brother Michaelo inclined his head. "Your Grace. Shall I advise petitioners to return after nones?" The thin lips fought a smile. Michaelo thought two habits of his master peculiar, his frequent bathing and his long walks.

Thoresby, in turn, found his secretary's characteristic languor distasteful. "You might walk with me. You must feel a prisoner in these chambers."

A flare of the nostrils. "Not at all, Your Grace. I am your devoted servant." Michaelo smiled. "And, of course, there are the petitioners to consider."

"A pox on the petitioners, Michaelo. Adam can tell them to return as well as you. Come along with me."

"And what of Brother Florian? According to his letter he might arrive today..." Michaelo looked down as if bored, brushed some crumbs off the table at which he stood, shrugged. "But he will be weary and glad of a chance to rest before he presents himself."

Thoresby was glad of his secretary's averted eyes, else he might see his master's confusion. He had forgotten about Florian's note of a few days past. The monk had been long in his service, and time and again had proved his skill in finding folk who hoped to disappear into the crowded city of London. Florian had sent word that a Don Paulus had recently arrived at a hospital in the city, and the monk would seek him out the following day, delivering the friar to Windsor if he proved to be the one Thoresby sought.

The very news Thoresby had awaited. He recalled his excitement upon reading it. And then to have forgotten it so completely, as if it were of no consequence. An unpleasant result of age, deeply disturbing to Thoresby, who had always prided himself on his memory. "I hardly think Florian will arrive so early in the day, but in the event he does, have Adam escort him out to the vineyard."

"With the friar if he has found him?"

Thoresby gave a brusque nod. "All the better to speak with him away from the ears of court."

Michaelo smiled. "I doubt you will be the only one enticed into the gardens by the weather."

Don Paulus was a round barrel of a man, his face ruddy and pleasant. Not at all what Thoresby had expected. "You come here willingly? You mean to tell me what you know?"

The friar bowed. "God has revealed to me my duty in this, Your Grace."

More likely the ranks of those seeking him convinced him, but no matter. "God bless you, Don Paulus. We are grateful, you may be sure. Are you comfortable walking, or would you return to my chambers?"

The keen eyes glanced down the tidy rows of vines, took in the emptiness. "This would seem an ideal setting for the dangerous confidences I am about to impart, Your Grace. We might see any intruders long before they could hear us." Paulus tucked his hands up his sleeves, rolled back his shoulders.

Dangerous? Thoresby found it almost amusing to think the round little man might bear dangerous tidings. "And you, Brother Florian?" Thoresby asked the white-haired monk. "Do you mind being on your feet in the fresh air?"

"I am yours to command, Your Grace. But I should like to participate. You know that you may trust me to be silent."

"Silence may not be sufficient in this instance," Don Paulus said, his tone incongruously pleasant.

"Do not condescend to me, Don Paulus," Florian growled.

"I meant nothing of the sort, I assure you," the friar was quick to reply.

"Then come, gentlemen, let us walk," Thoresby said with impatience. Yet he set a slow pace, noted the buds on the vines, the rich soil. "Beneath here lies chalk, apparently a benefit to vines, though not much else. A fortunate coincidence, eh?"

Don Paulus replied with a brief exposition on the chalky regions of France and the excellent wine produced. "Though of course the climate is gentler; for May, this would be a chilly day in Bordeaux."

"You are a herbalist who digs in the soil," Thoresby said.

"I rarely have the opportunity, but yes, I enjoy a day in the garden." The friar had withdrawn his hands from his sleeves and clasped them behind him, looking thoughtful. "But Brother Florian did not seek me out and bring me here to speak of gardens with the Archbishop of York and Lord Chancellor of England. Please, Your Grace. Ask me what you would." Paulus smiled down at the mounds of manure beneath some of the vines. "An experimenter, the vintner here."

Thoresby found the man's calm quite remarkable. "Why did you disappear, Don Paulus?"

A shrug. "I felt it was dangerous to know what I knew and to have communicated with a man marked for death." Don Paulus paused, turned to Thoresby with a serious face. "More to the point, and even less to my credit, fear drove me to keep silent about the young woman floating in the Thames. I knew I could not help her,

I could see she was dead—I have seen enough of death to know it before me—but her soul might have yet lingered. And I did nothing but sign a blessing over her and pray for her soul." Paulus closed his eyes, shook his head.

"And you come forward now?"

"Come forward?" Paulus chuckled. "In truth, it took much effort on Brother Florian's part to ferret me out. But then I was perversely relieved to see him. I felt unclean. And I feared that once such cowardice is permitted, it will shortly become habit. I prayed that would not be so, but I feared it was the inevitable outcome. Once soiled, never truly clean. The memory of the stain is in the fabric."

Thoresby began to suspect the pleasant face masked a dissembler. "Come now, Don Paulus, was it not reassuring to discover *I* had sent Florian? That someone of my stature was concerned about this?"

Don Paulus shrugged. "As I said, once soiled…"

Thoresby glanced at Brother Florian, who gave him a sidewise look that promised a good story when they were alone. Thoresby resumed walking. "How did you and Don Ambrose meet?"

The hands returned to the sleeves. "We studied together at Oxford." Paulus now walked with great concentration on his sandalled feet.

"You were good friends?"

Don Paulus sighed. "It is difficult in our order to develop lasting friendships. We move about…"

Irritated, Thoresby cleared his throat.

"No, Your Grace. We were not good friends."

"How did he come to confide in you?"

"I was at the leper house nearby. He came to me, remembering my knowledge of herbs. He wondered whether I knew of a way to detect poison in food or drink."

Poison? "And why did he seek this information?"

"At first he told me that he was to join the household of Don William of Wykeham, a man who had many enemies."

"Wykeham? Enemies who would poison him? I hardly think so."

Paulus nodded. "I told him that any enemies bold enough to

poison the King's favourite would be paying gold coin that would afford subtle poisons, undetectable by a layman. Or myself, even."

"Would they indeed?"

"Well, I should think so, Your Grace. But it is only a theory. In any case, Ambrose returned a few days later. 'What if the victim were not so lofty a person? What if he were one of us?' God forgive me, but that made me curious, for it was clear Ambrose feared for himself. He was a chaplain at Windsor Castle. I considered how easily such a chaplain might be drawn into trouble. So I asked him whom he feared." Paulus now glanced round, noted a gardener working in the next row. "Perhaps we might continue at the far end?"

They crossed the vineyard in silence.

"Continue, Don Paulus," Thoresby commanded when the friar stood with his hands behind his back, staring, apparently enthralled, at the unfinished wall of the castle, showing no sign of speaking.

The friar started, shrugged, smiled ingenuously. "Forgive me, Your Grace. The aspect of the castle is so lovely…"

"Tell me whom Ambrose feared before I have you dumped into the wall as fill," Thoresby growled.

Paulus brought his hands forward, clasped before him, and nodded. "He feared Sir William of Wyndesore and Mistress Alice Perrers, Your Grace."

Thoresby recalled the time he had come upon Alice arguing with a man in the courtyard at Windsor. It might have been Wykeham. He also remembered Alice's blush when she replied, *I know him.* "An interesting pair. Why did he fear them?"

"Because, Your Grace, he had married them. In a secret ceremony." The friar smiled smugly.

Thoresby was stunned. "Impossible."

Don Paulus threw up his hands. "It would seem so, yet Don Ambrose swore it, and he predicted the death of Perrers's maid after that of Wyndesore's page. They were the witnesses."

That gave Thoresby's stomach a twist. A logical connection, priest and witnesses. But so cold blooded. "Then there is no record of such a marriage?"

"A written record, Your Grace, which can be silenced more reliably than people."

"When Ambrose came to you with this story, neither witness had died?"

"Only the lad."

"Ambrose had feared poisoning. When he learned he was to ride north for the King, did he still fear poisoning?"

A shrug. "How can I know everything that was in his mind? He asked that I send a message to our house in York if I heard aught of Mary; he knew she was frightened. She had come to him several times to confess her sins, fearing death was near."

"Poor child," Brother Florian said, crossing himself.

Ah yes, the difference in rank; Brother Florian had the leisure for pity. Thoresby had to try to absorb all he heard and ask the right questions. Time later for pity. He wished to finish with Paulus, send this horrid little man away. "You say Ambrose feared Wyndesore and Perrers? They told him to keep silent?"

"Which he vowed he would."

"And yet he told you."

"As I have told you, he came to me about detecting poisons."

"Who did he fear would carry out his poisoning?"

"He did not know. He told me how Townley had quickly been declared innocent by Mistress Perrers after the page was found dead—too quickly, perhaps? So Ambrose was frightened when he heard that Townley was to ride north with him, if he was indeed involved with Mistress Perrers in some way. To make matters worse, two of Wyndesore's men were in the company."

Wyndesore. That name kept coming up. "After he received your letter in York Ambrose focused his fear on Townley. Perhaps he should have remained fearful of the others."

"I think not. One of my order in York tells me the commander of the company from York was a Captain Archer, not only a spy and Townley's friend but the spouse of an apothecary with access to poisons. No doubt Don Ambrose learned this."

"Don Ambrose was not poisoned."

A momentary hesitation. "No?"

Thoresby shook his head. "And what of Mary's death? Surely you do not think Townley had his leman murdered?"

"How sincere was his love, I wonder? Don Ambrose told me Townley was Lancaster's man. The Duke's disapproval of Don William is known in our order; we count him a friend. It seems plausible Townley allowed himself to be caught up in a plot to thwart Wykeham's ambitions by ruining the mission."

"With murder? Townley would not be so cold-blooded."

Don Paulus shrugged. "I came but to tell you what I know, Your Grace, not to argue for it."

"Indeed. Let us walk while I consider what you have told me. I may have more questions for you." Thoresby must put aside his disbelief and consider the friar's story. If it was possible, if Alice Perrers had married without the King's permission—for why else would it be kept secret—then where did the friar's story dissatisfy? Perhaps in the drawn out plot against Ambrose. The others had been dispatched quickly and within easy reach. "Why send Ambrose north? Why risk his escape?"

"I am afraid no one thought to tell me, Your Grace." A smirk.

Thoresby realised his hands were clenched. He relaxed them at his sides. "Any thoughts on the matter?"

"Ambrose was of higher station than the maid or page. His death might have warranted an investigation."

"But it still does."

"Perhaps three deaths at Windsor would cause too much gossip?" Paulus shrugged.

Why did even that slight gesture make Thoresby bristle? What did he despise so in the man standing before him? When this conversation had begun Thoresby had thought Don Paulus much pleasanter than he had earlier imagined him to be, much calmer. He was an actor, but he was useful. They had forced him from his hiding, but he had then co-operated as if he'd meant to all along. And he seemed to be enjoying himself. Brother Florian had expressed pity for the maid he had never seen; this man…Ah. There was a mystery.

"Don Paulus, how were you able to recognise Perrers's maid in the river? When had you met her?"

Paulus held up a finger. "The very question I expected. I had seen her with her mistress, in the town. I grew curious about Mistress Perrers after hearing Ambrose's story, and desired to learn more about her. Powerful young woman." He shook his head. "But who am I to judge? I discovered she had a house in town, near the river. I sold some herbs to her cook, dallied long enough to see the King's leman. And her maid. The maid was fair. I was heartsick to see her floating in the river, her midnight tresses a graceful cloud round her."

With every word Thoresby disliked the friar more. "You shall stay here at the castle until I release you, Don Paulus. In case I have more questions."

The friar frowned at Florian. "But you said…"

"Spend your time in penance, Don Paulus. To leave a young woman in the river like that…" Florian shook his head.

"See me after you have the friar settled," Thoresby called to Florian over his shoulder as he headed back to his apartment. He had an irrational desire to wash his hands.

Tom Merchet led the donkey cart across Ouse Bridge in the late afternoon. On the other side he turned off Micklegate at St. Martin's Lane and stopped in front of a small house that was almost built into the stables behind it. Owen slipped out from beneath a pile of flour sacks in the cart, disappeared into the shadows beneath the jettied second storey. A young woman opened the door to the house, disappeared a moment, then stepped out, basket in hand, glanced round, shut the door, put her hand on Owen's arm and took off down the lane. Tom clucked to the donkey and began to follow at a slower pace. They crossed Fetter Lane and continued up Bishophill in the direction of the Old Baile.

The Old Baile had been the twin of York Castle across the river before it had fallen into disrepair. It was now under the

Archbishop's jurisdiction, a sometime gaol, the yard occasionally a fairground. The last serious repairs to the buildings and walls had been undertaken forty-odd years before, when King Edward had moved the government of the realm to York while he'd fought the Scots. There were guards on the walls and at the gates, but a determined intruder could find a way in.

As did Matilda, picking her way across the boggy moat on stones, slipping through a breach in the wall behind bracken. Owen almost slipped when a stone proved slicker than anticipated, but he managed to catch himself and suffered only a wet boot.

Within, the bailey stank of damp and urine. Owen stood still, searching the dim waste with his one eye, thinking he had lost Matilda. And then, almost at his shoulder, she whispered, "Here is the gate, Captain. It will take your strength to open it."

He could see only a climbing vine. Matilda took his hand, guided it to an iron ring. He tugged with no result, stood back, wiped his hands on his leggings, blew on them, rubbed them together, then planted himself firmly and tugged once more. The door gave way a few inches. He went through the process once more, made more slight progress.

"This will take all afternoon," he muttered.

"I'll push, you pull," Tom hissed from the other side.

"God bless you, Tom."

They soon had it open, then Tom cautiously led the donkey cart across the rotting planks. Matilda took the lantern from the cart, led the way to a guardhouse, opened the lantern to show them the small room furnished with a cot, a table and chair, a small brazier.

"Who hides here?" Owen asked.

Matilda shook her head. "Show me how to tend him."

Owen and Tom helped Ned into the guardhouse, settled him on the cot. From his pack, Owen pulled the ointments. "Bring the light closer."

Matilda crept forward as Owen unwound the bandage. "Oh, Ned!" she knelt down, holding the light over his leg. "Is it very painful?"

He snorted. "Wasn't until this butcher took a needle and thread to it."

Matilda glanced over at Owen. "I don't think I could do that."

"It takes a strong stomach, aye," Owen said. "But you must only clean it, then dab on the ointment. Like this." He showed her. "And watch for fever, bring him plenty water, send for me if there is any change. Or trouble."

She nodded. "You can trust me."

"I see that," Owen said. "The usual resident of this den will not return for a while?"

"No."

"You are certain?"

She looked up at Owen, her eyes wide. "Is it a simpleton you think me, or a traitor?"

"Forgive me. I am only worried for my friend."

"He will be safe with me."

Owen rose.

Matilda put the cloths and ointments in her basket.

"A man in the livery of the Archbishop's household will await you here this evening," Owen told her as she rose. "Alfred will stand watch while Ned is here."

Matilda nodded. "I know Alfred."

Brother Florian touched his folded hands to his nose, hiding a grin. But Thoresby saw it. "What amuses you?"

"The ego of Paulus, thinking he could fool you. Surely he knew I would tell you how I caught him, trying to escape beneath a corpse being removed from the hospital for burial?"

"Sweet Heaven, no!"

Florian lifted his cup, nodded, drank, wiped his mouth on his sleeve. "I insisted he borrow a clean habit for the journey, impressing on his superiors that he was to be presented to you, Your Grace."

"You divulged my purpose?"

"Never, Your Grace. I suggested you needed an extra clerk."

"Who would believe that man would please me?"

"Other Austins, Your Grace." The sly face broke into a grin.

But Thoresby made little effort to smile. He swirled the wine round in his cup, thinking.

"His story sounds false to you, Your Grace?"

"Yes. And no. It is the only explanation I have that accounts for most of what has happened. The flaw is Townley's being sent away with the friar."

They grew quiet.

Thoresby was the first to speak. "Should it be true, we are now in possession of dangerous information."

Florian raised an eyebrow. "He did warn me."

"I doubt anyone would connect you with it. As far as I am concerned, you heard naught of this."

"Of course." Brother Florian drained his cup and slowly eased himself from the bench on which he sat. He never accepted a more comfortable chair with back and arms—too difficult to climb out of.

"You are leaving?"

"I have much to do while I am here, Your Grace. And, faith, I can be of little help in this musing stage. I find them for you; I do not pretend to understand them."

Fortunate man to be able to confine himself to what he excelled in. Thoresby should try that. But it was too late to change. Too late.

Florian turned stiffly at the door. "May God protect you, Your Grace."

"And you, my old friend."

Thoresby began to pace as the door closed. His mind was too active. Too full of questions. Was it possible? Would Alice Perrers risk her status at court for the loutish Wyndesore? Thoresby looked forward to his evening with her. How surprised she would be when he told her the rumour he had heard...Or should he mention it? But how else was he to know the truth?

First he must think of a secure hiding place for Don Paulus. Whether or not his tale was the truth, the man was in danger. And dangerous.

• • •

Lucie left Jasper in the shop and followed Owen into the kitchen. "What will you tell Jehannes?"

Owen sank down in a chair by the fire, ran his hands through his dusty hair. "I do not know, Lucie. Am I playing the fool?"

She leaned over, kissed Owen's forehead, took one of his hands, kissed the palm. "You would not rest easy abandoning Ned to his fate."

"Am I not risking him all the same? Using him as bait to lure two murderers who are out for his blood?"

"Perhaps they are not murderers."

"Then I am a fool."

"No you are not. You will get Ned safely to Windsor, where you will soon discover the truth. I have faith in you, my love."

Owen pulled her down on to his lap, buried his face in her neck. "I do not deserve you."

"It is Ned who might be undeserving, my love, not you."

"Poor Jehannes."

"You must go to him in the morning, try to explain."

"Aye. 'Tis much the worst part of this foolishness."

20

ALICE'S MISTAKE

The sun had set by the time Thoresby rode out of the castle gates along crowded Bishop Street, shadowed down its length by the castle walls and jettied second storeys of the houses. He turned down New Street, where the houses stood farther apart; Alice Perrers's was the last house on the street, overlooking the Thames. The torches set round her doorway illuminated a well-wrought structure of stone below, timber above. The windows were glazed, the area immediately before the door was set with cobbles—for the King's visits, Thoresby presumed. He wondered how long she might keep this house if Don Paulus's story was true?

Gilbert answered the door, showed Thoresby into a cosy parlour with a small fireplace, sturdy oak furniture, silver plate displayed in a floor-to-ceiling cupboard. Most surprising was the flaxen-haired lad who played in front of the fire, rolling about with a puppy intent on chewing his master's little hand. This was Thoresby's first glimpse of the King's son by Alice since shortly after his birth.

"Mistress Perrers asked that I make you comfortable, Your Grace," Gilbert said. He bowed Thoresby to a chair near the fire.

The lad's nurse jumped up. "My Lord Chancellor," she bobbed a curtsey, then deftly scooped the puppy up with one arm and grabbed the boy's hand with the other, lifting him to his feet. "Say *'benedicte'* to His Grace the Lord Chancellor of England, Master John," the young woman said.

The lad stuck a finger in his mouth, hid behind his nurse, then peered out cautiously to whisper something unintelligible that brought a proud smile to his nurse's charming face.

"*Benedicte*, Master John," Thoresby said. Now that he was a godfather he made an effort with children. Here was another risk Perrers had taken if the story were true: the King would never let her bring up his son if she had betrayed him. Surely she knew that. Would it mean nothing to her?

"Take him up to the chamber, Katie." Alice Perrers spoke from the doorway, where she stood, beringed hands stretched to either side of the door frame, her deep green gown shimmering in the firelight. Even at home she took care to make an elegant entrance. Alice smiled down at her son, stood aside to let him pass, recoiling slightly from the curious puppy.

"You are not fond of dogs, Mistress Perrers?" Thoresby commented as she slid into a seat half facing his.

A private smile was almost hidden as she had her head down, checking the drape of her gown. Alice raised her head, met Thoresby's eyes, wrinkled her nose. "Cats are so much cleaner, Your Grace. But puppies accept the brutality of children with more equanimity."

Such a confusing mix of artificiality and bluntness. "Equanimity? The pup seemed to be gnawing on your son's hand."

"I am sure John had done something far more horrible to the pup." Alice moved her smile from Thoresby to Gilbert. "Wine, Gilbert." She returned to Thoresby. "Thank you for coming, Your Grace. I know it must have seemed an odd request."

"Not at all. I assumed the nature of our discussion was private."

The smile flickered. Thoresby wondered what ghostly emotion had almost been revealed. "In truth, you will judge me a dizzy woman when I confess the topic. It is not so much private as—painful." Beringed hand to bare, beautiful throat, eyes cast down. All staged with her usual care. Thoresby should be flattered. Alice Perrers considered him someone to treat with caution. And he was. He was.

"It is a pleasure to retreat from court now and again," he said with his most charming voice and smile. He could be just as artificial. "Even if that was the sole reason for inviting me here, I should be happy to come." Oddly enough, he meant it. A pleasant house, interesting companion. Deadly, but interesting.

Alice was quiet as Gilbert poured the wine. They each sipped, sat back, relaxing into the occasion.

Thoresby looked round. "You have a pleasant house. It is close to the river, yet I feel the damp less than up at the castle."

"Thick stone walls hold in the damp once it penetrates," Alice said.

"You have studied architecture?"

Alice made a face. "Not voluntarily." She nodded slightly to Gilbert, who immediately and noiselessly left the room. "Wykeham delights in telling the King about the wonders of his works. Modesty is not one of his innumerable virtues."

"You have trained your servant well."

"In my situation I must have a trustworthy household, above reproach." Alice set her cup down on a polished table beside her, flicked a mote from her skirt. An uncharacteristic gesture. Alice Perrers was nervous. "This painful topic…" She took a deep breath. Her gown was not as low cut as usual; the scar which she usually brandished to remind him of his human frailty was covered. To put him at ease? "I wondered what your spy in York has told you about Ned Townley," she said. "Captain Archer is Ned's friend, is he not?"

Though Thoresby had guessed this conversation would centre round Mary's death, he had not expected this particular question. "His Grace the King has been fully informed, Mistress Perrers." He would not be accused of holding back information.

Alice glanced up, her cat eyes candidly surprised. "You think—? Forgive me, Your Grace, I did not mean to imply…I am clumsy because—." She pressed two fingers to her forehead, shook her head. "The King will tell me nothing. He will not speak of Ned." She did not meet Thoresby's eyes, but focused on his chain of office.

Losing her hold on Edward, was she? There was a time, just yesterday, in fact, when that would have improved Thoresby's mood more than the wine had, lovely as it was. But now it disturbed him. Could the friar's story be true? "His Grace will say nothing?" Thoresby knitted his brows, pretended to consider whether to speak, then shrugged. "I can think of no reason to keep it from you. You have heard that the King is sending men north to arrest Townley?"

The cat eyes lifted to meet his eyes. They were dark with emotion. Fear? Anger? That was the problem with all the artifice; when Alice had a true emotion, he could not decipher it. "Of what is he accused?" she asked.

Surely she had heard? "The murder of Don Ambrose, the Austin friar who accompanied the party from Windsor."

"Sweet Jesu," Alice whispered, bowing her head and crossing herself.

"Forgive me, but I cannot believe you did not know."

"It is what I heard, but I did not believe it."

This was a waste of time. "Mistress Perrers—"

She lifted a hand to silence him. "Does it look bad for Ned?"

"Is the letter Gilbert took to Walter of Coventry this afternoon an attempt to help Townley?"

Alice looked startled, but covered it quickly with a smile. "No. Walter will travel farther than York with my letter."

Was this the right moment? When might be the right moment to confront Alice Perrers? "Ah. The letter goes north to the Marches? To your husband?"

"My—" Alice's smile was unconvincing. "Is that meant as an insult?"

"An insult to have a husband?"

"*Not* to have one, and yet be a mother."

"My dear Mistress Perrers, were I to throw insults at every woman who bore a bastard and every man who sired one, I should find that a consuming occupation."

Alice fussed with her gown. "To the Marches, you said?"

Thoresby put down his cup, rested his elbows on the arms of the chair, steepled his hands. "Yes."

The cat eyes lifted to him, blinked. "Who is up there?"

This cat and mouse game would quickly bore him. "Wyndesore, who, I am told, is your husband."

Alice pressed a hand to her left side, asked quietly, "Who told you Wyndesore was my husband?"

Thoresby ached to move this from banter to confession. "A fat friar. The one who wrote the letter to Don Ambrose that ended up in Townley's possession. What was his name?" He glanced up at the ceiling, down towards the fire, returned to her, shaking his head. "The indignities of ageing…"

She levelled her amber eyes at him. "Don Paulus."

"Ah! The very man. Don Paulus told me of your marriage."

"Where is this man?"

"In a safe place. I should not care for another death along your path."

Already naturally pale, Alice now looked chalk white. She dropped her head back, closed her eyes. "I curse the day I ever met William." Her voice was tense with emotion. "He is the Devil."

"Perhaps you would tell me what this is about."

She lifted her head with a wide-eyed look of amazement. "Sweet Heaven, do you think me mad? To climb so far merely to go crashing down off such a treacherous limb?" Alice stood, walked away from him.

Thoresby set down his cup and rose. "Then I shall be taking my leave."

Alice did not call for Gilbert. Instead she knelt down by the toys scattered on the floor before the fire, lifted two wooden blocks, picked up a third, a fourth, then dropped them back on the ground. She rose, dusted off her dress, and resumed her seat. "Yet I sent for you." She pressed her palms to her pale cheeks, then dropped her hands. "I am a woman without friends, John," she clasped her hands in her lap, stared down at them.

"Without friends? Come now, you have powerful friends. The King and Queen—their friendship is a pearl beyond price." If she expected to stay him with that silly complaint and the use of his Christian name, she had grossly misread him.

Alice shook her head, eyes still downcast. "The King is not my friend. Lovers are never friends. He uses me, and he shall discard me when he will."

He would indeed. Thoresby had expected him to do so long ago. "But the Queen?"

A melodramatic sigh. To cover emotion? "Queen Phillippa is dying. There is no remedy. And then? The King is ageing. Soon he will follow the Queen. What is the position of a dead King's mistress?" Now the cat eyes met his. Did he see pain in them? Fear? "The King's favour has turned the kingdom against me. They say I insult the Queen, who is loved by all her people. It is worse that my kin are unimportant. And that I am plain."

What was her game? She echoed Thoresby's oft repeated opinion of her with the precision of someone who had memorised the words for a purpose. Thoresby forced a laugh. "Plain, Mistress Perrers? Do you question the King's taste?"

Alice made a face. "It is the King's subjects who question it. They say I am plain. My hair is a common brown; my eyes are too like a cat's eyes; I am too tall, too sharp-tongued." She smiled, her chin thrust up. "They cannot see why the King takes me to his bed, confides in me."

Oh, God forgive him, Thoresby could. All that she said was true, but by a devilish alchemy this woman of plain parts was made beautiful by a sensuality from deep within. Alas, Thoresby felt her power all too strongly. But he would not be caught in the web Alice spun round him. He would not be distracted from his purpose this night. "I confess I am still confused, Mistress Perrers. Are you admitting to the marriage?"

Alice's face was a blank. "Why else were Mary, Daniel and Don Ambrose murdered?"

Thoresby slowly resumed his seat, steepled his hands, pressing the forefingers against the bridge of his nose. If this was a joke, if she suddenly laughed, he wondered whether he would manage to restrain himself. "You knew all three were murdered and told no one?"

Alice shook her bejewelled head as if chiding a child for foolish talk. "I know little more than you do. I had suspicions. But you must see I had much to lose if I confided in the wrong person."

"Doubtless." Thoresby picked up his cup, sipped his wine, waiting.

The cat eyes held steady his gaze. "And now I see I must trust you. Very well. Mary witnessed my marriage vows. She and Daniel, Sir William's page. My marriage to Lucifer himself." The eyes unexpectedly shone with tears. The jaw was clenched.

It was true. *Deus juva me.* "I find this incomprehensible. You have schemed to get into the King's bed, and now you throw away your achievement with Wyndesore. A soldier."

Alice took a deep breath. "My uncles schemed to place me in the Queen's household, as you well know."

"But the King's bedchamber was doubtless beyond their reach."

Alice bowed her head slightly. "I have thrown nothing away but my peace of mind. The King has not put me aside."

Thoresby chuckled. "And yet you called me here because he would tell you nothing of Townley? Come now."

"I believe William has requested silence on the matter."

The woman was preposterous. "Do you claim the King is dancing to Wyndesore's tune? My dear Mistress Perrers, he has merely delayed putting you aside, though his restraint surprises me." Thoresby lifted the cup to his lips, was disappointed to find it empty. "But why Wyndesore?"

Alice rose and retrieved the flagon Gilbert had left on the table, returning to fill Thoresby's cup and her own. Wine in hand, she moved to the window, where she stood still a while, staring out into the dark. "William has made a lifelong study of devious paths towards wealth. He is cunning, ruthless. Of course you know how he used Clarence's trouble to gain the King's ear." Indeed. All the court knew. "And yet in Ireland William and the Duke were fellow thieves, keeping the moneys for themselves. The Duke was quite generous with his financial adviser." She smiled. "I even made some money in Ireland."

Thoresby studied Alice Perrers's profile. Sharp. Nothing soft and feminine about her face. "He bought you?"

Alice spun round with a tight smile, cold eyes. "A charming question. So like you. But no. The profit in Ireland was another matter."

This was inexplicable. Thoresby was finding it difficult to absorb. Alice Perrers had wed William of Wyndesore. "I *have* heard it said that women find Wyndesore handsome."

Alice still smiled. "I would never climb into a man's bed with no thought of pleasure. William is handsome, strong, quite remarkable for his years…" The smile faded. "The King was furious when he heard. He would not see me. He threatened to send William into exile. But William kept his wits about him, asked for an audience with the King. He fell to his knees, begged the King's forgiveness, swore he had not realised the King still loved me."

Thoresby had an unlovely vision of the household. Two consummate actors manipulating the world. "Wyndesore claimed you had lied about the King's affections?"

Alice shrugged. "It was not William's intent." She sat down. "He has a way of sounding a bumbling fool while weaving an intricate web round his victims. The eyes are innocent, the words are full of apologies, he stutters as he promises better behaviour." A nasty laugh. "By the time William left the King's audience chamber he had made it seem as if by tripping over his own tongue he had revealed a way in which the marriage would be useful to Edward."

Wyndesore was a man to watch. "And how is that?"

"It is to be kept a secret. A secret to be revealed only if necessary."

"When might that be necessary?"

"In the event the King gets me with child again. Then he can deny it is his, claim it to be the fruit of my marriage to Wyndesore." Alice threw back her head and drained her cup.

It was true the King had been bothered by the vicious gossip at court when Alice bore John. But to go to such an extreme, share his mistress with another man. That was not like Edward. "Is this why the King sent Wyndesore north? To be kept from you?"

Alice's cat eyes chilled Thoresby. "It is not a banishment, if that is what you ask. Joint Warden of the West Marches towards Scotland is an important step in William's ambitions. He is a good commander, ruthless when need be. The King will not regret promoting William. All the regrets shall be housed in my bosom."

"You express little affection for him. Why did you marry him?"

"I thought to ensure my future, to provide myself with a protector when the King died—or tired of me." Alice laughed. It was not a cheerful sound.

"Why did you not wait?"

Alice tilted her head. "Until the King discards me? I pray you, tell me who would have had me then?"

Thoresby nodded. "You say Daniel and Mary died because they witnessed this secret marriage. Who carried out the sentence?"

Was it Thoresby's imagination, a trick of the light, or did Alice's pale face seem suddenly more drawn, her eyes more sunken in shadow? "Of course it is not the King. He thought to banish them from court, but I had convinced him Mary was loyal to me, and that I was about to bind her to me even more closely with a good marriage, one for which she would have me to thank."

"So it is your husband you suspect of plotting the murders?" The eyes stared coldly. He took that for a yes. "Have you any proof?"

Alice closed her eyes, brought the cup up to her forehead, as if to cool a fever. "My only proof is the obvious motivation and pattern. Our witnesses, the priest…" she shrugged. "William is desperate that it should remain a secret, that he should not lose his advantage in the King's favour by letting someone discover we married."

"Why should the King wish to keep it secret at all?"

Alice looked amused. "You believe the King would be glad to be rid of me." She shook her head slowly, tauntingly. "No. He still desires me. Yet he would not be a cuckold. And he teases that if I am known to be William's wife I shall feel duty bound to act so."

"But already the news is spreading. How many besides Don Paulus and myself know, I wonder?"

"And who knows that you know?" A fleeting smile.

"Surely it has occurred to the King that these deaths are connected?"

Alice rolled her eyes. "The King chooses to look aside when it comes to intrigue at court unless he believes it treasonous."

Thoresby could not deny that. "Do you know what I oft wonder, Mistress Perrers?"

"How can I guess?"

"What is your hold on the King? God has not granted me an understanding of this."

An enigmatic smile. "Why do two people ever love? Beyond comeliness, what do we love in a person? A sympathetic ear? An intimate knowledge that affords insight? Would you laugh to hear I advise him on matters that have naught to do with bed sport?"

"Do you love him?"

The eyebrows lifted. "In my own way, yes, I do."

In her own way—a fascinating concept to ponder. "And Wyndesore?"

All humour left Alice's face. "I thought I had made my hatred plain." It was certainly plain in her voice. She rose to refill her cup, found the flagon empty. "I must see to this."

Thoresby hardly noticed her absence, so deep in thought was he. He heard the murmur of voices upstairs, the querulous cry of a sleepy child, stubbornly determined to stay awake, the whisper of wind in the chimney. Somewhere a loose shutter clattered in an irregular rhythm.

When Alice returned, Thoresby noted a dampness at either side of her forehead. Cool water against hot temples? She poured their wine with a grace and dignity befitting a King's mistress. He could not fault her self-possession.

"Let us return to the other matter," he said as he lifted his cup. "Did Ned Townley murder Don Ambrose?"

"How can I know? I do not know what William intended by sending them north together. But it sounds as if Don Ambrose suspected Ned had been ordered to do away with him and he tried to murder Ned first."

"So it was not you who chose Townley for the journey?"

"Me?" Alice frowned down into her cup. "I confess I was pleased to have him away from Mary, thinking to use the time to find her a more appropriate suitor, but no, I had no say in it."

"Did Townley murder Daniel?"

Alice shrugged. "Mary swore he was with her, and he was when I returned, but he might have slipped out, or arrived late. We shall never know."

"Why would Townley conspire with Wyndesore in this?"

"I knew him only as Mary's lover. I do not know what information William might have used to—recruit him."

"What of Mary? Who pushed her into the river?"

Alice looked away. "I fear I am of no help in these matters. William's men are very loyal."

"Loyal enough to drown a young woman?"

A sharp shake of her head. "I do not wish to speak of Mary's death."

"Are any others to die?"

Alice rose, poured herself more wine, brought the flagon to fill Thoresby's cup. As she poured with a steady hand, she said quietly, "We took care to limit the number of people who knew."

Thoresby sipped, watched her resume her seat. Yet more had learned of it. Himself, Paulus, Florian…"You realised any witnesses were in danger?"

Alice tilted her head to one side as if considering his question. "One does not climb so high without turning round now and again to study the lie of the land, the armaments of one's fellow climbers. I did not foresee the nature of the threat, but I was afraid it would exist. And that it would come from William."

"But they say you felt some affection for Mary. Why did you include her as a witness?"

A sly smile into the cup. "I wished to use either Cecily or Isabeau, preferably both. Pity I did not. But William knew neither of them would have kept the secret beyond the next day. He chose Mary."

"And you agreed."

"I had no choice. He gave me his word—" a shake of the head; tears glistened in the amber eyes.

Thoresby hardened himself to her tears. "It is a strange way to plan a wedding—by considering the murders which may follow."

"Such are the times."

"Such are always the times when ambition stifles virtue."

"My uncles chose my path in life."

"And you would have lived differently? Did you not dream of being leman to the King?"

Alice threw her head back and laughed. "Dream of lying with an old man? Surely you do not need to ask that."

"But now that you have tasted the power…?"

"Would I come this way again?" Alice ran a finger over the

pearls on her sleeve. "How can I know? I shall never have a day of peace. But the power is a heady concoction that makes me drunk with pleasure." She looked up at him through her long lashes. "And you, John? Would you work so hard to be in the King's favour, knowing what it costs?"

Thoresby grunted. "As you say, how can I know?" It grew late, he felt his concentration slipping. He put down his cup, sat forward to attempt one more thrust. "Why would Ned Townley have agreed to murder Don Ambrose?"

Alice smoothed her sleeve. "He is Lancaster's man; bound to work against Wykeham. I believe him devious enough to have foreseen the murder would disrupt the King's mission to the Cistercians, undermine Wykeham. But he stumbled into his own trap. He knew nothing of William's motives..."

"You do not believe anyone at court acts with honour, do you? You must find the King's Order of the Garter quite amusing."

"Men have not dealt honourably with me, Your Grace. How am I to feel otherwise?"

How indeed? Thoresby rose. His lower back was stiff, his knees ached, he was weary to the bone. "I have much to think about."

"Including the danger of knowing my secret."

"You will tell Wyndesore?"

"Not if you will keep me informed."

Thoresby nodded. "I shall."

Michaelo's eyebrows shot up. "Ride to York? Me?"

"You know the contents of the letter," Thoresby said. "Archer must have it as soon as possible. He must know from whom to protect Townley. And the magnitude of the danger."

"But why me, Your Grace?" Michaelo was using the querulous voice that usually so irritated Thoresby that he would send him away. The secretary had been drowsing in a chair by the fire when Thoresby had returned from town. His eyes were heavy lidded after an hour spent writing the letter Thoresby had dictated. "And tonight? I have not slept."

"You have slept more than I. I must trust the messenger, Michaelo, trust his loyalty and his cunning. Who better? And I have made it clear why you must leave tonight."

"You need me here."

"Suggest another so appropriate."

"Brother Florian."

Thoresby shook his head. "Too old to ride so quickly."

Michaelo's delicate brows pressed together. "You might be sending me to my death."

"To stay here might be more dangerous." A puzzled frown. "You are now in possession of information men have died for." Understanding widened Michaelo's sleepy eyes. "Ride out as soon as you can. I have told the watch that you are escorting Don Paulus back to London and seeing to critical business for me."

"Don Paulus, Your Grace?"

"You shall deposit him at Bishopthorpe. Tell the servants he is there to oversee the roof repairs."

"I must ride north with that noxious friar?"

"Offer it up as penance, Michaelo."

"I may yet go to Heaven, Your Grace."

Thoresby smiled. "Thank you for cheering me at the end of a very disturbing day, Michaelo."

Michaelo looked genuinely puzzled. "Do I also return with Don Paulus?"

"No. My hope is that you will return with Captain Archer. I need him here."

"Why do you not ride with me? You are in more peril than I, Your Grace."

Thoresby shook his head. "I have duties. My absence would be noticed. Stay close to Archer, assist him as you can so he may hasten to Windsor."

21

UNWELCOME ADVICE

In a chill, grey dawn Thoresby knelt in St George's chapel and listened to the chanting of the office. Sleep escaped him. His mind would not rest; he fidgeted, wanting action. He envied Michaelo, out on the road, headed north—though he did not envy him his companion. Thoresby's opinion of Don Paulus had not been tempered with the proof of his story.

Holy Mary, Mother of God, I must leave this court. The kingdom was ruled by a lecherous old man who sought the counsel not of his chancellor, trained in law, but of his young, scheming mistress. Was it possible that the King was now too old to rule wisely? Forty years ago they had set Edward on the throne while his father was yet alive, and he had shortly proven himself a worthy successor. But of late he had squandered the wealth of England in his futile attempts to win the crown of France, antagonised most of his councillors with his preference for Wykeham, and insulted the Queen with the presence of Alice Perrers.

There had been several Austin friars, Giles of Rome the first, William of Cremona the latest, who had preached that the authority of a lord was null and void unless he was in a state of grace. Was Edward in such a state? Thoresby thought not. Though it was perhaps a matter of power rather than Edward's particular weaknesses. Could a man hold power and maintain innocence? Thoresby had long ago decided that was impossible.

He did not consider himself in a state of grace, a situation that bothered him now that he felt his age so keenly, so constantly.

Archer had been disillusioned by Thoresby's ability to bend with the wind; particularly because he had chosen to serve Thoresby rather than Lancaster, expecting an archbishop to be a godly man. He had not found Thoresby so, nor had he accepted Thoresby's explanation that as Archbishop of York he must weigh matters in light of the good of all his flock, and thus justice became more complex.

But of late Thoresby wondered whether as Archbishop he should look first to spiritual matters. Was that not what Pope Urban actually wished to bring about? Not a petty victory over Edward, but a reformed Church guided by saintly men dedicated to the cure of souls. That is what His Holiness sought. That is why he distrusted Wykeham, a man who owed everything to his secular lord. That is why the Cistercian abbots distrusted Wykeham.

Which was rather hypocritical, as the abbots were tainted themselves; they were powerful men in the kingdom, clever businessmen not above questionable financial practices. In the reign of the King's grandfather the abbots of Fountains had speculated in future wool yields, almost ruining the abbey's treasury.

Say what they might, Wykeham, though unarguably the greatest pluralist in the kingdom, was not the greatest sinner.

Was Alice Perrers? She claimed her uncles had set her on her path. Thoresby knew that to be true. He knew of the merchant family who had raised her until her uncles reclaimed her and educated her for court. And so she had made the best of her circumstances. Was that not true of most intelligent, ambitious folk? Had Thoresby not done the same as a second son? He might have been a better man had he followed a cloistered path. But how did one so young develop such cunning as Alice Perrers? Had she now tripped with this marriage? Had her precocious talent proved temporary?

Raising his head to silence, Thoresby realised prime had ended and the chapel was emptying. As he slowly rose, his joints sore from kneeling so long, he noted a tall, familiar figure gliding past. Quietly, Thoresby followed Wykeham from the church. He wished to learn more about the soldier, William of Wyndesore.

• • •

Wykeham greeted Thoresby with a puzzled smile, his hands in his sleeves, his nose red in the damp early morning chill, looking as if he had just awakened rather than attended the service. He had not bothered to fuss with his attire, wearing a dark clerical gown with a patched elbow. "'Tis early to be about, Your Grace."

"I have not slept, so it is late for me, not early."

"Not slept, Your Grace? What keeps you wakeful?"

"In faith, something I would speak of with you. But not here. In your chambers."

Wykeham smiled. "You wish to pass your wakefulness on to me?"

"Whether or not I wish to, I soon shall."

"For those of us who slept, it is far too early for clever speech."

"I promise you that what I wish to speak of is not clever."

Wykeham bowed. "Then come along. We shall break our fast together."

Before Wykeham's servant, Peter, opened the door, Thoresby warned the councillor that their discussion must not be overheard. Wykeham told Peter to serve them and depart, he might entertain himself as he liked for the next hour. Peter looked disappointed, but did as he was told, leaving them in possession of a fire and ample food.

Without more ado, Thoresby came to the first point of his visit. "What do you know of Sir William of Wyndesore?"

Sniffing the cheese set before them, Wykeham nodded to himself and cut a piece, tore off some bread. "Why do you ask about Wyndesore?" He took a bite of the cheese, the bread, chewed with an eye on Thoresby.

"He has entered into a liaison with Mistress Alice Perrers. I wish to know more of this schemer." Close enough to the truth for now.

Wykeham swallowed, washed the dry food down with ale, thought for a moment. "Unremarkable family. Good soldier.

Nothing brought him to notice until he turned on the Duke of Clarence after the Irish troubles."

"Tell me about that."

A frown. "Surely you know about that."

"I know the King was furious with the Duke of Clarence, said he was no son of his, antagonising the Irish as he'd done, wasting the treasury. But what was Wyndesore's role?"

Wykeham considered his cheese. "I have no doubt he profited from the war treasury, as did the Duke. They both returned to court better dressed, better horsed. But when the King questioned Wyndesore about the Irish troubles, he blamed them all on the Duke and his bullheadedness, his self-conceit." Wykeham nodded at Thoresby's frown. "Oh yes, a delightful man, Wyndesore, as I have said before. How appropriate for him to befriend Alice Perrers."

"Why would the King take Wyndesore's word over his son's?"

Wykeham shook his head. "When Wyndesore first accused Clarence, the King was furious. And then suddenly I heard the King had not only forgiven him, but had pardoned Wyndesore his debts and made him a joint Warden of the West Marches towards Scotland. Had the King discovered evidence of Clarence's guilt? Had he in some other way come to appreciate Wyndesore?" Wykeham shrugged his bony shoulders.

Thoresby sat with his cup of ale halfway to his mouth, thinking how tidily it all fitted together. It would seem that Perrers was right, that Wyndesore had convinced the King that this foolhardy marriage might be useful if kept hidden until needed.

"I have said something that satisfies you?" Wykeham asked.

Realising how he must look, Thoresby slaked his thirst, put down his cup with decision. "I believe I know what brought about the King's change of heart. But before I speak I must in good conscience warn you that some might stop at nothing to keep it secret."

"Indeed?"

"You were right to question the death of Wyndesore's page."

Wykeham pushed aside his food, leaned on the table, his slender fingers entwined. "Is it what kept you wakeful?"

Thoresby nodded. "Two disturbing conversations since last I slept. One with Don Paulus, one with Mistress Perrers."

The shadowed eyes widened, a smile softened the long, narrow face. "Already I am intrigued. Don Paulus? He is here at the castle?"

Everyone was eager to talk with Don Paulus. Thoresby thought they might not be so keen once they had met the amoral, jolly friar. "He *was* here."

"Ah." Wykeham nodded. "You saw to his disappearance."

"I did. And if you choose knowledge over caution, you shall shortly understand why I thought it important."

The smile vanished. "I would know this secret."

Thoresby nodded, poured himself more ale, settled back in his chair, and as succinctly as possible told Wykeham what he had learned. It was gratifying to watch the privy councillor's eyes grow rounder and rounder. He had been unaware of the affair.

"Why are you telling me this?" Wykeham asked when Thoresby raised his cup to his lips, signalling the end of his tale.

"You chose to hear it."

"This is indeed dangerous information—you risk much by repeating it. Why do you trust that I shall not go straight to the King and tell him you have told me? Or to Wyndesore?"

"Because I do not believe you are the sort of man to betray a confidence, particularly when it is offered in your interest."

Wykeham tilted his head, studied Thoresby. "In my interest? What do you mean?"

"I must reply by explaining my concern over the state of my soul."

Wykeham bent over a plate of cold meat, pushed it, too, aside. "You wish to use me as a confessor? At table?"

Thoresby laughed. "I merely wish you to understand how I came to tell you of the Perrers business."

"It has to do with your soul?"

"When a man comes to the point in his life when his bones ache for no reason other than the rain, or his memory deceives him into thinking he placed something here when it is there"—Thoresby shook his head—"he thinks much on his state of grace, how he should answer to God if taken suddenly from this mortal shell."

Wykeham raised his cup to his lips, then paused. "Surely you are not thinking on your death?"

"Of course I am. A wise man thinks on his death from the cradle. But at my time of life I ponder it with a sudden urgency. And I find I am uneasy with what I see."

"You are a good man, Chancellor."

Thoresby gave Wykeham a slight bow. "God bless you for your kind words, Councillor. But I know my sins. I have contemplated them time and again. I know that I chose the life at court out of vanity. My parents had thought I would take my vows as a Cistercian, or perhaps a Benedictine, but not a lay priest, then an archbishop. Nor had they planned for me to study law."

"Your parents were disappointed in you?" Wykeham's eyes more than his voice expressed disbelief.

"No, I do not mean to say they were not content with my elevation. On the contrary, they were proud of me, glad of the prestige I brought to the family. No, it is I who believe I would have been a better man, a holier man, had I shut myself away from the world."

Wykeham wiped his knife with a linen cloth. "You have recently been to Fountains, I hear. You know the Cistercians have the world in their abbeys. Not precisely what one thinks of when speaking of being shut away from the world."

"Indeed. But the intrigues of the court. The compromises one makes in deference to the King, his family, the welfare of the diocese…" Thoresby lifted his hands, palms up. "Surely you see the difference?"

Turning his knife this way and that in the lamplight, Wykeham was satisfied, tucked it into the scabbard at his waist. "The Cistercian abbots were quick to find fault with your messengers so that they might exercise their power and prevent my becoming Bishop of Winchester."

"Winchester. Yes. And then Lord Chancellor."

Wykeham sat back in his chair, folded his hands in his lap, faced Thoresby with a level look. "Indeed, I believe that is the King's intention."

Thoresby nodded. "Which is why I wished you to understand what a nest of vipers the court has become."

An uncomfortable silence as Wykeham held Thoresby's gaze while his pale face was washed with an angry crimson. "You would trick me out of becoming chancellor? You are sly, I grant you that. I almost believed you meant to help me."

The councillor's suspicion did not surprise Thoresby. They had not been confidants. "In the past months I have watched you, Councillor, and I have come to believe that I formerly misjudged you. You are a good man who hopes to act for the good of the people, for the good of their souls. And I am telling you—awkwardly and unconvincingly, it seems—that you must understand what it means to be the King's bishop, how impossible it will become to act contrary to the King. For you will owe him everything, and he will not hesitate to remind you."

Wykeham shook his head as if puzzling over a surprisingly disappointing child. "It is not so much your chain of office I seek, Chancellor. It is the see of Winchester. I grew to manhood there, Bishop Edington was my teacher in all things I count best in myself."

Thoresby raised an eyebrow. "You would reject the chancellorship?"

"No. But it is Winchester I covet."

Thoresby did not believe him. Though it was said that the see of Winchester was the richest in the kingdom. "I did not realise…"

"No. You would not. It is something personal, and we have not been on such terms."

Thoresby bowed to Wykeham, began to rise. "I understand. You feel I have overstepped the bounds you have set for us." He shrugged.

Wykeham lifted a hand, stopping Thoresby, then gestured towards the table. "God has provided us this goodly feast. Shall we not give thanks and enjoy it?"

"Do you wish to do so?"

"I do."

Thoresby resumed his seat.

They finished their meal idly wondering about the bones found beneath a floor in an old building being razed for the new construction in the upper ward.

It was not until Thoresby was at the door, taking his leave, that

Wykeham said, "I am puzzled why Mistress Perrers has not told the King of her suspicions about her husband, the deaths for which she believes him responsible." His lean face was drawn, almost pinched. "The King would surely wish to know."

Thoresby put a hand on Wykeham's shoulder. "My noble, godly Wykeham. It is not the sort of information the King welcomes. You would be wise to remain silent. It is enough to know. To watch."

"That is impossible. We should *do* something."

"What? We have no proof. And if we did? And the King judges the secret marriage more important? What then?"

"He would not do so."

The man had heard nothing Thoresby had said. "When you are the King's bishop, you will understand."

He felt Wykeham's eyes on him as he disappeared down the stone steps. But he did not turn, did not retrace his steps to try to explain. He was headed for sleep.

Owen woke when Gwenllian cried out for her midnight feeding. As he lay quietly watching Lucie feed their daughter, he felt a horrible dread. He had so much to lose; what if Ned were not to be trusted? What if he *had* murdered Don Ambrose? Might Ned have attacked the friar in a fit of rage, as Abbot Richard believed?

No. That would go against Ned's nature. He had a temper, there was no denying that. Many a time he had bloodied a face, broken a nose. When in his cups, mostly. That was a problem. Matthew had described Ned as drunk that night. But after the friar had disappeared, not before. *After* Ned had learned of Mary's death. And who could blame him for drinking to lessen that pain?

Owen turned on to his side, sighed at the dark sky glimpsed through the chinks of the shutters. Try as he might, Owen could not imagine Ned losing his head and attacking Don Ambrose, not unless he had found some sort of evidence that Ambrose had been responsible for Mary's death.

And how could he have been? Ambrose had been with the party from the beginning.

Lucie put Gwenllian back in her cradle, turned to Owen. "You sigh over Ned." She brushed back his damp curls, kissed his forehead tenderly.

"I risk much to help him."

"I would do the same for Bess."

"Time and again Ned saved my life, I am certain."

"Then I am beholden to him."

"You cannot imagine the half of it. You did not fight alongside Bess."

A sudden chuckle.

Owen raised his head, frowning. "What can you possibly find amusing in this?"

"The thought of Bess in battle."

Owen could not help but smile. "She would make an excellent captain."

"That she would."

"I would not want her for an enemy."

"No, nor I. I wonder…Would she wear ribbons on her cap in the field?"

Owen pulled Lucie to him. "Thank you for making me smile tonight."

Lucie nestled close. "It is my pleasure. Now rest, my love. Think of Bess going to battle starched and grim."

Alfred leapt from his chair, dagger in hand.

Owen gave him a kick that sent him sprawling. "'Tis your captain, you slugabed. What are you doing inside? You were to stand guard, not sit!"

"I was awake, wasn't I? Came for you soon as you stepped within." Alfred rubbed his booted groin and spat on the floor beside him.

"Charming company you've provided me with," Ned said. He

lay on his back on the cot, fully dressed.

"Outside with you, Alfred," Owen barked. "I want no one listening from the shadows."

"'Tis naught but shadows out there, Captain," Alfred complained.

Owen turned slowly, a warning look on his face.

Alfred grabbed his cloak, a shuttered lantern, and hobbled out.

Owen sank down on the chair vacated by Alfred, opened his lantern further to get a better look at his friend. "Do you always sleep with your boots on?"

"Only in hellish surroundings. This is worse than a gaol." Ned propped himself up on one elbow. "So what's amiss?"

"Amiss? My man knows nothing of guarding, that's what's amiss."

Ned grunted. "I know you, Owen. An early morning walk means troubling thoughts robbed you of sleep."

"I must see Jehannes, give him some explanation for what I have done."

"Ah."

Owen stretched out his legs, tilted the chair back against the stone wall. "Tell me again. Why were you chosen for the journey north?"

Ned dropped on to his back, stared at the damp stones above. "The ceiling leaks, you know." He rubbed his cheeks briskly with his palms as if to wake himself. "I believe Alice Perrers arranged it to separate Mary and me."

"Who told you this?"

"No one. But what else makes sense?"

"Do you believe Mistress Perrers had aught to do with Mary's death?"

Ned closed his eyes, clenched his fists. "Without her interference, it could not have happened. I would have been there to protect Mary, as she wished. As she begged."

Owen saw the tension in his friend's face, gave him a moment with his grief. He did not doubt his friend's feelings for Mary.

"You are keen to blame the King's mistress. What do you know of Alice Perrers?"

"Far more than you might think."

"Lancaster is interested?"

"She is his father's mistress."

"But there are too many males between Lancaster and the throne. Why does he take such an interest?"

"He believes someone must. His brother Edward lives for the next chance to don his black armour and Lionel is ever busy running from his own troubles."

"Tell me about her then."

"Mistress Alice was a plague child, born in the year the death first walked among us. It is said such children have unholy strength. Or unholy powers. Many believe the King's mistress has both. She bewitched the Queen, who took her into her bedchamber; soon she had crossed over to the King's."

"What of her parents?"

"Landed family. Modest income. Both died of the plague. Uncles placed her with a merchant and his wife who had lost a daughter to the plague. They raised her as their own with a small allowance from the uncles. A sudden family feeling led them to tear her from her foster parents, the only folk she remembered. Put her in a convent school for manners, reading, writing."

"Fortunate young woman."

"You would not think so to hear her tell it."

"This is your Mary talking, isn't it? Is that how you came to woo her, to spy on Alice Perrers?"

"May God forgive me. Aye. 'Tis just so. But God soon put it right. Mary won my heart. I did love her, Owen. I would have done anything for her. But the one thing she begged me…"

"She did not tell you why she wished you to stay?"

Ned shook his head. "I wish to God I knew why. What prevented her from confiding in me about her fear?"

"Wyndesore's page. What was that about?"

"He befriended her. When I asked her why, she took it as an insult." Ned put his knuckles to his temples, pressed.

"Pain?"

"Nothing you might cure."

"The deaths of Wyndesore's page and Perrers's maid. Any connection?"

"If there is, I am the last to know."

"Bardolph and Crofter, Wyndesore's men. How can you be certain they are after you?"

"When we began the journey, Don Ambrose feared them. After York, when he turned against me, they encouraged that, elaborated slights, made him think I placed him in particular danger."

"Why?"

"They believe I murdered Daniel?" Ned shrugged. "Only God knows their black hearts."

"Still believe it has to do with your being Lancaster's spy?"

"Does it matter?"

"If they do not come after you, will you give me your word to continue to Windsor?"

A hesitation. "You will deliver me up to the Lord Chancellor?"

"I will."

Ned nodded. "I promise to continue to Windsor."

Jehannes, Archdeacon of York, paced his parlour, hands clasped behind him. "God give me strength. This is an impossible situation, Owen. Impossible."

Owen wished he were up and pacing, too, but one of them must be calm. He sat with his elbows on knees, one hand pressing the patch against his left eye, in which a shower of needle pricks alerted him to his own uneasiness. "We are merely trying to keep Ned alive until the King's men arrive for him," he said slowly, in the calmest tone he could manage.

Jehannes was suddenly within arm's length, peering down with an anxious expression. "You are certain they will come?"

Owen sat back, stretched his legs. "Do you doubt it?"

With an exasperated sigh, the Archdeacon pulled up a chair and sank into it, grasping his knees through his gown. "They would take him back to Windsor and put him to death, Owen. The King does not send men after a captain unless he means to do so."

Owen nodded. What was there to say?

Jehannes touched his palms to his cheeks, as if feeling their heat, then dropped his hands to his sides. "I cannot let that happen unless we know he deserves death."

"What?" Owen straightened up, amazed by what Jehannes implied.

"So." Jehannes nodded to himself. "Unless the Archbishop has managed to intervene..." He shook his head. "I have never to my knowledge disobeyed my King."

Owen grinned. "Think of it as thwarting a group of soldiers out for blood."

"Ralph was here last night, warning me that Townley might count me dangerous. That I might be his next victim."

Bloody minded bastard. "He seemed a sensible man."

Jehannes shrugged. "He believes Townley murdered his comrades. It is not senseless to feel that such a man is dangerous. It is senseless to take the law into one's own hands and eliminate the danger."

"Senseless and soldierly," Owen muttered, wondering how long it would be before Ralph and his companions descended upon the shop. "There is no need for you to continue feeding Matthew."

Jehannes had turned towards the window; now he spun round. "You would have him guard Townley again?"

"No. But I may have need of him."

"You will not tell me where you are hiding Townley?"

"You know you trip over yourself when you attempt a lie."

Jehannes pressed the bones beneath his brows. "What shall I tell the King's men?"

"Tell them I've removed Ned to Bishopthorpe."

A frown. "Bishopthorpe?"

"That is all you need tell them."

Jehannes nodded. "Go in peace, Owen. May God watch over you."

22

MICHAELO RIDES NORTH, BRINGING TURMOIL

Crowder rolled about the floor with a knot of cloth while Jasper bit his lip and poured powdered orris root into a mortar, trying not to raise dust, which would make him sneeze and ruin the physick he had worked on most of the morning. Lucie saw to customers and pretended she was unaware of Jasper's little cries of dismay, knowing that his yelps usually signalled only his fear of an accident rather than his having made a mistake. Owen was with Ned, removing the stitches; after four days the threads were itching horribly, a sign of healing.

When the door opened, Lucie squinted, thinking her eyes tricked her. But it still looked like Brother Michaelo, though not as meticulously groomed as usual. "I thought you were in Windsor with His Grace."

Michaelo closed his bloodshot eyes and nodded. "I left His Grace four days ago with an urgent message for Captain Archer. Is he here?"

Lucie wondered where Michaelo's loyalties would lie, with the King or with justice. "He is out at present. Might I see the letter?"

Michaelo bowed to her. "Forgive me, Mistress Wilton, but it is for your husband. If he decides, having read it, that you are to be privy to its contents, so be it. But that is not for me to judge."

Lucie did not like the secretary's solemn tone. "I presume it has to do with Ned Townley?"

"God sorely tests Captain Townley. I must warn you that the

King's men are a day behind me. They come to arrest your friend."

One day. So little time. "That is why you rode so hard your eyes are bloodshot and you've not stopped in the city to change?"

"Just so. I refreshed myself at Bishopthorpe, but I did not risk a long pause."

"They will take the Captain to Windsor?"

"Those are their orders, Mistress Wilton. Accompanying them is a clerk with a letter for Captain Archer from His Grace. But I carry a more recent one."

The Archbishop had obviously learned something that forced him to make haste getting word to Owen. "Come through to the kitchen, Brother Michaelo. Tildy will give you refreshment while I fetch Owen."

"What of the shop?"

"Jasper can watch it. I shall not be long away."

Lucie met Owen on the bridge. He did not like the news.

"Can Ned ride?" she asked.

"If he must. But his leg will be the worse for it later."

They returned to the shop arm in arm. Lucie left Owen there; he took Michaelo over to the kitchen of the new house, where they made a place for themselves among the supplies Tildy was gradually moving there. Michaelo gazed out at the apothecary garden while Owen read.

Thoresby had carefully described Don Ambrose's fear for his life, Alice Perrers's secret marriage, her suspicions of her husband's part in the deaths of the witnesses, and the danger all shared who had knowledge of this. Owen read quickly, then read it through again.

"So, Michaelo, Mistress Perrers may be a victim of her own heart, eh?"

"Heart? I should rather say she is a victim of her own ambition." He sat down by Owen. "The King's men will arrive tomorrow to take Captain Townley back to Windsor for trial. I rode hard to arrive before them, pausing only to sleep a few hours each night and give my horse a rest."

"You travelled alone?"

"Faith no, more's the pity. I had the companionship of Don Paulus."

"*Jesu*. He is at Bishopthorpe?"

Michaelo's nostrils flared. "I trust he will eat through the larder and drain the wine cellar if left too long."

"What does the Archbishop suggest I do?"

"That you take some of his retainers and head for Windsor with Captain Townley."

A tidy coincidence in plans. "He will do what he can for Ned?"

"His Grace is particularly eager that you should come, Captain. He wants you by his side. In return, he will give Townley his support."

Owen slapped his thighs, rose. "I must discuss preparations with my wife. We must leave before the gates are barred tonight."

"You will tell Mistress Wilton all that you have learned?"

Owen's eye met Michaelo's. "I shall weigh the danger, you may be sure. Now let me tell you of the plan." He was pleased to find Michaelo agreed to it.

"Bardolph and Crofter." Michaelo shook his head. "It was they who lifted Daniel's body from the ditch. I've no doubt they hurried out so that others might not see the welts on the lad's wrists."

"What about his ankles?"

"The others were bound at the ankles also?" When Owen nodded, Michaelo shook his head. "I regret I had not the leisure to examine him further, Captain. As it was I worried the men might notice my interest."

"Is that why His Grace sent you? Fearing you knew enough to be in danger?"

Michaelo bowed slightly. "Strange, is it not? He calls me his penance, yet he seeks to protect me."

Strange indeed. But Owen had noticed the subtle changes in the secretary. It was difficult to believe he had once been the toady of Archdeacon Anselm. "Let us return to the shop."

As Michaelo and Owen walked back through the garden, the secretary complained about his journey north with Don Paulus.

The friar had eaten and drunk more than his share, been difficult to wake, accident prone…

"You must remember not to mention his presence at Bishopthorpe until Ned has ridden off ahead."

"I am no fool, Captain."

"I depend on that, Brother Michaelo."

While Owen packed, Lucie fretted in the shop, forgetting a customer's name, dropping a pestle, answering in monosyllables. She had seen the grim set to Owen's jaw. There was a danger beyond what they had discussed. Obviously something in the letter Michaelo carried. At last, able to bear it no longer, she put Jasper in charge, told him to shout up the stairs if he had an urgent need, and hurried up to Owen.

She found her husband near the door, pack slung over his shoulder.

Lucie closed the door, blocked his way. "You shall not pass until I know the danger you face."

Owen closed his eye, shook his head. "Not this time, Lucie. The knowledge of it will place you in peril. I will not do that."

"Do you think anyone would believe I knew naught of it?"

"Many men keep their business to themselves."

"What have you done with the letter?"

"I have it in my pack. I shall dispose of it."

"How easy it is for you to deny me this. You are not the one who stays at home and waits. Worries."

Owen rolled his eye. "There is no one better at worrying than me." He tried to take her hand.

She kept her arms crossed, hands tucked behind elbows, and told him of her mistakes in the shop. "They will multiply and worsen once you are gone. Better that I know the truth. My mind will conjure such horrors…"

Owen dropped his pack, pulled Lucie close. "I would not endanger you, my love. Or the children."

The hands uncrossed of their own volition, wrapped round Owen. Lucie peered up at his dear face, so grim at the moment. "We are one household, Owen. If someone means to silence you, they will come for us for good measure. There is no escaping it with foolish silences."

He opened his mouth to argue, cursed instead. Backing away from her, he sat down, untied his pack, handed Lucie Thoresby's letter. She read it by the window in the gentle spring sunshine, fighting her trembling hands as she realised the enormity of the affair. "But surely too many now know. They cannot all be silenced," she whispered.

"Let us pray that is so, Lucie." She handed him the letter. He returned it to his pack. "Forgive me for the trouble I bring to this home."

He brought? "How can you blame yourself? It was the Archbishop who began it. But go now. Ride quickly. Get Ned to Windsor and safety."

"I do not know how much security Thoresby can provide."

"More than the open road, for certain."

They held each other tight for a long moment.

"They will come here in search of Ned."

"All for naught." Lucie forced a smile. "What shall I tell them?"

"Tell them I heard rumours of two rough-looking men asking his whereabouts, so I took him off to Bishopthorpe, where I am steward."

Lucie took a deep breath. "That is where Ned and Matthew ride off ahead?"

"Aye. Ned believes Bardolph and Crofter are watching him and will follow when he leaves me. Michaelo, Alfred and I shall stop at Bishopthorpe overnight, then ride hard to close in on them from behind."

"There is much risk in the plan."

"Aye."

Lucie bit her lip. "And how shall you explain an armed company to the gatekeeper?"

"I shall be telling him that I've had word an Austin friar is hiding at Bishopthorpe and I mean to oust him. It will explain my having armed men riding with me."

"What of Jehannes? What will you tell him?"

Owen shook his head. "Nothing. It is my revenge for his silence."

"Poor man. His house will be turned up so down."

Owen grinned.

"Should you collect more men, Captain?" Michaelo fretted as they led five horses from the stable of Matilda's father.

"More might be useful but I cannot ride out with a group of men without alerting Ralph and his mates; they would follow, you can be sure of that."

They led the mounts slowly through the narrow streets to the Old Baile.

Tom Merchet had alerted Alfred, Matthew and Ned earlier so they would be ready when Owen and Michaelo arrived. The three crept out from the vine-clad wall, slogged through the muck of the old moat, Alfred and Matthew assisting Ned so that he might not slip and open his wound.

"The innkeeper gave us no reason for the haste," Matthew complained.

"He knew not the reason, and neither will you, Matthew. If you obey orders, ask no questions, it will be better for you."

Matthew straightened up. "Aye, Captain. I meant naught—"

"The less talk the better." Owen handed him a rein. "We ride out Micklegate for Bishopthorpe. Lead your mount until we are out of the gate." The procession quietly began.

Harold opened the door to the King's men with trembling hands. The Archdeacon had warned him that they were bound to come soon.

"God go with you," Jehannes called from the parlour, "come in, come in." Six of them; tall, broad shouldered, well-armed soldiers looking travel-stained and stiff from riding. Jehannes offered them ale and a repast of vegetable stew, cold meats, cheese, and bread.

"Where is Captain Townley?" the gruff spokesman of the company asked. He was a burly redhead named Rufus.

"The Captain is in a safe place," Jehannes said, grateful that he was already damp with nervous sweat; Rufus would hardly notice an increase of what was already there.

The men sat and ate.

The delay was not absolutely necessary, but Jehannes wanted to give his servant Ann time to warn Lucie Wilton that the men would soon be at her house.

"Has the Duke of Lancaster been notified of the pending arrest of his man?" Jehannes asked as the appetites slowed.

"This is King's business, not the Duke's," said Rufus, rising and adjusting his belt to his full stomach. "But my lord of Lancaster would not wish a murderer to go free, his man or no. We will go to Captain Townley now, if it please you, sir."

Jehannes nodded. "You must ride south, I am afraid. To the Archbishop's manor of Bishopthorpe."

Rufus shook his head. "We were told he was in your custody."

Thinking quickly, Jehannes said, "He slipped out of my house while in my custody. I thought it best to hand him over to someone more practised in such matters."

"And who might that be, sir?"

"Captain Archer, captain of the Archbishop's guard."

Rufus frowned. "Are you mad? They fought together under Henry of Grosmont."

Jehannes nodded. "I am aware of that. But Captain Archer is an honourable man."

Rufus muttered something Jehannes did not care to decipher and strode from the house, shouting to his men to follow at once.

Lucie greeted the soldiers in the shop, informed them of Owen's departure for Bishopthorpe, saying he had gone the previous day.

"But stay." She walked over to one of the soldiers who held a bandaged hand close to him, nodded to another with a nasty cough. "Let me put your men at ease before you ride forth."

"Where's your husband, Mistress Wilton?" Rufus demanded.

Lucie did her best to look puzzled. "I have told you. He rode to Bishopthorpe yesterday."

"How many men with him?"

"Captain Townley, his man Matthew, and one of Owen's men. Three travelled with him, Captain." It seemed unwise to mention Michaelo. Rufus turned to his men, ordered two of them to the quarters of the Archbishop's guards. "See whether any others rode along."

Lucie could not believe the insolence. "I would thank you for trusting me, Captain. I am Master Apothecary in this city. I am not accustomed to having my word questioned."

"I pray you pardon me, Mistress Wilton, but I don't like what I find here. I shall find the truth for myself."

Lucie bit her tongue. The sooner the arrogant knave was out of her shop, the better.

Jehannes suddenly appeared in the shop doorway as Rufus paced back and forth. "'Tis a crowded house you have here, Mistress Wilton," Rufus muttered. "Pity the only man we want is missing."

Archdeacon Jehannes stepped into the room. "*Benedicte.*" He blessed them all. "I must warn you, Captain Rufus, that Mistress Wilton and her family are under the protection of Archbishop Thoresby, who is godfather to young Gwenllian."

Rufus glared at the Archdeacon. "Mistress Wilton is seeing to my men before we depart once more, sir. I would not harm the innocent family of a soldier, no matter what he had done."

Jehannes sank down on a stool, fanning himself. Lucie feared he might faint. "Go to the kitchen. Tildy will give you something to drink," Lucie told him. "I will not have you passing out in my shop." She herself looked forward to a good measure of brandywine when the men departed.

23

UNLIKELY ALLIANCES

Ralph rapped sharply on the Archdeacon's door. Harold informed him, and the three standing behind him, that the King's men were searching the house and his master could not be disturbed.

"It's Captain Rufus I would see," Ralph said with an unfriendly snarl.

Harold withdrew quickly. Ralph stood with hands clenched behind him and waited until the red-haired captain darkened the door. "We were part of the company sent up from Windsor, Captain. We would join you in your search and return with you to our station."

Rufus peered past him. "How many?"

"Curan, Edgar, Geoff, and myself, Captain."

Rufus considered. "You have your own mounts?"

"Aye, Captain."

He nodded. "Then return at dawn. It is too late to depart tonight."

At midmorning, within sight of the gates to Bishopthorpe, the company halted. Owen brought his horse alongside Ned's. "No unnecessary risks, eh? We mean to be right behind you, ready to close in when they appear. You are to lure them, not dispose of them."

Ned grinned, slapped Owen on the thigh. "No pinning them to a couple of sturdy oaks to await their fates?"

"No."

"Pity." Ned turned, noted the alarm on Matthew's face, and

shook his head. "You know me better than that, you daft man."

Owen watched the two ride off with a gut full of worry. But they must move ahead.

The three entered the gates of Bishopthorpe and rode into the yard of the Archbishop's favourite home, an imposing stone house with chapel and extensive stables. Owen was pleased to see men at work on a corner of the roof. But he was not pleased by the news that Don Paulus had departed the previous day.

"How can that be?"

Maeve, the Archbishop's cook, hurried from the kitchen wiping her hands and shaking her head. "I had my doubts, Captain Archer, but the two were wearing King's livery. And I can't say as I was sorry to see the fat back of that friar."

Her descriptions fitted Bardolph and Crofter. "A day ahead of us." Owen wondered whether they were now in flight and would not rise to the bait. "Damn them. They must have seen the King's men headed this way, thought to take the friar prisoner just in case."

Michaelo was crestfallen. "Does this mean we ride tonight?"

Owen stared at the secretary. "Are you mad? I would charge after Ned and Matthew to alert them if they were not riding slowly because of Ned's injury. Even so, we can afford to stay only long enough to gather what provisions Maeve can spare. We leave after midday."

At midday on their second day out from York, Owen's company came upon two familiar men and a third having some food and a rest. Owen, Michaelo and Alfred crept close to the camp site as the men were mounting. With Bardolph and Crofter was a black-robed friar. "Do you recognise the friar, Michaelo? Is it Don Paulus?"

Michaelo's delicate nostrils flared. "Can you not smell the corruption?"

It was odd that Wyndesore's men did not appear to have the friar bound, nor did they watch him so much as they watched their backs. The friar sat his horse comfortably, his expression one of enjoyment. The three men picked up speed as they reached the road.

"Shall we take them, Captain?" Alfred asked.

"Expecting trouble, they are," Owen said, reining in. His companions followed suit. "We shall do best to keep them in sight. When they find their prey, we shall surprise them as they think to surprise him."

"How is it we come upon them before the Captain and Matthew?" Michaelo wondered.

Owen shook his head. "Ned is riding faster than I'd thought? They allowed Ned and Matthew to pass? God help me, I wish I knew."

Thoresby's nights of little or no sleep finally took their toll at supper in the great hall of Windsor. As a Welsh harper played a sweetly pensive melody, Thoresby listened with thoughtful pleasure. But soon his eyelids fought to close, his focus blurred, his head nodded forward. Worst of all, he caught Alice Perrers glancing at him with amusement.

She bent to the Queen. "My lady, I would confer with the Lord Chancellor on the legal matter we spoke of earlier."

Queen Phillippa, her own lids heavy with wine and the smoky room, glanced over at Thoresby, inclined her head towards Alice. "Speak with him now, child, then come to my chamber and amuse me till I sleep." The Queen laboriously pushed herself from the table. A servant was immediately behind her to assist her difficult rising.

The King smiled at Alice, Queen Phillippa. "My ladies desert me so early in the evening?" He kissed Phillippa's hand. "May God grant you sweet dreams," he said gently.

Alice rose, curtsied to the King and Queen. Thoresby stood, feeling revived. He had meant to seek Alice out. It had occurred to him last night, as he tossed on what only weeks ago had been a comfortable bed, that Alice had omitted an important item in her story: who had informed the King of her marriage?

"Let us walk out into the courtyard, take some air," Alice suggested. "There is a legal matter I wish to discuss with you."

Thoresby bowed and gestured for her to precede him. Heads turned, tongues wagged as they passed the lower tables. Gilbert and Adam raced each other to open the door. Gilbert won. Thoresby thought it a tribute to him that his lad had not needed to learn speed in order to avoid physical abuse. He knew Gilbert was frequently slapped.

The damp, chilly evening was a relief after the hall. Thoresby drew his cloak round him and began to stride forward.

"More slowly, please, Your Grace," Alice cried. "I wear dancing slippers, not boots."

Thoresby paused.

Alice lifted her skirt to show him the delicately embroidered velvet shoes in the lantern light provided promptly by Gilbert.

Thoresby bowed. "Forgive me, Mistress Perrers. I must be more accustomed to your booted stride."

Gilbert did not raise the lantern to reveal his mistress's expression.

"I am amazed that a man who so recently nodded over his wine now strides forward with such energy and purpose," Alice said with false sweetness.

Enough of this babble. "I have thought long on the matter we discussed, Mistress Perrers, and I find myself with more questions."

"Oh?" A brief pause. "Walk ahead, Gilbert, gossip with Adam."

That brought another question to mind. "How is it that Gilbert has been spared?" Thoresby asked. "Why was he not a witness?"

"William said he needed but two, one from each household." The voice was flat.

"Ah."

"Was that your question, Your Grace?"

"Oh no, quite a minor matter about Gilbert. No, I wondered… you see, it seems to me that you strove for secrecy and then…my good Mistress Perrers, who betrayed you to the King?"

Alice cleared her throat. "The question is one I have asked myself over and over, Your Grace. Who indeed?"

"Come now. You are too shrewd to have let that go unanswered, Mistress Perrers. Far too shrewd."

"I swear I do not know, Your Grace. I hope to discover it.

I would know my enemies. But where do I look?" Alice sighed. "Your Grace, I see that you mean to learn all that you may about this affair." She paused, touched his arm, a fleeting, importunate gesture. "If you learn anything—I pray you will tell me."

Indeed. Tell her what she already knew and refused to tell him. "Of course. I would be remiss to keep it from you. Now what was the legal question you wished to discuss?"

"It is a matter of my property and how my marriage affects it."

"I should require the deeds, Mistress Perrers. The wording is critical. I suspect the King has been careful with it, as I was when I prepared the contract for your house in Windsor town."

"You would not mind reviewing this matter for me?"

"It would be my pleasure."

"God bless you. I shall send Gilbert with the deeds in the morning."

Thoresby smiled as they parted. It would be enlightening to see the extent of Alice Perrers's holdings.

In the morning, Thoresby had Adam watch Alice's movements. When Alice left the Queen's apartments on an errand, Thoresby presented himself to the Queen's receiving chamber. Phillippa sat with her legs cradled in soft cushions, her feet draped with a silk coverlet. Apparently shoes were a pain she endured only when necessary these days. Her face was swollen and unnaturally flushed. Yet the Queen welcomed Thoresby with a sweet smile as usual. "Come, sit near me. You have become a stranger to these rooms, my friend. The King works you day and night, I fear?"

"And now Mistress Perrers."

"Ah. Yes. I assured her she might trust you with her secret."

Thoresby glanced at the lady in waiting who hovered nearby. "You are kind to show such faith in my discretion, my lady."

"I know that you are not fond of Alice." Phillippa waved away his protests. "It is kind of you to look into these matters for my sake." She turned to her lady, asked for her to leave them for a moment.

"Talk with the gardener. Coax some early blooms from him."

When they were alone in the large, yet comfortable chamber, Thoresby grinned at the Queen. "You enjoy this intrigue."

The bloodshot eyes brightened. "It provides diversion."

"Sir William of Wyndesore. Such an unpleasant choice for Mistress Perrers. Would you have encouraged her in her intent? Had you known, of course?"

The Queen closed her eyes, pursed her lips. "Sadly, it is a common fault in otherwise shrewd women; they spy a rogue, sense danger, and think it love." She shook her head. "Happily for me I fell in love with the best of men."

"You have been blessed in your marriage."

"It is a rarity, such perfection." Phillippa smiled. "Even now, when I am not pleasant to look on and move with the gait of a crippled beast."

"You are the beauty you ever were, my Queen."

Phillippa patted Thoresby's hand. "Alice is unhappy. No, that is too weak a word for it. She is cursed in her lot. Sir William is a ruthless man. He has defamed Lionel, my precious son." Tears glittered, the cracked lips trembled. She had a particular affection for her second son.

Thoresby took the plunge. "So you had not blessed the marriage? Who had the temerity to tell you? Who told the King?"

"That Austin friar of whom the privy councillor thought so highly." She frowned, having forgotten the name.

"Don Ambrose?"

Phillippa nodded. "Yes. Poor man. May he rest in peace." She crossed herself. "He told Edward. It was Alice's request. You see, almost at once she saw her mistake. She hoped that Edward would be worried that the marriage would look like a reward to Sir William for revealing Lionel's errors in Ireland, that he would order its dissolution. But alas, Edward thought it a good match. Rather than dissolving it, he chose simply to keep it secret until the problems in Ireland are forgotten."

Poor man indeed. Don Ambrose must have feared for his life many times before it ended.

24

A PLAN GONE UP IN SMOKE

Owen's company continued south, following Wyndesore's men and the friar. The pace was swift. Owen wondered whether Ned was sleeping in the woods, as they were, or finding nightly comfort in the abandoned cottages that dotted the countryside, grim reminders of the terrible toll of the plague. They had just ridden past a village of collapsing buildings, some weed-choked shells, others partially roofed. Considering how his own legs rubbed against saddle and steed, Owen knew Ned must be in agony with the pace. Unless he had found some trick to riding in an odd position, his wound would surely have reopened. Loss of blood, continual pain—how strong would Ned be by the time Bardolph and Crofter reached him? But they were not the ones controlling the pace. Ned must know what he was doing.

His head thick with pain, Ned yearned to stop, but early that morning he and Matthew had detected a fire upwind. Creeping close, they'd discovered their pursuers—Bardolph and Crofter, falling right in with the plan. But Ned was puzzled by the addition to their company, the black-robed friar. Might it be Don Paulus, the bastard who had left Mary floating in the Thames? Should Ned attack now? He itched to do that. But they were two against three, and Ned was weak from the wound which stained his bandages though bound as tight as he could manage. The scar had long since torn, the wound reopened. Ned regretted having talked Owen into staying behind him. Together they would have fallen upon the three with no doubt as to the outcome. But he would not attempt an assault with Matthew—he was too hesitant a fighter to risk it.

Now, as he rode, Ned fought the temptation to stop at an inn, pay good coin for a private room, slake his terrible thirst and then close his eyes on the spinning, too-bright world, rest his pounding head. He feared his pace had slowed, and his frequent pauses at streams to refill his water-skin were surely costing him time. In fact, he was puzzled why Bardolph and Crofter had not already overtaken him. They had camped so near him last night; was it possible they were unaware of how close they were?

And then he saw a tumble of crumbling buildings, one a substantial ruin. He, Matthew, and the horses might easily hide in there and take a day to gather strength, then move on in pursuit of today's pursuers. Ned suggested it to Matthew, who judged it a wise move.

As evening fell, the forest canopy hastening the night, Brother Michaelo noted that he had seen no signs of riders ahead for some time. Alfred and Owen agreed. All were uneasy. They reined in together to consider.

"Do you think they knew we followed? Perhaps hid to let us pass?" Michaelo suggested.

Alfred scratched his straw-coloured hair and pulled on his nose. "'Twas the farm gone to weeds we passed, mid-afternoon." He nodded. "That's when last I noticed movement ahead."

Owen remembered the farmhouse. It had reminded him of one in Normandy, recently gutted by fire. He, Ned, Gaspare, Bertold and Lief had spent a hellish night hiding within, amongst the ashes and splintered wood, waiting for enemy scouts to pass by. It might have touched Ned's memory, too, coaxing him to stop there, rest his leg. The ruins had been sufficiently intact to hide them.

Michaelo was nodding. "I recall nothing since." He and Alfred looked to Owen for a decision.

"We turn round, pick our way there in the dusk."

. . .

Walter of Coventry at last arrived at the camp of Sir William of Wyndesore, soaked, chilled to the bone and exhausted. For the last few hours of the ride he had been composing in his head a letter of complaint to Mistress Alice Perrers, insisting on more generous pay for bringing this letter so far. To be fair, she could not have known that Sir William had quit Alnwick Castle to go on patrol with his men up into the Cheviot Hills. Walter had not come prepared for late snow in the higher elevations. He would be laid low with a fever, he had no doubt. The additional funds would compensate for lost income. The money should by rights come from Sir William; but knowing the soldier's foul temper, Walter preferred to make his complaint to the lady.

Sir William greeted him with a grunt and snatched the letter from his gloved hands, stood with his back to the tent opening, examining the seal by what little daylight there was. "Good." He broke the seal, read with the squint and moving lips of one who does not read with ease. Walter, curious what business the King's mistress might have with the handsome but surly soldier, moved closer in hopes of reading the man's lips.

Too late. A snort. "Women. Always fretting over things they don't understand. Huh. I've dealt with worse." Wyndesore glanced up through heavy brows, noticed Walter's intent gaze. "Still here, are you?"

Walter cleared his throat. "A matter of supplies, Sir William. I had not provisioned for a mountain journey…"

"Alan! Give the messenger what he requires. I'll not have him dying in the mountains. He's served me well."

Rising to follow the squire, Walter bobbed his head at Sir William. "God speed, Sir William."

"Aye. Off with you, now."

As they picked their way through the slush to the cook's tent, Alan asked, "The letter you carried. From Mistress Perrers?"

"Aye."

Alan nodded. "I am glad he's sending you off with supplies.

That bodes well for us all."

Walter could imagine life in camp with a commander such as Wyndesore.

After Matthew had cleaned Ned's wound and bandaged it as best he could, Ned had dosed himself with some wine and lain down to nap. "Keep your eyes on the edge of the wood, Matthew. They will come from there if they come."

But they had not. Bardolph and Crofter had ridden in straight from the road, bold as could be. By the time Matthew had spotted them setting up camp, he and Ned could no longer slip out of the house without being seen.

Ned cursed Matthew as he struggled to the mossy hole that had once been a window. But seeing the activity, he shrugged. "They may not know how close we are, just thought to stop early tonight. This could be where we carry out the plan, Matthew, if Owen and the others are riding right behind them. We must be prepared for battle."

They retreated into the shadows and ate some dried meat, drank enough wine to quench their thirst, no more, and then settled in to wait. The daylight faded. Ned crept back to the lookout. A small campfire lit the twilight. There was but one figure sitting beside it.

"I am much afraid we have eased ourselves into a trap, Matthew." Ned drew his daggers. "Come. Let us use the shadows to our advantage."

As Owen and his companions drew near the derelict farmhouse, Alfred rode on ahead to scout. The three had caught sight of what appeared to be a substantial campfire, guessed that perhaps the King's men were upon them.

As he rode closer, Alfred's uneasiness mounted. He had to fight not to cough in the smoky air; it was no mere campfire up ahead.

Dismounting and tethering his horse at the edge of the wood, he put a cloth to his face and crept among the tumbledown farm buildings to the farmhouse. As the lopsided ruin came into view he halted, crossed himself. The bonfire was heaped before the door; a fire built with a base layer of dry wood and plenty of it, creating enough heat now to burn damp wood, making a smoky, slow-burning fire. The sort used to smoke someone out of an enclosed space. As Alfred watched, the rotting wood round the door caught fire.

Feeding the flames was the black-robed Don Paulus.

Alfred ducked behind an outbuilding. Somewhere before him, most likely in the house, he could hear the terrified horses.

With a pounding heart, Alfred crept back to his horse and led it into the wood where he mounted and galloped back to Owen and Michaelo.

With cautious, exploring steps Owen and Michaelo crept through the dark wood. Alfred had gone round the front, his mission to incapacitate Don Paulus, then soak a blanket in the pond by the outbuildings and throw it upon the fire. For Owen the way was doubly difficult; a man with both eyes has poor sight at night, but a man with a single eye is almost as good as blind. And with the increasing smoke, the one eye must blink far too often. Michaelo was soon way ahead of Owen. How odd to depend on Thoresby's secretary to assist him in saving Ned. Owen pressed a damp cloth to his nose and mouth as the smoke thickened. Sweet Heaven. Let them find the bloody bastards before Ned died of a lung full of hellfire.

Michaelo had paused, his hands out, palms up. Owen hurried towards him. They were now at the edge of the clearing directly behind the house. It was a nightmare scene, the ruin haloed in firelight which weirdly illuminated the billowing smoke. The crisp crackle of the blaze was shattered now and again by the cries of the terrified horses within.

"Step out farther," Michaelo said.

As Owen did, he understood Michaelo's stance. It had begun to rain. A good, steady rain. "Let us pray it is enough to slow the fire."

"Two men," Michaelo said, pointing to a darkness Owen could not yet make out, his eye still affected by glancing at the fire.

They edged forward cautiously, staying within the thickest smoke. Blinking rapidly, Owen now made out the two figures, one on either side of a yawning opening through which the flames were visible.

"The bastards await Ned and Matthew."

Michaelo crossed himself. "And their horses."

Suddenly a horse rushed from the opening, knocking over one of the men in its desperate escape. "Now!" Owen shouted, pushing forward. "Get the one on the ground."

Owen leapt aside as the second horse came crashing through a burning wall. Mud splashed up at him as he landed in a puddle. He looked up, kicked out in time to trip a man lunging for him. Grabbing the muddy figure, Owen rolled him over, wincing as he discovered the man's dagger. He knelt on the man's gut and snapped the wrist to the ground, grabbed the knife, held it at the man's throat.

A groan. "You've broke my arm."

Only then did Owen know his opponent. "Only your wrist, Crofter." The man's throat was tempting; but Crofter had much talking to do. "Is Townley still in the house?"

"Wouldn't you like to know?" Crofter spat in Owen's eye.

Owen slid the knife across the throat more gently than he would have liked, then shifted his weight to the knee on Crofter's groin, dug in, grinning at the curses Crofter spewed forth.

Nearby someone was winding a rope round an inert body. Owen prayed it was Bardolph on the ground.

Once Brother Michaelo had landed on the fallen man, he hesitated. It had been so long since he had indulged in a brawl he was uncertain what should be his next move. The man moaned, clutched his head. Michaelo reached down, found the rock the man's head had struck when he fell. Lifting it high, he brought it down at the nape of the man's neck with a prayer of thanks that God had shown him the way.

After Michaelo had bound the unconscious man, he limped over to assist Owen—Bardolph's struggle had bruised the monk in muscles he'd forgotten he had.

The King's men complained when they paused only briefly at twilight to refresh themselves.

"We must move ahead," Rufus said. "There's a storm coming, and a scent upon the air I do not like."

He sent the scouts forward with less rest than the others. They returned shortly with news of a friar lying in front of a burning house and two horses crashing through the wood.

When they reached Don Paulus, he did not at first respond to their presence. At last he lifted his head, trembling. There was dried blood on his forehead. Geoff helped the friar rise, but the poor man fell on one leg and cried out, "God bless you, men, but they've done for me. Leave me. Find the two who did this to me. God would wish you to stop them before they injure another innocent soul."

"Where are they?" Rufus asked.

Don Paulus closed his eyes, pressed his forehead gingerly. "Behind the house."

Leaving a skin of wine for the wounded friar, Rufus led his men round the burning house.

The rain came down hard now, finally waking Alfred. He groaned, rolled over, coughed until his lungs burned.

"You'll feel better now." Someone knelt beside him in the damp straw, handing him a bucket. "It's rain water. Drink all you can."

Captain Townley. Alfred tried to say the name, managed a croak.

"No talking. Just drink. You swallowed too much smoke wrestling with the friar."

Alfred grabbed the bucket and drank. "Must help them," he managed to whisper after enough water.

"All is well, Alfred. The King's men have come. Matthew's helping Owen and Michaelo. So just drink deep and save yourself. You did a good night's work."

Upwind from the fire Owen stood guard over the trussed up men. Nearby, Rufus's men were setting up camp for the night. Suddenly two pairs of boots approached. Owen peered from beneath the rain-heavy cloak he held over his head to shield his eye from the smoke and the steady downpour. He groaned to see Ralph and Curan.

"How do you come to be here?"

"We ride with the King's men, as is proper. Where's Townley?"

"Somewhere nearby, I hope. Do you still think him guilty? After what Wyndesore's men have done this night?"

"This proves only that they want Townley dead," Curan said. "And if he murdered Gervase and Henry, we mean to succeed where they failed." He moved close to Ralph.

Rufus, sensing trouble, slogged through the ashy mud, shouted to Ralph and Curan to fetch the friar, find him some shelter while the rest searched for the missing men. The two went off grumbling.

"Captain Archer. I would speak with you and your companions in my tent." Rufus motioned two of his men forward. "They will guard Wyndesore's men now."

Owen, Brother Michaelo, and Matthew followed him without protest, eager to be out of the rain for a while.

"What happened here? Why had you separated?" Rufus demanded.

"Townley and his second left us at Bishopthorpe to lure Bardolph and Crofter after them," Owen said.

"Why?"

"He is convinced they committed the murders of which he's accused, and now they are after him."

"Why?"

Good God. What could Owen say? "Politics. Some trouble between Lancaster and Clarence."

Rufus grunted. "I wouldn't know about that." He turned to Matthew. "Where is your captain?"

Matthew looked pathetic, with a filthy bandage holding up a broken arm and half his hair burned to a stubble. "He dragged Captain Archer's man away from the fire, into one of the outbuildings. Too much smoke."

"And now he's bolted, no doubt."

"Permit us to search for him," Owen said quietly.

Rufus grunted. "Nay. I'll put my men to it. I want Townley bound. Curan is right, what Wyndesore's men have done does not prove Townley's innocence."

Michaelo stepped forward, managing his usual haughty dignity even with muddy clothes, a split lip, and a pronounced limp. "I have papers from the Lord Chancellor entrusting Captain Townley to Captain Archer."

Rufus studied Michaelo. "I thought I knew you. The chancellor's secretary."

Michaelo gave a little bow.

"So where are these papers?"

"Back with my horse."

Rufus nodded at Michaelo. "So it was the chancellor plotted to make a fool of me?"

"His Grace means to see that Townley has the opportunity to clear himself."

"It is for the King to decide that. We shall escort your party to Windsor."

"I have no objection to that," Owen said. "But I ask you to allow Captain Townley to ride unshackled."

Rufus shrugged. "If we find him. But you will have charge of him."

"We shall find him. And I shall watch him."

Rufus nodded. "He would not slip away easily." He gestured towards some camp stools round a makeshift table. "Sit, have some wine. It has been a long night; it will be longer still."

Shortly after the wine was poured, Ned appeared with Alfred, each seemingly propping the other upright.

"Your men are about to come through and announce the flight of Don Paulus," Ned said. He leaned against a tent post, closed his eyes, caught his breath. Alfred unceremoniously sank to the ground, wheezing.

By morning it was established that Don Paulus had slipped away with his horse and those of Bardolph and Crofter.

"And how to decide what direction?" Rufus rubbed his cold hands over the fire outside his tent and yawned. "He is not our concern. We must forget him, head for Windsor."

Though Ned cursed, Owen realised that Rufus was right. "As far as we know, Don Paulus has committed no crimes, has sought merely to save his own neck."

"He fed the fire, the bastard," Alfred protested.

"We cannot know whether he did it willingly or under duress," Rufus said. "I don't suppose you thought to ask him before you beat him?"

25

A REMARKABLY BRAVE LADY

The company stopped for the night at an inn just north of the Thames to clean themselves and see to their wounds; they would cross the river in the morning and ride on into Windsor.

Ned had become increasingly agitated as the day wore on. Now he chose to lie on his pallet rather than sitting below with his fellows over tankards of ale. "'Tis the river, Owen. The scent. Makes me see her, floating there." He pressed the heels of his hands to his eyes.

Owen had not thought how Ned would be once they reached Windsor. "You will feel better when you've visited her grave, old friend."

Ned said nothing.

"Let me see to your leg before I go down to the men." As Owen unwrapped the soiled bandage, he shook his head. "This will be a nasty scar, my handsome friend. What will your ladies say?"

"Save your breath. I've not thought of ladies since Mary's death. And I'll not be cheered." Ned jerked and took his hands from his face as Owen pressed a hot towel on the wounds. He propped himself up on his elbows to observe. "What are you doing to me?"

"Drawing out the poison." Owen studied his friend's face as he waited for the wound to soften with the heat. Ned looked healthier, more like himself than when Owen had found him on the moors. His brown eyes were focused now, but they still shifted uneasily. "What are you plotting now?" Owen wondered.

Ned dropped back on the bed, eyes closed. "I am plotting nothing, for pity's sake. Did I not give you my word I would go straight to Windsor?"

"Aye, you did." Owen lifted the hot cloth from the wound, washed it with a calendula rinse to stop the bleeding and encourage the skin to close over it, then rubbed in a soothing marshmallow salve.

"That wash stung as if you were slitting me open again. I begin to wonder whether you mean to heal me or kill me."

"I did not come all this way to lose you, you fool. I've fought for you and have the wounds to prove it. Lucie won't thank you for that."

"With all your scars, how will she notice?" Ned opened his eyes, propped himself up again. "I do thank you, old friend. I doubt I'll ever find a way to repay you."

"I pray I never need such help."

"How did you know to come back to the farmhouse?"

"It put me in mind of one in Normandy."

Ned was quiet, his eyes had a faraway look.

Owen stuffed everything into his pack, rose with a sigh. "And now I'm off in search of a sorely needed ale. Matthew waits without. He is your guard this evening. I am trusting you, in other words."

"We have fought long and well together, Owen."

"Aye, that we have."

"I'll entertain Matthew with tales of chivalry," Ned said to Owen's departing back.

Michaelo could not sleep. He rose from his vermin-infested bed and slipped quietly out of the inn to pace the courtyard and work out the stiffness in his hip and knee. The night was clear and chilly. Exhilarating.

"Who goes there?"

"*Benedicte.* 'Tis Brother Michaelo. I would walk a while in the courtyard."

"God go with 'ee." The guard walked on.

The excitement of the past week had stirred Michaelo's blood, made him restless. But for what? Some would say he had a most exciting, varied life. What did he lack? Would he wish to ride through the countryside in search of miscreants as a regular occupation?

Indeed not. God had protected him on this journey; but most soldiers died painful deaths. Even if they survived their exploits, they returned with wounds, missing limbs...Old age seemed disagreeable and ugly enough without a body malformed by years of limping or performing every chore with but one hand, or with old wounds and scars that ached in damp weather, grew stiff in the cold.

Consider Captain Archer. A handsome man, but for the scarred cheek and blind eye. Michaelo had noted how often Archer rubbed the scar, pressed the eye beneath the patch. And his left shoulder bothered him, too. Every morning the Captain paced back and forth, shrugging that shoulder round and round to warm it before mounting his steed for the day's long ride.

Even Archbishop Thoresby had scars from his early days when he had accompanied King Edward on campaign and travelled far and wide as a negotiator.

Still, what had Michaelo done with his life? Where had he ever been? Was his unmarked body the sign of intelligent caution or a life that had never begun?

Michaelo paced back and forth, shivering, but with no desire to withdraw to his bed. Why this restlessness? Was it his vows? Did he wish to be freed from them? Why would he wish that? A cleric's life was to his liking, comfortable and organised. He had never desired women; and his taste for men had been tamed into a chaste appreciation of beauty. It was perhaps odd to wear the habit of the Benedictines when he no longer lived among his order, but he was still of the order. What would happen when the Archbishop passed away? Michaelo had been granted special dispensation to serve as Archbishop Thoresby's secretary. Would he be sent back to St Mary's? He shivered and crossed himself at the prospect of the cold reception he would find there—too many still alive remembered his earlier self...His fellow Benedictines were a long-lived brotherhood.

The guard passed without comment, disappearing round the side of the inn. As soon as he was out of sight, a door creaked nearby. Michaelo stood still in the dark courtyard, held his breath. A cloaked man headed across the open space towards the stables, glancing round as he moved, a man who did not wish to be observed. Tingling with a sense of danger, Michaelo followed.

"Two empty pallets, two missing horses, and a man proving precious slow to wake. What were you playing at last night, eh? What were you drinking that you saw naught?" Rufus bellowed at the three men who had stood the night watch.

"I saw the monk," one replied, shame-faced. "He was pacing to and fro in the courtyard. I thought naught of it." The guard winced when Rufus raised a hand as if to strike.

But the large hand continued to Rufus's brow, the fingers soon engaged in rubbing as if to clear the head. "Why would His Grace's secretary flee with your friend, Captain Archer?"

Owen sat on the counter, draining a tankard of ale to wash down the night. He set down the empty tankard with a clatter. "He's no friend of mine. Never again shall I count him that. I went through hell to bring him safely to Windsor and he thanks me with flight." Owen jumped down, kicked a bench out of his way, strode out of the inn. But where to go?

Alfred and Rufus followed cautiously.

"I thought he swore he would go straight to Windsor Castle," Alfred said.

Owen glowered at the river mist. "Clear night and misty morning. What is God's purpose in that, I wonder?" And what had possessed Owen to leave Ned with Matthew last night? "I was a fool to trust him." And a fool to leave him.

"Where might he run, Captain?" Rufus asked. "Surely we cannot expect him in Windsor town, enjoying a brew at the tavern."

Owen rubbed the scar beneath his patch wearily. "Where indeed? Not away from trouble. We cannot hope for that." Windsor. Ned had vowed to go to Windsor. But castle or town? "Does Mistress Alice Perrers live at court or elsewhere at present, Rufus?"

"Both. At the castle her rooms are near His Grace's. In the

town she has a house on the river. You can see it from the bridge."

A house on the river. Ned would know the house from Mary. In Windsor town. "The Lord means to confound me," Owen growled. "Come, men. We must ride as fast we can to Mistress Perrers's house. There is a ferry before the bridge, eh?"

"You're thinking he would not trust the bridgekeeper to let him pass?"

Owen nodded. "To the ferry, Captain Rufus."

Shortly before dawn, a castle guard escorted Brother Michaelo to Archbishop Thoresby's quarters. Adam, nonplussed by the odd procession, woke his master for instructions.

"Michaelo is here?" Thoresby muttered, rubbing his eyes. "That is as it should be. Why wake me in the middle of the night?"

"Forgive me, Your Grace. But he comes with an armed escort. He wished them to follow him back into town. To Mistress Perrers's house."

By now Thoresby was reasonably awake. Michaelo and Alice Perrers? "Did he wish them to arrest her, Adam?"

Adam shrugged.

Well, there would be no more sleep this night. "Get me dressed, dammit, boy. But first tell them I am coming."

There was a commotion in the parlour as Thoresby awaited Adam's assistance, and Michaelo poked in his head. "Might I dress you, Your Grace, while we talk?"

"You?" Michaelo had always considered it beneath his station to dress Thoresby. "No. Adam shall do it. But stay here and tell me what's ado. I understand you wished for an armed guard to escort you to the bed of the King's whore."

"I wished to *save* her, Your Grace, not *ravish* her."

"Who *is* ravishing her, then?"

Michaelo stepped into the room, followed by Adam, followed by the guard.

"Remain just outside the door, if you will," Thoresby barked to the guard. "But do not hesitate to break down the door if I cry out."

The guard's look was one of alarm as he slipped out.

Thoresby nodded to Adam to prepare his clothes. "Now, Michaelo, quickly and without drama."

Michaelo took a seat, impatiently smoothed out the damp hem of his habit. "Captain Archer and company are yet across the Thames, perhaps even now discovering that Captain Townley and I are gone. I was wakeful last night. A curse under which I suffer, as you know—" at Thoresby's glare, Michaelo nodded. "Forgive me for wandering, Your Grace. I happened to be in the inn yard when Captain Townley slipped to the stables, retrieved something, I do not know what, and then made his way to a ferryman, waking him to demand passage at once across to Windsor town."

"Indeed? Why did he not cross by the bridge?"

"I doubt he trusted his right of passage, Your Grace."

"And you followed him?" Thoresby had a delightful image of Michaelo hanging to the edge of the ferry, being dragged through the muddy river water. But he did not look wet, though the journey had certainly taken its toll. "Did you offer to pay your share if invited to accompany him?"

Michaelo sniffed. "I did not. I had no worries about the bridge guard."

Thoresby stared at his secretary in amazement. "You rode alone? At night? You?"

Michaelo shrugged. "I waited for Townley on the other side and followed him to the house of Mistress Perrers. He is quite convinced that she is the cause of his troubles. I believe he means to kill her. So I hurried to the castle to enlist the aid of guards to come to her assistance. Instead they led me to you like a naughty child who must be punished for being abroad at night."

Thoresby was alarmed. "My cloak, Adam." He took Michaelo's arm. "Did you tell the guards your story?"

Michaelo shook his head. "Of course not. They need not know our business. I merely said I needed an armed escort to accompany me to the home of Mistress Perrers."

"They have wasted much time. Come."

Adam opened the door just in time for the Archbishop and his secretary to sweep through.

The maidservant who opened the door to Ned recognised him at once. "Master Townley! Oh dear. Oh. Did you not know about poor Mary? She is"—she wrung her hands—"not here."

"I know, Agnes. I know all about what has happened here." Ned clenched his hands, fighting for calm. The river mist swam round him in the open doorway, permeated the house. "I want to see your mistress."

Agnes clutched the shawl beneath her chin. "'Tis but the middle of the night. I cannot wake her."

"You need do naught but stand back from the door. I shall wake her." *Wake her so she knows death is near.*

"*You* wake her? You shall not!" Agnes set down her lamp with a clatter and rushed to close the door against the intruder.

Ned pushed; Agnes stumbled backwards. "Sit and behave, Agnes, and no harm will come to you."

Whimpering, Agnes sank down on a bench near the door.

Ned grabbed the lamp and peered round the room. Little to see in the dim light, but there was no need. He saw it all in his mind, Mary sitting by the hearth, bent over her sewing… "Mistress Perrers sleeps up in the solar?"

"Aye." Agnes sniffled. "With little John. You must not hurt little John."

Would Mary have borne a raven-haired son? "The child sleeps in the same room?"

"A partition separates the nurse and John from my mistress."

It was enough information. Ned climbed the open, ladderlike stairs awkwardly, his wounded leg dragging behind the other. Another thing for which to curse Perrers. At the top, Ned came face to face with the mistress.

"Down the stairs," Alice hissed, a knife flashing a warning. "I will not have you frightening the boy."

Armed though she was, Ned was taken aback by how young and vulnerable Alice Perrers seemed without her courtly trappings. Still, while he backed down the stairs he looked for a perch for the light so he might draw both his daggers. He had reached his goal and would have his revenge.

The ferryman cursed as he was once again wakened from a deep sleep by his equally cranky wife. "You see to them, woman. I cannot go till I've had me sleep. It matters nowt *who* they be."

"They be King's men, Colm. They want to know who you ferried tonight. And they say you must ferry them straightaway, else the King will have your head!"

"He's got everything else, why not that?" Colm grumbled, but he pulled himself out of bed, rising to find a stranger in his doorway. "King's man? A one-eyed rogue?" Colm spat on the floor.

Owen lifted Colm up by the cloth of his shift. "You shall row us across as soon as you are clothed, and you will be silent all the way, Ferryman," he said. "The man you ferried over earlier may be murdering one of the Queen's ladies at this very moment."

Alice ordered Agnes to stoke the fire. It now burned smokily. Even so, it produced some warmth. Yet Alice still clutched a length of cloth round her shoulders, much as Agnes had done. Her hair, pulled back from her face by an embroidered cap, tumbled in brown waves down her back. Not as beautiful as Mary's raven hair. But the King's bitch looked young with her hair down. Young, but never innocent. The cat eyes were far from innocent.

"I understand why you blame me, Ned," Alice was saying. "But I, too, am the victim of Sir William."

"Why were Wyndesore's men after me?"

A thin eyebrow raised. So calm. "Captain Archer has said nothing?"

What was this? Owen knew the cause and had not said? "What are you talking about?"

"My secret marriage. Poor Mary and Daniel were witnesses. I have no proof, but—"

"You married Wyndesore?"

A modest lowering of the lashes, a brief nod. "But the King would call it treason to speak of it."

Did he believe it? "What had I to do with it?"

Alice shrugged. "Mary might have confided in you?"

Ned closed his eyes, wiped sweat from his brow. "And Don Ambrose?"

"Officiated."

Ned shook his head. "No matter. You handed Mary over to Wyndesore, that's enough for me to know."

"I did not plan for her to have aught to do with him."

"Oh, aye, you planned to marry her off to someone better than me. She told me. But Wyndesore got to her first."

"I meant to help Mary. Ensure that she had a good life."

"Then why did you choose her as witness? You might have chosen Cecily or Isabeau as witness."

"Sir William chose her, not I."

"Stinking cow." Ned took a step towards Alice. She flashed her knife. He reached out and knocked it from her hand, enjoying the expression of alarm on her face. "Who murdered Mary?"

Alice pulled tight her shawl, a protective gesture, shook her head. "Some of Sir William's men, or men for hire. I swear I do not know."

"I do not believe you, Mistress Perrers." Ned began to toss his daggers from hand to hand.

• • •

Thoresby ordered the two guards who accompanied them to stand on either side of the door, out of sight but not of earshot. He would pretend he and Michaelo had come without escort.

A weeping maidservant opened the door. Thinking the worst, Thoresby pushed past her into the room.

"My lord Archbishop, are you come to rescue me?" Alice asked sweetly. She sat on a bench near the hearth. Ned stood behind her, one dagger to her throat, the other to her breast. Her arms appeared to be pinned at her side by a length of cloth.

Thoresby regretted the drama of his entrance. How did one reason with a cut-throat when it was plain one knew precisely what he meant to do? Why should Ned believe Thoresby would give him clemency? How could he possibly guess Thoresby would thank him for the murder of the common upstart? Or would he? Damn the woman, her soft brown hair undone, the gauzy shift. "Forgive me, Mistress Perrers, but it is Ned Townley I would save."

"Me?"

"I swore to Captain Archer that I would give you such protection as I was able, allow time to investigate the matter. But I warn you, Townley, should you commit any violence on Mistress Perrers, the King will have your head, no matter your reason, no matter my argument."

"He means to have it—" Ned stopped as Thoresby raised a hand to silence him.

"If my secretary speaks true, you have Bardolph and Crofter, the very men you claim can prove your innocence. Save your martyrdom for another time, a nobler cause. Mistress Perrers is not worth your life."

Ned's eyes suddenly moved to the door. "Your secretary? So it was Michaelo betrayed me?"

Michaelo stepped into the house. "I followed you from the inn."

Alice shifted slightly, gave a little cry as the dagger grazed her neck. "Sweet Heaven, if you mean to slit my throat, do it and be done with me!"

The prick had drawn blood. Ned glanced at it, grinned. "Not

long now, Mary," he whispered.

Thoresby must think how to dissuade Townley from injuring Alice. It was difficult, once tempted, he knew.

"God bless you for your effort on my behalf, Brother Michaelo," Alice said, "though it may yet come to naught. Could Agnes bring a cloth and see to my throat?"

Thoresby stared at Alice. The woman was remarkably calm.

Once over the Thames, Rufus had led Owen and company straight to Alice Perrers's house, where they found guards standing watch. Owen identified himself as Thoresby's captain.

"The Lord Chancellor is within, Captain Archer," the guard whispered, "and his secretary."

"And Mistress Perrers?"

"Aye. Captain Townley with her. He is in a murderous rage."

"Why are you not inside?"

"His Grace ordered us to stay without and listen for his call. He has not called."

"Townley has a skill with daggers," the other guard said. "If we were to rush in, he would use them, I've no doubt."

"Is there a rear door?"

"Aye. By the kitchen."

"Any others?"

"Nay."

"Alfred. Come with me. Rufus, choose two men to guard the back."

Alfred and Owen moved round the house to the back. As they drew close to a shuttered window, a woman's tearful voice cried, "The mistress is bleeding! Lord have mercy on us sinners! Help her!"

The back door, hung so that the cook did not struggle with it, swung easily inwards. Owen and Alfred entered the house silently.

• • •

Ned pressed the knife closer, drew another trickle of blood, glanced up at Thoresby, smiled to see him wince. "Why should Bardolph and Crofter admit to anything?"

Thoresby tried to keep his face impassive as he watched Owen creep into the room behind Ned. "They will confess to save their souls."

"Why worry about their souls now? They knew they were committing sin when they—" Ned stiffened, began to turn his head.

Blind on the left, Owen chose to grab Ned's right hand, the one holding the dagger at Alice's throat.

Ned stumbled backwards. Owen spun him round, knocked the dagger from his left hand, and threw him to the ground.

"Alfred, keep him down," Owen commanded.

Alfred dropped on to Ned.

Alice had slumped forwards. Agnes knelt before her, weeping and dabbing at something with a cloth.

Owen pulled the maid away, saw a crimson stain blooming on the cloth that bound Alice's arms. When he untied the cloth, her upper left arm bled freely.

Alice touched it. "It is nothing, Captain. I expected far worse."

"You are a brave woman, Mistress Perrers. I know something about wounds. Both that and the cut on your throat are causing some pain."

Thoresby noted the light in Alice Perrers's cat eyes as she studied the scarred face bent towards her.

"A little, yes, Captain. But I can bear it."

26

OWEN INTERROGATES

Unable to sleep, Owen paced his bedchamber in the great castle of Windsor. His sleeplessness was not lack of comfort. He had been given an officer's billet in the lower ward with a brazier that heated the room and two small windows that aired it. It was rather Ned's fate that set him to pacing. Ned had attacked the King's mistress, wounded her, no matter that the wounds were superficial, and had therefore been taken into custody. It was impossible that he should be spared. The fool. Had he but stayed with the company he might have been proved innocent and set free.

He might still have a chance. With Bardolph and Crofter under lock and key in Winchester Tower there was the possibility of a confession. Owen's hope lay in Bardolph. That moment in York when the man had risked discovery to beg Jehannes's blessing. Panic? The right words, the right mixture of sympathy and suggestion might coax the truth from him. Owen must try.

Hands idly playing with the papers strewn before him, Thoresby listened to Owen's proposal, a smile gradually brightening his face.

"You are amused?" Owen asked.

Thoresby pushed the papers aside, leaned across the table with an excited air. "If you managed a confession, naming names..." The deep-set eyes shone. "Do your best, Archer. If you can get him to state that Wyndesore gave him the orders—" head flung back, a throaty chuckle.

Owen thought the Archbishop had gone mad. "I do not understand this mood, Your Grace."

The dark eyes levelled at Owen. "The King could not ignore such an accusation. This would bring Wyndesore down."

"I had no idea you had such an ambition for the man."

"Not him. Alice Perrers. The ambitions of both were at stake in this deadly game. The King would cast her out."

His petty court intrigues again. "I do this for Ned and justice, Your Grace. Not to bring down a lady I barely know."

"Yes, yes," Thoresby said, waving aside Owen's protest. "Michaelo will arrange for your meeting with Bardolph. And he will be your witness. There is a room in Winchester Tower partitioned with a thin wall. Michaelo will be your invisible scribe the other side."

Bardolph had haunted eyes and stank of fear. He winced when Owen handed him a cup of ale, as if expecting a blow.

"Rest easy. I want to talk, no more." Owen was grateful for the half-dozen lamps Michaelo had provided. The high window did nothing to freshen or light the tower room. Even here at ground level it was damp, dark, cold. What must the dungeon be like? As Owen studied the man who had spent the past several days down below, he held his breath, listening for Michaelo. Silence. "Go ahead. Drink."

Peering at Owen, disbelieving, Bardolph shakily raised the cup to his cracked lips.

"They have denied you drink?" Owen asked.

Bardolph gulped, wiped his mouth on his sleeve, shook his head.

"Your lips. I thought perhaps..."

"Nay. I lick 'em in the cold."

Or when nervous, more like. "I have a balm that would help."

"'Tis no matter." Bardolph drained the cup.

Owen raised the pitcher. "More?"

"Won't say no." But as Owen brought the pitcher forward, Bardolph frowned, as if remembering something, and covered his cup. "Men say you're Townley's old friend."

"Aye, that I am."

A shake of the shaggy head, as if warding off flies. "How do I know you don't mean to poison me?"

"Why would I do that, Bardolph?"

Bardolph's eyes slid sidewise. "Being in gaol makes a man wary."

"No doubt. But why would I poison you?"

Bardolph sniffed, said nothing.

"Have you done something to Captain Townley?"

The shadowed eyes blinked. Bardolph gripped the cup, confusion clouding his face momentarily. "Our last meeting was not friendly."

Owen nodded. "No, not friendly. But I could see you meant to smoke him out, not burn him alive. Go on. I've shared this pitcher with you and we're neither of us on the floor, eh? I want to talk to you is all."

"Why?"

"I would like to understand what drove my friend to attack the King's mistress."

Bardolph shook his head. "I know naught what's between them." He lifted his hand from the cup, held it out to Owen.

While Owen poured, he considered his next words. Bardolph was no subtle thinker, but neither was he stupid.

"I thank you, Captain," Bardolph said, raising the cup and nearly draining it. He belched with satisfaction as he set it down. But the hands still trembled.

"What was your business in York?"

Bardolph squinted. "Eh?"

"You were in York?"

The man squirmed. "Who says I was?"

"Don Jehannes, the Archdeacon of York. Was he mistaken?"

Bardolph's lower lip dabbed at the sweat beading on his upper lip. "I passed through York."

"And you asked the Archdeacon's blessing—and forgiveness."

A wince. The eyes searched the room for a safe reply. "We are all of us sinners in this world, Captain."

"Aye. That we are, Bardolph, that we are. And you were feeling the weight of your past that day, were you?"

"Sommat like."

Owen nodded. "As soldiers we live with troubling memories." He rubbed the scar beneath his patch. "Killed the woman who did this to me. And her man."

Bardolph studied Owen with sympathetic eyes. "I remember the night you told the tale in York Tavern. You had reason to kill them."

Owen took a long drink, placed his cup carefully on the table. "Doesn't help in the middle of the night, when I lie awake wondering about the state of my soul."

Bardolph squirmed. "Aye. 'Tis worst in the dark." The lower lip dabbed at the sweaty upper. The eyes looked even more haunted.

"Fair is fair. I've told you my nightmare. What's yours?"

A shake of the head. "I did not ask for your confession."

Owen settled back on the bench, leaning his head against the wall, stretched out his legs, closed his eyes. "Sometimes a scent brings it back. Blood, salt air and damp earth." He was quiet a moment, listening to Bardolph's laboured breathing. "Sometimes I hear them. In my sleep. Their cries. I suppose that's God's way of making sure we don't forget our sins. The memories that haunt us."

"Some folk aren't bothered." The voice trembled.

Still with his eyes closed, Owen shook his head. "I don't care to be round a man with no conscience. No better than a beast, to my mind."

"Beasts. He calls us that."

"Who?"

Sharp intake of breath. "No one."

"Someone calls you and Crofter beasts?"

"Train us till we snarl and snap like mad dogs, pet us when we kill the right folk, prod us with a pitchfork back into the pit when we act on our own. 'Tis ever the same."

"Is that what you were doing? Acting on your own?"

The brows came together, lower lip over upper. Shake of the

head. "Don't know what you mean."

"Someone called you beasts because you acted on your own?"

A shrug. "Trouble in Dublin. Got drunk. We didn't know who he was."

"And Sir William called you beasts?"

"Aye."

So Wyndesore had something on them. Promising.

"You would have nightmares about Gervase and Henry had you seen them after they had been left up on the moor." Owen took his time describing the bloated, torn bodies. It made his own stomach lurch. Bardolph sweated freely now in the chilly room, his trembling worsened. "I cannot believe Captain Townley would murder them," Owen said, "leave them like that, then lead me to the site and show me what he had done. Can you, Bardolph?"

The head hung low. "You buried 'em?"

"Aye. Up there on the moors."

"God ha' mercy," Bardolph muttered, crossing himself.

"What I cannot understand is why? Why did Gervase and Henry die?"

"Ask your friend." An attempt at a sneer, but Bardolph almost choked on the words.

"How can you be so certain it was Townley? For that matter, did you see him murder Don Ambrose? What makes you think he's such a—beast? I have known him"—Owen shrugged—"a score of years? Almost. And in that time he never to my knowledge committed such a deed."

"They say he attacked Mistress Perrers."

"Aye. He did. Scratched her throat and arm, no more than that. He holds her responsible for the drowning of his ladylove. Have you ever been in love?"

"I've had my sport."

"But love?" Owen poured himself more wine, held the flagon towards Bardolph. "You look thirsty."

Bardolph held the cup out for more, took a long drink. His nose reddened. "Don't know as I've ever found that sort of woman.

Crofter did. He's got wife and children."

Owen nodded. "Why were you ordered to murder Don Ambrose?"

Bardolph shook his head. "You mean to confuse me."

"I've no need to confuse you. I know you are guilty, Bardolph. You killed Gervase and Henry because they discovered you'd killed Don Ambrose. But why did you kill the friar?"

"I did not kill him. Nor the other two."

"We've found a shepherd who swears he saw you and Crofter dragging Gervase and Henry to the stream." A lie, but God would surely forgive him.

The head shot up, eyes wide with shock. "No one saw"—he ducked—"Lord ha' mercy." Bardolph crossed himself.

"If it wasn't because of Don Ambrose, then why did you murder them, Bardolph? They were your comrades."

Bardolph shook his head. "Nay. Hardly knew 'em. But we didn't plan it. Swear to you, Captain."

"Then why?"

Bardolph frowned into his cup, breathing shallowly and blinking as sweat dripped on to his eyelashes. "We heard them talking about us. Thought something stank about the friar's disappearance, you see. And Crofter said when we caught up with Townley those two'd want to take him straight to Windsor. But we did not mean him to reach the castle."

"Why?"

A shrug. "Crofter said so."

"Who gave Crofter his orders?"

"No one."

But Wyndesore. Say it, dammit. "You told Abbot Richard that Sir William of Wyndesore sent you north to watch Townley, just in case he had murdered the page."

"Aye."

"But he sent you north to murder the friar and Townley, eh?"

A sharp shake of the head. "No."

Who was he protecting? "You are marked for death, Bardolph. Don't you want to confess your sins?"

"You're not a priest."

A deep breath. "So you dumped Henry and Gervase near the monk road, hoping Abbot Richard would accuse Captain Townley?"

A nod.

Owen remembered Michaelo listening, writing. "Do I have that right?"

"Aye."

Owen rose, paced back and forth a while, sat down, raking his hand through his wiry hair. Bardolph peered at Owen over the rim of his cup, his breath a laboured wheezing.

"No." Owen shook his head. "It does not fit together."

"What?"

"You were sent north to eliminate Don Ambrose and Captain Townley, weren't you?"

A pause as Bardolph wiped his glistening face on his sleeve. "Crofter said we must."

At last. "Why?"

Bardolph shook his head slowly back and forth, back and forth, like some great woolly beast. "As God is my witness, I do not know, Captain. I do not know." He reached up his large hands to his head and pulled at his greasy hair. His eyes seemed to grow larger, his face crumpled. He sobbed, "I am damned for all eternity and I don't know why!" He dropped to his knees on the stone floor and rocked, sobbing.

Owen found it difficult to pity the man with so much blood on his hands. "Sir William ordered you to do this. And because of that accidental slaying in Dublin, you obeyed."

"No." The woolly head rocked from side to side. "He knew naught of this."

"Why did these men need to die?"

"Ask Crofter."

"I am asking you, Bardolph."

"Something to do with honour. And ours, being his men. Crofter said we must do this."

"Wyndesore's honour?"

"He is our lord."

"And you did all this without his knowing?"

"Aye. Crofter said we must."

"And you do all Crofter tells you?"

"He's smart."

"I am surprised, Bardolph. You seem to be a man with a conscience."

A shrug.

"Did you tell the friar something to make him fear Townley?"

"Nay. 'Twasn't us. But we used his fear."

"Mary and Daniel. What of them?"

Bardolph stopped rocking. His eyes slid to the partition. "What was that noise?"

"Rats. Surely they visit you below?"

"'Tis a hellish place."

"What did you have to do with the deaths of Mary and Daniel?"

"We didn't touch those two. Had others see to them."

"Two innocent young people and you never asked why?"

A shrug. "Crofter said we must."

Crofter snorted. "Knew he would fall apart. But he wouldn't've told you we had orders, because we didn't."

Owen doubly despised this man, for the murders and for pulling Bardolph down into the mire. "Then what made you do it?"

A sly smile. "Sir William's a good lord. When he has good fortune, so do his men. I heard there were some knew something might ruin him. They had to be silenced. For the good of us all."

"Sir William told you this?"

A roll of the eyes. "He's not one to complain. I keep my ears pricked, is all."

"And you took it upon yourself to murder—how many, Crofter?"

"You're the cunning spy, Captain. I'll leave it to you to count 'em."

. . .

Thoresby paced his parlour. "Damn them. How can two common soldiers confound my purpose?" He threw Michaelo's account down on the table. "Damn them."

"They will soon be dead, and damned I'm sure, Your Grace," Owen said. He yearned for a long sit with a tall tankard of Tom Merchet's ale.

"I fear she has won, Archer. Her stench is everywhere at court."

The man was obsessed. "This has naught to do with Alice Perrers. Wyndesore is far more a demon than she is."

Thoresby shook his head. "You are wrong there. It has everything to do with her."

27

CONFESSOR TO THE DAMNED

A chilly dawn rain fell as Wykeham hurried to Winchester Tower in the middle ward. He was acting as confessor to Bardolph and Crofter, condemned for arranging the murders of Daniel and Mary, and carrying out the murders of Don Ambrose, Gervase, and Henry. King Edward thought the councillor's offer a harmless act of penance for being more disappointed in the outcome of the mission to the Cistercian abbeys than sorry for the deaths. But Wykeham's motive was morbid curiosity.

To murder three people, arrange for the murders of two others, all for the protection of a lord who, they claimed, knew nothing of these deeds was an act of sublime madness. Had they in good faith believed Wyndesore would wish for such protection? If not, what had inspired such violence? Surely not hatred. They hardly knew their victims. Wykeham could not sleep for the unease the questions aroused.

The guard jerked to his feet, rubbing his eyes, and bowed to Wykeham. He had been nodding, not surprising at this early hour. Wykeham blessed the guard. "I am here as confessor to the two men who are to die tomorrow."

The guard shook his head. "They be murderin' thieves, *Domine*. Have a care."

As he gingerly descended the narrow stone stairs, Wykeham wondered what lie the guard had been told; the entire business was still shrouded in mystery, the King still insistent that the marriage of Perrers and Wyndesore be kept a secret.

The guard stopped at a heavy door, used a large key to open it. "I shall stand guard, *Domine*. Call out if they give you trouble."

Wykeham bowed his tall frame through the low doorway, rose cautiously; his head brushed the ceiling while he yet bent forward. Awkward for a tall man. He wondered who had designed this tower; had it been intended for a prison? Was the low ceiling part of the punishment?

Lifting the lantern to shoulder height, he saw that the condemned men lay at opposite ends of the small room, each asleep on a pile of clean straw. One stirred as the light shone on him. Crofter. The other remained still. A table with two stools stood between them, on it a pitcher and cups, bowls, spoons, and an oil lamp. The men were neither chained nor bound. Wykeham wondered who had seen to their decent treatment—it was comfortable for a dungeon.

"Who goes there?" Crofter demanded, struggling to rise.

"Sir William of Wykeham, come to hear your confession."

"We have confessed already."

"I am here to shrive you."

"The King's man? Are we such important prisoners, then?"

"All men's souls are important to the Lord."

"But not the King? Or is His Grace curious? Wants to hear how we grovel?"

Wykeham paid him no heed; the man had cause to be bitter, taking the blame for crimes he may have been ordered to commit. "You might confess to me in private before your friend wakens."

"We have no secrets, Bardolph and me." Crofter glanced towards Bardolph. "Still. He isn't waking." He shrugged, rose to his knees, folded his hands. "I confess to those sins for which I stand accused."

"Do you feel remorse for your sins, Crofter?"

"I do."

"Then why did you commit them?"

Crofter squinted at Wykeham, puzzled. "I judged it my duty, sir."

This had been his claim throughout the past days. He never varied in his explanation. "Had Sir William ever ordered you to perform such a task?"

"He knew naught of this. I've said that."

"I understand that Wyndesore knew nothing of your scheme, but were there other occasions when he asked you to risk your salvation? Something to convince you he would condone such a solution?"

Crofter shrugged. "We are soldiers, sir. 'Tis the sort of thing we do. Only difference is whether the Church has blessed the act, seems to me."

Wykeham crossed himself.

"Ever kill a man, sir?"

"No. God has spared me that need."

Crofter nodded. "That is why you cannot see it. Duty. A soldier's duty is to defend by force."

Wykeham wondered who had put that simple-minded idea in the man's head. "Your comrade did not appear to agree with you when he begged forgiveness of the Archdeacon of York."

Crofter shrugged. "Bardolph has ever been a worrier. Not cowardly, mind you. Just thinks too much. Perhaps he asked forgiveness in case we were wrong to protect Sir William in such way. But you must ask him." Crofter rose, stooping slightly under the low ceiling, shuffled over to his mate. "Bardolph. Chaplain has come. He's an important man. He won't wait." Crofter shook his inert friend. Bardolph did not move. "Bardolph, did you hear me? Bardolph!"

Alarmed, Wykeham joined Crofter, touched Bardolph's neck, his wrist, felt no flutter of life. The flesh was cold. He had been a fool not to question the deep sleep. "Has he been ill?"

Crofter met Wykeham's eyes, shrugged. "He's been sweating a lot. Wakeful. 'Tis why I was relieved he slept so sound."

"Sweating and wakeful?"

"Aye. Frightened of dying, frightened of the fires of Hell." A deep breath. "He's dead, isn't he?"

"I fear he is. Though not long dead." Wykeham shone the lantern on Bardolph, turned his shaggy head this way and that, examined his arms. He saw no obvious signs of violence. The man seemed as if resting peacefully.

But Crofter was too quiet, too calm for a man who had just discovered a friend's death. Nor would he raise his eyes to Wykeham's. The privy councillor sent for Owen Archer.

Owen stood at the window staring out between the iron bars to the grey May sky. Rain drummed on the grill; the damp seeped through the chinks in the stone and glistened on the walls like a fine sweat. "I once considered myself exiled."

"But it is not the same thing at all, is it?" Ned said wearily. "You could return to Wales."

"What were the odds, eh?"

"As high as the odds of my being pardoned, I suppose."

Owen turned towards his friend, watched as Ned paced back and forth from corner to corner of the tiny cell, working the stiffness from his joints. Tomorrow he must leave for Dover; he would have three days to make his way there and take ship. After that he was an outlaw, subject to immediate execution if caught in the kingdom. It would be a hard ride, with only enough money to buy his way on to a ship as crew. "From Lancaster's spy to this. You've been a fool, my friend."

Ned stopped in front of Owen, grabbed his friend's shoulders, squeezed them. "I did what I felt honour-bound to do. For Mary. I only regret that I involved you and your family. And that the King won't grant me a few moments at Mary's grave."

Owen looked away from the intensely sad eyes. "I tried."

"I know you did, my friend. I'll never forget all you've done."

Owen had attempted to sneak Ned out in Alfred's clothes, but the guards were too well-trained.

"Where will you go?"

"Where the wind takes me."

Forcing himself to meet his friend's eyes, Owen clasped Ned's still upraised arms. "I shall miss you, despite the fool's chase you led me."

Their arms fell away.

Ned resumed his pacing. "Neither of her wounds were serious."

"It was the threat, not the wounds, Ned. And she protested the King's initial sentence." The King had ordered Ned beheaded, but Alice Perrers had begged for clemency.

"Aye, she did that. But what of Wyndesore? What will he pay for this?"

Owen turned back to the iron-crossed sky. "His men have sworn he knew nothing of their effort to protect him."

"He does not deserve her. She is a brave, elegant lady," Ned said, sounding wistful.

"Mistress Perrers?"

"Aye. Have you ever seen such courage?"

The dreamy look in Ned's eyes cheered Owen a little. It was more like the Ned he had known as an archer. "You said you no longer thought of women."

Ned shrugged. "She liked you. 'Twas plain in those cat eyes of hers."

"No doubt she would have looked kindly on anyone come to rescue her."

"You deny it for Lucie's sake?"

Owen laughed. "Will you write from exile to tell her?"

A rap on the door. "Message for Captain Archer," the guard called out.

"Important man, you are, my friend."

Owen opened the door.

"Sir William of Wykeham asks that you come right away, Captain. He found Bardolph dead in his cell."

"Murdered?" Owen asked.

"The messenger did not say."

Ned crossed himself. "Some hasten their own end, fearing the axe."

Owen shook his head. "In Bardolph's case I very much doubt it. He was worried for his soul. I doubt he would take his own life."

"Crofter?"

"I am sure of it. Those cold eyes. Let us pray it was less painful than what the King planned."

"I cannot share your concern for his comfort."

• • •

Bardolph's body had been moved to a room with more light. Wykeham greeted Owen, beckoned him over to the table where Bardolph lay. "I doubt he died unaided, Captain Archer. But I find no marks about him."

"Poison?"

Wykeham shrugged. "I have no training in such things. But as your wife is a master apothecary and you have studied the craft, I hoped you might tell."

"Only in the case of some poisons is there aught to see, Sir William. And only a foolish man uses such poisons, or a man who need not worry about being punished. But Bardolph's behaviour and appearance before he died might tell us something."

"His comrade said he was sweating and wakeful."

"Do you trust Crofter?"

Wykeham grimaced. "He seems too calm about the death of his comrade."

Owen nodded, turned to look Wykeham in the eye. "The King's surgeon might be more knowledgeable in this."

Wykeham dropped his eyes to his folded hands. "We wish to keep this matter as quiet as possible, Captain."

Adam poured wine for three, set the flagon in front of Thoresby, and departed. Thoresby nodded to Owen and Wykeham, who lifted their mazers. "May God grant an end to this plague of murders with Crofter's death at dawn," Thoresby said, "though he be guilty only of poor judgement in his loyalty." The three drank.

Owen put the mazer down before his thirst was quenched. It was after compline and he must yet tell the chancellor and the councillor what he had learned in an exhausting day of poking and prodding guards and comrades of Bardolph and Crofter. He must stay awake.

"Shall we ever know the truth of it, Captain?" Wykeham asked.

Owen glanced up at the councillor to see whether he meant the question in jest; surely he understood by now that the truth was not meant to be known. But the heavy-lidded eyes held no guile. "Crofter has ceased to speak to anyone. Neither he nor Bardolph shared confidences with their other comrades, or if they did they frightened them into silence. I did learn this: Crofter's wife has received the deed for a sizeable property in the fens to hold for her eldest son's maturity, property that formerly belonged to the Wyndesore family. It is said that Wyndesore did not wish the family to suffer for Crofter's sins."

"He did not wish Crofter to reveal his orders before he died, more like." Thoresby said, his disgust apparent in his voice.

Owen wondered when Thoresby had aged so. His lids crinkled over his deep-set eyes, he had jowls, though his face had little flesh elsewhere.

Wykeham seemed quite young in contrast. His face was unlined, his eyes were clear and earnest. "And Bardolph's family? Has Wyndesore provided for them?"

"He had none."

"Ah." Wykeham sat back in his seat, frowning slightly.

Thoresby nodded. "He could not be bought, who had no heirs."

"What did you learn from the guards about Bardolph's condition in his last days?" Wykeham asked.

Owen allowed himself another sip of wine. "They describe him as by turns quiet and frantic, wrapped in blankets with chills and then suddenly throwing them off and crying that he could not breathe, the air was too heavy. I am unsure what he was being fed, but I've little doubt he was receiving or had received a slow poison. I witnessed the sweating, thought it fear."

"A poison administered by Crofter?" Thoresby asked.

"That is my guess, but we'll never know for certain. As I said, Crofter is suddenly dumb."

"You searched Crofter and the room?" Wykeham asked.

"I did."

"And?"

"I found nothing. Of course."

"But you thought he had been ill with fear."

"But now he's dead. And the men had been travelling with Don Paulus, who is known in some quarters as a herbalist who asks no questions. It is curious that the friar survived his journey with Crofter and Bardolph. Others were not so fortunate."

"Have they found Don Paulus?" Wykeham asked.

"No."

"They must continue to search."

"To what end?" Thoresby demanded, pressing the bridge of his nose, his eyes closed. "He will not speak. Why should he? What would he gain?"

"We must know whether Crofter poisoned Bardolph," Wykeham insisted.

"For Heaven's sake, give it up!" Thoresby cried. "No one wishes to know that but you. Bardolph would have been dead come morning. What does it matter if the man who was to die with him hastened the end for him? How would we know whether it was out of fear of exposure or charity? Eh? Speculation. All speculation. We have no proof. We shall never have any proof." Thoresby nodded to Owen. "You look weary to the bone. I shall keep you no longer."

"Weary I am," Owen said, rising. He wondered at the Archbishop's outburst, but not so much that he wished to linger.

After Owen had taken his leave, Thoresby refilled his mazer, passed the flagon to Wykeham. "You must pardon my temper. It comes of frustration." He shook his head as Wykeham began to reply. "The King has commanded me to cease my probing. He wishes for some peace. He will hear no more of this."

"Because of Prince Edward's illness?"

"Aye. The Queen is concerned by Lancaster's report that the Prince cannot rise from his bed, though the Prince himself sends word that he is well, recovering as quickly as ever."

"It is fortunate that Lancaster is with his brother so we may know the truth."

"Fortunate? To frighten the Queen when she is herself so ill?" Had Thoresby been Phillippa's son, he would have kept the worry from her. But he did not care to discuss the Queen with Wykeham. "I understand you volunteered to be confessor to the condemned men, Sir William."

Wykeham sat with flagon in hand, one finger tracing the intricate silverwork on the lid. Eyes still on the flagon, he said quietly, "I beg you to forgive my accusation that you meant to trick me out of the chancellor's chain. I feel ill tonight, thinking of six lives lost for an ageing King's vanity and a soldier's plotting." Slowly, as if fearful it would shatter, Wykeham rested the flagon on the table. He lifted his mazer, raised his eyes to Thoresby. "You came to me in friendship and I mistrusted you. May God bless you, my Lord Chancellor, and forgive me for my ignorance."

Thoresby shook his head. "There is no need for forgiveness. What man would welcome the revelation that the jewel he had just won in an honest, exhausting contest had a flaw that rendered it worthless?"

Wykeham's head shot up. "Worthless? Hardly that. Requiring cautious handling, perhaps, but not worthless. I seek to influence the King for the good. His reign has been glorious; it shall be again."

Thoresby found Wykeham absurdly idealistic for one who had been at court so long. Sadly, he recognised much of himself in the councillor. He was vain. Naive. Thoresby despaired. There would be no enlightenment for Wykeham. He would push through to the chancellorship. He would work hard, hoping to ensure that justice was served. And slowly, after years of puzzling over the King's judgements, he would realise how personal were Edward's decisions, how he saw the law as his to bend and form to his taste. And when the King detected the sorrow in Wykeham's eyes, the disapproving purse of his lips, he would find another ambitious, clever man, acquire for him a bishopric, and transfer the chain.

"What saddens you?" Wykeham asked.

"I have been foolish. I thought to save you. But you will not be saved."

28

DIPLOMACY

Impatient with the tailor's hesitant tugs and anxious mutterings, the King yanked at the costly cloth, a blue background embroidered with gold garters for his Order. "Are you a tailor or a gnat? Fit me and be done with it!" Edward's roar was as loud and resounding as ever.

Thoresby had sought the King with a matter that could not be discussed in front of the tailor. And so the chancellor sat near the hearth and attempted to distract the King from the annoying little man so that they might still speak civilly before the day was out. Thoresby fortunately had some fresh anecdotes heard at last night's dinner with Archer and a courtier whom Thoresby had been surprised to learn was a poet, Geoffrey Chaucer. Leave it to a Welshman to sniff out the bards at court.

"Master Chaucer has a sly wit," Edward said. "Clever man. He has the eye of a master tailor when sizing up a man's worth." A meaningful glance at the anxious face focused on the royal shoulders. "I find Chaucer useful. I warn you, John, do not think to add him to your staff. Phillippa would not have it."

"I have no intention of adding to my household, Your Grace."

An eyebrow raised. "No? Hm." The broad shoulders twitched under the exploring hands of the tailor. "Why did he dine with you?"

"I thought to cheer Captain Archer. Chaucer is one of the few folk at court can tease laughter from my grim spy."

"Ah." The King nodded. "Your Welsh archer. Discourage that friendship, John. Spies should not become friends. Tomorrow they may need to betray each other."

"I am finished, Your Grace," the tailor murmured. He clumsily folded the cloth and backed out of the room, bobbing obsessively.

"A runt of a tailor. The French are all runts," Edward muttered. "So." The fading blue eyes rose to Thoresby's suddenly solemn face. "What is amiss, John? Your good cheer strikes a false note. Something troubles you."

Thoresby sucked strength from deep within, used it to lift the heavy chain from his shoulders and, holding it out before him, voiced the words he had rehearsed throughout the night. "Forgive me, Your Grace, but I believe it is God's will that I resign the chancellorship. I grow too old and vague to serve you well and wisely." He handed the chain to the servant who hovered at the King's shoulder.

The King narrowed his eyes, gazing on the chain dripping through the servant's outstretched fingers. Slowly, Edward raised his head to Thoresby, his lined face flushed unattractively with anger. "God's will, John? And what of *my* will? What of your King's will? Is there treason in your heart? Do you agree with the upstart Austins who claim I forfeit my right to rule when I fall from grace? You condemn me for Alice, John. I know that you do. And I know what you've been about with your spy, trying to save the bastard who attacked Alice. So that he may try again!"

Jesu, what could Thoresby say to that? "My stepping down has nothing to do with Mistress Perrers. Nor did I make enquiries to annoy you, Your Grace. I merely wished to know the truth."

The blue eyes narrowed, sharp chin lifted. "You know too much and you grow frightened, John, that is the truth of it. Because you have divulged Alice's secret? Is that what worries you so?"

"I have not spent a lifetime at court without learning the wisdom of silence, Your Grace." Or of lies carefully chosen.

"Who knows of Wyndesore and Alice? Your ferret Florian? Your Welsh spy? Your elegant secretary?"

"None of them, Your Grace. My sole confidant has been your privy councillor."

"Wykeham? You are the sly one. You stink of the moors. Perhaps that is where you belong. Leave me."

. . .

As Owen lifted his hand to knock on the door he felt an excitement that surprised him. A private supper with Mistress Alice Perrers. A rare privilege. She had sent word that she wished to thank him for coming to her aid against Ned, whom she knew to be Owen's friend. How could he refuse?

Thoresby had raised an eyebrow, pronounced Owen a brave man.

"Brave? To dine with a beautiful lady?"

"To dine with the King's lady. In private."

Owen remembered the look in the cat eyes, the look that even Ned had noted. Should he worry?

Alice Perrers rose from a thronelike chair as Gilbert showed Owen into the gaily lit chamber. Her silk gown matched the candlelight; her eyes glowed with it. Her hair, caught up with gold netting sprinkled with amethysts, shone gold and red. A trick of light and jewels, yet so like the colour of Lucie's hair that Owen wondered about Alice's purpose. But she had never seen Lucie.

"God be with you, Captain Archer," Alice said. She had a deep, resonant voice that caressed the ear. "I have ordered a feast fit for the courageous man who saved me."

Owen felt like a fly caught in a spider's web—by his own fascination. There was something compelling in her eyes, voice, movements. "It was my duty, Mistress Perrers."

Alice smiled sweetly. "You are modest, Captain. Come. Sit. Gilbert, pour the wine." Her silk gown whispered as she moved gracefully, gesturing for Owen to sit, resuming her own seat.

Candlelight reflected off silver spoons and plates, Italian glass goblets. The table at which Gilbert stood ready to serve was laden with costly covered serving dishes from which came mouth watering aromas. Owen had thought Thoresby's table grand, but it was nothing compared with this. And surely there was far more food here than two could eat.

"Who else joins you this evening?"

Alice's delicate eyebrows lifted in surprise, then her entire face brightened with amusement. "No one else. Please, do sit down, Captain." She waved Owen into the chair opposite her. "I have heard much about you that intrigues me." As they sipped their wine and Gilbert served, Alice entertained Owen with stories she had heard about him, some accurate, most not, but all complimentary.

Owen, feeling more and more as if he were being wrapped up in a silky cocoon, at last begged Alice to tell him something of her own life. She told him of her foster parents, how jolly life had been among their large brood, how confusing it had been when her uncles had taken her away, put her in a convent school. Owen assumed he was meant to pity her, but looking round at the splendour of her apartment at court, he found it difficult.

"My wife and I took in an orphan," he said.

"But you have a child of your own."

"You seem to know a great deal about me."

"The chancellor is proud of his godchild."

Owen's scar itched, reminding him that he must tread this web with care, that it could be deadly no matter how charming the weaver. Alice Perrers knew too much about his family. He was not here merely as a courtesy.

When they had progressed from the meat to a plate heaped with dates and nuts, Alice remarked, "I imagine you are puzzled why I insisted on a private meeting."

"I did wonder whether it was wise, when courtiers take such pleasure in gossip."

Alice inclined her head slightly. "I wished to tell you that I tried to convince the King that Ned Townley had reason to act as he did. But His Grace did not find it sufficient cause. He insisted on exile."

"I have heard you argued for exile rather than execution."

Alice's right hand, on which an amethyst ring twinkled, rose to silence Owen. "Since I could not save Ned from exile, I have provided him with letters of introduction. They should help him find service in the Aquitaine, if not with Lancaster, then with someone suitable."

A generous act, were it not for the fact that Alice's reputation, her standing at court had been saved by the death of Ned's lady.

Owen saw that Alice Perrers expected gratitude; instead he tasted gall. He lifted his goblet. "To your efforts on Ned's behalf."

Alice tilted her head quizzically. "Drink to my efforts? No. Let us drink to Ned's future."

"Odd to drink to such an uncertain thing as my friend's future."

The amber eyes studied Owen over the rim of the exquisite goblet. Alice sipped, set the goblet down. "You are not pleased. How have I offended?" Her look of dismay was almost convincing.

"You have caused Ned immeasurable pain. You owe him far more than letters."

A hand to her delicate throat. "Indeed?" How did she manage a blush? Or was it controlled anger? "What do I owe him?"

Owen was intrigued now. How far would she take this act of innocence? "You owe Ned Mary's life. But of course it is impossible to bring her back."

"You accuse me of Mary's death?" The question was a whisper. The eyes glistened with tears. The too bare bosom moved as with a restrained sob.

"You might have protected her. And warned Ned and Don Ambrose of their danger. To my mind you are as guilty of the deaths as your husband is."

The painted lips opened slightly in surprise. "My husband? Who told you of that?"

"Do you know, Ned was sent away without a chance to visit Mary's grave." Owen closed his eyes, bowed his head.

"I did what I could."

Owen glanced up, surprised by the emotion in the quiet voice.

But Alice had regained control. She lifted an embroidered napkin, dabbed at her lips. "Surely you understand the power of the men involved? Not just the King. Wyndesore, too."

"Are you saying that power excuses murder?"

"I am saying that I have little freedom, Captain. I am in the clutches of two powerful men."

Owen glanced round the room. "A comfortable clutch."

A becoming rose flushed her skin from neckline to veil.

"Thoresby has poisoned your mind against me."

Owen set down his goblet, rose with a courteous bow. "On the contrary, Mistress Perrers, His Grace does not care to speak of you. I thank you for your hospitality."

Alice rose also. "He does speak of me. I know that he does. What does he plan, Captain?"

Owen feasted on her one last moment. "Our King is a fortunate man, Mistress Perrers. I thank you for a delightful evening."

Alice crossed to him, placed her hands on his shoulders, looked into his eye, then kissed him on the lips, a lingering kiss. When she stood back from him, her smile was that of a cat who has just tasted of forbidden cream. "Mistress Wilton is also fortunate."

"I think, Mistress Perrers, you have nothing to fear from the Lord Chancellor. He tires of court and would be quit of it."

"God go with you, Owen Archer."

As Owen walked back through the castle precinct he thought it a good thing that for Ned he must hate Alice Perrers.

Thoresby sat quietly, reading the compline service, when Adam tiptoed into the chamber. "What is it, lad?" the Archbishop asked wearily.

"The Queen sends for you. She asks that you come at once."

"So late in the evening?" Was she ill? Did she send for him for confession? "I shall be there at once."

The Queen sat on her canopied bed, swathed in silk. She held her right hand out to Thoresby while her left hand stroked a puppy that lay curled on her lap. Two ladies of the chamber fussed with pillows and a tray of wine. "Sit here, where I might speak quietly," Phillippa said, patting the top of a chair pulled up beside her. Her round face had some colour this evening, the bags under her eyes were less evident. But she trembled when she moved, as if weak.

Thoresby sat, troubled by this new symptom, yet relieved by the normal domestic activity in the room. "God be thanked that you are well, my lady."

"Well?" Phillippa shrugged. "God has spared me, though I would not say I am well. Still, I shall not complain. I have had a long, happy life." She nodded for a servant to pour wine, then waved her away. "We would have a moment of quiet," she said sharply in her accented French. Ladies and servants melted away. Phillippa sat back, arms crossed, pursed her lips, shook her head. "And where is your chain of office?" Even now, her voice stern, her head trembled.

"Forgive me, my Queen, but I felt myself unworthy..."

"Nonsense. Have we been friends or have you offered me empty courtesies, John?"

"We are friends, my Queen."

"Then do me the courtesy of speaking true. You grow weary of court. Heaven knows it is a thing of which we all grow weary soon enough."

"I would retire to the north, my lady. I wish to devote my last years to God."

Phillippa closed her eyes, lay her head back on the pillows. "I understand, John. I do understand. It is a wish I share." She lay there quietly a moment, then opened her eyes, sat forward, reached for Thoresby's hand. He grasped her swollen hand, looked into her watery eyes.

"Do not break Edward's heart. Remain chancellor until Wykeham wins his bishopric. Do this for Edward. And for me."

The hand trembled in his grasp. Thoresby bowed his head over it. "Whatever you wish, my Queen."

Owen laughed in the face of the man who asked him whether the rumour about Thoresby was true, that he had resigned as Lord Chancellor. And then, returning to his room, he settled back with a flagon of ale and considered the likelihood. He had soon decided it might be true. Was very likely true. For who would fabricate such a fabulous story that was yet possible, though none but Owen was likely to know what was in Thoresby's heart? Owen knew of the

Archbishop's deteriorating relations with the King, which had been greatly affected by the ever growing influence of Alice Perrers. Owen also knew how time weighed on the Archbishop's shoulders. He had watched Thoresby painfully ease himself out of a chair after sitting overlong at supper, pause halfway up stairs to catch his breath, pass his hand over his brow and push the wine away. Thoresby felt his mortality.

But when Thoresby sent for Owen, he wore the chain of office.

"Then the rumours were untrue. You yet wear the chain."

Thoresby glanced down at the heavy links. "I resigned, that is true enough. But the Queen persuaded me to stay yet a while. Until Wykeham can truly assume the title. Queen Phillippa grows worse with each passing season. I could not refuse the gentle lady."

Owen shrugged as he sank into a chair, stretched his legs. "I had hoped you summoned me to prepare for a journey."

Thoresby smiled. "Despair not. I shall not trap you at Windsor indefinitely. I intend to depart tomorrow for York."

"Tomorrow?" That smacked of flight.

"Can you be ready?"

Owen felt light-headed. "I shall count the hours, Your Grace." They were pleasant hours, now he knew he was leaving. He dined with the poet Chaucer and his wife, a round apple of a woman with a practical turn of mind that complemented her husband's dreaminess. While the husband described all at court with amusing anecdotes, she tempered the humour with analyses of their importance to the King. They had parted with promises of a meeting some day that would include Lucie.

Michaelo did not think the departure a moment too soon. His Grace had agreed to keep the chain of office until Wykeham's confirmation, but he still insisted on delegating the work that kept him in London to his staff at Westminster. Michaelo prayed that they were well away when the King called for Thoresby and discovered Brother

Florian instead. He feared the King's roar.

Nor did he wish to be at Windsor when the gossip about Archer's private supper in Mistress Perrers's apartments reached the King. Tongues wagged about the handsome captain who had used his charms to convince Mistress Perrers to beg the King for Ned Townley's life. Or was it Townley who had been her lover?

It was never safe to be in the household of those who aroused the court's interest. Thoresby's abrupt decision to leave had lifted Michaelo's spirits.

Now Owen rode beside a brooding Thoresby, who kept glancing back at the grand castle, which appeared a mirage in the morning fog.

"Are you worried it will disappear from your life for ever, Your Grace? Or do you expect to see Wykeham raise yet another tower before you are out of sight?"

Thoresby chuckled. "You have heard of the words one of the King's clerks discovered on an inner wall of the new buildings at Windsor?"

Owen had. *This made Wykeham.* "Aye. But they say he explains it as meaning that without the chance to prove his worth as Clerk of Works on such a grand project, he never would have risen so high."

"He is a good man, Archer. But foolish. An eager pup."

"A bit old for a pup."

"I live for the day when I am truly through with court."

"You will not be quite rid of it, even when Wykeham wears that chain. As Archbishop you will still be on the King's council, eh?"

Thoresby gave Owen a sideways glance. "You enjoy ruining my daydream, Archer. I see the pleasure in your eye. But at least I shall be free to stay in my own house in London. I hope never to see my apartment at Windsor again. Or Alice Perrers."

"Ah. Mistress Perrers."

"Do I hear a smile in your voice?"

"I confess I find myself wondering why you despise her so."

"Indeed? I have been meaning to ask how you enjoyed your supper."

"I felt pampered. A kingly repast, a gracious, witty woman who is more of a beauty than I had been led to expect..."

"She bewitched you."

"Fascinated me, yes. She knows her powers and uses them with consummate skill."

Thoresby crossed himself. "It is all the worse that she is intelligent, a shrewd judge of character. You are quite right, she is absolutely aware of what she is doing. It is all purposeful. And she cares not a whit for her soul."

"Perhaps she is still too young."

"She is a plague child, Archer. She has faced death since birth."

"Well, that might be even more to the point."

"You do not despise her, Archer?"

"Of course I despise her—for Ned's sake."

"*Deo gratias*. I began to worry for my godchild."

EPILOGUE

Jasper shuffled into the shop, gathered a squealing Crowder into his arms, and plopped down beside Lucie at the counter, cuddling the wriggling kitten.

Lucie recognised the signs of worry. "I thought you were helping Owen in the garden."

"Aye," Jasper muttered glumly.

Lucie put a hand on his shoulder, looked him in the eye. "He has been brusque with you?"

Jasper shrugged. "He's had bad news, hasn't he? About Ned Townley, wasn't it?" His pale eyelashes blinked, fighting tears.

"No! Gaspare wrote with good news of Ned." Which was true. But there was sad news as well. Why of all mornings did the letter come today? It was Gwenllian's first birthday and they were hosting a dinner in their new hall for her godparents. Lucie had hoped Owen would watch the shop this morning while she helped Tildy and her youngest sister with preparations. But shortly after the messenger had arrived Owen had donned his oldest clothes and gone out to attack the garden. It was true the apple trees in the Corbett garden must be moved, the carpenters would be ready in two days to begin the passageway that would connect the houses and create a courtyard screening the garden from the bustle of Davygate, and the trees were in the way. But Owen suddenly behaved as if they must be moved this morning.

Jasper's face screwed up in a question. "Gaspare has seen Ned?" He had prayed for Ned ever since he had learned of his exile. No matter how lengthy Owen's explanations, Jasper was convinced that exile meant death. Lucie had hoped the news from

294

one of Owen's and Ned's old comrades would reassure the boy.

"No, Gaspare has not seen Ned, but he has had a letter from him. Ned has joined the Duke of Lancaster's household in the Aquitaine."

Jasper's face was solemn. "Gaspare serves Lancaster, too. Why has he not seen Ned?"

"Because Ned is at the Duke's residence, not with his fighting men, Jasper. That is what it means to be of the household." Lucie knew even as she spoke that the boy saw this as another adult lie to keep at bay the nightmares that plagued him.

"Gaspare can neither read nor write."

The shop bell jingled. Lucie knelt to brush the boy's flaxen hair from his eyes. "Gaspare would use one of the clerks travelling with his company, as most soldiers do." She kissed Jasper's forehead, shook her head at the suspicious look he gave her. "You are such a doubting Thomas. I shall leave it to Owen to explain to you. Go back to him, now. But no worrying about Ned." She chucked him under the chin and sent him off.

Mistress Ketel, the wife of a Flemish weaver, stood timidly waiting. Lucie greeted her in French and the young woman beamed. Her husband would not allow anything but English spoken in the house so that their children might be fluent; but Katrina had a limited vocabulary. "The words tangle in my head," she had once explained to Lucie. "Frederick says I take a little of this word, a little of that, and create nonsense. God help me, I cannot seem to learn."

Nor did she look as if she would carry her next child to term. "You are unwell, Mistress Ketel?"

"I am well, Mistress Wilton. It is the baby. She crawled too close to the fire and burned her hand."

While Lucie filled a jar with a burn ointment she wondered about Katrina's thinness, her almost grey complexion, her trembling hands. Might it be a wasting sickness? "You should see the Riverwoman about little Anna," Lucie suggested. "She is good with burns." And might take Katrina in hand.

Katrina shook her head and crossed herself. "Frederick would not approve, Mistress Wilton." She thanked Lucie for the salve, paid her money, and hurried away.

A wasting sickness. Gaspare wrote that the Prince of Wales was wasting away. He had been bedridden since spring. The journey through the snow and ice to Najera had weakened the army; many men had died before enjoying the victory. Many more had fallen prey to a sickness that purged the body until there was nothing left but skin and bones. It was thought that the Prince had the same sickness, but his courage and faith kept him alive. Owen's old friend Lief had not been so lucky—hence Owen's mood. Lucie said a prayer for Agnes, Lief's widow, and their babe.

Customers kept Lucie occupied for the rest of the morning. As soon as the last one strolled out she closed the shop and hurried out to see the state of the trees. Three were already planted and staked, and Jasper was soaking them with buckets of water from a wagonload brought up earlier from the river to supplement their well water. Far in the back of the garden Owen was at work on another tree. Lucie crossed herself when she saw the fury with which he threw the dirt, stomped, yanked at the tree when it tilted. She backed out of his way as he went for the cord and stakes, sank down on the bench by the roses to wait for him to exhaust his devils. There would be time enough for him to wash himself for their guests.

And indeed, when Tildy and her sister came out to tell them it was time to dress, Owen called to Jasper to gather the tools while he joined Lucie.

She wiped Owen's grimy face with her apron. "We must don smiles for our daughter now."

Miraculously, Owen managed a crooked grin. "Aye. Lief would not be the cause of gloom on such an anniversary. I have done with my mourning for now."

It was an assortment of guests that one would find only in such a household, with Owen's standing as steward, retainer and spy, and Lucie's as Master Apothecary and the daughter of a knight: John Thoresby, Archbishop of York; Camden Thorpe, Lucie's guildmaster, and his wife Gwen; Tom and Bess Merchet of the York Tavern; and Lucie's father, Sir Robert D'Arby, and his sister Phillippa. Magda Digby, who had been midwife at Gwenllian's birth, had declined, amused that Lucie and Owen had even thought to ask her to sit at table with the Archbishop. "Magda has no mind to drink wine with the Carrion Crow, no matter that Bird-eye is his man. Magda has a longer memory than most."

Thoresby, conspicuous in his Archbishop's robes, offered a toast to Sir Robert, "Who in his delight at the news that his daughter was with child gave her and her worthy husband this gracious property."

Sir Robert, who stood in the window of the new hall watching his sister fuss with the children out in the garden, bowed and held up his glass with an apologetic glance at Lucie, who had not at first been keen on his extravagant gift.

But she, too, held up her glass. "To Sir Robert."

All toasted.

Sir Robert then stepped forward. "Let us also toast to the Lord Chancellor's generosity in providing this splendid wine."

"The Archbishop, Sir Robert," Bess said. "His Grace is no longer Chancellor."

Thoresby had just returned from London, where he had handed the Great Seal and the chain of office to Wykeham.

Sir Robert scratched his thin white hair and frowned. "Ah. Now it comes back to me. My daughter did say something about it. Forgive me, Your Grace."

Thoresby held up his cup. "No need, Sir Robert. Why should you be bothered to remember the shifting fortunes of court? Let us drink rather to Captain Archer, Mistress Wilton and my beautiful godchild."

When they had also toasted the house, the workmen, Owen's miraculously successful moving of the apple trees, Thoresby stepped forward once more. "And lastly, let us drink to Sir William of Wykeham, who is consecrated this day Bishop of Winchester."

Camden Thorpe frowned. "But, Your Grace, should not the

Archbishop of our great city have been included in the ceremony? How is it that you are not at St. Paul's?"

"He is well attended by the Archbishop of Canterbury and the bishops of London and Salisbury. I shall not be missed, Guildmaster."

"But did you not wish to go?" Camden asked, a man who delighted in ritual.

"Not when it falls on the first anniversary of my goddaughter's birth," Thoresby said with a gentle smile.

Owen and Lucie exchanged puzzled looks.

"To the Bishop of Winchester," Gwen Thorpe said, raising her glass.

After the toast, as the guests moved towards the gaily lit table, Bess touched Tom's arm, and, leaning close, whispered, "'Tis a proper house for them."

Tom looked round at the glazed casements opened to the garden, the tiled firepit in the middle of the room, the raised platform at the head of the table. He shrugged. "Too grand for me. The old kitchen was more to my liking."

"Well, they will be glad of the extra room when the next babe comes."

Tom glanced over at Lucie, shook his head. "Lucie is with child? She looks right slender to my eye."

"You've a good eye for a tiny waist, as always, husband. But mark my words, with His Grace come home to stay there will be ample opportunity for bed sport."

"Oh, aye." Tom drained his glass. "Come, wife, let us join them at table before that fine roast is cold."

AUTHOR'S NOTE

Two historical threads entwine in this book: King Edward III's battle to make William of Wykeham the bishop of Winchester, and Alice Perrers's intriguing relationship with Sir William of Wyndesore. I find William of Wykeham and Alice Perrers complementary souls because of their dependence for their standing on Edward's affection. I put this thought into the mind of John Thoresby, who balances precariously on the edge of retirement as Lord Chancellor, his close friendship with King Edward having soured over his obvious disapproval of the King's low-born mistress. And now the King is grooming another commoner, William of Wykeham, to take Thoresby's place. Historians have treated Wykeham with more kindness than they have Perrers, but both have come down to us with the taint of King's favourites.

Froissart, the Flemish chronicler who resided at court at Queen Phillippa's invitation, said of Wykeham: '…everything passed through his hands. He stood so high in the King's favour that, in his time, everything was done in England by his consent, and nothing was done without it.'[1] No doubt an exaggeration, but Wykeham did rise to become Lord Chancellor of England from a modest beginning as King's chaplain and surveyor of the works at Windsor Castle, and it was his success with the completion of the castle that endeared him to King Edward. During this period the lower ward of the castle was largely rebuilt to house the chaplains who served St George's Chapel. Timber buildings within the keep, or Round Tower, were rebuilt or renovated to house the royal family (chambers, a hall, and probably a chapel), whilst extensive building in the upper ward

---

1. *Froissart Chronicles*, ed. G. Brereton (London: Penguin Books Ltd., 1978), p. 67.

was completed. This ward, with the royal apartments and lodgings for courtiers, essentially took its present form at this time. Though modernised, enlarged, refaced over the centuries, much of what we see today stands on the foundations planned by Edward III and William of Wykeham. The work in the upper ward is described thus by the continuator of Ranulph Higden's *Polychronicon*:

> About the year of our Lord 1359 our lord the king, at the instance of William Wikham, clerk, caused many excellent buildings in the castle of Windsor to be thrown down, and others more beautiful and sumptuous to be set up...The said William was of very low birth...yet he was very shrewd, and a man of great energy. Considering how he could please the king and secure his goodwill, he counselled him to build the said castle of Windsor in the form in which it appears today to the beholder.[2]

I mention in the book an inscription found on a wall in the castle, "This made Wickam".[3] It is said that when King Edward objected to the inscription, Wykeham explained that he had not meant to take credit for the castle, but rather to acknowledge that its completion was what made his career. This story is probably a myth, but the point is well taken. Windsor was close to the King's heart. Here it was that he had envisioned his recreation of Arthur's Round Table. Though that early plan was aborted, it was revised as the Order of the Garter. And Wykeham had seen to it that Edward had a glorious, mighty castle in which his noble order could gather and celebrate chivalry, with a college of chaplains to serve them.

By the time this book opens, Wykeham is Keeper of the Privy Seal. Now Edward wishes to make him Bishop of Winchester, a sufficiently high office from which to choose a Lord Chancellor. But Pope Urban V stalled in conferring the bishopric on the King's

---

2. *The History of the King's Works*, Vol. I, *The Middle Ages*, ed. HM Colvin (London: Her Majesty's Stationery Office, 1963), p. 877.

3. The spelling of names was at this time as creative an endeavour as all other spelling. The spelling of Wykeham's name that I use is the one I came upon most frequently in 20th century historical writing.

favourite. Although it appears that enemies of Wykeham (jealous of King's favours?) had begun a campaign against him, the issue was not entirely personal. Edward had been in continual conflict with the papacy over what he saw as the popes' meddling with patronage, which the English kings had always claimed as a temporal, not a spiritual matter, and thus in their jurisdiction. With Urban V the conflict was compounded: the Pope wished to cleanse the Church of pluralism (clergy holding multiple benefices, or ecclesiastical livings) and saw Wykeham as the richest pluralist of the time. Edward had, indeed, generously granted benefices to Wykeham; it was a common, convenient way to pay such a cleric without dipping into the royal purse. Hence the stalemate, and a controversy that divided the English Church into two camps.

In the present novel Edward seeks support for Wykeham from the abbots of two major Cistercian abbeys in Yorkshire, Rievaulx and Fountains. While we know that Edward sent at least twenty-five letters to cardinals enlisting their support (actually one to an abbot who was soon to become a cardinal), we have no indication that Abbot Robert Monkton of Fountains and Abbot Richard of Rievaulx were so approached, but it was not a random choice on my part. The Cistercians were not known for blind allegiance to the King of England; their bonds were to their mother house in France. Their support might well have impressed His Holiness.

Another drama is unfolding, this one in Alice Perrers' life. Alice was an orphan who began her reign at court in Queen Phillippa's household. She quickly became a favourite of the Queen, and shortly thereafter of the King. As the King's mistress, Alice's situation at court was precarious; in fact, her relationship was one of the great scandals of the times, as I mention briefly in the note to *The Lady Chapel*. If the birth of her son by the King was greeted with hostility among the courtiers, a young woman of nineteen, no matter how self-possessed, might well have sought a protector who would be bound by law to stay by her side. Alice Perrers had no powerful family to protect her when she fell from favour.

Historians do not agree about when it occurred, with theories ranging from 1367 to after King Edward III's death, but at some point Alice married Sir William of Wyndesore, who held command under Lionel, Duke of Clarence, in Ireland from 1362 to 1366. Wyndesore appears to have been as financially cunning as Alice. He returned from his second tour in Ireland in disgrace for extorting money from the people for his military campaigns. It seems that the money allocated to him for his expedition had been shared with Alice before his departure. This would suggest the early closeness of the relationship that I have chosen. But they made public the marriage only after Parliament denounced Alice following King Edward's death; the couple argued that Alice had been tried as a single woman when she was in fact married, and thus the property Parliament sought to take from her was Wyndesore's. Alice stated at this time that the marriage had taken place long ago. She and William lived together occasionally thereafter, but only when it was politically expedient. It appears to have been a cold marriage between two ambitious people; William essentially disinherited Alice's children after her death and made claim to all her property. I begin in this book to unfold my own version of this marriage.

In reading about Wyndesore (I take this spelling from Burke's peerage solely to avoid confusion with the castle and town of Windsor), I found it peculiar that a man of whom no one had good things to say rose so quickly upon his return from Ireland with Clarence. In the winter and spring of 1367 the King rewarded Wyndesore with pardon of all debts owed him, granted him a weekly market and yearly fair at Morland (a healthy source of revenue), and made him Joint Warden of the West March towards Scotland. Shortly after the action of this book Wyndesore became Sheriff of Cumberland and Keeper of Carlisle Castle, then returned to Ireland as the King's Lieutenant for several tours beginning in 1369. A man well rewarded for his soldiering...

Or was he being rewarded for something else? Might the King have discovered the relationship between his mistress and the soldier and seen it as potentially useful if revealed at the proper time? Meanwhile, he paid Wyndesore well for his silence and kept him busy away from court, whilst Alice remained at Edward's side. Might this not explain the later chill to the marriage? I think it might, though I doubt the relationship was ever warm except between the covers.

I do not condemn Alice for her scheming. In the fourteenth century a woman's best hope for security was to marry well. And yet even this could be temporary, as in the case of Lucie Wilton's Aunt Phillippa, a childless widow who discovered she had no role when her husband died. Because of this reversal, Phillippa encouraged the marriage that secured Lucie her position as apothecary. Once Lucie proved her skill and was accepted by the guild, she was remarkably secure. Her marriage to Owen neither improved her standing nor reduced it; only her professional integrity could affect it. Lucie did not seek a protector in marrying Owen; she married him for love. Perversely, she is the one who finds a protector. For all Alice Perrers's scheming, she wound up with a man who will prove more of an adversary than a partner.

THE OWEN ARCHER SERIES

THE APOTHECARY ROSE

In the year of our Lord 1363, two suspicious deaths in the infirmary of St. Mary's Abbey catch the attention of the powerful John Thoresby, Lord Chancellor of England and Archbishop of York. One victim is a pilgrim, while the second is Thoresby's ne'er-do-well ward, both apparently poisoned by a physic supplied by Master Apothecary Nicholas Wilton. In the wake of these deaths, the archbishop dispatches one-eyed spy Owen Archer to York to find the murderer. Under the guise of a disillusioned soldier keen to make a fresh start, Owen insinuates himself into Wilton's apothecary as an apprentice. But he finds Wilton bedridden, with the shop being run by his lovely, enigmatic young wife, Lucie. As Owen unravels a tangled history of scandal and tragedy, he discovers at its center a desperate, forbidden love twisted over time into obsession. And the woman he has come to love is his prime suspect.

Lovingly detailed, beautifully written, *The Apothecary Rose* is a captivating and suspenseful tale of life, love, and death in medieval England.

THE LADY CHAPEL

Perfect for fans of both Ellis Peters and CJ Sansom, *The Lady Chapel* is a vivid and immersive portrait of court intrigue and a testament to the power of the medieval guilds.

Summer in the year of our Lord 1365. On the night after the Corpus Christi procession, a man is brutally murdered on the steps of York Minster. The next morning his severed hand is found in a room at the York Tavern—a room hastily vacated by a fellow guild member who had quarreled with the victim.

Archbishop Thoresby calls on Owen Archer to investigate. As Owen tracks the fleeing merchant, he uncovers a conspiracy involving a powerful company of traders, but his only witness is a young boy who has gone into hiding, and his only suspect is a mysterious cloaked woman. When Owen discovers a link between the traders and a powerful coterie in the royal court, he brings his apothecary wife Lucie into the race to find the boy before he is silenced forever by the murderers.

THE NUN'S TALE

Based on an enigmatic entry in the records of Clementhorpe Nunnery, this authentic, gripping mystery conjures a 14th century ripe with forbidden passions and political intrigue.

When young nun Joanna Calverley dies of a fever in the town of Beverley in the summer of 1365, she is buried quickly for fear of the plague. But a year later, Archbishop Thoresby learns of a woman who has arrived in York claiming to be the resurrected nun, talking of relic-trading and miracles. And death seems to ride in her wake.

The archbishop sends Owen Archer to retrace the woman's journey, an investigation that leads him across the north from Leeds to Beverley to Scarborough. Along the way he encounters Geoffrey Chaucer, a spy for the king of England, who believes there is a connection between the nun's troubles, renegade mercenaries, and the powerful Percy family. Back in York, however, Owen's wife Lucie, pregnant with their first child, has won the confidence of the mysterious nun and realizes that there are secrets hidden in the woman's seemingly mad ramblings...

THE RIDDLE OF ST. LEONARD'S

In the year of our Lord 1369 the much-loved Queen Philippa lies dying in Windsor Castle, the harvest has failed, and the pestilence has returned. In York, the atmosphere of fear and superstition is heightened by a series of thefts and violent deaths at St. Leonard's Hospita, as well as rumors that these crimes are connected to the hospital's dwindling funds. The Master of St. Leonard's, Sir Richard Ravenser, hurries north from the queen's deathbed to summon Owen Archer, soldier-spy, to investigate the scandal before it ruins him.

While his wife Lucie faces the plague-panicked townsfolk at the apothecary, Owen encounters a seemingly random series of clues:

a riddle posed by one of the victims at the hospital, a lay sister with a scandalous past, the kidnapping of a child from the hospital orphanage, and a case of arson. The answer to the riddle of St. Leonard's lies in the past, and as Owen's family is caught up in the sweep of the pestilence, he must abandon them to race across the countryside to save the next victim.

A GIFT OF SANCTUARY

Under the pretense of escorting his father-in-law and the archbishop's secretary on a pilgrimage to the sacred city of St. David's in Wales, Owen Archer and Geoffrey Chaucer, in truth, are carrying out a mission for the Duke of Lancaster. England and France are at war, and the southern coast of Wales is vulnerable to invasion—Owen and Geoffrey are to recruit archers for the duke's army and inspect his Welsh fortifications on the coast, while quietly investigating whether the duke's steward at Cydweli Castle is involved in a French plot to incite rebellion in Wales.

But trouble precedes them in the cathedral city of St. David's. On Whitesands Beach beyond the city a young man is beaten and left for dead, then spirited away by a Welsh bard. Shortly afterward a corpse clothed in the livery of the Duke of Lancaster is left at the city gate, his shoes filled with white sand. Meanwhile, at Cydweli Castle, a chain of events begun by the theft of money from the castle's exchequer ends in a violent death and the disappearance of the steward's beautiful young wife. Owen and Geoffrey begin to see connections linking the troubles in city and castle, and learn they must unravel the complex story of betrayed love and political ambition to prevent more deaths. But in the course of his investigations in the land of his birth, Owen is haunted by doubts about his own loyalties...

A SPY FOR THE REDEEMER

Late spring in the year of our Lord 1370, and Owen Archer is anxious to leave Wales for home. His mission for the Duke of Lancaster complete, he attempts to arrange safe passage on a ship sailing for England, but the hanging of a stonemason interrupts his plans. On the surface it appears the young man was driven to suicide by a broken heart, but to Owen the signs all point to murder. As his investigation stretches on, however, Owen finds himself drawn into the influence of the leader of a Welsh rebellion whose manifesto speaks to his heart, and a choice is offered to him: join or die.

Meanwhile, at home in York, Owen's wife Lucie is troubled by rumors that her husband's long absence is permanent, as well as threats by a customer who claims she was poisoned by a physic from the Wilton apothecary. Meanwhile, Lucie is tempted by the attentions of a friend's steward, even as she uncovers a shattering betrayal in her own household.

THE GUILT OF INNOCENTS

Winter in the year of our Lord 1372. A river pilot falls into the icy waters of the River Ouse during a skirmish between dockworkers and the boys of the minster school, which include Owen Archer's adopted son Jasper. But what began as a confrontation to return a boy's stolen scrip becomes a murder investigation as the rescuers find the pilot dying of wounds inflicted before his plunge into the river. When another body is fished from the river upstream and Owen discovers that the boy Jasper sought to help has disappeared, Owen Archer convinces the archbishop that he must go in search of the boy. His lost scrip seems to hold the key to the double tragedy, but his disappearance leaves troubling questions: did he flee in fear? Or was he abducted?

On the cusp of this new mystery, Owen accepts Jasper's offer to accompany him to the boy's home in the countryside, where they learn that a valuable cross has gone missing. A devastating fire and another drowning force Owen to make impossible choices, endangering not only himself, but the two innocents he fights to protect. The bond between fathers and sons proves strong, even between those not linked by blood.

A VIGIL OF SPIES

Archbishop Thoresby of York, the second most powerful cleric in England, lies dying in his bed. The end of his life is seen by the great families of the North as a chance to promote one of their own as his successor, and Thoresby himself announces he will leave the matter to the dean and chapter of York. On the eve of this decision, the dying archbishop agrees to a visit from Joan, Princess of Wales, wife of the Black Prince, heir to the throne of England. Thoresby's captain of the guard, Owen Archer, has no doubt that trouble will follow.

As soon as the company rides into the palace yard he is proved right: they arrive burdened with the body of one of their party, and Owen finds evidence that the man's death was no accident. Within days of this discovery, a courier carrying an urgent message for the archbishop is found hanging in the woods. With guards surrounding the property, it is clear that the murderer walks among the palace guests. The powerful Percy and Neville families are well represented in the entourage, including a woman who remembers an afternoon tryst with Owen as much, much more. Even the princess' son is suspect. As Owen races to unmask the guilty and rid the palace of the royal party, his final wish for his lord is that he might die in peace.

THE MARGARET KERR SERIES

A TRUST BETRAYED

In the spring of 1297 the English army controls lowland Scotland and Margaret Kerr's husband Roger Sinclair is missing. He'd headed to Dundee in autumn, writing to Margaret with a promise to be home for Christmas, but it's past Easter. Is he caught up in the swelling rebellion against the English? Is he even alive? When his cousin, Jack, is murdered on the streets of Edinburgh, Roger's last known location, Margaret coerces her brother Andrew, a priest, to escort her to the city.

She finds Edinburgh scarred by war—houses burnt, walls stained with blood, shops shuttered—and the townsfolk simmering with resentment, harboring secrets. Even her uncle, innkeeper Murdoch Kerr, meets her questions with silence. Are his secrets the keys to Roger's disappearance? What terrible sin torments her brother? Is it her husband she glimpses in the rain, scarred, haunted? Desperate, Margaret makes alliances that risk both her own life and that of her brother in her search for answers. She learns that war twists love and loyalties, and that, until tested, we cannot know our own hearts, much less those of our loved ones.

THE FIRE IN THE FLINT

Scots are gathering in Murdoch Kerr's Edinburgh tavern, plotting to drive out the English forces. Margaret takes her place there as innkeeper, collecting information to pass on to William Wallace—until murder gives the English an excuse to shutter the tavern. The dead man was a witness to the intruders who raided chests belonging to Margaret's husband and her father, the latest in a string of violent raids on Margaret's family, but no one knows the identity of the raiders or what they're searching for.

Margaret's uncle urges her to escape Edinburgh, but as she flees north with her husband Roger, Margaret grows suspicious about his sudden wish to speak with her mother, Christiana, who is a soothsayer. Margaret once innocently shared with Roger one of Christiana's visions, of "the true king of Scotland" riding into Edinburgh. Now she begins to wonder if their trip is part of a mission engineered by the English crown...

A CRUEL COURTSHIP

In late summer 1297, Margaret Kerr heads to the town of Stirling at the request of William Wallace's man James Comyn. Her mission is to discover the fate of a young spy who had infiltrated the English garrison at Stirling Castle, but on the journey Margaret is haunted by dreams—or are they visions?—of danger.

He who holds Stirling Castle holds Scotland—and a bloody battle for the castle is imminent. But as the Scots prepare to cast off the English yoke, Margaret's flashes of the future allow her to glimpse what is to come—and show her that she can trust no one, not even her closest friends.

A Cruel Courtship is a harrowing account of the days before the bloody battle of Stirling Bridge, and the story of a young woman's awakening.

CPSIA information can be obtained
at www.ICGtesting.com
Printed in the USA
LVHW091337131020
668687LV00003B/1054

9 781682 301043